GOOD TIME COMING

GOOD TIME COMING

C. S. Harris

This first world edition published 2016
in Great Britain and the USA by
SEVERN HOUSE PUBLISHERS LTD of
19 Cedar Road, Sutton, Surrey, England, SM2 5DA.
Trade paperback edition first published
in Great Britain and the USA 2017 by
SEVERN HOUSE PUBLISHERS LTD

Copyright © 2016 by Two Talers, L.L.C. JUL 2 6 2017

British Library Cataloguing in Publication Data
A CIP catalogue record for this title is available from the British Library.

ISBN-13: 978-0-7278-8649-1 (cased)
ISBN-13: 978-1-84751-751-7 (trade paper)
ISBN-13: 978-1-78010-815-5 (e-book)

This is a work of fiction. Names, characters, places and incidents
are either the product of the author's imagination or are used fictitiously.
Except where actual historical events and characters are being described for
the storyline of this novel, all situations in this publication are fictitious and
any resemblance to actual persons, living or dead,
business establishments, events or locales is purely coincidental.

Typeset by Palimpsest Book Production Ltd.,
Falkirk, Stirlingshire, Scotland.

For Samantha, Danielle, and Steve.

There's a good time coming, boys.
A good time coming:
War in all men's eyes shall be
A monster of iniquity
In the good time coming.
Nations shall not quarrel then,
To prove which is the stronger;
Nor slaughter men for glory's sake;–
Wait a little longer.

The Good Time Coming, 1846,
words by Charles Mackay; melody by Stephen Foster.

One

I killed a man the summer I turned thirteen. Sometimes I still see him in my dreams, his eyes as blue as the Gulf on a clear spring morning, his cheeks reddened by the hot Louisiana sun. His face is always the same, ever young and vital. But the bones of his hands are bare and stained dark by the fetid mud of the swamps, and his scent is that of death.

Yet even worse are the nights when I lie awake, when a hot summer wind shifts the festoons of Spanish moss hanging from the arching branches of the live oaks down by the bayou and whispers through the canebrakes in a sibilant rush. That's when the fear comes to me, cold and soul-shriveling, and I find myself listening lest the hushed breath of the dead betray the secret of what we did that day.

I tell myself his mouth is filled with earth, his tongue turned to dust. But the dead don't need to speak to bear witness to the wrongs done them. And though I tell myself the wrongs were his, and that no just God could condemn my actions on that fateful morning, it is a desperate reassurance that brings no real rest. If this war has taught us anything, it is that convictions of righteous certitude can be soul-corrupting illusions that offer no dispensation from hell.

I first saw him late one hazy afternoon in the spring of 1862, when I was nearly twelve. Finn O'Reilly and I had come after school to splash around in the lagoon near Bayou Sara's train depot, using a broken copper dipper he'd found in a paddock to catch tadpoles. The warm water lapped pleasantly against our bare calves, the mud billowing up around us with each step as the fine silt squished between our toes. The light had taken on that golden, slanted quality that comes in the hours just before evening, and from up high in the nearby green curtain of vine-draped cypress and willow branches came an endless chorus of birdsong.

Thanks to the cracks in the dipper's bowl, the long-tailed polly-wogs simply wriggled to freedom in the streams of water that escaped in a sun-sparkled rush every time we raised the dipper high.

'It's worse than a sieve!' I said, laughing out loud. Then I paused, aware of an unnatural hush that had fallen over the afternoon. The raucous shouts and laughter from the workmen down at the wharves stilled, along with the rattle of cartwheels and the click of the grist mill and the myriad other sounds that normally formed the background noise of our lives. Even old Toot Magill's liver-colored hound stopped his infernal barking. It was as if the entire town had suddenly paused to catch its collective breath.

A woman's high-pitched voice sang out, 'Oh, Lordy, Lordy, Lordy! They be acomin'!'

Finn's head jerked up, a heavy hank of dark hair falling into his eye, so that he had to put up a hand to shove it back. He was a year older than me but still short, his features sharp, his green eyes disconcertingly pale and tilted in a way that made him look vaguely exotic. He wore a pair of patched canvas trousers rolled up to his knees and a plaid shirt of homespun woven by his mama, the bare skin of his arms and legs sun-browned and still nearly hairless. After more than a year of the Federal blockade, shoes had become so precious that most folks put them on only when they went visiting or to church. But Finn had never worn shoes much anyway.

A lot of folks looked askance at the O'Reillys. They weren't just Irish, they were Black Irish. I wasn't sure exactly what that meant, but it sounded pretty darn bad. Finn confided to me once that he'd been born smack dab in the middle of the Atlantic Ocean, halfway between Dublintown and New Orleans, in what his mama called a coffin ship. He said the Irish were packed in the hold so tight and with so little food and water that at least three or four died every day, their bodies thrown overboard to the schools of sharks that followed in their wake. Neither his mama nor his papa could read or write, and though they worked hard, they'd started from nothing and were still dirt poor. I often heard my classmates' mothers wondering aloud why my mama let me play with him. They usually came to the conclusion she must not know how much time Finn and I spent together. But when they tried to tell her, she'd just change the subject.

I'd been holding my skirts and pinafore bunched up in one fist, but as the shout from the waterfront was taken up by first one voice, then another, I let them slip so that they trailed in the water. 'Reckon it's the Yankees?'

Finn's gaze met mine. Tadpoles forgotten, we raced each other to the levee.

Finn and I lived on the outskirts of the town of St Francisville, which perched like a dainty lady high above the Mississippi on a narrow ridge overlooking the river. But the depot was half a mile below at the foot of the bluff, in a technically separate town called Bayou Sara. Once, Bayou Sara was the busiest port between New Orleans and Memphis. It's all gone now, its mile of brick warehouses reduced to blackened rubble, its bustling shops and banks, hotels and taverns, sawmills and livery stables only a memory marked here and there by a solitary chimney thrusting up from a tangle of vines. When the river is high, its raging brown floodwaters sluice over the crumbling levees and forgotten foundations, and creepers reclaim what were once streets and lovingly-tended rose gardens. Yet on that hot spring day, I thought it as permanent and eternal as the sky. I'd no notion, then, how quickly life can change, how ephemeral everything I took for granted around me actually was.

We climbed the levee to find the grassy slope thick with folks, knots of dockworkers and field hands in white jean cloth trousers and loose shirts mingling with hoop-skirted women and gray-whiskered men in black broadcloth coats and tall silk hats. The air was thick with the reek of working men's sweat and ladies' talcum powder and the stench of burning cotton as planters up and down the river set fire to their stores rather than see them confiscated by the enemy. We had to duck low under boney elbows and squeeze around wide hips, murmuring, ''Scuse me, Mr Marks, 'scuse me, Miss Jane,' until we finally reached the water's edge.

The Mississippi was running treacherously high that year, a mile-wide torrent yellow-brown with mud. Great spreading trees, washed from distant banks to the north, swept along on the fast current, and a smoky haze muted the dazzle of the sun off the water as the wind kicked up choppy waves flecked with foam. But what made my breath catch and my scalp pull tight was the sight of a massive sloop of war, its high prow riding above the raging floodwaters, a colossus of gleaming wood and wind-snapped lines and deadly, dark-bored cannon mouths. In its wake steamed a flotilla of smaller, two-masted gunboats guarding a procession of confiscated paddle-wheelers that had been pressed into service as troop transports. Streams of white smoke belched from their stacks, joining the black smudge from the burning cotton.

'Holy mackerel,' whispered Finn. 'Look at 'em all.'

The wind off the river snatched at the loose hair from my braids and whipped it around my face, so that I had to put up both hands to catch it back. As the flotilla drew closer, I could see the flags and brightly-colored streamers that flew from every mast and peak, an incongruous note of gaiety that added one more bizarre element of unreality to the scene. From every deck, a thick horde of blue-coated men stared at us.

We stared silently back at them, as if they were some exotic species, as if we hadn't seen men in these familiar uniforms marching back and forth across the Baton Rouge parade ground all our lives, as if our own loved ones hadn't worn similar uniforms in the wars to wrest Texas and California from Mexico and the western territories from the Indians.

My own Uncle Bo still wore blue, although we didn't talk about him much – and not at all when my Grandmother Adelaide was around.

The first of the flotilla was drawing abreast of us now. Rolling swells curled away from the endless hulls and churning paddle-wheels to crash against the slope at our feet and throw up a fine spray that seemed to sting my cheeks.

'Reckon they're comin' here?' asked Mr James Marks, Bayou Sara's portly, middle-aged mayor. His face was soft and round and pink with the heat, his watery eyes blinking rapidly as if struggling to bring what he was seeing into focus.

'Not here. Vicksburg.'

The answer came from a tall, mahogany-bearded man in home-spun who stood at the edge of the crowd. He had blade-like features and the hard, whipcord body of a man who spends his days in the saddle or on the march. He kept his slouch hat pulled low, his eyes narrowed against the sun as he cradled a new Enfield rifle in his arms. He wasn't from around here and I didn't know his name, although I had seen him before. I'd heard rumors that he was an observing officer sent by General Ruggles, but I knew better than to believe too much of what was said.

All kinds of wild talk had been flying up and down the river in the two weeks since New Orleans fell without a shot being fired in her defense. Oh, a fierce enough battle had raged lower down at the mouth of the Mississippi, a nightmare of screaming shells, choking fire, and sobbing, dying men that ended with the Federal fleet blasting its way past the two red-brick, star-shaped forts that guarded the river's access. Once Forts Jackson and St Philip surrendered, the city did, too.

'Jimminee, there's a mess o'em,' said the Widow Carlyle's Tom, his dark face shiny with sweat, his eyes hooded in that way habitual to those who must learn early to hide their feelings and reactions from the world. I looked over at him. But it wasn't until later that I found myself wondering what *his* thoughts were, watching that fleet.

'Reckon Vicksburg'll surrender without a shot, like New Orleans and Baton Rouge?' someone asked.

'If it does, the war is as good as lost,' said Bernard Henshaw, the gloomy, stoop-shouldered owner of the town's book and stationery store. But no one paid much attention to him beyond a few mutterings and foul glances. A fussy little Englishman with dainty features and gold-rimmed spectacles he was always pushing up with the pad of his thumb, Henshaw had been loudly prophesying ruin and defeat for over a year now.

'If them Yankees think Vicksburg's gonna surrender, they've got another think comin',' said William T. Mumford, the graying, barrel-chested proprietor of the grand China Grove Hotel. A bunch of the men nodded and grunted in agreement. But something about their posture and air of forced bravado reminded me of Finn sticking his hands in his pockets and whistling every time he had to pass a graveyard.

By now the fleet stretched out in both directions up and down the river. Folks were breathing easier, their shoulders sagging in relief. The slouch-hatted stranger was right; the Federals weren't coming to Bayou Sara. We were safe – at least for now.

Then the Reverend Samuel Sweeney, whose steepled, white clapboard Methodist church lay on Sun Street, said, 'Look at that boat – one of them low ones with the two masts. What's it doing?'

Executing a slow, ominous turn, the nearest gunboat swung wide to point its bow in towards shore, its whistle shrill as it pulled away from its fellows. We could see the name emblazoned on its side as it plowed toward us, and though the sun still shone hot and intense, I shivered.

USS *Katahdin*.

'Holy cow,' said Finn. 'They're fixin' to tie up at our wharfboat!'

Two

The rat-tat-tat of a drum floated to us from across the water as the gunboat steamed toward us. Singly or in groups of two or three, the assembled townsfolk on the levee began to melt away.

I glanced over at Mr Marks. The mayor's plump face was slick with sweat, and he kept opening and closing his mouth like a fish left stranded in a crevasse after the spring floodwaters receded. He was a journalist by trade, editor of *The Bayou Sara Ledger*, although lately his newspaper had been shrinking steadily as paper and ink grew harder and harder to get. From the looks of things, he'd rather be anyplace but where he was. Yet he stood his ground, a small, rotund man with widely spaced eyes, protuberant ears, and a dark stain of perspiration soaking the back of his threadbare coat.

The slouch-hatted man with the shiny new rifle had disappeared.

'Why you reckon they're stopping here?' asked one of the few men who'd chosen to stand with the mayor.

Mr Marks only shook his head, although I heard him mutter under his breath, 'Please God some young fool doesn't get it into his head to take a potshot at them.'

He moved to position himself in the muddy lane leading down to the ferry landing, the wind off the river fluttering his black tie and the tails of his coat. He'd always been something of a figure of fun to us children, with his earnest way of leaning forward when he talked and the plump, ink-stained hands he had a habit of fluttering in the air. But it occurred to me, watching him, that maybe I needed to reassess my estimation of Mr Marks.

The *Katahdin* didn't pull up to the wharfboat, but anchored off the ferry landing with a loud rattle and splash. We watched as a longboat full of seamen and marines began to pull toward us, its oars throwing up arcing cascades of water that glistened in the sunlight. One of the ship's officers, a slim lieutenant with a boy's smooth round face and turned-up nose, stood at the prow. But for some reason I found my gaze inexplicably drawn to the tall, golden-haired man at his side. The bugle embroidered on the front of his

black felt hat and the light blue straps on the shoulders of his dark
frock coat marked him as an infantry captain.

'Amrie,' whispered Finn, bumping his elbow against mine.
'Maybe we oughta go.'

I shook my head and took a step closer, drawn by something I
couldn't begin to understand.

Sometimes I wonder how my life would have turned out if I'd
listened to Finn, or if he and I had simply stayed catching tadpoles
rather than running with everyone else to see the Federal fleet.
What if the *Katahdin* had steamed on toward Vicksburg without
turning into Bayou Sara? Would things have turned out differently?
Or were we fated, this golden-haired man and I, to meet and play
such a pivotal, tragic role in each other's lives?

The infantry captain looked to be somewhere in his late twenties
or early thirties, his cheeks reddened by sun and wind, his lips so
thin they seemed to disappear as he pressed them into a tight,
determined line. I stared at him, and I knew the strangest sensation,
as if this moment had happened before, as if I had seen *him* before,
although I knew that I had not. And somehow I also knew, with
that clear certainty that sometimes comes to us, that this was one
of those moments I would always vividly recall long after an untold
multitude of my life's moments had slipped irrevocably from my
memory.

I watched him step ashore, one hand resting on the hilt of his
sword, his head lifting as his gaze took in Bayou Sara's rows of
sunbaked brick storerooms, the neat streets now quiet and eerily
deserted. The pungent reek of burning cotton drifted to us on the
breeze as another planter upriver set fire to his stores.

Mr Marks cleared his throat, his hat held in his hands. 'Gentlemen,'
he said, his voice shaky, 'this is a trading town, full of women,
children, and old men. Not a military instillation.'

The boy-faced lieutenant glanced at him, then turned pointedly
to address the diminished crowd on the riverbank. 'We are here
under orders from President Abraham Lincoln, Flag Officer David
Farragut, and Major General Benjamin Butler.' He spoke loudly and
clearly in formal, flowing periods he must have repeated dozens of
times coming up the river. 'Know you that we are on this river for
the purpose of enforcing the laws of our common country and
protecting its loyal citizens. But understand this, as well: if any
hostile demonstrations are made upon our vessels or transports as

they pass before your town, you will be held responsible for such actions, and a terrible vengeance will be visited upon you all.'

The mayor's face hardened and took on a deep, angry hue. 'You would make war against innocent women and children? For the impulsive act of some hothead?'

'We do not make war on innocent persons, but on those in open rebellion against our mutual country. If there are any hotheads amongst you, I suggest you curb their zeal. The fate of your town is in your hands. Good day to you, sir.' The lieutenant started to turn away.

Mr Mark's fingers tightened on the brim of his hat. 'No country of mine would ever collectively punish the innocent for the actions of a few.'

The lieutenant paused to look back at him, his upper lip twitching in a way that crinkled his nose, although whether it was in suppressed revulsion at the pronouncement he'd just been ordered to make, or in disdain for us, I couldn't tell. 'You have been warned,' he said, and strode toward the boat.

The infantry captain lingered a moment longer, a strange, almost bemused light in his eyes as he looked out over the scattered towns-people. 'God's retribution is a terrible thing,' he said, his voice as deep and melodious as a preacher's. 'Fear it.'

He was close enough now that I could read the Co. M, 4TH REG, WISC. VOL. on his unit badge. *Company M, Fourth Regiment, Wisconsin Volunteers.*

Then I realized his gaze had landed on me, and I found my fingers creeping up to touch the small gold cross that hung around my neck on a fine chain. It was a gift to me from my father's mother on the occasion of my christening, and I had worn it always for as long as I could remember.

He walked up to me, his gaze still locked with mine, and I saw that his eyes were blue and clear, and that sweat sheened his high-boned cheeks. 'Pretty necklace,' he said. My hand dropped to my side, but it was too late. Reaching out, he closed his fist around the cross and jerked. I felt his rough knuckles brush the skin of my throat, felt the clasp give way. 'My little girl will like it.'

'But you can't—'

'Amrie! Don't,' warned Reverend Sweeney, catching my arm when I would have thrown myself after the blue-coated man now sauntering back to his waiting boat.

'But it ain't right! He can't just—'

'Hush, child. Let it go.'

I was never very good at listening when people told me what to do, especially when I was riled up and convinced of the justice of my cause. But something in the reverend's tone stopped me cold. I stood at his side, quivering with rage and hot tears and a sense of violation I couldn't begin to explain.

The reverend kept his hand on my arm, just in case, as we watched the seamen lean into their oars and the boat pull away from the bank. With his free hand he fumbled a tattered handkerchief from his pocket and wiped his face. 'Please God we'll never see them again.'

'They'll be back,' said Finn.

It was the first time I'd looked at Finn since the Federal longboat knocked against the ferry landing. He stood rigid, his fists clenched white at his sides, his face held so taut it was as if the skin had somehow been stretched tighter across the bones.

'Did you hear that?' he demanded. 'Did you hear what they said? What kind of men talk about murdering women and children and are *proud* of it?'

'Those without the wisdom to know that the Lord God watches us always,' said the reverend.

I heard the bookseller, Bernard Henshaw, give a harsh, ringing laugh, and craned my neck around to see him, surprised to find him still here.

'On the contrary, my dear reverend,' said Henshaw. 'Those men are utterly convinced that God marches at their side. As far as they're concerned, they've embarked on a holy crusade against evil personified, with you and I cast into the role of Satan. And in a war against the devil, anything is permissible. Anything.'

I waited for someone to tell him he was wrong.

Only, nobody did.

Three

I took off running as soon as the reverend removed his restraining hand.

Finn shouted, 'Amrie!' But I just kept running, up the long, steep slope to St Francisville.

My name wasn't really Amrie. I'd been christened Anne-Marie St Pierre, a good Catholic name my grandmother Adelaide loathed. A Boston-born Episcopalian, Adelaide Dunbar could never find her way to forgiving her daughter for marrying a French Creole doctor from New Orleans. Yet she was one of the few people who insisted on always calling me Anne-Marie. To everyone else, I was Amrie.

When we were little, my older brother, Simon, had a hard time wrapping his tongue around my name. It came out sounding like 'A'm'rie.' And so I became Amrie, even after he grew old enough to say it right.

Even after he died of yellow fever in his twelfth year.

Simon had been gone nearly two years. But it was to him that I ran, racing to the top of the bluff where the new Episcopal church stood, its tall brick bell tower thrusting proudly above the oak trees that dotted its vast churchyard.

The church might be new, but the graveyard was not. In fact, St Francisville had been a graveyard even before it was a town. Back in the days when Louisiana was Spanish territory, some monks had established a monastery across the river at Pointe Coupee. Once they learned what the Mississippi's rampaging floodwaters could do to a grave, they started rowing their dead across the river to bury them on high ground beside a small wooden chapel they dedicated to St Francis.

The monks were all long gone now. Only their dead remained, mingled with ours.

Simon lay beneath the spreading limbs of a young oak not far from the church's eastern transept. I knelt in the grass beside him, my hands shaking as I brushed a scattering of dried leaves from his stone and yanked at the weeds that had grown up since my last visit. Another girl in my position might have run to her mother.

Not me.

Finn knew me well enough to know where to find me, once the last of the Federal fleet had disappeared around the bend toward Vicksburg. He came to sit on the other side of Simon's grave, his legs bent and his elbows resting on his spread knees. After a minute, he said, 'Reckon maybe I oughta join up.'

I glanced over at him. That pinched look was still there around his face. 'You're twelve years old, Finn.'

'I'll be thirteen soon enough. I could go as a drummer boy.'

He could. I'd heard of drummer boys as young as nine or ten. I said, 'Your mama needs you here.'

Finn's daddy, Patrick O'Reilly, had joined up that March, even though his Irish brogue was so thick most folks couldn't understand more'n one word out of ten he said. The O'Reillys had a small farm not far from our place. They were too poor to own slaves and Finn was the eldest of their four children. I asked my mother once why Mr O'Reilly would volunteer to go off and die in a war that wasn't any of his making.

She said, 'I doubt he thinks he's going to die. Most men don't.'

'But why does he want to fight at all?'

'Why do you think Nico Valentino sighed up? He came here from Italy less than eighteen months ago. Or Archie Finley? He's from London.'

'I don't know why,' I answered, exasperated. 'That's why I'm asking.'

But all she'd said was: 'Maybe your father can explain it, because I certainly can't.'

The problem was, since Papa was off with the Louisiana Tiger Battalion in Virginia, we both knew it'd be a spell before I'd be able to ask him anything.

Finn picked up a stick and poked at an ant battling its way through the grass. 'I'm sorry about your cross, Amrie. I know how much it meant to you.'

I nodded, not quite trusting myself to answer. That cross had been my most prized possession. Yet its theft seemed somehow inevitable, a symbol of all that I'd cherished yet now perceived ever so dimly was slipping away forever.

Four

The St Francisville of my earliest childhood memories is a place of soft morning mists sweetly scented by jasmine and honeysuckle, its winding lanes edged with tumbled hedgerows of Cherokee roses that burst into glorious bloom every spring. Bayou Sara, sprawling along the base of the bluff, was mostly all bustle and business. But on the narrow ridge above, stately homes with white-columned porches and sunken brick walkways lined quiet, shady streets. In my recollections of the years before the war, the sky is always a clear crystal blue, the watermelons always juicy to the rind, the harsh sunlight filtered by a leafy canopy of moss-draped live oaks. Yet every Eden hides its own serpent. Ours was not native to this land, but an evil brought by forefathers too ambitious and self-righteous to recognize their own original sin.

I've often pondered what Grandmother Adelaide disliked most about my father: his Catholicism, his French ancestry, or his unabashed hostility to slavery.

I suspect it was the latter.

My father, Anton St Pierre, was the son of French planters who traced their lineage back to some of the first settlers in Ascension and Plaquemines Parishes. By all accounts those earlier St Pierres were a rowdy, disreputable lot, running slaves with Jean Lafitte, dueling beneath oaks at sunrise, and carrying on in ways that adults talked about only in hushed whispers that ended as soon as I walked into the room. When my Grand-père died, Louisiana's French-derived inheritance laws meant that half of his vast plantations went to my Grand-mère St Pierre, with the other half divided equally between my father and his younger sister, Claire. Papa ended up with 920 acres, part of which he sold, and thirty-eight slaves, all of whom he immediately set free.

At that point, my parents had been married only a year. His magnanimous gesture scandalized Adelaide – but not nearly as much as what happened less than two years later when Grandfather Dunbar died. My mother freed every one of the twenty-three slaves she inherited.

Adelaide never forgave her for it. Any time they were around each other for long, at some point Adelaide inevitably ended up saying, 'I can't believe he made you do that.'

My mother would cross her arms at her chest and throw back her head in that way she had. 'Anton didn't *make* me do it. It was my choice.'

But I knew that was only partly true. The gratuitous forfeiture of so much wealth had severely tried my mother's thrifty Scots' soul. Her opinions of slavery pretty much ran even with Papa's, but if she'd had her way, she would have required her slaves to earn their freedom.

Papa would have none of it. 'How in God's name can we ask a man to pay us for what is not rightfully ours to possess?'

And so all twenty-three were freely manumitted. To Adelaide's way of thinking, my parents had jointly cast forty to fifty thousand dollars to the four winds, impoverishing themselves in the process.

This happened before I was born, but the tale was a part of my heritage, often told, for my parents' actions were not popular with their neighbors, either.

There was a time, particularly back in the days of the French and Spanish, when manumission had been common in Louisiana. As a result, tens of thousands of *gens de couleur libres*, or free people of color, lived and worked amongst us as tradesmen and landowners, shopkeepers and laborers. There were nearly as many free blacks as slaves in the city of New Orleans, while one of the biggest slaveowners in our parish was a black woman named Rose Lacroix whose vast plantation lay to the north of Bayou Sara, near the river. But something changed around the time I was born. Folks started getting more defensive in their postures, more angry, more afraid. When my parents freed their slaves, their neighbors took it not just as a moral indictment of the peculiar institution itself, but as a criticism of anyone who practiced it – which I suppose it was. Most folks don't like to be criticized, especially about something they know deep down in their secret heart of hearts is as wrong as wrong can be.

When the abolitionists up North began talking about arming the slaves and setting them to slit the throat of every man, woman, and child in the South, folks around town started getting downright unfriendly, treating us like they treated the Black Irish or the old Choctaw woman who ran a tavern near the wharves in Bayou Sara. It got even worse when the war started, with lots of sullen mutterings about 'traitors in our midst'. Fortunately, that pretty much ended when Papa volunteered as a surgeon.

I thought that might've been why Papa joined up, because I knew what he thought of the war. But when I asked him, he said no.

He'd been gone nearly a year now. Yet sometimes I still caught myself listening for his ready laugh, his quick footstep in our house's wide central hall. Sometimes I'd see a flicker of shadow in the yard and, for one joyous instant, I'd think it was him. Then I'd remember, the truth rushing back with a burning vengeance. It was in those moments that I missed him with a fierceness that was like a physical ache.

But it was at night, when thunder rumbled in the distance and a thick darkness lay heavy and oppressive over the land, that I'd be seized by the unshakable terror that this war he hated so much was going to claim him. That he might at that very moment be bleeding to death alone on some distant battlefield, and I wouldn't know it. I wasn't sure how I could bear it if I never saw him again, never again heard his deep, melodious voice or pressed my face against his vest to breathe in the tobaccoy, horsey scent that had meant safety and comfort to me for as long as I could recall.

I often wondered if my mother shared my silent torments. But whatever her hopes and fears, however frequent her quiet moments of despair, she kept them to herself. With each passing day, she grew a little more aloof, a little more withdrawn into herself in a way that reminded me of the months after Simon died. Consequently, along with missing Papa, I found myself missing my mother, too.

I brooded on these thoughts as I followed the winding, rutted lane that led home. The sky was growing pale, the air cool and hushed, the shadows beneath the oaks and willows a deep violet alive with insects.

We lived in a modest Creole-style raised cottage on the north-eastern outskirts of town. Built of cypress boards painted white, it had two dormered rooms built into a high gabled roof and tall, French-style windows that opened onto deep galleries stretching across both front and back. There were nearly four hundred acres of cleared land attached to the house, and another fifty or so that were still a wild tangle of woods, swamp, and cane breaks. My father leased most of the cleared land to his neighbors, leaving us with enough space for an orchard, a truck garden, and pasturage for our horses and mules, a few sheep, a cow named Queen Bee, and one ornery goat named Flower. The house itself sat in a park-like clearing scattered with live oak and pecan trees and an assortment of smaller structures that had been erected haphazardly with no regard to symmetry or aesthetics: kitchen and laundry, smokehouse, corncrib, woodhouse, stables, and barns. The two-room building Papa used as his doctor's office stood near the front gate.

I thought I might find Mama there, because now that Papa was gone, she did what she could for folks in the area. But as I drew closer to home, I saw her standing in the yard talking to someone I didn't recognize.

Her gaze shifted to me, and in that moment I saw myself through my mother's eyes. The bottom six inches of my skirts, which had trailed in the lagoon, were now brown and grubby with ground-in dirt; a rent I had no recollection getting showed the dark green of my dress through a triangular rip in my pinafore. To top it off, I'd lost one of the leather thongs I used to bind my braids, so that half my hair had come unplaited and was now hanging in a tangled brown mess down my back.

My mother had probably spent the day doing all manner of tasks she never would have needed to set her hand to before the war. Yet the thick, honey-toned chignon at the nape of her neck was still neatly coiled, her white apron clean and starched, her air one of calm serenity. She was well into her thirties now, but she was as slim and beautiful and elegant as in the days when she'd been Miss Katherine Dunbar of Misty Oaks, one of the grandest plantations in Livingston Parish. Once, I used to wonder how a woman as cool and exquisite as my mother could possibly have produced a daughter like me. I eventually decided I must take after one of those disreputable St Pierres no one ever wanted to talk about.

As I turned in through the front gateway, our big old black and white hound, Checkers, came bounding joyously to meet me, tongue lolling, rear end wiggling his welcome. He was nearly as old as I was, and I loved him with a fierceness that sometimes scared me, for reasons I was never quite willing to put into words. As he barreled into me, I let him bowl me over, laughing with delight as he shoved his big head up under my chin. For one eye-squeezing moment, I hugged him to me with all my might.

It wasn't until I stood up, with Checkers running in circles around me, that I realized I did recognize the man Mama was talking to – sort of. It was the mahogany-bearded stranger in homespun I'd seen down by the river. At my approach, he touched a hand to his hat with a nod and strode away into the gathering gloom.

'Who was that?' I asked, staring after him.

'A friend of your father's.'

Her answer surprised me. He didn't look like anyone I could imagine Papa being friends with.

I expected her to give me what-for over being late and tearing my pinafore. But she just pressed her fingertips to her lips, her eyebrows drawing together in a frown, her thoughts focused on some inner, troubled place.

'He told you about the Federal fleet?' I said, relieved that someone

else had already carried the tale to her. I didn't want to talk about
it.

She nodded. 'Although he mainly came to tell me about a man
found drowned this morning in Thompson's Creek. They think he
was one of General Butler's men.'

'*Here*?' Thompson's Creek ran just to the south of us, between
St Francisville and Port Hudson, and was currently flooded by water
backing up from the Mississippi. As much of a shock as it'd been
to watch the Federal fleet steaming boldly up the river, I found it
even more disturbing to realize that the enemy could be creeping
through our woods right now and I wouldn't know it. 'Do they
think he could've come from the gunboats?'

She shook her head. 'No; he wasn't wearing a uniform.'

'So what makes them think he was a Federal?'

'He was carrying a message intended for a woman in St
Francisville.'

I stared at her. 'What woman?'

'There's no way to tell; it was simply addressed "Dear Madam".
But from the contents it was obvious this woman has undertaken
to supply General Butler with details of Confederate troop movements in the area, and other such things.'

By now the sun had disappeared behind the treetops, the last of
the light leaching fast from the sky. A faint mist drifted through the
trees, the cicadas starting up a hellish rhythm that suddenly sounded
unnaturally, almost maddeningly loud.

I said, 'Why did that man come to tell you this?'

'Because he considers your father a friend. He wanted to warn
us.'

'Warn us? About what?'

'At the moment, only the men who found the body know about
the message. But amongst those who do, there's obviously been
some speculation as to the identity of this woman.'

I took an involuntary step back, my head shaking in silent denial
as I finally understood what she was saying. 'They can't think . . .
Oh, surely they don't think that message was intended for you!'

A strange smile touched the corners of her mouth. 'I was born
in Boston.'

'But lots of folks come from up North! You've lived here your
whole life!'

'I have a brother fighting for the Union.'

'And Papa and your two other brothers are all fighting for the South!'

Yet even as I said it, I knew none of that mattered. Mary Todd Lincoln, wife of the Federal president himself, had three brothers fighting for the South. This was a war that had divided brother from brother and son from father. Surely it had also divided husband from wife?

Back in the early, heady days of secession, when patriotic fervor was running red hot and most everybody was convinced that if war came the North could be defeated quickly and easily, Papa had argued vehemently with anyone who'd listen to him and more than a few who wouldn't. But once the war actually started, he and Mama had gone for a long walk along the stream. When they came back, Mama went off to work in her garden, her face set hard, her cheeks wet. She didn't even look up when Papa saddled his horse and rode away to sign up.

I still remember standing in the doorway to his room a few nights later while he packed his knapsack, haversack, and blanket roll. The oil lamp on the round, lace-covered table beside the bed cast his shadow long and distorted across the far wall. I felt the same way I'd felt as I watched them shovel the dirt onto the top of Simon's casket – as if this couldn't be happening. As if I should be able to wake up and the nightmare would all go away. I was desperate to do something – anything – to keep him from leaving.

I said, 'I don't understand why you're doing this. You didn't want this war.'

He folded his extra shirt and carefully nestled it in the soft leather case. 'No. But whether I wanted it or not, war has come, and I must do what I can to protect our new country, our home, and those I love.'

'But you've always hated slavery!'

He hesitated, then left his packing and came to stand before me, his hands resting on my shoulders. 'Make no mistake about this, Amrie: slavery caused this war. If there'd been no slavery, these dark days would never have come to pass. But it's not the passion fueling the fight. Oh, it's obviously what's driving the more war-like amongst the Northern abolitionists to sign up. But while they're certainly vocal, they're not all that numerous. Most folks up North will tell you they're fighting to preserve the Union, while folks down here will say they're fighting for the same reasons their grandfathers fought the Revolution against England – to resist oppression and unjust tariffs, and to safeguard their liberty.' His hands slid from my shoulders as he turned back to his packing, his voice so soft that I barely heard it when he added, 'The ironic contradiction between all their stirring verbiage and the persistence of chattel slavery doesn't occur to them any more than it occurred to their slave-owning forebears.'

'Mr Mumford says that if the Federals win, they're going to outlaw slavery.'

'It's possible. It's not one of their stated war aims, but it is the one sure way to preserve the new western states for free white men – which is what started all of this in the first place.'

'So in a sense, you are fighting for slavery.'

He paused in the act of buckling his knapsack, his head bent, his shoulders stiff. Then he thrust the last strap home and straightened slowly. 'No. I'm fighting to keep you and your mother safe, and to keep our house from being looted and burned, and to keep us from being overrun by the kind of ruthless speculators and profiteers who always follow in the train of a victorious army.'

I stared at him. 'But none of that's going to happen, is it? Folks are saying all it's gonna take is for us to win one big battle, and then Lincoln'll give up and let us go our own way.'

Whatever he saw in my face must have made my father regret what he'd already said, because he came to wrap his strong arms around me and hug me close to his chest. 'I hope so, sweetheart,' he said, turning his head to press his cheek against the top of my head. 'I really hope so.'

But that was a year ago, and I realized now that Mr Mumford and the others like him were wrong, and my papa had known what he was talking about.

Now, to my mother, I said, 'Who do you think that message was intended for?'

My mother shook her head. 'I don't know. Nor do I have any intention of speculating about it – and don't you either, Anne-Marie.'

My mother only called me Anne-Marie when she was seriously peeved at me. At first I couldn't figure out what I'd done to provoke her – muddy hems and torn pinafores not normally being seen as dire enough to warrant it. Then I realized her irritation was both accumulative and preemptive. She was remembering all the times I hadn't listened to her, and anticipating that I'd do it again.

She said, 'I mean it, Amrie. What's at stake here is too serious – and the consequences of a false accusation too dire – for you and Finn to turn it into a game.'

'We wouldn't—'

'I still remember how you tormented poor Hilda Meyers, trying to prove she was a witch.'

I kept quiet. Hilda Meyers was a dour, German-born shopkeeper with a broad, plain face, iron-gray hair, and a body like a lumpy sack of potatoes. Unabashedly avaricious and mean-spirited, she had been locked in perpetual warfare with the children of Bayou Sara and St Francisville since the day she opened her dry goods emporium some seven years before. She'd been known to chase boys out of her store with a broom; she rapped their knuckles with the ramrod from an old musket when they tried to sneak candy out of her jars. Once, she even threatened to turn Finn into a mouse and feed him to her big black cat, which is what made us start thinking that she might be a witch.

We knew better now, of course; she was just a malevolent old woman who hated everyone. But it occurred to me . . .

'*Amrie,*' my mother snapped, as if aware my attention had wandered. 'Don't make me regret having told you.'

I wondered why she had told me, since I knew by the familiar tightening of the skin beside her mouth that she had little expectation of being heeded. Then the furtive rustling of a small, unseen creature in the tangled stretch of gardenias and azaleas bordering the lane made her head jerk around, her hands fisting in her apron, the rest of her body held breathlessly still as she sought in vain to probe the impenetrable darkness that had by now engulfed us.

The night air smelled of sour mud and damp vegetation and distant, stale smoke. I sucked in a deep breath, and it came to me that she'd told me because she feared our lives were about to become exponentially more difficult, and she wanted me to be prepared for it.

We turned to walk together toward the house, with Checkers frisking ahead of us. The faint, sickly glow of a single tallow candle flickered in the parlor window, the marshy, willow-lined stream at the base of a nearby gully alive now with a chorus of croaking bullfrogs. The familiar white house, the myriad of stars, the dark shapes of the mules grazing lazily in the distant pasture, all looked the same as they always had; sounded the same, smelled the same. But that comforting, illusory sense of safety and certainty that I'd known all my life had vanished. I felt small and vulnerable and isolated, and I found myself wondering how many of our friends and neighbors knew about the drowned Federal agent in Thompson's Creek, and how many of them suspected us of being the intended recipient of his message.

Yet as disconcerting as that thought was, I recognized an even more bone-chilling realization: someone I knew and trusted was at that very moment working to destroy everyone I loved.

Five

I awoke the next morning to gray skies and an unseasonably cool wind that shook the fragile leaves of the willows down by the creek and filled the air with the smell of damp earth and coming rain.

My room was one of two nestled beneath the eaves and reached by a steep staircase that led up from an arched alcove off the wide central hall. Downstairs, the parlor and dining room lay on one side of the hall, my parents' room and a guest bedroom on the other. But as I stared out the dormer window at the churning clouds, I became aware of an unnatural stillness that hung over the house.

I knew I should be getting up for school. Instead, I lay with one arm crooked over my eyes, the fingers of my other hand touching the hollow at the base of my throat where my cross should have been. And I felt it again – that swelling of outrage and anger and a tumultuous host of other emotions for which I had as yet no name. I felt as if my world were flying apart. In times like these, how could anyone expect me to go to school and sit quietly listening to Mr Fischer droning on about the agricultural production of the steppes of Russia or the difference between subjunctive and subordinate clauses?

I'd never liked school, which I considered a pitiful waste of precious hours I could fill far more productively and pleasantly on my own. I'd gone through a stage a few years before the war came when I'd advocated endlessly for a private tutor, like the children of the big planters in the area. A tutor would not only free me from such torturous tediums as having to sit through the halting attempts of my fellow classmates to read aloud, but also eliminate the need for me to endure the proximity of the likes of Christian LeBlanc and Meredith McKinney and Isaac Underwood, all of whom I loathed.

Papa put up with my pestering for a time, before finally telling me quite frankly that while he heartily sympathized with my boredom and frustration, private tutors were beyond the means of simple doctors. Then he'd looked at me over the rims of the glasses he always wore when reading the New Orleans papers, and added, 'Besides, it wouldn't hurt you to learn to get along better with other children.'

The statement left me beyond indignant, for it implied that the fault was mine, which it most certainly wasn't.

Or at least, I thought it wasn't.

Yet as bad as things had been, before, my troubles at school took a severe turn for the worse in the fall of 1860, when the election ratcheted up folks' emotions to the snapping point, and my parents' well-known abolitionist sympathies and open opposition to secession brought me more than my usual quota of sideways glances and whispered taunts.

I'd responded to those insults with all of a ten-year-old's ferocious righteousness and a few dirty tricks I'd learned from Finn. But it didn't take me long to realize that while grinding Spencer Caine's face into the mud of the schoolyard or pulling one of Sarah Henley's braids until she hollered, ''Nough!' might get my classmates to shut up and leave me alone, it was worse than useless when it came to changing their minds.

I was still pondering the uses and limitations of violence when I heard Mahalia holler up the stairs, 'Amrie! You gonna drag your lazy bones outa that bed? Don't make me come up there and git you!'

I got up.

Mahalia had been with us for as long as I could remember. A full-bosomed, shapely woman in her early thirties, she had golden skin and the startling, turquoise eyes one sometimes saw in those of mixed race. She'd been born down on the Bayou Teche and lived her early years amongst the French-speaking Acadian settlers there, which left her with their distinctive accent and syntax. She was one

of the twenty-three slaves my mother inherited from my grandfather
and freed. I asked Mahalia once why she'd decided to stay with us
when most of the others had gone their separate ways, but all she
said was, 'I like yor momma, and I like it here. Why should I go
off and live amongst strangers, hmmm? I wouldn't be any more
free.'

I always thought there was more to the story than that, but I'd
never managed to ferret it out.

'There you is,' she said when I wandered onto the back gallery,
still rubbing my eyes and with Checkers padding at my heels. In
those days, food was still relatively plentiful – at least for us – and
she plunked a breakfast of buttermilk, eggs, and corn muffins down
on the round rattan table we used for our meals when the weather
was fair. 'Miss Lavinia Carter's baby done decided in the middle
of the night that it was ready to be born. Yor momma drove off
with Avery hours ago, and I ain't heard nothin' since.'

Avery was the younger of the two men my parents employed,
thin and gangly, with long arms and legs and a big, wide smile.
When my mother was called off to help someone in the middle of
the night, Avery usually drove her.

Only men could be licensed as doctors in Louisiana, as in most
other parts of what had been the United States. But anyone, male
or female, with the money to pay the fees could attend lectures at
the medical schools in New Orleans, and my mother had attended
every lecture they offered.

Her long-standing fascination with medicine both scandalized
and shamed my Grandmother Adelaide. But my grandfather had
been more open-minded – or maybe he was just more indulgent.
He made arrangements for her to live with his sister, whose banker-
husband had just built a big house on St Charles Avenue. While
other young women her age were attending balls and dinner parties
and moving through all the formal rituals that were a traditional
part of finding a husband in her world, my mother attended lectures
on anatomy and physiology. She met my father over the dissection
of a cadaver pulled from the river. Papa always said her tiny hands
and manual dexterity would have made her a better surgeon than
he could ever hope to be. But he had the license from the state, and
she didn't.

Sometimes in the evening when the wind was blowing wild,
when thunder rumbled in the distance and a hum of tense expecta-

tion charged the air, I'd see her standing at the end of the gallery, her arms wrapped around her waist, her gaze fixed on something in the distance I could never see, her features drawn with a bleak combination of longing and frustration.

I'd learned early to leave her alone on such occasions.

Now, with my father and most of the other doctors in the parish off to war, folks had started coming to my mother for help, license or no license. I thought at first it might make them like her better, but it didn't. I could never figure out why they still held the freeing of those twenty-three slaves against her, but shrugged away my father's freeing of his thirty-eight. I figured it had something to do with her being a woman, but I couldn't untangle the details.

'Why you just playin' with that food, you?' Mahalia demanded, her delicately arched eyebrows puckering together in a frown. She was a beautiful woman, her face and figure such as to turn the heads of most men – and women – who saw her. I asked her once why she had no children of her own, but she just got a funny look on her face and told me to finish my grits before I was late for school.

Mahalia and I had never got on easy together. She was constantly picking on me, poking me to stand up straight, and worrying me something fierce over one thing or another. I knew Simon had been her favorite, although I didn't hold that against her because he'd been my favorite, too. She had mourned his death nearly as hard as my mother, but it didn't lead her to go any easier on me.

'I ain't hungry,' I said, giving up on the cornbread. Time was, I'd loved cornbread. But we hadn't seen any wheat flour for nearly six months, and a steady diet of cornbread gets tiresome quick.

'I'm *not* hungry,' she corrected. 'Don't you let yor momma hear you talkin' like ignorant, common folk.'

This was one of our constant battles. I knew she blamed Finn, which was a surefire way to set up my back. 'You say *ain't*.'

'That ain't the point.' She took my plate and scraped my leavings into the slop bucket she would later carry down to the hogs. 'I is what I is. You is not.'

I stared at her, baffled by her logic.

I knew *gens de couleur libres* who spoke better than most white folks, who'd been educated in Paris and seen places I could only dream of visiting – London and Rome, Venice and Istanbul. They were always as careful as careful can be to differentiate themselves from the field hands and house servants, not just by their speech, but by their dress and their mannerisms and their fastidious adherence to the designated 'done thing'. So why didn't Mahalia?

It would be a long time before I came to understand that different people can have different ways of coping with the pressures that strain and constrict their lives.

Our schoolhouse was wood-framed and small, since even those who couldn't afford to hire a private tutor used to send their older children off to finishing school or college. Some went to Virginia and Philadelphia or even Paris. But most didn't go far, the boys heading to Centenary College up the road in nearby Jackson, Louisiana, and the girls to Silliman in Clinton.

With the coming of the war, most colleges in the South were now closed.

We sat on rows of long pine benches with low desks that faced the schoolmaster's raised platform and a blackboard. Girls sat on one side of the room, boys on the other – except when a boy was punished by being forced to sit with the girls. It was intended to humiliate the boy, and it did, for he would sit there with his face bright red with shame. But it always humiliated and angered me, too, in a way that took me a long time to pin down. I noticed that girls were never punished by being made to sit with the boys, and I eventually figured out that was because sitting with the boys would have been considered an honor.

As I slid into my place, I cast a quick glance around the room, wondering if the whispers of my mother's supposed treasonous activities had leaked out. But everybody was talking about the Federal fleet; I didn't hear a peep about drowned Federal messengers. I caught Finn's eye, but he just threw me a big grin and went back to trading marbles with Tad Cooper.

Our schoolmaster was a thick-bodied recent immigrant from Vienna named Horst Fischer, who still spoke with a heavy Austrian accent. At the time, we considered him old, although he was probably only in his late twenties or early thirties. He just seemed old, with his slow, ponderous movements, his fussy ways, and the thin cornsilk-fine hair he wore long on top in a futile attempt to disguise his prematurely balding pate.

I'd nursed a personal grudge against the schoolmaster ever since he confiscated my copy of Voltaire's *Candide*. I'd had the slim blue volume open on the bench beside me, surreptitiously reading while he was trying for the hundredth time to explain the intricacies of long division to the slower children, and he'd somehow spotted it. He said he'd give it back to me when I learned to pay attention in class. But it'd been nearly a year now, and he still had it. I'd sometimes see him reading it himself. I couldn't understand why if he liked it so much, he didn't just buy his own copy and give me mine back.

In that self-centered way of children, we were cruel enough to hope that he would enlist, since that would be the end of school for us. But he kept insisting this wasn't his war, and that was all there was to it. As more and more young men left to fight, folks started calling him a stay-at-home and a fireside brave. Some of the boys stuck white feathers in his books when his back was turned and clucked like a chicken when he walked down the street.

He set his jaw hard and worked at ignoring them.

After my earlier, unsatisfactory conversation with my mother, I'd once considered asking Mr Fischer why men like Finn's daddy and Nico Valentino had enlisted when it wasn't their fight, either. I figured he could surely explain it to me. But I decided against it. He got enough grief from everyone else; he didn't need me adding to it. I might not like him much, but I did feel a bit sorry for him. He always struck me as dreadfully lonely.

Before the war, Mr Fischer would ring a bell to 'take in' school. But the school bell, like the big brass bell in the tower of Grace Episcopal Church and plantation bells up and down the river, had been donated to the war effort. Instead of beating its swords into plowshares, the South was melting down its bells and molding them into canons.

As a result, Mr Fischer had to tap his ruler on the side of his desk to call his pupils to order. It wasn't very effective under the best of circumstances and even less so that morning, for the room was abuzz with talk of yesterday's first sighting of the Federal fleet, and those children unlucky enough not to have witnessed it in person were eager to hear from those who had – or who were pretending they had. I was probably the only child in the room who simply sat with my fingers laced tightly together and my gaze fixed straight ahead as I tried to ignore the swirl of excited voices and rampant speculation around me.

'I reckon Farragut himself musta been on that sloop of war—'

'I heard them paddle-wheelers is carrying General Williams's army. They embarked from Kennertown—'

'My grandpa says if they take Vicksburg, they'll be able to cut the Confederacy clean in two. My grandpa says—'

Mr Fischer practically broke his ruler banging it on his desk again and again, trying to get everyone's attention. '*I vill have silence!*' he screamed, spittle flying from his mouth as he shook with rage, his face such a deep, purple hue that he reminded me of old Mr Blackburn when he choked on a fishbone and nearly died.

Struck dumb, the entire class stared at him.

'There. Goot.' He adjusted the collar of his coat. 'Ve vill began.'

I breathed a silent sigh of relief. Then he told us to haul out our spelling books, and my brief, uncharacteristic enthusiasm for school-work evaporated then and there.

But I didn't need to endure that day's tedium for long. I was just cleaning my slate for our geography lesson when a shout went up and someone ran past the schoolroom door hollering, 'Confederate cavalry squadron coming!'

Horst Fischer gave it up and let us go.

Six

The cavalry squadron was from Camp Moore, the big Confederate training camp to the east of us. Camp Moore was Louisiana's largest training camp, and it lay on the railroad line between New Orleans and Jackson, Mississippi. When New Orleans surrendered, the troops who had been guarding the city were withdrawn north up the tracks to Camp Moore.

The cavalry thundered through town, horse hides dark with sweat and rain, filling the air with the pounding of hooves and the creak of saddle leather and a welcome reassurance after yesterday's humiliation and intimidation. They talked to Mr Marks for a time and then rode on.

With the sudden, unexpected freedom of the day stretching before us, Finn wanted to go off with some of the other boys and practice drilling. Because we'd spent so many hours hanging around the green to watch the militia drill, all the children knew the commands and maneuvers by heart. We could 'file left' and 'about face' far better than any batch of new recruits. Wielding broomsticks and pokers rather than muskets and rifles, we regularly shouldered and presented arms with precision.

Usually, no one said a word in disparagement when some of us girls joined in the drilling. But today seemed somehow different, yesterday's sighting of the Federal fleet having worked the boys into a fever pitch. They swaggered around with their hands in their pockets and their straw hats tipped back on their heads, boasting to each other about which unit they were going to join when they got old enough. Finn might have welcomed me, but I knew from their sideways scowls that wasn't true of the other boys.

Normally, that wouldn't have stopped me. But I had something else I wanted to do – something I didn't want to tell Finn about.

After he'd run off with the other boys, I headed down the bluff to Bayou Sara. Once, Bayou Sara had been a rough town, akin to Natchez-Under-the-Hill. It was considerably more respectable now, with its grand emporiums and fancy hotels and ostentatiously imposing banks. But there were still parts of town I was forbidden to enter, mainly the Point, where Irish bargemen and mulattoes and Houma Indians mingled in seedy taverns, and painted women in various stages of undress lounged in doorways or leaned out of upstairs windows.

Like all forbidden things, the Point fascinated me. I listened with rapt attention to snatches of conversations I knew I wasn't supposed to be hearing, tales of wild brawls and knife fights, of men's naked bodies dumped in the river and women found slumped with their throats slit.

Yet as much as the Point intrigued me, it also repelled me. No one had ever explicitly explained to me what might happen were I to wander alone down those forbidden alleyways. But I knew. I'd grown up surrounded by pigs and cows, sheep and horses, dogs and cats. The mechanics of the creation of new life were no mystery to me, and I hadn't been very old before I figured out the connection between what I saw happening in the fields and the swelling bellies of the talcum-scented, hoop-skirted, oh-so-respectable ladies who filled our church pews every Sunday. My mind boggled at the details, for I was still very ignorant and innocent. But I grasped the essence of what men did to women, even though I gathered they generally did it at night, in bed, rather than out in the fields.

Just the thought of such an intrusion into the very core of my being revolted me. I'd long ago decided that, while I'd probably like to be married some day, I would never allow my husband to do *that* to me. I couldn't understand why any woman would willingly submit to it.

I'd expressed this conviction to my mother, once. A strange, secret smile softened her features and she said, 'I remember feeling much the same way when I was your age. I think you'll find you've changed your mind when the time comes.'

I knew I never would.

But I knew, too, that such congress could also occur outside the matrimonial bed, in which case the consequences were dire. As with so much else, these matters were never explicitly addressed. Yet every girl my age understood quite clearly that her purity and innocence were considered her most prized possessions, to be safeguarded at any cost. We knew that an unmarried woman would be utterly 'ruined' if she had relations with a man, even if such attentions had been forced upon her against her will. Whether she succumbed willingly or under threat of violence made no difference; any woman known to have done *that* with a man not her husband became an object of scorn and pity, forever outcast from polite society. Yet when I look back on it, I can't recall anyone actually using the word *rape*. The expressions of choice included 'outraged', and 'grievously insulted', and, of course, 'a fate worse than death'. As far as most people were concerned, that's exactly what it was.

I stayed away from the Point.

My objective that day was the dry goods emporium of Mrs Hilda Meyers. My mother might be unwilling to speculate on the identity of 'Dear Madam', but I had never been known for my self-restraint.

Meyers Dry Goods Emporium and Grocery Store stood just off Principal Street, beside the livery stable owned by Castile Boudreau, a free man of color, and his son, Leo. Meyers Emporium was an impressive establishment, two stories tall and built of brick, with a covered gallery shading the broad wooden sidewalk across the front. Beneath this overhang clustered baskets, barrels, and crates heaped with everything from blackberries and potatoes to tomatoes and sweet peppers and goober peas. Before the war, the shelves inside had been generously stocked with all sorts of wonders: ladies' parasols and high-top shoes, delicate linen drawers and chemises, dresses of silk and cashmere, stays and hoops and handkerchiefs, crochet hooks and skeins of brightly colored wool, lace tablecloths, buttons, tapes, bolts of cotton, and any manner of other delights, while the smell of new leather, starch, rose water and lavender filled the air. But the blockade had bit hard into Hilda Meyers' business, depleting her shelves as well as her customers, as men marched off to war and the women they left behind found themselves scrambling just to feed their families.

I had to draw up just inside the entrance, for despite the cloud cover the day was bright enough that the sudden gloom of the shop's interior left me momentarily blind.

'Vhat are you doing here?' Hilda Meyers's husky voice boomed out of the darkness. 'Vhy aren't you in school?'

I squinted in the general direction of the voice. 'Mr Fischer let us off for the rest of the day 'cause of the cavalry in town.'

She snorted. 'Vhat a fool.'

I could see her now. She stood behind the massive, heavily carved wooden counter that stretched along one wall of the emporium, her upper lip pinched in a way that made her nose wrinkle as if she'd smelled something foul. She was probably in her early sixties, although there was nothing frail about her. She towered over the other women in town and most of the men, too. Her carriage was fiercely upright, her movements quick and strong, and when she walked, her stride was so long that most folks had to trot just to keep up with her.

If she'd been a more pleasant person, I might have admired her, for her strength and her shrewdness and the bull-headed courage that had brought her halfway around the world to open a shop in a strange land. But she was a sour, brusque, and unhappy person, the lumpy features of her face having long since settled into a scowl that only deepened whenever she saw me. She knew I was Finn's friend, and she hated Finn with a special passion that was more than mutual.

'Vhere's that good-for-nothing Irish thatch-gallows I see you with all the time?' she demanded.

I wandered the aisles, unexpectedly saddened at the sight of empty, dusty shelves that had once been overflowing with goods. 'He's off practicin' drillin' with the other boys.'

She let out a grunt that heaved her massive, shelf-like bosom. 'Huh. They've ambitions to become canon fodder, have they? More fools. This state is full of fools. This *country* is full of fools.'

I threw her a quick, studied glance. Hilda Meyers had never made any secret of her contempt for the idea of Southern independence. She owned three slaves she frequently hired out as day laborers, so I knew she was no abolitionist. But I suspected she'd give just about anything to bring back the flow of commerce up and down the river.

I said, 'D'you see the Federal fleet yesterday, Miss Hilda?'

'I did not.' Her frown deepened with her suspicions. She knew I was up to no good; she just couldn't figure out what. 'I've better things to do with my days than spend them on the levee, gawking at the river with all the riffraff in town.'

'Some folks are saying there's Federal messengers in the woods, too. You believe that?'

I watched her face. But I couldn't tell if her fierce scowl was because I'd hit a nerve or if she was just fed up with me.

'Vhat you doing here?' she demanded again. 'Hmmm?'

'Just lookin' around.'

'Vell, go look someplace else.' She reached for her broom. 'You heard me. Go, go, go!'

I knew better than to turn my back on that broom. I retreated slowly toward the door, one foot behind the other, my gaze locked with hers, my hands tense at my sides, ready to do battle if it came to that.

'Don't come back; you hear?' she shouted after me. 'Not unless you got money to spend. And I mean *real* money; not that worthless paper script.'

I backed to the end of the gallery, then stopped, one arm wrapped around the support post, my gaze fixed thoughtfully on the emporium's plate glass windows. I wasn't sure what if anything I'd learned, although there was no denying the encounter had underscored my antipathy for the woman.

'I guess Mizz Hilda don't want your bidness, child,' said a deep, amusement-filled voice behind me.

I turned to find Castile standing at the entrance to his stable, a bridle dangling from one hand. He was a big man – big enough to tower over even Hilda Meyers. His skin was a deep ebony, his head bald and bullet-shaped, his nose wide and flat, his lips full. He told me once he figured he was somewhere in his fifties, although he didn't know exactly where.

He might be free now, but you didn't need to see the scar tissue on his back to know that he'd once been a slave. He'd been branded with an 'AD' on his face, the letters seared into both cheeks. I'd never had the impudence to ask him what it stood for, or who'd put it there, or why.

Castile was one of Finn's and my favorite people. He came often to see Priebus, the older man who worked for Papa. Over the years, Castile had taught us all sorts of wondrous things – how to make and bait bird traps, how to track animals in the woods, and how to fashion a bow from hickory and sinew. Priebus told us once that Castile had lived with the Choctaw for a spell when he was a young man, back in the day when the tribe could still be found along the banks of the Mississippi and up the bayous.

I let go the post and hopped off the end of the boardwalk, my face still hot from my recent encounter. 'I think she has to be just about the nastiest person I've ever known.'

He laughed out loud, his amusement crinkling the skin beside his eyes into fan-like creases. But all he said was: 'She's had more than her fair share of sorrows.'

'Huh. She don't strike me as sorrowful; she's just mean.' I watched a heavy freight wagon labor up the street, its massive high wheels plowing deep ruts in the mud. 'What's a thatch-gallows?'

'A low-down no-account.' He nodded toward the emporium. 'She call you that?'

I shook my head. 'Finn.'

He laughed again. 'Well, she don't like Finn much, that's fer sure.'

Then his eyes went out of focus, and I realized he was looking behind me. Turning, I saw two men coming out of the door of Miss Nell's eatery. The man in the lead was tall and lean, his long beard unkempt, his clothes of simple homespun. Across the width of the rutted street, his gaze met mine.

Then he looked away.

I said to Castile, my voice low, 'See that man – the one with the mahogany-colored beard? You know who he is?'

'Reckon I do, seein' as how he keeps his horse wit me. Name's Gallagher; Sean Gallagher. He come down the river a few weeks back. Stayin' over Mr Gantry's, he is.'

Devon Gantry ran Bayou Sara's post office, stage station, and telegraph office. Several years ago he had moved with his new wife and baby girl into a neat white house with green ventilated shutters up in St Francisville, and let out the rooms over his offices. The significance of the association between the two men would not occur to me until later, although I suspect Castile had already figured it out.

The other man with Gallagher moved forward now to stand beside him, a man wearing a short gray Confederate jacket, kepi cap, and sturdy trousers. Built thick through the chest and shoulders, he had a broad face with a thick black mustache and small, widely set eyes the translucent gray color of fish scales.

I didn't need to ask Castile about the second man, for I recognized him the instant I got a good look at him. His name was Hiram Tucker, and he and his brother Rufus ran a sawmill and brick factory on the south side of town. Once, late last summer, he'd called my mother out to the mill to attend an injured worker. Hiram claimed the man had fallen onto a pile of logs. But my mother didn't believe him. She was convinced somebody had taken a board to the man and beat him half to death with it. She told Hiram to his face that there was a special place in hell for anyone who abused those under his power.

Hiram looked at her through slitted eyes, his jaw tight, and said, 'You think I'd risk killin' a man I paid twelve hundred dollars fer? If I got somethin' really dangerous needs doin', I hire me some Irishman fer a dollar a day. If he gets kilt, there's always more where he come from, and if he gets his back broke, it ain't none of my affair. I tell you, that stupid nigger fell.'

'I've seen the way you treat your dogs and your horses,' said my mother, climbing into her buggy. 'That tells me all I need to know.' And then she'd given her horse the office to start, the buggy jerking forward to leave the sawmill owner standing in the middle of the road, his hands clenched into fists at his sides, his hat pulled low as he watched her drive away.

The injured workman survived, although he always held his left arm kinda funny. He never would talk about how he got hurt.

But there was something about the look in Hiram Tucker's eyes now, as he stared at me from across the street, that told me he still hadn't forgiven my mother for her unvarnished expression of contempt. Instead, he'd hugged his indignation and sense of grievance to himself, nurturing and feeding it until it had grown into something vile and dangerous.

And I realized now with a chill that the man's burning malevolence also extended to me.

Seven

Leaving Castile's livery, I turned toward the steep street that ran up the face of the bluff.

Since yesterday's appearance of the Federal fleet, a palpable air of foreboding had descended on both Bayou Sara and St Francisville, an eerie kind of tension that reminded me of the breathless hours that can come just before the fierce winds and deadly rains of a hurricane.

As I walked, I kept having to detour around huddled bunches of women and aging men. They gathered together outside the telegraph station, on street corners, at garden gates, some arguing heatedly, others simply standing with shoulders hunched, eyes darting this way and that as they waited desperately for word of what was happening just up the river at Vicksburg.

Like St Francisville, the city of Vicksburg sat high on a bluff overlooking the Mississippi. But Vicksburg lay at a strategic hairpin bend of the river and was well fortified. If the Federals wanted control of the Mississippi, they were going to have to take Vicksburg. So the question on everyone's mind was: would the city resist? Or would Vicksburg simply surrender, the way New Orleans had?

'The situation is entirely different,' I heard Mr Marks insisting. 'Vicksburg is defensible; New Orleans was not. Why, when New Orleans fell, the river was so high the Federal gunboats were actually looking *down* on the city. To have refused to surrender would have been an act of suicide!'

Jane Gastrell, the bony, pinch-faced woman who ran the hardware store now that her husband Jack had gone off to war, twitched and sputtered with a corrosive combination of outrage and stung nationalistic pride. 'Did the three hundred Spartans surrender at Thermopylae? No, they did not! They fought to the death. Would you suggest that Southerners are made of lesser stuff? Well, let me tell you right now, Mr Marks, we are not! The people of New Orleans should have burned their city themselves, the same way the Russians fired Moscow rather than let it fall to Napoleon. That's what proper Southerners would have done. If you ask me, the problem is all those Irish and Germans in the city these days.'

I had to force myself to keep walking, because what I really wanted to do was stop and kick Jane Gastrell in the shins. I'd heard that kind of talk before and I could never understand it. My grand-mère lived in New Orleans. Just the thought of her high-ceilinged, pastel-colored house with its dark green slatted shutters and honey-suckle-draped iron balconies going up in flames was enough to make my chest hurt. Why would anyone want to see such a beautiful city destroyed? Whether the Federals had moved into a bustling city or a smoking ruin, they'd still be there. So what would've been the point? The only difference would've been a hundred thousand or so people without homes – and probably a good many of them dead, too. No one ever seemed to think about what happened to those residents of Moscow who were too old or sick or young to run away from the flames. I figured they'd died; that's what happened to them, along with a heap of their cats and dogs and other hapless creatures. And now our fireside braves were advocating the same fiery end for Vicksburg.

My Aunt Em and Cousin Hannah lived in Vicksburg.

Feeling suddenly tired and oddly alone, I climbed the bluff and went home.

I spent what was left of the day helping Mahalia weed the vegetable garden. The morning's light rain had left the earth soft and crumbly, the sky an opaque white with high clouds, the breeze warm and smelling of freshly turned soil and the animals grazing in the nearby pasture.

I did not tell my mother about seeing the mahogany-bearded man with Hiram Tucker, just as I had kept silent about the infantry captain who stole my necklace. As I pulled out pokeweed and chopped at the chickweed that threatened to choke our rows of corn and beans, melons and potatoes, I found myself wondering at my new, uncharacteristic reluctance to share the worrisome details of my life with the people I loved. I hadn't even told Finn about the drowned Federal found in Thompson's Creek and the dangerous speculation that the intended recipient of his message was my own mother.

Why?

I had a feeling the answer was not one I cared to name.

Despite the cloud cover, the afternoon was hot, and I had to keep stopping to wipe the sweat out of my eyes with one crooked arm. We'd always had a vegetable garden to supply our own needs. But when talk of secession heated up after the election, my mother decided to triple our garden's size, ordering seeds for all sorts of stuff we didn't normally bother growing for ourselves. And at the end of the season, she'd carefully saved seeds from our harvest, because seeds, like so much else in the South, came from the North and disappeared when the Federal blockade slammed down on us.

At the same time she expanded the vegetable garden, my mother also widened the patch of medicinal herbs she grew behind a picket fence near the front gate, everything from pennyroyal and feverfew to wormwood and angelica and peppermint. This was a garden she always tended herself, and when Simon and I were little, we were under strict, don't-even-think-about-disobeying-me instructions never to touch anything that grew there.

Simon was never interested anyway. But I was. I found the scraggly, wild-looking, yet mysteriously powerful plants endlessly fascinating, and I listened with rare attention as my mother patiently taught me their names and histories and reputed properties. I knew that pennyroyal could keep away ants and kill a baby growing inside a woman – or the woman herself, if she ingested too much of it. I knew that mint helped a bad stomach, and that a salve made of arnica soothed aching muscles. But none of my mother's plants intrigued me more than the long-stemmed, brightly hued poppies.

I could see them swaying gracefully in the breeze that evening when I left the vegetable garden and cut toward the front gate with Checkers trotting happily at my heels. The sun was sinking low in the west, throwing long shadows that stretched before us across the grass. The poppies were a recent addition to the herb patch. My mother had planted them with the first talk of war and she tended them with a careful vigilance that underlined in a way nothing else could how valuable they were. For from the unripe seed heads formed by these exuberant, carefree-looking flowers came opium, with its magical ability to take away pain and melancholia – and life itself.

When I reached the picket fence around the garden, I could see her moving along the rows of poppies, methodically scoring the big, unripe seedpods. With each slice, a milky white resin oozed out like thick tears that would dry overnight into golden-brown globs of opium.

For the past year, she had been sending her balls of raw opium to New Orleans, where it was turned into the morphine needed so badly by the sick, maimed, and dying soldiers who overflowed our military hospitals. But with the fall of the city, who would take it now?

I paused with one elbow looped over the picket gate, quiet for a time as I watched her move on to the next fat seed head. Then I said, 'What's the point of collecting the opium when you can't send it to New Orleans anymore?'

She glanced over at me before refocusing her attention on the poppy head, slicing it carefully so as not to go too deep. 'Morphine works better than raw opium at deadening pain. But even raw opium is better than nothing, and they need it to help control the dysentery over at Camp Moore.'

I'd heard that folks up North had the idea that when New Orleans fell, Louisiana fell. But the truth was, the Federal presence in our state was limited only to New Orleans and to the gunboats on the river. They'd stopped briefly at our capital, Baton Rouge. But they'd only stayed long enough to tear down the Confederate flag and run up their own. Then they'd continued on up the river to Vicksburg without leaving even a squadron of troops.

'Although this isn't just for Camp Moore,' she said, moving on to the next plant. 'We're going to need it, too.'

'Us?' I echoed, not understanding. 'We're not sick.'

'I meant "we" as in the people of St Francisville and Bayou Sara. Too many of my medicines are running low already, and I don't see this war ending any time soon.'

With the firing on Fort Sumter, Lincoln had placed an embargo on all medical supplies, along with the myriad of other things we normally imported. Lots of folks claimed the Federal blockade was the first real act of war between our two nations. But that was a nicety that didn't concern my mother overly much. What riled her was its effects. As I watched her lips tighten with anger, I knew exactly what was coming.

She said, 'Isn't it enough to stop the importation of food and necessary supplies? What kind of inhuman monsters deny medicines to sick women and children, to the old and the dying? What kind of twisted moral contortions could ever justify that? How do they sleep at night? By blaming us? Do they really think God believes the comfortable lies they tell themselves?'

'Yes,' I said. I might have been only eleven, but I'd already figured out that one.

She looked up again, and I knew by the faint widening of her eyes that she had been speaking as much to herself as to me. Then her gaze narrowed and she said, 'What happened to your cross, Amrie?'

I felt my cheeks flame for reasons I couldn't even begin to explain. 'I lost it when I was playin' with Finn.'

I thought she might scold me for my carelessness, but she only said, 'I'm sorry, honey. I know how much it meant to you.'

I glanced away, my vision of the dark, spreading branches of the oaks and their streamers of gray, wind-ruffled moss suddenly blurred by an unexpected uprush of tears that I struggled to keep back. The heat had gone out of the day, the air sweetening with the smell of the coming dew and the night-blooming flowers just beginning to open as the horizon turned pink.

And I found myself wondering, again, why I felt the need to hug the truth to myself, as if I had somehow invited the theft by running to the levee to watch the dark presence of the Federal fleet steaming into our quiet world.

Eight

Within a few days, the news came singing over the telegraph wires: Vicksburg hadn't surrendered. Its mayor had answered Commodore Farragut's threatening demands with a tersely worded message of defiance.

But the Federal fleet didn't take no for an answer. They immediately opened fire on the crowded city, indiscriminately hurling bombs and shells toward homes and churches, schools and hospitals, screaming women and frightened children. So the new question became: how long could Vicksburg hold out? We understood only too well that if the Mississippi fell under Federal control, no town along the river would be safe.

What we did not yet realize was that the vestiges of safety to which we still clutched were only an illusion.

That Sunday, the long rows of pews in Grace Episcopal Church were crowded.

The big, red-brick church was far grander than the earlier wooden structure it had recently replaced, with rows of narrow, high-pointed windows and a massive organ that took up nearly all of one transept. It was so new it still smelled faintly of paint and plaster and linseed oil, and folks in town were enormously proud of it.

I'd noticed the war was having an uneven effect on people's churchgoing habits. There were some, like old Mr Sprague, who lost his faith when his twin sons, Adrian and Daniel, fell together on the battlefield of Manassas just a week before their eighteenth birthday. But most folks clung to their religion the way a half-drowned raccoon hangs onto a log in the swirling waters of a raging flood. It was the one thing keeping them afloat, and they wondered aloud how Sprague got through his days.

My own faith in God was something I'd never questioned. It was taught to us in Sunday school the same way spelling and the times tables were hammered into us by Horst Fischer during the week: by rote, and with the steely expectation that we would accept what we were told.

Like my father and all the St Pierres, much of New Orleans and south Louisiana was still French and Catholic – or, at least, Irish and German and Catholic. But St Francisville and the rest of West Feliciana Parish had been heavily settled by Anglo-Americans, many of them from New England, which was why the biggest church in town was Episcopal. We didn't even have a Catholic priest in the area; he came over from Clinton and Jackson every few weeks to say mass in the big room over the market building.

I'd never been to one of those masses. But whenever I visited Grand-mère on the rue Sainte-Anne not far from St Louis Cathedral in New Orleans, she'd take me with her to mass. I accepted the differences between the two churches with no sense of incongruity, for both had always been a part of my life. No one had ever asked me to choose between my parents' religions. To my Grandmother Adelaide's disgust, my mother and father had long ago agreed to expose their children to both Catholicism and the Episcopal Church, and let us decide when we came of age.

I sometimes wondered how that affected my brother, Simon, who had died before he'd had a chance to make his selection. I asked my mother, once, if she thought God held Simon's indecision against him, or if his early death had actually worked in his favor, since he might have chosen wrong if he had lived long enough. She'd given me a funny look, then said she didn't think God cared overly much about what tenets people claimed to believe; what mattered was the way they behaved and what was in their hearts. I thought at the time she hadn't answered my question, but I later realized that she had.

For reasons she'd never particularized, Mama was usually careful to choose a pew at the back of the church, unlike Grand-mère, who liked to sit as close to the altar as she could, her head tilted back in rapt attention to the mass, the jet black beads of her rosary moving silently through her gnarled, boney fingers.

I found myself thinking about Grand-mère as Mama and I took our usual seat near the door, and I missed her with a sudden fierceness that was part selfish need and part nagging worry. She was a tiny woman, Grand-mère, about my height and wispy thin, with a thick head of white hair and sharp black eyes and an elegant bone structure she had bequeathed to her son but not, alas, to me. She'd always been a wonder to me. My other grandmother, Adelaide Dunbar, and, to a lesser extent, my mother herself, were both undemonstrative and endlessly critical. But Grand-mère was effusive and unabashedly emotional, a refuge of lavender-scented hugs and kisses and exuberant laughter.

In the weeks that had now passed since the fall of New Orleans, we'd heard no word from Grand-mère, for the coming of the Federals had utterly severed our normal mail services. We didn't know if she was well, or if she was even still alive. It was as if an iron cordon had slammed down around New Orleans, separating parents from children, husbands from wives, and imposing a silence that weighed heavily on anyone with loved ones in the occupied city. Soon, the heat of the summer would be upon us, when those who could normally fled the city to escape the yellow fever epidemics that all too often raged as the temperature climbed. Usually Grand-mère would spend the summer months with the family of her daughter, my Aunt Claire, in Ascension Parish. But this year, Grand-mère was trapped; a seventy-five-year-old widow living alone with only a couple of aged servants, at the mercy of men like the golden-haired infantry captain whose image floated before me unbidden as I opened my prayer book.

In an effort to banish the memory, I let my gaze rove over my fellow parishioners. These days the pews were filled almost exclusively with drawn-faced, anxious-eyed women and fidgeting children, their homemade palmetto hats, threadbare ruffles and bows punctuated only here and there by a dark-suited, sweating man of middle age or older, with a scattering of soldiers wounded at Shiloh and home on medical furlough.

Sometimes in the past when I grew bored in church, I'd occupy myself by covertly studying my fellow parishioners and wondering what each person was praying for. But I suspected we now all prayed for the same things: for the health and safety of the men away at war, for victory, for peace. I imagined I could actually *feel* the fervor of all those prayers, a mighty chorus of beseechment rising up not just from our church but from every church – Episcopal and Catholic, Baptist and Methodist – scattered across Louisiana. I thought of all the churches across the South; tens of thousands of them full of millions of women and children and aging men, heads bowed and hands clasped in desperate prayer for an army of beloved sons and grandsons, husbands and fathers, brothers and nephews, cousins and friends.

How could any merciful God not heed such heartfelt pleas, I wondered? But then I thought about those millions of other women and children, to the North, who at this very moment were likewise kneeling to assail the heavens with prayers for the safety of *their* loved ones, for the victory of *their* armies.

For our death and destruction.

How did God choose whose prayers he answered, I wondered? Did He flip a coin? Weigh the strength of our respective voices? They were four times as plentiful; did that mean they could out-pray us as well as out-fight us? Or did He weigh the justice of our respective causes? I had no doubt that whoever won would think so, puffed up in the certitude of their righteousness as well as in the glory of their victory and the smug conviction that God had chosen *them*.

I wished I could be that sure.

People were always saying, 'The South *must* win! Our cause is just, and God is on our side.' I'd said as much to my father, the morning he rode off toward Camp Moore and the train that would carry his battalion away to join the Army of Virginia. But he just shook his head with a strange, sad smile and said, 'Amrie . . . God isn't on anyone's side in this or any other war. Not the abolitionists screaming for our blood, not Abe Lincoln with his grim determination to preserve the Union even if it means a million dead, not the planter's son with his high-flown ideals of honor and chivalry and a strange notion of freedom that somehow involves the right to keep the slaves down in his quarters.'

'But we're fighting to protect our homes!' I argued.

He'd opened his mouth, then closed it, but I knew what he'd wanted to say because I'd heard him say it to my mother late the night before, when they thought I was up in my bed asleep. 'I keep remembering what this Federal government did to the Choctaw and the Cherokees,' he'd said. 'The officers leading their armies against us now are the same ones who burned all those Indian villages and killed and mutilated their women and children.'

My mother had said, 'I can't believe they would massacre us. I can't.'

'Perhaps you're right. We are white, after all. But then, so were the French settlers in Canada, and that didn't save them.'

When we were little, my father used to tell Simon and me bedtime stories – not the usual children's fare of dancing princesses and magical beanstalks, but real tales, drawn from history. He told us of William Wallace, and his courage and death in the Wars of Scottish Independence, and about Acadians like Evangeline, driven by the British and the New Englanders from their homes in French Acadia and forced to wander for decades before finding a new home here on our own bayous. I'd often wondered how they coped when they realized all their fervent prayers had failed, that their God had deserted them.

Now I found myself staring at old Mrs Foster. She knelt beside me, her eyes closed in fervent prayer. She had six sons, five already fighting for the Confederacy. How could she ever forgive God if none of those sons came home? How could anyone survive such a loss? How could God ask anyone to survive such a loss?

'*Amrie.*'

My mother touched my arm and frowned at me, and I obediently bowed my head and closed my eyes in a simulation of devout prayer.

But my questions remained unanswered.

Nine

Midway through the following week, word reached us that Commodore Farragut had given up his attempt to take Vicksburg. They said the town was perched so high above the Mississippi that his gunboats couldn't hit it properly with their canons. And with the river still in flood, he couldn't put General Williams's army ashore, either.

Everyone in St Francisville cheered when we heard – until we discovered that Farragut had decided to sail back down the river and occupy Baton Rouge instead.

For the next several days, Finn and I spent the hours after school perched in a big old oak whose branches stretched out over the rushing river. The tree's thick green leaves hid us from sight, so that we could watch unobserved as the Federal gunboats and troop transports steamed past us again, headed south this time.

But eventually, even the sight of the strange, low-riding, ominous-looking ironclads that had been added to the Federal fleet began to pall, and we decided to go fishing for bass in the bayou for which the town of Bayou Sara was named. The late afternoon sky was clear and blue, washed clean by a brief rain shower; the air smelled of cypress and wet willow trees and mud, with the sunlight flickering down through the heavy canopy to cast shifting shadows across the algae-skimmed water. Finn had just hooked a good two-pounder when he went suddenly still, his head lifting as he turned to stare toward the south.

'Did you hear that?' he asked. Finn had the keenest hearing of anybody I knew.

'No. What?'

'Listen.'

I strained to hear, and this time, I caught it: a faint, rolling *boom* away to the south.

'Maybe it's thunder,' I said.

He shook his head. 'That's not thunder.'

He'd let his line go slack, so that the fish slipped its hook and darted away. But Finn didn't care. He was already gathering our gear. 'Come on; let's go!'

We raced to the top of the bluff. As we reached the crest of the hill, the wind shifted, blowing hot and dry out of the south and bringing us a sound that would soon be all too familiar to us.

Boom. Boom. Boom.

There was no doubt in my mind now that I wasn't hearing thunder. 'Finn,' I said, unable to put my thoughts into words.

All around us, children stopped jumping rope or chasing hoops; folks came out of their houses, bareheaded women with their hands clenched in wet aprons, joined by stooped old men with watery eyes that narrowed as they stared solemnly to the south.

Toward Baton Rouge.

It was early the next morning that the Widow Carlyle's Tom came pounding at our front door.

'Mizz St Pierre! Mizz St Pierre!' he hollered, gasping from his run. 'Come quick! It's the widow's cousin from Baton Rouge! Them Yankees done shelled her house just as she was fixin' to birth a babe!'

My mother sent Avery to hitch our big white mare Magnolia to the buggy while she scrambled into her clothes and grabbed her bag.

'Can I come?' I asked.

She paused halfway out the door to look back at me. Behind her, the sky was gray with the coming of day, the cool air alive with a sweet chorus of birdsong. She started to shake her head. Then she stopped, as if arrested by a thought the nature of which she kept to herself.

To my surprise, she tightened her fist around the handles of my father's medical bag and said, 'Yes; come. I may need you.'

Magnolia's big hooves ate up the short distance to town. The fragrant dawn mist that lay in wispy drifts across the road half-obscured the thick dark trunks of the oaks that flashed past us, and I could smell the fecund odor of the dew-dampened fields and the distant bayou. On the horizon the morning sky shimmered like a flat lake of orange fire streaked with pink.

While Avery drove, my mother hugging her bag to her chest, her thoughts focused on some inner, private place. But as we swung onto Royal Street, still deserted in the early-morning light, she turned her head and looked at me.

'You're certain you're up to this?'

I stared back at her, wondering if she was already regretting allowing me to accompany her. I said, 'Do you know why I asked to come?'

She shook her head. 'No. Why?'

I wasn't sure I could explain it. It was just that, somehow, catching tadpoles and drilling with a broomstick seemed to belong to a world I no longer lived in, a world where gunboats didn't darken our river, where men didn't steal children's necklaces with impunity and the sound of thunder in the distance really was thunder.

I said, 'It seems to me we're all gonna need to be learnin' how to do things we've never had to know before.'

Her gaze met mine, a strange light shining in the depths of her eyes as she reached out ever so briefly to touch my hand. 'That's why I wanted you to come.'

We reached the widow's house to find an unfamiliar bay horse and buggy drawn up on the verge. The bay was splashed with mud up to its withers, its head hanging in exhaustion. But what riveted my attention was the fresh blood that smeared the buggy's seat, floorboards, bar – everywhere I looked. I didn't see how anybody could've lost all that blood and still be alive.

My mother cast one look at it and said to Avery, 'Take care of that poor horse,' before disappearing into the house.

From inside came the thin, reedy wail of a newborn babe. I tore myself away from the sight of that gruesome-looking buggy and raced up the front steps. By the time I reached the wide, central hall, my mother was already yanking off her gloves and hat, and barking orders.

'Mrs Carlyle, I'll need brandy and strips of cloth – linen, if you've any left, but homespun will have to do if that's all there is. Amrie, get me hot water and a clean basin, and tell the cook to rustle up a good strong chicken bullion.'

She paused beside the man who stood in the doorway to the widow's spare bedroom. He looked like a storekeeper or a clerk, his bony face ashen with exhaustion and fear, his thick sandy hair in disarray, the bare sleeves of his shirt and the front of his vest stained bright red with blood. In his arms he held a baby wrapped in his own dark coat, and my mother lifted the babe from him and unwrapped it.

The baby looked a god-awful mess to me, all streaked with blood and something white and waxy. But my mother seemed satisfied with what she saw, because she just nodded and wrapped the babe up again to hand it back to its father, saying, 'How long ago was he born?'

'Late last night, in a farm house that offered us refuge after we fled the shelling.' His voice was a shaky whisper. 'She just keeps bleeding and bleeding, so I brought her into town to try and get help. I—'

But he was talking to air. My mother had already pushed past him into the bedchamber, yelling over her shoulder, 'Amrie! The water.'

The next hour was a blur of helping Tom tote water and ripping up the Widow Carlyle's last set of clean linen sheets and helping my mother cope with the blood that just kept coming and coming and coming.

'Why's this happening?' I asked at one point.

But my mother simply shook her head.

I shifted my gaze to the woman in the bed. She was such a tiny thing, and so young. Grace, was her name. Small-boned and fragile-looking, she had a heart-shaped face and fine flaxen hair that looked dark where it was plastered by sweat to her face.

'My baby,' she kept saying, over and over again, her head moving restlessly against the pillow. 'Is he all right?'

'Your babe's just fine,' my mother would say.

But I knew from the way she said it that while the babe might be fine, the mother was not.

After another hour, the woman was too weak to say much of anything, her eyes drifting almost closed. Her breath came in peculiar little jerks, and her skin had taken on a gray, slack quality that scared me.

'Amrie!' my mother yelled as I stared at that pale, beautiful face. 'Get me more hot water!'

I fled the room, my bare feet slapping the floorboards of the Widow Carlyle's long, wide hall. By the time I made it back, my mother was simply sitting in the low chair near the empty hearth, her bloodstained hands resting palm up in her lap. The Reverend Lewis from our Episcopal church was there, and I could hear his voice droning in prayer, the familiar cadences punctuated by the sandy-haired man's gut-wracking sobs. 'And the Lord said, my kingdom is not of this world. Look not—'

I stared at the Baton Rouge woman's pale, still face. We'd worked so hard, and she'd wanted so desperately to live. She couldn't be . . .

'Is she dead?' I whispered.

My mother nodded, her lips pressed into a tight line, her throat working hard as she swallowed. 'They killed her. All of them, North and South. With their arrogance and their refusal to compromise, with their righteous demands and their blind hatred and their *God damned* gunboats, they killed her as surely as if their bullets and shells and bombs had ripped her apart.'

She sat for a long moment, her shoulders slumped with exhaustion, her gaze staring at nothing. Then she pushed up from the chair and came to use the water I'd brought to wash the dead woman's blood from her hands.

Ten

That evening I sat on the top rail of the pasture fence and watched Magnolia canter across the grass, mane flying, pounding hooves kicking up chevrons of turf, the setting sun warm and golden on her back.

My mother's hack, a big bay gelding named Hennessey, was so old that she seldom rode him these days. But Magnolia was young, and she circled the pasture, shying in mock terror when our milk cow, Queen Bee, raised her head. Then she trotted up to thrust her big white head against my chest and nuzzle my pockets for carrots. I wrapped my arms around her neck and pressed my face against her warm silky hide.

My mother and Mahalia were taking down a load of washing from the lines strung near the laundry, and I could hear occasional snatches of their conversation carried on the soft evening breeze.

'I shouldn't have taken her with me,' my mother said to Mahalia. 'I'm afraid the experience was just too . . .' She paused, as if searching for the right word. '. . . raw for her.'

The words surprised me, for my mother rarely questioned her own judgment about anything. Mine, yes; her own, no.

Then I heard Mahalia say, 'She's tougher than you give her credit for. And she's gonna need to be a whole lot tougher soon enough. I reckon she'll be seein' a heap worse before this dreadful war is over.'

The breeze gusted up, rustling the leaves of a nearly willow, so that my mother's reply was lost to me. But it was Mahalia's words that continued to haunt me. I'd noticed no one ever talked about 'the war' anymore. It was always 'this dreadful war' or 'this cruel war' or, with increasing frequency, 'this *damned* war' – used even by folks who up until six months ago had probably never said such a thing in their lives.

We'd heard by now what had happened in Baton Rouge. It seems an officer from one of the Federal gunboats had bundled up his dirty laundry and ordered himself rowed ashore to the shacks along the riverfront inhabited by some colored laundresses. The problem was, four young hotheads who'd recently joined the guerrillas happened to be down there at the same time. They took some potshots at the boat, wounding the officer and a couple of the seamen at the oars. They'd then skedaddled, no doubt laughing uproariously and well-pleased with themselves for what they'd done.

Commodore Farragut responded to the incident by ordering his gunboats to open fire on the city without warning.

He pulverized the shacks along the river and, once those were in flames, he turned his guns on the upper streets of the city.

Women and children fled screaming from their homes as shells whistled and bombs burst, drowning out the wails of small, terrified children separated from their mothers in the panic and the pitiful cries of those too old or sick to save themselves. Even after the shelling ceased, the terrified inhabitants spent the night in the surrounding woods and swamps, unsure of what might happen next.

In the end, no one knew how many had died. At least two women had been killed along the riverfront, but it was probably more. Several children were said to have drowned, and some old folks' hearts gave out in the panic. A babe born that night in the woods had died within hours, and some folks were so badly bit by snakes and mosquitoes it was doubtful they'd survive. I wondered if Grace's name would be added to the list of the shelling's innocent victims.

That was before I realized that no one on either side was bothering to keep count of the dead.

It was one afternoon a few days later when my mother asked me to go with her to Locust Grove plantation, where a couple of babies in the quarters were sick with what might be chickenpox.

I tried to wiggle out of it, saying, 'Finn and I were gonna make gigs so we could go gigging frogs.'

But my mother said, 'I'd like you come, honey. There's something I want you to see.'

And so I went.

Locust Grove lay a few miles to the east of St Francisville. We drove through sun-warmed, gently rolling hills cut by shady hollows thick with old growth pine, oak, and persimmons. The sky overhead was a deep, heart-rending blue arching over the vast fields of cotton, sugar cane, and corn that stretched out on either side of the road. My mother handled the reins herself, her gaze fixed straight ahead, her attention already focused on the sick she was going to see. The air was hot and dry, the dust raised by Magnolia's hooves and the rattling wheels of our buggy drifting behind us to catch the sunlight that filtered down through the branches of the oaks lining the road.

Locust Grove was the home of Mrs Anna Davis Smith, a formidable old widow who'd managed the plantation since the death of her husband some thirty years before. But we didn't drive up to the big house, a red-brick, federal-style structure that wouldn't have looked out of place in the hills of Vermont or New Hampshire. Instead, my mother skirted the rambling gardens of camellias and azaleas, sweet olives and gardenias, and headed straight to the neat rows of whitewashed houses that faced each other across a wide swath of Bermuda grass, each with its own garden, its own hogs and chickens, and an occasional goat or two.

Some of the hands were already coming in from the fields, their voices and laughter and the spicy aroma of simmering gumbo and etouffée spilling from the houses' open doors. Once, when I was younger, after a visit to my Grandmother Adelaide's plantation in Livingston Parish, I'd remarked to my mother that the house servants and field hands I'd seen there seemed happy enough. She'd looked at me with that withering scorn I'd learned to dread and said, 'What do you expect them to do, Amrie? Sit around all day and weep and wail about their condition? They're people, just trying to live their lives as best they can, like anybody else. The fact that they can laugh and sing and dance and smile doesn't mean they're contented not being free; it just means they're *people*.'

The big building that served as the quarter's nursery stood at the end of one of the rows, its long windows thrown open to catch the breeze. Here babies slept in cradles and the youngest children of the quarters played beneath the watchful eyes of two, aged woman. As we pulled up before the nursery's wide gallery, I could see one of the mammies, her ebony skin spotted with age, sitting in a rocker with a squalling infant in her arms.

'Thank the Lord,' she said, pushing to her feet. She was a big woman, her arms flabby with fat, her hips swelling wide beneath the calico of her dress. 'I done give this poor babe snakeroot and saffron tea, but there ain't nothin' that'll quiet her. Burnin' up, she is.'

I watched my mother go to take the sick, feverish child in her arms and disappear into the nursery's large, open room.

I followed her, wondering why my mother had been so anxious for me to accompany her here. I'd had the chickenpox years before, right after I started school, so I was in no danger myself. But I didn't see how I could be of much use to her, and she didn't ask for my help, but simply moved through the children with an air of gentle tenderness that always surprised me, for she was not a particularly tender woman.

She checked each child in turn, measuring out packets of dried herbs and speaking to the mothers as they came to collect their offspring, their calico dresses dark with sweat across their backs, their hair wrapped up in vibrant tignons secured with gold and coral pins. I was watching one pretty young woman, her teeth flashing white in a wide smile as she swung her squealing toddler high in the air, when my mother came up behind me and said, 'We can go now.'

I waited until we were descending the wooden front steps before asking, 'Are they gonna be all right?'

'I think so.' She nodded toward a grove of spreading oaks in the distance. 'What I want to show you is over there.'

We followed a shell lane that curved around the edge of the big house's gardens toward a white picket fence I now realized enclosed Locust Grove's graveyard. As plantation cemeteries went, this one was surprisingly large and filled with an assortment of moss-covered headstones, low, flat tombs, and box-like crypts. By the time we let ourselves in the latch gate, the shadows were deepening beneath the trees, the last lingering rays of the sun slanting golden across the grassy sunken graves and aging monuments.

'You know someone buried here?' I asked, annoyed now by her continuing silence.

'Several people, actually. But that's not what I want you to see.'

We cut across the long grass, the branches of the oaks making a soft shifting sound as they lifted against the sky with the evening breeze. Our destination was a waist-high crypt, plain except for the pilasters at each corner. Built of white limestone now grayed and covered with lichen, it had a flat top with a timeworn inscription. Peering at it, I could just make out the faded letters.

'"Sarah Knox Davis",' I read aloud. '"Beloved wife of Jefferson Davis. Died 15 September 1835, aged 21 years".'

Puzzled, I looked over at my mother. I knew that Mrs Anna Davis Smith was an older sister of the Confederacy's president. But Jefferson Davis's wife was very much alive and the mother of a passel of children. I said, 'I don't understand. Who was she?'

'She was the daughter of Zachary Taylor.'

'You mean *the* Zachary Taylor?'

'The very one.'

Every schoolchild in Louisiana knew about Zachary Taylor, for his plantation lay just outside of Baton Rouge, and he had the distinction of being the only man Louisiana ever sent to the White House. A lot of Southerners had supported his election as president because they figured that, as a slaveowner himself, he'd favor their drive to extend slavery into the Western territories. Instead, he'd opposed it. More than that, he'd been an outspoken critic of secession, saying he'd already seen enough people die in war in his lifetime, and that anyone who advocated rebellion against the Union ought to be shot.

'Of course,' said my mother, brushing off the scattering of dried leaves that covered the worn surface of the crypt as carefully as if the grave belonged to someone she'd loved, 'in the 1830s, Taylor wasn't president. He was just a colonel, stationed at Fort Crawford in Wisconsin. Knox – that's what they called her; not Sarah – was eighteen and vivacious and mischievous. She was also very beautiful.'

My mother paused for a moment, and I could hear the chatter of the squirrels in the oaks overhead and the caw of a distant crow. 'Jeff Davis was a young West Point graduate assigned to the fort, a lieutenant. Knox fell in love with him, much to Zachary Taylor's dismay.'

'Why? What was wrong with him?'

'Nothing except his profession. You see, Colonel Taylor knew only too well how hard army life can be for a woman. His older daughter,

Ann, had almost died giving birth on a frontier post, and he didn't want to expose a second daughter to all the risks that a young army wife faces in the wilderness.'

'So what happened?'

'The colonel refused to give his consent to the marriage. So rather than give up the woman he loved, the young lieutenant resigned his commission in the army. He and Knox were married, and they sailed down the river to Vicksburg, where Davis intended to establish a new plantation to be known as Brierfield.'

'When was this?' I asked, my gaze on that faded inscription.

'The summer of 1835. Before they settled at Brierfield, Jefferson brought his bride here, to St Francisville, to meet his sister. While they were here, Knox fell ill with fever; they both did, actually. Jefferson Davis eventually recovered.'

'But Knox died.' I traced the letters of her name with one fingertip, imagining the woman she'd once been, laughing and in love.

'He eventually remarried,' said my mother, 'but not for another ten years.'

'And now he's President of the Confederacy, while Knox is just . . . dead.'

'Long dead.'

I looked up at my mother. 'Why did you bring me here?'

She gazed toward the big house, where a snowy white ibis stalked elegantly across the clearing, its long legs lifting soundlessly, its head turning from side to side as it searched the grass for lizards and hoppers. She said, 'Zachary Taylor insisted that his future son-in-law leave the army because he didn't want his daughter to die young on some lonely frontier post. So she died instead of fever on a Louisiana plantation, while her older sister – the army surgeon's wife – is still alive . . .' She hesitated. 'I suppose the point is, life is capricious. We can never know the outcome of our actions or decisions, and the idea that we can control our lives is more often than not an illusion. All we can do is what we think is right, and acknowledge that sometimes things will turn out horribly wrong anyway.'

I thought about my mother's words as we drove home through the gloaming of the day. But her reasons for choosing that moment to impress such a lesson upon me continued for a time to elude me.

Eleven

A few weeks later, a family came through town, driving a tired horse hitched to a broken-down old buggy. The man was a once-wealthy hotelier from New Orleans who'd been expelled after having his home and business confiscated by the Federal occupation authorities. His name was Pascal Rochon, and he stopped by to see us because he had smuggled a precious letter from my Grand-mère St Pierre out of the city.

rue St Anne
29 May 1862

Mes Enfants,

I pray to our *Seigneur* this letter finds you well and safe. I write quickly, as Monsieur Rochon has graciously offered to carry a message to you on his way to his sister in Pointe Coupee. He will doubtless tell you of the treatment he himself has received at the hands of our city's new masters. For a people supposedly enamored of their constitution, they do have a most cavalier attitude toward the sanctity of law.

My health remains essentially as before, although I find myself consumed always by fear for you, your father, and Claire and her family. I have received news from no one since the Federals' arrival. Our parish priest, Father Paul, was a great a comfort to me, but he has recently been arrested for refusing to lead us in prayers for the victory of President Lincoln and the United States. They say he will be sent to prison in New York. Who does such things?

But please, do not worry about me. Perhaps because I am old and seldom venture out, I myself have not suffered as have so many others here. Every day brings word of more arrests, more businesses seized and sold, more homes 'searched for guns' and stripped of all valuables. This Federal general has well earned his nickname, 'Spoons', although some have taken to calling him 'Beast' since the proclamation of this new Woman Order. He has declared that any woman of New Orleans who dares show her contempt for the Federals, whether by word, gesture, or movement, is now subject to being treated as 'a woman of the streets plying her avocation'. I thank Our *Seigneur* every day that you are not here to be exposed to this barbarism, and pray that He will keep these demons far from you and your home.

I miss you and think of you always, and pray that Our *Seigneur* keeps me alive until this cruel war's end, so that I may see you again.

> *Le Seigneur vous bénisse et vous garde.*
> Grand-mère

We fed the poor, wretched family of refugees well, and put them up for the night before seeing them off on their journey again the next morning.

It was the last news we would receive from rue St Anne until the war's end.

Twelve

June came, and Finn and I were finally free of school for the summer.

In the past, the summer holiday had always stretched before me as a season of unalloyed bliss, a time of fish fries and barbecues and tramps through the woods with Checkers, of long lazy days spent fishing and riding Magnolia, or just reading curled up in the crook of my favorite oak.

But this year, an air of tension and uneasy expectation hung over us all. Everyone's focus turned anxiously to the south, where the Federals had set about occupying Baton Rouge with the same authoritarian brutality they'd demonstrated in New Orleans. The difference was, Baton Rouge was only thirty miles away from us.

The damage to the city itself from that brief spurt of retaliatory shelling was reported as minimal, which I suppose it was – unless you were a washerwoman whose riverfront shack had been burned, or a loved one left alive to mourn someone who'd been killed. The unspoken question on everyone's mind was: what were the Federals going to do next?

I was awakened early one Saturday morning by a low murmur of voices from beneath my dormer window. Curious, I threw on my clothes and scrambled down the steep stairs to the hall. No one was in sight, although both the front and back doors stood open to encourage a cool, sweet crossbreeze that brought with it the smell of dew-dampened grass and the clear, heartbreaking song of a mockingbird.

Across the front of the house, the gallery still lay in deep shadow. But beyond that, the golden morning light was already soaking the spreading branches of the oaks and the thick green Bermuda grass that stretched toward the lane. I could hear my mother's low voice interspersed with a vibrant baritone I now recognized as belonging to Castile Boudreau, the free man of color who owned a livery stable in Bayou Sara.

'I saw it hangin' by the gate at dawn,' he was saying to my mother, 'when I drove past on my way out to talk to Hitch about gettin' another load of hay. I stopped right then and there and ripped it down, so I don't think you gotta worry. As early as it was, I don't reckon nobody but me noticed it.'

I could see my mother now. She stood near the top of the front steps, her arms crossed at her waist, a scrunched up length of red and white striped cloth held clenched against her. 'I don't know how to thank you, Castile,' she said. 'Won't you stay and have some breakfast?'

He shook his head, his soft white palmetto hat twisted in his hands, the branded scars on his cheeks pulling with his smile. 'Thank you kindly, Mizz Kate, but I oughta be gettin' back.' He glanced over to where I stood just inside the open door and nodded as if he'd only just noticed me, although I knew him well enough to be certain he'd heard my bare feet creeping down the hall. 'Mornin', Missy Amrie. You and Finn like to go huntin' wild turkey with me sometime?'

'Oh, yes, please!' I said, coming out from behind the door.

He laughed out loud. 'We'll do it, then. You still got your bow?'

I shook my head. 'It broke.'

'Ah. I reckon that's 'cause we didn't season the wood proper-like. I got me some hickory I laid by last winter; you and Finn come see me later this week, and we'll make a couple new ones.'

My mother and I stood side by side at the top of the steps and watched as Castile climbed up onto his high wagon seat, the big wheels clattering as he urged his mules out the gate and turned toward town.

I nodded to the bundle in my mother's arms. 'What's that?'

Wordlessly, she unfurled the cloth. It looked like a length of red- and white-striped bunting, of the kind we'd once used to decorate St Francisville's courthouse and bandstand back in the days when we still celebrated the Fourth of July. The wind caught the length of fabric, billowing it out, and I saw that someone had scrawled across it in heavy black letters: TRAITORS LIVE HERE.

I felt my stomach give a funny lurch. Somehow in all the excitement of the past month, I'd forgotten this other danger that threatened us. 'It's because of that drowned man they found in Thompson's Creek, isn't it? Whoever hung this thinks the message he carried was for us.'

'Probably.'

'So who done it?'

'*Did* it,' she corrected. I sometimes thought the world could be coming to an end, and my mother would still be correcting my grammar. 'I don't know who did it.'

I stared out across the garden to the pasture where I could see Magnolia and a couple of the mules grazing lazily in the morning sunshine. But I wasn't really looking at them; I was remembering a mahogany-bearded man in homespun talking to another man with a bushy black mustache and eyes that reminded me of something dead.

'I bet it was Hiram Tucker,' I said before I could stop myself.

'Hiram Tucker joined the Partisan Rangers. I heard he's over at Camp Moore.'

'He might be a ranger, but I saw him just the other day in Bayou Sara. And he was talking to that fellow who knows Papa.'

'Sean Gallagher?' She paused in the act of wadding up the bunting, her head coming up. She stared at me a moment, then shook her head. 'No. I can't believe he'd tell someone like Hiram Tucker.'

'Maybe he didn't need to tell him. Maybe Tucker was one of the men who found that dead Federal.'

She finished winding the cloth into a tight ball. 'Amrie, you can't do this.'

'Do what?'

'This war is destructive enough without our allowing it to pitch neighbor against neighbor. We need to work together – all of us.

You can't start suspecting anyone and everyone you don't happen to like. It's that kind of thinking that led someone to hang *this* –' she shook the wad of cloth at me – 'by our gate.'

'But—'

'No *buts*. I won't have any more of it. Is that understood?'

I swallowed the retort that burned within me and said, 'Yes, ma'am.'

But, childlike, I clung to the consolation that she hadn't made me promise.

I'd never been able to figure out how a group of women could all talk at the same time and yet still manage to follow every conversation in the room.

'What did you use to dye that dress? It's a lovely shade of—'

'—Beast Butler sent her to prison for giving her child a birthday party on the same day as some Federal's funeral. And her the mother of seven! They say she's not well—'

'Sophie Wright was telling me she heard that both France and Spain have recognized the Confederate States of America. I *want* to believe it, but—'

The grand double parlors of the big house known as Bon Silence were so crowded with ladies that I had to crane my neck around to identify the right speaker. It was Mrs Henshaw, and she sat on one of the brocade-covered settees grouped near the front parlor's elegant oriel window, barely glancing at her work as she simultaneously talked non-stop and laid down a row of neat stitches in the hem of a white flannel shirt.

Unlike her husband, who'd been born and raised in Cambridge, England, Madeline Henshaw hailed from Gulf Port, Mississippi. As big and robust as her husband was small and fussy, she was one of fifty-odd ladies and young girls who'd gathered together that Friday afternoon to sew for the Soldiers' Aid Society. With the outbreak of the war, hundreds of these societies had sprung up across the South as women got together to knit socks, sew shirts, scrape lint, and roll bandages ripped from their own donated linen sheets and tablecloths. St Francisville's society hadn't met much lately, mainly because they'd used up their own supplies, and things like material, wool, needles, and thread had become pretty near impossible to find. But General Ruggles had somehow managed to get his hands on ten bolts of soft flannel, along with a supply of needles and thread, and a bunch of the city's women had volunteered to sew shirts for the new recruits training at Camp Moore.

I myself sat perched on the edge of a lyre-backed, satin-covered chair next to a gilded console with swan-shaped legs. A half-sewn sleeve lay neglected in my lap, and I was feeling nearly as out of place as a buffalo at a barn dance. As far as I was concerned, Soldiers' Aid Society meetings fell into the same category as spelling bees and Sunday school, and were to be avoided. It wasn't that I begrudged doing my bit for the war effort, because I didn't. Finn and I had rolled bandages and scraped lint, and gone door-to-door collecting scrap iron and brass in a wheelbarrow. But concentrated gatherings of ladies inevitably made me feel like I was coming down with the hives. Fortunately, since my seams were so uneven and crooked that any soldier unlucky enough to receive a shirt sewn by me was truly to be pitied, my lack of attendance in the past had never been mourned.

But for some reason, my mother had insisted that I accompany her here today. When I'd asked why the blazes I needed to spend the afternoon with a bunch of ladies sitting around yakking when Finn and I had planned to work on the new hickory bows Castile was going to help us make, she'd gotten a funny, pained look on her face and said, 'That's why.'

I made a mental note to try to drop 'blazes' from my vocabulary.

I knew I was in trouble when I found out the sewing meeting was being held at the home of Rowena Walford. The Walfords owned three plantations, but they spent most of their time here at Bon Silence, a dazzling white Greek Revival house just up the road from us. Fronted by massive Doric columns, it had fourteen-foot-high ceilings, a grand, sweeping central staircase, and so many rooms you could get lost in there if you weren't careful. Up until recently the Walfords had employed a private tutor to teach their three children. But the tutor had enlisted practically before the smoke cleared from the firing on Fort Sumter, and when the Walfords weren't able to secure a suitable replacement, they sent their children to our school. The eldest, Laura, was my age, and it hadn't been more than a month since I'd dipped one of her pigtails in my inkbottle.

I was pretty sure her mother hadn't forgotten the incident.

Yet Rowena Walford was all smiles when she met us in her elegant, elliptically-shaped entry. While I might not care much for Laura, I'd always liked Rowena Walford. She was charming and open and funny in a way my mother never could be. As elegant as her house, she was still slim and small-waisted, with big blue eyes and golden curls and a cute little nose that combined with dimples to make her look like a girl, even though she was only a few years younger than my mother.

'Kate,' she said, stopping my mother to give her a kiss on the cheek as the Walfords' stately, white-haired butler showed us toward the parlors. 'Thank you so much for coming. And I see you brought Anne-Marie with you.' One delicate eyebrow arched higher as she turned to me. 'Bless your heart. Laura is here. Perhaps you two can sit together. I'll just tell Aunt Babs to hide the ink bottles.' And with that she sailed away, leaving my mother looking pained and me to slink off to the opposite end of the room from where I could see Laura, her own golden curls clustered short around a face as pretty as her mother's.

Miss Rowena had had to cut her hair after the inkbottle incident.

'Old Mr Mason got hold of a recent edition of the *Vicksburg Whig*,' I heard Old Mr Mason's stout, sandy-haired daughter-in-law, Margaret Mason say. 'They're saying the town sustained little material damage from the Yankee shelling, although one shot went clean through the Methodist church—'

My feet were hurting. My shoes had grown so small over the past year that they pinched something awful, but I didn't dare take them off. I picked up my assigned sleeve again, only instead of setting a stitch, I found my gaze wandering over the ceiling's detailed cornice work and the four crystal chandeliers that hung from ornate medallions carved with pineapples, grapes, and what I realized were human faces. I'd spent enough time in my Grandmother Adelaide's house and the various St Pierre plantations that the magnificence of Bon Silence didn't overwhelm me, but it was still impressive. The twin parlors' two matching mantelpieces were of marble, surmounted by massive gilded and beveled French mirrors that soared all the way to the high ceilings. Yet only simple mats covered the gleaming hardwood floors.

It was the custom in the South to take up all wool carpets in the spring and replace them with mats for the hot summer months. But I suspected that the Walfords' carpets – like our own – had been cut up into squares last winter and sent off to Virginia and Tennessee for the soldiers to use as blankets.

'Do you find you're having trouble with your house servants?' I heard Mrs Irvinel ask of anyone seated nearby who cared to reply. 'Ours have been dreadfully lazy and disobedient lately. If they don't settle down, we're going to need to send a few down to the fields and replace them with new ones from the quarters.'

'I think the problem is all the excitement in the air,' said Rowena Walford, her voice as sweet and pleasant as if she were discussing blackspot on her roses. 'It infects them.'

I glanced over at the young woman serving the ladies small glasses of sherry from a silver tray. She kept her gaze downcast, her expression inscrutable. But I found myself watching her as she moved gracefully around the room. Her name was Josephine, and she had skin the color of polished oak and an elegantly arched nose that gave mute testimony to the mixed nature of her ancestry. Rowena Walford's own husband, Major Morgan Walford, now off with the First Louisiana in Tennessee, was said to be hopelessly devoted and rigidly faithful to his beautiful wife. But Bon Silence had originally belonged to Miss Rowena's family, and everyone knew that her father, old Mr Gilbert Vance, had spent more nights down in the quarters than he had in his own wife's bed. I did the calculations and figured this silent, gazelle-like house servant might well be Laura Walford's aunt.

Just the thought of it made my stomach feel queasy.

'I find I want to believe that all the encouraging rumors are true, and all the discouraging ones are false,' I heard Delia Stocking say with a soft laugh. 'If only it were so.'

I glanced over at her. The wife of a dentist now off with the army in Virginia, she was wearing a pretty, tuck-fronted yellow homespun gown trimmed with lace that was probably salvaged from an older dress. Time was, the women here would have been wearing elegant gowns of organdy, muslin, or foulard, their hats stylish confections from New Orleans' or at least Bayou Sara's milliners. But there wasn't a woman here today who wasn't wearing homespun, and most of their hats were of bleached palmetto they'd woven and trimmed themselves.

Many of these women probably still had silk gowns hanging in their cupboards at home, for they were seldom used these days and so hadn't worn out. But everyday dresses soon fell victim to the harsh soaps we were reduced to using since the blockade. And the bolts of linen and cotton, cashmere and silk that normally lined the shelves of places like Meyers Emporium had all come from the mills of England and the North, and had long ago disappeared.

And so, as the blockade took hold, women of all walks of life had dragged dusty old spinning wheels down out of their attics. Grandmothers who'd been girls at the time of the Revolution were pressed to teach this lost art to their daughters and granddaughters, while plans were circulated for the construction of homemade looms. Soon almost everyone was weaving their own cloth and exchanging formulas for dyes with the same enthusiasm they'd once exchanged recipes for peach cobbler. Wearing homespun became a matter of pride, a way for women to show their patriotic fervor.

My own mother was wearing a gown of soft blue homespun she'd sewn herself. But the cloth had come not from her own loom but from Maisie Sparrow. After Mama set little Roy Sparrow's broken arm, Maisie had given her the cloth in payment. Unlike me, Mama had always been handy with a needle. But it was a good thing she could get our homespun in exchange for her doctoring, because she was hopeless at it.

'Amrie,' my mother said softly.

I picked up my half-sewn sleeve and set to work undoing a nasty snarl in my thread.

Someone said, 'The latest word out of New Orleans is that General Butler was furious with Farragut for breaking off the attempt at Vicksburg. They're saying the Federals are gathering their forces to try it again.'

I glanced over at the speaker. It was Mrs Gantry, the telegraph operator's young wife.

The ladies had mostly fallen silent, listening to her.

'This time they're going to try using mortar boats with canons fixed in such a way that their shells will reach the city,' Sophie Gantry continued. 'They're saying they intend to wipe Vicksburg off the face of the earth.'

'But that's barbaric!' said someone. 'Has Lincoln decided to become the new Genghis Khan?'

A chorus of disbelief and outrage swelled around the room.

I felt the muscles of my neck and shoulders suddenly bunch and constrict as I glanced around the assembly of women. I was remembering the crudely lettered banner hung at dawn beside our gate.

And I had the uncomfortable realization that one of the gaily chatting, smiling women here today might well be the 'Dear Madam' someone had accused my mother of being.

I looked at Sophie Gantry, with her soft blue eyes and flaxen hair drawn neatly back into a bun, and I heard the echo of my mother's voice saying, *You can't start suspecting anyone and everyone you don't happen to like.*

But I wondered if Sophie Gantry realized she'd just revealed that she must be in contact with one of the confidential agents at work in New Orleans – agents General Butler was frantic to root out. Or at least she knew someone who was. Had one of these diligently sewing ladies quietly picked up on the slip and filed that bit of dangerous information away for a future report?

This war is destructive enough without us allowing it to pitch neighbor against neighbor, my mother had said. But wasn't that what rebellions and civil wars did? Set brother against brother, father against son, neighbor against neighbor?

It hadn't occurred to me yet that war could also set mother against daughter.

Thirteen

We watched the river.

For those of us who lived along its banks, the Mississippi had always been a lifeline. Louisiana's low-lying, soggy ground and frequent teeming rains made a muddy mess of the roads. So freight, supplies, people, and the mail all typically moved up and down the river.

Now, the river had now become something to fear.

Finn and I arrived at Castile's livery stable early that Saturday morning to get to work on our bows. The lengths of hickory he'd dried were about four and a half feet long and an inch and a half around. He patiently showed us how to locate the center and allow for a six-inch grip in the middle. After that, it was just a matter of carefully thinning and tapering the upper and lower limbs. Castile made sure our knives were as sharp as they could be.

'A dull knife is more dangerous than a sharp one,' he said, 'because you need to apply more pressure to a dull knife, and you never know what it's gonna do.'

Finn and I were sitting in the cool breezeway of the stables, the horses nickering softly in their stalls, the thin shavings of hickory wood curling away from our knives to settle in fragrant drifts around us, when Finn suddenly stilled.

'What is it?' I asked, watching him.

'Listen.'

'I don't hear nothing,' I said. The town had gone oddly still around us.

'That's the point.'

We dropped our bows and knives and bolted for the door.

'Look!' said Finn, pointing toward the river. The tall masts of a steam sloop stood out dark against the blue sky.

The air filled with the roll of a drum, the ominous tramp of marching feet, and a man's guttural shout. I felt my breath back up in my throat. 'Not again.'

Castile came to stand behind us. 'Where they headed?' he shouted to a boy dashing up the street, one elbow crooked skyward as he held his hat clapped to his head.

'The telegraph office!'

We could see them now, a detachment of seamen trotting at double time up the street in tight formation, their breach-loading carbines dull in the sun. At their lead strode a craggy-faced officer wearing a long, double-breasted navy frock coat and brandishing a saber bayonet over his head as if leading his landing party into battle. 'This way, men!'

'How'd they know where to go?' Finn asked, watching them.

'Reckon somebody musta told 'em,' said Castile.

An unnaturally silent crowd streamed along at a safe distance behind the Federal landing party, although whether drawn by curiosity or fear or the age-old desire to witness a spectacle, I couldn't have said.

The Federals marched straight to the telegraph office. It had rained that morning; I could see lighting still trembling in the dark bank of clouds that hung over the river, and the air smelled of mud and wet wood and fear. Nodding to his sergeant, the officer leapt up onto the boardwalk and strode to the office door.

It was locked.

Finn and I exchanged glances. If Devon Gantry was in there, he was a brave man.

The Federal officer pounded on the doorframe with one gloved fist. 'Open up! Open up, I say!'

When no one appeared, he tightened his jaw and turned to his sergeant, 'Have the men break it down.'

A couple of burly seamen rammed their shoulders against the door, wood splintering and hinges snapping beneath their weight. The officer and his party of men disappeared inside. He reemerged only a moment later, his bony, homely face set in harsh lines. Drawing up at the edge of the boardwalk, he scanned the crowd of anxious townspeople.

'Where is it?' he demanded.

When no one answered, he grabbed a nearby Negro in patched trousers and a ripped shirt, and shook him hard enough to make his head flop back and forth on his neck like a dead duck on a string. 'Damn you! Where's the telegraph apparatus?'

The man's eyes went wide, his tongue poking out to lick his lips as he looked wildly about for help that wasn't coming. 'Some fellers done took it away!'

'When?'

'Last night.'

'How the devil did they know we were coming? *How*?' He shook the hapless man again, but he only stared back at the officer with a baleful look of assumed ignorance that he'd been practicing his entire life.

With a foul oath, the lieutenant shoved the man away from him and turned to the big, redheaded sergeant who'd emerged from the office behind him. 'The vitriol and batteries are still here. Destroy them.'

'Yes, sir.'

'And send some of the men out to cut the wires. I want to take away at least a quarter mile of it.'

We could hear the clatter of heavy boots as the Federals rampaged through the telegraph office, laughing as they tore the lists of Confederate dead, wounded, and captured off the walls and splashed them with vitriol.

'Careful, men,' I heard the lieutenant warn. 'That's acid you're dealing with.'

A chair came crashing through the front window, the splintered frame and shards of glass flying across the boardwalk and into the rutted street. A table followed, the seamen inside the telegraph office whooping and cheering. Someone shouted, 'Here, let me clean up your office for you, Mr Jeff Davis!' An oil lamp sailed through the shattered window to smash against a post, followed by a waste bin and an umbrella.

With a whoop, the men inside fell to chucking the office's contents out the window, everything from ink bottles and ledgers to a big brass spittoon that landed with a splat in the mud.

'Why are they doing this?' I said.

It was Castile who answered me, his bald head shiny with sweat in the sun. 'Because they can.'

When there was nothing left to destroy, the seamen fell into formation again. This time, one of the men pulled out a fife.

'Now what?' muttered Finn.

The lieutenant took his place before the men, his saber bayonet held like a drum major's baton. And away they marched, the pipe and drum striking up a tune I suddenly realized was 'Yankee Doodle'.

Only, they didn't march straight back to their ship. Up and down the streets of Bayou Sara they paraded, the familiar strains of what had once been a beloved song washing over the silent townspeople drawn up to watch them.

'Golly, look!' shouted a man's gleeful voice. 'A parade!'

Craning around, I spotted Nathan, the Widow Rove's simple-minded son, his bony, freckled face split into a wide, delighted grin. Gleefully slapping the thighs of his tattered trousers, he fell into step behind the seamen, long, spindly arms pumping, knees raised high as he stepped in time to the music.

'Yankee Doodle went to town, a ridin' on a pony,' he sang, his head tipped back, eyes shining with pride. 'Stuck a feather in his h—'

A hand reached out from the crowd and his face fell, ludicrously, as the widow's brother yanked him out of line.

No one laughed.

I wondered at the purpose of this odd little parade. Did the Federals imagine it might awaken within the townspeople some nostalgia for our lost common heritage? Was it intended to inspire the silent women, children, and old men with awe? Or was it merely intended as a demonstration of our own relative impotence – something they did, as Castile had said, because they could?

We would learn all too soon that they could do much worse.

Fourteen

The next few days saw a constant stream of Federal gunboats, troop transports, and mortar schooners steaming past us again, headed north. Then came the news we were all dreading: the Federals were shelling Vicksburg again. I thought about my Aunt Em and her little blue-eyed, curly-headed daughter, Hannah, and felt a heavy weight pressing on my chest, a growing sense of ominous dread as we waited to hear what would happen next.

The end of June brought my birthday, but it seemed hard to celebrate. Mama gave me a pair of gloves she knitted herself, and Mahalia baked a cake from rice flour that was so awful we all laughed so hard we cried.

Afterward, I climbed the stairs to curl up on the window seat built into the dormer of Simon's old room next to mine. Everything was much as he had left it the afternoon he died. My mother was normally ruthless about cleaning and throwing stuff out, but I guess even she didn't have the heart to get rid of his collection of bird nests and driftwood, or his battered editions of The Leatherstocking Tales and Sir Walter Scott.

I rested my head against the glass and whispered softly, 'Hey, Simon.' There were times the silence of the room daunted me, but not today. I said, 'Today's my birthday, you know. Funny, I've always thought of you as my big brother. But now I'm a whole week older than you were when you died. I guess I should feel bigger than you. Only, I don't.'

My voice trailed off and silence returned to the room. My eyes started stinging and my nose was running, but I sniffed and said, 'I miss you, Simon. We all do. I know Mama never says anything, but I can tell. I reckon she'd be a lot easier about this war, if'n you was here.'

I thought, *You'd only be turning fourteen, so we wouldn't need to worry about you going off to war, too.* But I didn't say it out loud, because I knew if Simon were here, he'd be raring to go off to war, just like Finn, and worrying it might end before he had a chance to fight so that someday he'd have to admit to his grandsons that he'd had no part in the struggle for our independence.

I slid off the window seat and went to fiddle with Simon's collection of old Indian points. It was Simon who'd pestered Castile into showing us how to make our first bows. I cleared my throat and said, 'Finn and me are making new hickory bows, Simon. Finn says he don't reckon I'll have the gumption to actually kill anything. But I figure maybe I could shoot a turkey. I mean, they're sorta like big, overgrown chickens, right?'

The last time Castile had taken us hunting with our old bows and arrows, when Simon was still alive, I'd cried something fierce when Simon brought down a deer. But I'd been only nine at the time. Now I was twelve . . .

I fell silent again. And for a moment, in the stillness, I thought I caught the distant sound of a boy's familiar laughter.

But it was only wishful thinking. I squeezed my eyes shut too late to stop the tears from spilling down my cheeks. 'Oh, Simon. God, how I miss you.'

One hot, still afternoon in early July, Castile rode out from Bayou Sara with the latest news from up the river.

'Word is, them new mortar schooners ain't no better than the gunboats at hitting Vicksburg's defensive batteries,' he said, his hat dangling from one big, blunt-fingered hand as he leaned against the trunk of the old oak near the kitchen door. 'So now they're fixin' to dig a canal across that little spit of land made by the river's bend and turn the river into it.'

'You mean, cut off De Soto Point?' My mother had been busy working with Mahalia putting up peach and fig preserves. But she'd come out of the kitchen, drying her hands on her apron, to talk to him. 'You can't be serious.'

Castile let out a soft huff. 'Well, *they're* serious, ain't no doubt about that. I hear tell they reckon all they gotta do is dig a ditch four to six feet wide, and about as deep, and then once they let the water in, the Ole Mississippi'll do the rest of their work for them. At first they was jist talking about usin' the force of the river to dredge out a channel deep enough for them to send their ships through and bypass the guns at Vicksburg. But now they're crowin' about how they're gonna change the course of the whole river and leave Vicksburg stranded high and dry.'

'Could they do that?' I asked.

Castile scratched his chin and looked thoughtful. 'Well, maybe – if they did it right. The thing is, the river is already fallin'. And I hear tell the angle they're diggin' at is all wrong.'

Mahalia came to stand in the doorway from the kitchen, her face shiny from the heat of the fire. 'I reckon them Northern boys ain't none too happy, trying to dig through that clay in this heat.'

'That's just it,' said Castile. 'They ain't the ones doing the diggin'. They got raidin' parties impressin' blacks up and down the river, and they're settin' *them* to doin' the diggin' for 'em. Mostly, they're takin' men off the plantations – they git hold of the plantation books and just call off the names of the young, healthy men they want. But they're impressin' free men of color, too, if they like the looks of 'em. That's why I come out here to warn y'all. Don't reckon they'd want old Priebus, but Avery better look sharp. I'm worried about my boy Leo, I am.'

'How many men have they taken?' asked my mother.

'Over a thousand, last I heard. Most of the men they're takin' are happy to go. They march off laughin' and a'singing, 'cause they reckon they're gonna be earning their freedom. But it don't make no difference if a man say he don't wanna go, or that he cain't leave his wife and children. They make him go. And if he try to resist, they jist shoot him. That way they know they won't have no trouble with nobody else.'

I stared off across the yard toward the sunlit pasture. The long fingers of gray moss dripping from the oaks hung still and lifeless against a hard blue sky. 'How long is this canal gonna have to be?' I asked. The idea of trying to turn a river as big and wide as the Mississippi struck me as too fantastical to be believed.

'Pretty near a mile and a quarter, I reckon. Not as long as the New Basin Canal.'

We all fell silent. The New Basin Canal had been dug several decades before, to connect uptown New Orleans to Lake Pontchartrain. But its making was so callous, its toll in lives so gruesome as to forever haunt all who knew of it. Because the canal cut through snake-infested swampland ravaged by Yellow Jack and intermittent fever, no one ever considered using valuable slave labor. The work was done by poor Irish and German immigrants, who worked for a pittance a day and died by the thousands. No one knew exactly how many because no one kept count. Most weren't even given proper marked graves, but were simply pushed to one side where they fell, their bodies buried beneath the levees that rose up on either side of the canal.

'Maybe it won't be that bad,' my mother said after a moment.

Castile shook his head. 'I hear they're already dyin' up there. The Federals are workin' 'em to death without givin' 'em enough to eat or even a proper place to sleep at night. We might not've seen any of their press gangs around here yet, but at this rate, I reckon we will, soon enough.'

I watched my mother and Mahalia exchange a silent look I could not understand. Then a breeze kicked up, lifting the branches of the oaks against the sky and bringing us the earthy scent of coming rain.

It was just a couple of nights later that old Mr Pierce Becnel rode up from Port Hudson with a letter from Papa.

We hadn't had a letter from Papa since the fall of New Orleans destroyed our mail system. This particular letter was over two months old and had come via a circuitous route, passed hand to hand, friend to friend, until it was finally carried to West Feliciana by Mr Becnel's son, Peter, who'd contracted typhoid fever and been sent home to convalesce.

Mr Becnel was a sweet, white-haired old man with three sons off fighting in the war. Mama invited him in for dinner and okra coffee, and listened with attention and concern while he talked about his sons. But I knew that, inside, she was as fidgety as I was for him to go so that we could read Papa's letter.

He'd barely turned his horse through the gate toward town when she tore open the envelope. Two dried, pressed violets fluttered out, their faint fragrance filling the room.

'What does he say?' I demanded impatiently when she paused to pick up one of the flowers, a faint smile pulling at her lips and lightening her eyes as she held it to her nostrils. Violets were amongst Mama's favorite flowers, and I guess Papa knew that.

'Well?' I said again. Patience was never one of my virtues.

She had to clear her throat a couple of times before she could start reading. '"My dears",' she began.

It was how he always addressed his letters to us. *My dears*. I waited expectantly for her to continue.

I pray to our Lord this letter finds you all well. I have been tolerably healthy, although I must admit that I don't find sleeping on the hard ground quite as easy as the younger recruits. The morning frequently sees me hobbling around as stiff as an old man until the sun warms these aging bones. You'd think I was nearer fifty than forty.

I gathered these violets from one of the old British trenches here at Yorktown. We are camped on the old battlefield in a maneuver to halt McClelland's latest advance on Richmond. So I suppose it's inevitable that, as I sit down beside my crackling campfire to write to you, I find my thoughts drifting to the war our grandfathers fought on this same ground eighty years ago. They were fighting – or thought they were fighting (isn't that the same thing?) – for the same causes we say we're fighting for: liberty, and independence, and freedom from tyranny and oppression. Their old battle songs remind me so much of our own, today, that they could be from the same war.

But General Washington had the Comte de Rochambeau and his French troops at his side, and the French fleet just off shore, while we have only ourselves. I know there is continued hope the French and British will recognize us and perhaps even join us, but I don't see it, myself. True, the United States' efforts to enforce their blockade against us have caused outrage in Europe, just as the British navy angered us in 1812, when they seized our ships in their war against Napoleon. Perhaps if we are seen to be winning, they will jump in. The world does love a winner.

But what I find myself coming back to is how the British offered freedom to the thousands of black slaves who fought against us in 1776 and again in 1812. When Cornwallis was forced to surrender here, in Yorktown, his black recruits were dragged back to slavery – or shot. Yet Cornwallis has gone down in our history books as the villain, while Washington is revered as a hero. So perhaps there is hope that future generations will not see us as the villains of this piece. Or is that dispensation available only to victors?

Of course, unlike the old tyrant, King George, Lincoln has not yet offered freedom to the slaves of his enemies. I suppose the fact that nearly a third of all slave states are still in the Union makes such a proclamation difficult. Still, I suspect that in the end he will do so, for expediency's sake. I've heard he often says that if he could save the Union without freeing one slave, he would do it, so I cannot believe his convictions are involved. If the North had won a speedy victory, the South would have been dragged back into the Union with its peculiar institution intact. Now, however, the longer we fight, the more certain it becomes that Lincoln will inevitably attempt to use the South's African population against us and that slavery will be abolished, no matter who wins. If anything good could come of this accursed war, that would be it. But at what cost? The other former colonies of the New World have found a way to end slavery without the slaughter of hundreds of thousands; why couldn't we have done the same? Is it somehow because of that very war, fought here on this battleground, so many decades ago? Did the Revolution bequeath to us a legacy of violence and rebellion, a too-ready propensity to solve problems with bloodshed? If so, what will be the effect of this war on our nation? I can't think it will be good.

I find myself looking out over this old battleground and thinking about how different our land would be today, had the French not joined our grandfathers, if Cornwallis and King George had won. Heresy, I know. And yet . . . had the British won, would we as a people be so enamored of violence, so stirred by the rhetoric of rebellion? Even more ironic to realize that, had our grandfathers lost, slavery would have ended here long ago – peacefully, as it has already in the rest of the British world.

Useless thoughts, I know. But a man must have something to fill the long lonely hours of the night.

I keep telling myself that, someday, this cruel war will be over, and I will be able to go home. I miss you and think of you both constantly. It's an ache I carry with me always, this yearning to be with you, to sit on our front gallery and watch the mist gathering beneath the oaks in the gloaming of the day, to hear the chorus from the frogs down by the creek and breathe in the scents of the honeysuckle and night-blooming jasmine. Someday, I'll be able to hold you both close to me again.

Until then, good night, my dears. Keep safe. All my love forever, Papa.

My mother's voice cracked as she reached the letter's end, so that she had to sit quietly for a moment, the closely-written pages clenched in one hand as she stared off toward the lane, her eyes blinking rapidly.

I had never seen my mother cry, not even when Simon died. She did not cry now. I used to envy her ability to control her emotions, for my own anger and sorrow raged all too often unchecked. But lately I've come to wonder if she might have found the vicissitudes of her life easier to bear if she could have vented some of the turmoil she was surely feeling, even though she steadfastly refused to let it show. But perhaps she did express her sorrow, alone, at night, in the privacy of her room. At the time, that was a possibility that did not occur to me.

She cleared her throat again and carefully refolded the letter. I knew it would join the stack of other letters, tied up in a white ribbon and kept in a small camphor box on her bedside table. I knew she reread them often.

Sometimes I would creep into her room, open that box, and hold the stack of Papa's letters in my hands, taking some kind of comfort from the knowledge that these pages had come to us from him, that they represented a tangible expression of his love for us, his thoughts of us. Yet I could never bring myself to reread them, although I could never quite explain why.

I suspect perhaps it had something to do with the slim packets of letters I'd seen in other homes; bundles that would never be added to, for they were tied up with a black ribbon. The ribbon was always frayed and worn from constant untying and tying, as those few precious letters were read over and over again, a last tangible link to a loved one who was never coming home.

I never acknowledged it, but it was as if I'd somehow convinced myself that if I never reread one of Papa's letters, I could ensure that a new one would always eventually arrive. And then someday he himself would come riding up our lane – perhaps in the gloaming of the day, when the mist gathers beneath the oaks and the scent of night-blooming jasmine hangs sweet and poignant in the air.

Fifteen

The week after my birthday, Finn and I finished our new bows and started work on a supply of arrows.

We tramped through the woods collecting strong, straight shoots of wild rose and black locust, which we then shaved and sanded before tipping them with points fastened with sinew. Castile chipped some of the arrowheads for us from old bottle glass, but we made others ourselves from antlers or bones or even thin scraps of metal.

'The best feathers for arrows come from wild turkeys,' Castile told us one rainy afternoon as he showed us how to strip some of the barbs from a feather's vane and attach three of them to a shaft with more sinew. 'But you can use eagle and hawk feathers, too.'

He held up the first completed arrow, balancing the shaft on the pad of his finger. 'You need the feathers because of the weight of the arrowhead. Without the fletching, the arrow'd jist tumble end over end.'

'When do we git to go after wild turkeys?' asked Finn, ever impatient.

Castile glanced over at him and grinned. 'When I can be sure that if you see one, you're gonna be able to hit him.'

And so Finn and I started spending time in the open wood behind our barn, shooting our newly finished arrows into a target Castile fashioned of hay. Before the war, most folks hunted turkeys with guns. But both powder and shot were now growing scarce. And since at that point the whole idea of hunting wild turkeys was mostly just a grand adventure for us anyway, creeping through the woods with bows and arrows only made it all the more fun.

We didn't realize, then, that the time was rapidly approaching when hunting for food would become very serious indeed.

One afternoon in July, I came back from practicing shooting with Finn to find the house, kitchen, and yard oddly deserted.

Puzzled, I set aside my bow and quiver and began searching the outbuildings, Checkers padding happily at my heels. I finally heard a familiar *whoosh-whooshing* sound and followed it to the barn, where I found Priebus seated on a three-legged stool beside our black and white cow, Queen Bee. 'Come on now, darlin',' he crooned softly. 'You ain't sayin' I done lost my touch, are you?'

The milking was normally Mahalia's chore, and I could tell from the angle of Queen Bee's ears that she wasn't taking kindly to Priebus's technique.

'Whatcha doing that for?' I asked.

He looked up at me. 'Mahalia done gone off wit yor momma to Hidden Hills.'

Hidden Hills was a vast plantation to the north of St Francisville owned by Rose Lacroix, a free woman of color. Tall, proud, and beautiful even in her fourth decade, she owned more than seventy slaves and was known to rule them with an iron hand. It was no secret that my mother didn't like Rose Lacroix much.

I came to rub the whirl of short, stiff hairs between Queen Bee's soft brown eyes. 'Why? What's the matter?' I'd never known Mahalia to go with Mama before.

Priebus sat back on his stool, his hands resting on his thighs. He was only a few years older than Castile, but he seemed much older, his thin body racked with rheumatism, his short, tightly-wound hair grizzled, the majority of his teeth long gone. Like Mahalia, he had come to us from the Dunbar plantation in Livingston Parish and chosen to stay. 'Reckon maybe you oughta ask yor momma 'bout that,' he said.

I looked over at him and laughed. 'What? Why?'

He straightened slowly to his feet, then stooped to grasp the pail's handle. 'Yankees done been there, impressin' men to dig their canal up by Vicksburg. But that ain't all they done.'

'What's that supposed to mean?' I asked.

But he simply shook his head and refused to be drawn any further.

My mother and Mahalia returned late in the afternoon, when the sky swirled with clouds as black as smoke, and veins of lightning trembled in the distance.

Mahalia went off to start dinner, but my mother simply walked into her bedroom, tore off her hat, then stood beside the front windows looking out at the gathering storm.

'Priebus says the Yankees have been to Hidden Hills,' I said from the doorway.

She turned her head to look at me over her shoulder. 'What else did he tell you?'

'Nothin'. He said to ask you. Why? What happened?'

The rain swept in with a clatter, shuddering the leaves of the trees in the yard and drumming hard on the roof.

'A press gang came ashore from a Federal gunboat,' she said. 'Early this morning. They'd rounded up a dozen men before Rose Lacroix heard what was happening and came down from the big house . . .' My mother paused, as if choosing her words carefully. 'You know what she's like. She was furious, and not the least bit hesitant to let it show. She started screaming at the soldiers, saying they were stealing her property and demanding compensation.'

'So what happened?'

'The officer in charge – a captain – just laughed at her. He refused to believe the plantation was hers and accused her of being the planter's slave mistress, putting on airs while her master was away fighting for the Confederacy. He treated her . . . abominably.'

'What did he do to her?' I asked, my voice so quiet it was nearly drowned out by the thundering of the rain.

Instead of answering me, she walked over to her washstand, poured water in the bowl, and carefully washed her hands and face.

'What did he do?' I asked again, my heart pounding, although I suspected I already knew the answer.

She paused with her wrists resting on the edge of the bowl, her head bowed. 'He had his soldiers strip her fine clothes from her and hold her down while he forced himself on her. He wasn't the only one – although most of the men were more interested in the young girls from the quarters they caught.'

I felt a strange vibration in my body, a humming in my ears, so that my voice sounded as if it were coming from far away when I said, 'Didn't anyone do anything to stop it?'

'The grandfather of one of the girls tried. The soldiers bayoneted him.'

'Is everybody gonna be all right?'

'I don't know about Rose Lacroix. She wouldn't let me help her – she's refusing to admit it even happened and threatening to whip any slave who says it did. One of the girls . . . She was only thirteen. If she survives, I don't think she'll ever be the same again. Her grandfather is dead.'

I watched my mother dry her hands on her towel and then fold and hang it on its ring with studied care. 'I never liked Rose Lacroix.

Not only is she a harsh mistress, but I could never understand how a black woman could possibly own slaves.'

I'd never understood it, either, although Papa always said that greed and cruelty are both color blind. Ironically, some *gens de couleur libres* were amongst the loudest opponents of abolition, selfishly guarding the freedom that separated them from the field hands and house servants, as if the liberation of millions of their black brethren would swamp them and destroy their own tenuous position in society.

'I never liked her,' my mother said again. 'But no one deserves what happened to her. No one.' She smoothed the folds of the towel, then went outside to stand at the top of the steps.

The air filled with wind-swirled eddies of rain, the thrashing of the oaks, and the roar of water sluicing off the eaves. In the distance I could hear Mahalia shouting at Checkers, saying, 'You get out of my kitchen, you. You so much as think of lookin' at that chicken again, and I swear, I'll crack your big ugly black head with this here rolling pin. You hear?'

My mother kept her gaze on the teeming rain.

I walked up to stand beside her. 'I don't understand why they did that. Those soldiers, I mean.'

I'd thought soldiers were supposed to be disciplined. Wasn't that why they spent all that time drilling and learning to obey orders? The idea that they could behave like the worst kinds of thieves and murderers from the Point was new to me. But I understood, for the first time, some of the whispers I'd heard, a part of the fears inspired by those armies of angry men marching against us that I hadn't grasped before.

She slipped her arm around my waist and drew me close, a gesture of affection that surprised me. When I was little, my mother was always holding me and hugging and kissing me. But somewhere along the line she'd quit, so that these days her demonstrations of affection were generally limited to an occasional awkward peck on my cheek.

Now she rested her head against the top of mine, her voice oddly strained as she said, 'I don't understand it either, honey. But part of it, I think, is an ugly expression of anger toward the rich man they thought owned that big house and all those slaves. It's as if they didn't see Rose Lacroix and those poor young girls as human beings, at all – as people with feelings and hopes and dreams and needs – but simply as tools to be used for revenge.'

'Revenge for what?'

'For rebelling against the Union. For being rich. I don't know.' She brought up one hand to smooth my hair, which was a tangle from my afternoon's rambling. 'You need to be careful, Amrie. We all need to be careful.'

I was afraid she was going to tell me she wanted me to start sticking closer to home, but she didn't. It was only later it occurred to me that her failure to do so was an acknowledgment of a grim reality: I was probably more vulnerable here, in our house and yard, than I was roaming the swamps and bayous with Finn.

Sixteen

A week or so later, Mama and I were in St Francisville, picking up a plow that Avery had brought in earlier to Cyrus Pringle's black-smith's shop to be fixed, when we heard the pounding of running feet punctuated with shouts of excitement and laughter.

Stepping to the front of the shop, my mother snagged a boy dashing past. 'What has happened?'

'The Yankees done give up tryin' to take Vicksburg again!' said the boy, his face split by a wide grin, his thin chest jerking as he sought to catch his breath. 'And they're evacuating Natchez, too. We're winnin' the war!'

The boy wiggled out of her hold and darted off. She turned to look at me.

'You think it's true?' I asked.

She shook her head. 'I don't know.'

Cyrus Pringle came to stand behind us. He was a big man in his late forties, sweat staining his worn, homespun shirt and gleaming on his thick bare forearms. He was one of those who had quietly opposed succession. Now his only son, Isham, was off fighting with Beauregard. A deeply religious man, he could often be seen sitting on his porch of an evening, his worn Bible open on his knee, as if he could somehow pray Isham home safe.

'Maybe they're finally admittin' they can't win this war, and they're gonna sit down and talk peace,' he said, although he didn't sound as if he really believed it.

The day was hot and overcast, the sky a flat gray, the atmosphere so humid that breathing was like trying to suck air through a thick wad of wet cotton. For a moment I felt as if I couldn't catch my breath. I was remembering what happened the last time the Federals left Vicksburg and came down the river. Except that we'd heard General Williams's army had now joined up with another force from the north, so this time there would be even more of them.

'Could be just a rumor,' said my mother. There were so many rumors flying around these days, some wishful thinking, some telling of disasters that were simply the figment of someone's frightened imagination.

Only, we soon found out this one was true; the Federals really had decided to break off their attack on Vicksburg. The remaining question was: why?

Some said it was because the big iron Confederate ram, the *Arkansas*, had sailed down the Yazoo River and scattered the Federal fleet, destroying dozens of their boats. Others claimed it was because General Butler had heard the Confederates were planning a move to retake Baton Rouge and he wanted to concentrate his forces back down the river. And then there were those who said it was because the Federal troops camped in the marshes below Vicksburg were sickening and dying at a fearful rate. About the only thing we knew for certain was that they'd also given up their plan to shift the channel of the Mississippi into a canal.

In so doing, they abandoned the twelve hundred slaves they'd impressed to dig it.

Left far from their homes and families, without food or protection, their dreams of freedom shattered, the forsaken men waded out into the river behind the departing Federal boats, arms raised in beseechment, crying out in anguish as they begged to be taken, too. But the decks of the troop transports were already crowded with sick and dying soldiers.

It was a day or so later that Finn and I found the first of those soldiers washed up, dead, on the bank below Bayou Sara.

The river was falling rapidly, leaving the levee strewn with driftwood and pieces of raft all tangled up with a variety of weird and wonderful things carried away by the floodwaters from settlements up river: everything from barrels and pirogues to broken chairs and old boots. We were scavenging the piles of wreckage, Finn a ways

ahead of me as we poked around for anything useful, when I saw
him go suddenly still.

'What'd ya find?' I called.

'Looks like a dead Yankee,' said Finn in a queer, tight voice.

Leaving the birdcage I'd been trying to free from a tangle of
rope, I scrambled down the bank to where the body of a man lay
face down in the silt-heavy water, his arms flung out at his sides
in a way that reminded me uncomfortably of the crucified Christ.
'How'd he get here?' I asked, my own voice thick in my throat.

Finn grabbed a handful of the soldier's sodden blue uniform and
dragged him over, one arm splashing in the water.

'*Ew!*' I said, my hand coming up to cover my mouth as the sweet
scent of decay rose up strong and a big black water beetle skittered
across the dead man's blue, slack face. 'What'd you want to go and
do that for?'

''Cause I wanted to see how he died.' Finn hunkered down beside
the pale, stiffening corpse. 'I don't think he's been shot, Amrie. He
looks like somebody who was sick for a long time.'

'Maybe he fell overboard.'

Finn pushed to his feet, his gaze narrowing against the glint off
the water as he stared down the riverbank. 'Look; there's another
one!'

At first I didn't believe him. But I've never known anyone with
eyes like Finn. Stepping gingerly over the mounds of tangled
branches and logs, I followed him to where another dead Union
soldier floated, this one face up in a gentle eddy.

'Reckon we oughta tell somebody?' I said.

Finn glanced over at me, his face screwed up as he squinted into
the westering sun. 'What for?'

'Why you think? So they can bury them!'

'Why the heck should *we* bury them when their own officers
didn't bother? They just tossed 'em overboard like they was dead
hogs or somethin'.' He jerked his chin toward the dead man at our
feet. 'He come down here aimin' to kill us; I say, let him rot in the
sun.'

I stared down at the dead soldier's pale face. I wanted to hate
him. I kept thinking about the soldiers ravaging New Orleans and
what that raiding party had done up at Hidden Hills, and wondering
if he'd been a part of it. But what if he hadn't? What if he was just
some poor farmer who thought he was doing the right thing, fighting

for his country, the way Papa was fighting for his? What if he had a little girl somewhere, just like me? A little girl whose daddy was never coming home.

I said, 'Everybody deserves a proper burial.'

Finn just let out a disgusted snort and turned away to go back to picking through the flood's leavings.

And so I left him there, and went and told Dr Daniel Lewis, our reverend at Grace Episcopal Church. Not only was he a good Christian man, but he was also originally from Schenectady, New York; I figured I could trust him to do what was right by the dead Northerners.

He borrowed a cart and mule from Cyrus Pringle, and then he and Mr Pringle went out to collect the bodies. They found another one, too, further down the river, and brought all three back to bury them behind the church. He asked me if I wanted to attend the brief graveside services.

I said no. My charity toward dead Yankees only extended so far.

It took the Federal fleet three days to steam past us. And all that time, dead soldiers and seamen kept washing up on our riverbanks. We heard later that so many men were dying, the commanders didn't want to take the time to stop and bury them along the levees. But that didn't explain why they didn't order them sewn into blankets and weighted down before being thrown overboard, as was the custom. Some folks reckoned the Federals were hoping the rotting corpses would infect the settlements along the river with whatever sickness had struck their men so savagely in the marshes before Vicksburg. But from the sound of things, their troops had succumbed to swamp fever, which was something we battled all the time. If anyone sickened and died from those rotting Federal corpses, I never heard of it.

I thought it was a nasty thing to do, nevertheless – to us and to the Northern women and children whose loved ones were left to putrefy in our hot sun, or else coldly laid to rest by the resentful hands of those who wished them only a speedy trip to hell.

Church was crowded that Sunday, both because the sight of all those rotting corpses had folks thinking uncomfortably about the state of their own souls, and because a famous visiting preacher named Garette Hale was in town, and everyone was anxious to hear his sermon. After more than a year of war, our sources of entertainment had narrowed down something pitiful.

I scooted in behind Mama as we took our usual places in the last pew nearest the door. The day had dawned clear and brutally hot, so that the air in the church quickly grew stifling and close as more bodies pressed into the confined space. A ceaseless, hummingbird-like beating of scores of handheld fans joined the usual stray coughs, rustling skirts, and murmuring voices.

I leaned in closer to my mother and whispered, 'How come this preacher is so famous?'

'You'll see,' she said.

That's when I noticed the martial light in her eyes, and I knew a heavy, sinking feeling in the pit of my stomach.

My mother was a curious mixture of contradictory inclinations, her instinctive Scots reticence combined with a fiery temper that could be instantly roused to unbridled, caustic condemnation by the sight of someone kicking a dog or beating a tired horse. But nothing riled her more than slavery and war.

Slewing around in my seat, I eyed the unfamiliar, rotund man I could see talking to a woman in the pool of golden morning sunshine just outside the church's wide open doors. I'd always been quick to judge people; it was one of my many grievous faults, constantly catalogued in painstaking detail for me by my Grandmother Adelaide. So as I studied the visiting preacher, I tried to practice the charity in which I'd been told I should view each new acquaintance.

I'd heard the Reverend Garette Hale came to us from Georgia. Only, I could catch snippets of his conversation with Mrs Fox, and he reminded me more of Bernard Henshaw than somebody from Macon or Atlanta.

I said to my mother, 'He don't sound like nobody from Georgia I ever met.'

'He *doesn't* sound like *anyone* from Georgia,' she corrected me. 'That's because he's originally from Oxford.' Then she added, 'England' in case I was confused, since the nearest Oxford to us was in Mississippi.

'Oh,' I said.

I eyed him more intently. He had a pink, puffy face sheened with sweat by the sun. But his smile was cherubic, a glow of amiability that crinkled the flesh beside his small blue eyes and suffused his face with good cheer tinged with a touch of amused indulgence that for some reason set up my back.

I realized I was doing it again – judging – and redoubled my efforts to be charitable. He had a blobby nose, which I sorta liked, and the heaviest eyebrows I'd ever seen, of the same silken silver as the ring of hair that circled the sides and back of his head but left the top bald and shiny. The effect was somewhat like that of a tonsured monk, so that he reminded me of a holy picture Grand-mère had of St Francis of Assisi. Only, the Reverend Hale was better fed.

Much better fed.

The rustling and coughing inside the church reached a crescendo, then fell abruptly silent as we all rose. Mr Garette Hale swept into the church, followed by our own Reverend Daniel Lewis. I liked Dr Lewis. A small, sparse, scholarly man, he was beaming with pride at the honor of having such a famous orator visiting his church. But there was something else in his face that confused me; something that looked almost like nervousness as the two men took their places.

The Reverend Lewis often struggled to project his thin, nasal voice to the back of our church. Not Garette Hale.

'The Lord is in his lofty temple,' declared the Reverend Hale, his deep baritone booming out like a clarion call from heaven itself. 'Let all the earth keep silent before him.' He spread his hands wide, his smile one of beatific forbearance. 'Enter not into judgment with thy servants, O Lord; for in thy sight shall no man living be justified.'

I found myself focused for some reason on his big, puffy fingers, which were white and soft, with bejeweled rings that sparkled with fire in the light streaming in through the high arched windows of the nave as he brought his hands together again and bowed his head. 'Let us pray.'

We all bowed our heads except for one small child who whined, 'I'm thirsty!' before being quickly hushed.

'Lord God, author of peace and lover of concord, to know you is eternal life and to serve you is perfect freedom. Defend us, your humble servants, in all assaults of our enemies, that we, surely trusting in your defense, may not fear the power of any adversaries, through the might of Jesus Christ our Lord, Amen.'

A heartfelt 'Amen' echoed around the church.

I'd obediently bowed my head along with everyone else. But I'd long ago discovered that by tilting it slightly, I could present a semblance of devotion while still looking around a bit. If my Grandmother Adelaide had been there, she'd have thumped me, and glared me into a stricter posture of attention. But she wasn't there, and if my mother noticed my wandering focus, she didn't let on.

I let my gaze rove over the pews full of women of all ages, shapes, and sizes; planters' wives and daughters mingled with the wives, daughters, and mothers of shopkeepers, tradesmen, and laborers. We were a church full of women and children, left alone while our men went off to war. And not for the first time I found myself wondering if one of the women in church with us that day was the intended recipient of that letter carried by the dead Federal down on Thompson's Creek.

As I pondered these thoughts, the Reverend Garette Hale's voice rolled on through the confession and the anthem, the congregation standing and kneeling when appropriate, the old folks' knees popping and creaking as they labored to comply, the air in the church getting hotter and smellier with a mingling of sweat and onion breath and the occasional squirt of chewing tobacco spit discretely into a half-hidden can. Then, at last, came the moment for which all were waiting: Mr Garette Hale stepped up to the pulpit, and we settled thankfully onto our pews to listen to the famous man's sermon.

Our Reverend Lewis always delivered his sermons from a sheaf of notes he prepared every week, sometimes laboring over their composition by candlelight late into the night. But Mr Hale took the pulpit with only a worn black Bible in his hands, which he laid unopened before him as he said loudly and clearly, "'The statutes of the Lord are right.'"

He paused theatrically, his gaze traveling over the congregation as he waited for his words to sink in. 'This is what God tells us in Psalm 19:8. It is an instruction we do well always to remember, and never more so than at this grievous hour. At this hour, when our benighted brethren to the north have unleashed the hellhounds of war upon us and seek to steal from us the sweet blessings of liberty granted to us not merely by that Constitution writ nearly four score years ago by our forefathers, but –' he paused to lift one pointed finger – 'by God himself, as our birthright.'

I cast a quick sideways glance at my mother. She was beating her pretty little painted wood and silk fan kinda fast, but other than that, she appeared calm, her gaze intently focused on the man at the pulpit.

'"The statutes of the Lord are right",' he said again. 'We obey the Lord's statutes every day. We honor our fathers and mothers. We resist the urge to covet our neighbor's donkey or bash him over the head to steal his pretty new pocket watch.'

A faint titter of amusement rippled through the pews.

'We know all that. But what does God say about slavery?'

All traces of laughter disappeared as a new seriousness gripped the congregation. One or two glances were thrown our way, and I wanted to sink down behind the back of the pew before me.

'It's a timely topic, isn't it?' asked Mr Garette Hale in a mastery of understatement. 'So what *does* the Bible say about slavery? Actually, it tells us a lot. It tells us in the Book of Genesis that when Ham transgressed the rules of God, his father, Noah, cursed his descendants for all time, darkening their skin and saying, "A servant of servants shall he be unto his brethren. *Forever*."'

I shifted my gaze from the man at the pulpit to our own Reverend Lewis. He was sitting with his gaze downcast, a faint flush on his cheeks, and I thought I understood now the source of his earlier discomfort. Reverend Lewis might hail originally from New York, but he was a fervent Southern patriot. Every Sunday, he called for prayers for the Confederacy and Jefferson Davis and all our boys in gray, and vehemently condemned the wickedness of Abraham Lincoln for ordering his armies to burn our farms and kill our cows. Yet I'd never heard him try to use the Bible to justify slavery – not once. I wondered if he'd known Garette Hale's chosen topic for the day, or only suspected it.

Hale's plumy Oxford vowels continued to boom out over the small Louisiana church. 'Now, some people say, "Oh, that's the Old Testament" – as if we can parse the Lord's word, believing some parts and ignoring others as the fancy takes us. But let's play their game, shall we? Let's look at the New Testament. Did Jesus condemn slavery? No, he did not. Just pause for a moment and think about what that means. Jesus lived in a world in which slavery was a common institution; he was literally *surrounded* by slaves. Don't you think that if he considered slavery an evil, he would have condemned it? Of course he would have! He chased the money-lenders from the temple, didn't he? But where's the parable about Jesus freeing the slaves? It must be here somewhere . . .'

The preacher made a show of thumbing through his Bible as if hopefully searching for such a passage. Another titter spread through the flock, and he looked up with a smile. 'You know why I can't find it? Because it doesn't exist! Jesus never said a word in condemnation of slavery. But the Apostles talked about slaves. And what did they say? Well, in the First Epistle of Peter, slaves are clearly instructed to obey their masters – "as to the Lord"! Slaves are ordered to submit to their masters just as wives are ordered to submit to their husbands: "as to the Lord".'

I didn't dare look at my mother. I knew that part of the Bible always riled her.

Hale's voice rolled on. 'In The Epistle to Philemon, St Paul tells us how he returned a slave named Onesimus to his master. That's right; St Paul *returned* a slave to his master! Now, it's true; Paul does entreat Philemon to treat Onesimus with the kindness to be expected of a good Christian. But does he tell Philemon to free Onesimus? No! Does he tell Philemon that he must free all the other slaves he owns? No! In fact, in the Epistles of Paul to Titus, Paul actually tells slaves they must obey not only those masters who are good and kind, but even those who are severe and unjust!

'So, ask yourself for a moment: why did Paul say these things? Because Paul knew – as Jesus knew – that in this imperfect world bequeathed to us by Original Sin, slavery is not only appropriate, but *necessary* for the preservation of the natural order. Slavery was established by the decree of the Almighty God himself. That's why you find it reinforced everywhere in the Bible – ' he brought his fist down on the book with a mighty thump that made some folks jump, and woke up Miss Delia, who'd been gently snoring at the end of the pew – 'from Genesis to Revelation. The stability of church and state, the very survival of civilization itself, rests upon our defeat of the pernicious, misguided doctrine of abolitionism.

'Now, I know that some folks are as kind-hearted as they are wrong-headed.' He gave a tight, sad little smile and shook his head at the folly of such ignorance. 'They want to believe that slavery is wrong, that it goes against God's teachings. But this is a dangerous, misguided error. Yes, the Negro has a soul – don't let anyone try to tell you otherwise! But just because he has a spiritual soul does not mean that he is in any sense the intellectual, moral, or *civil* equal of the white man. The truth is, anyone who would try to free the Negro from slavery does not have his best interests at heart. Slavery is the African's natural condition, the God-mandated institution by which the superior white race, in their benevolence and generosity, has turned the ignorant, heathen savages of Africa into civilized Christian laborers, guiding them and protecting them from the consequences of their own sloth and folly. The Negro is so intellectually and morally deficient that he is simply fundamentally incapable of surviving on his own.'

My face grew hot, and I shifted uncomfortably on the hard wooden pew. I felt as if I were somehow besmirched, just by sitting there and listening to this kind of talk. I could not begin to imagine what all the free people of color and the slaves in the gallery must be thinking, listening to this. I thought about all the *gens de couleur libres* I knew, like Castile and his son, Leo; they were surviving just fine with their livery stable. And what about Rose Lacroix, with her vast plantation to the north of Bayou Sara? There were something like a quarter of a million free people of color scattered across the South, and a few hundred thousand more up North; how did this preacher think *they* managed not only to survive, but often prosper?

I glanced around me. But if these thoughts were occurring to any of my fellow parishioners, it didn't show on their faces. They stared up at the Reverend Hale in rapt attention.

'The Negro,' said the preacher with a sad smile, 'is like the Irishman—'

I heard Margaret O'Sullivan, a plasterer's wife from Ulster who sat beside me, draw in a quick, indignant breath.

'He's like the Irishman, and like our own dearly loved and cherished women and children: of inferior mental faculties, foolish and overly emotional, and in constant need of guidance and control by his betters. And just as we protect, guide, and chastise our women and children when necessary, we take loving care of the black members of our families, too. Anyone committed to the abolition of slavery is in effect advocating the destruction of our families. That's right; abolitionism is one of the seeds of socialism and communism. Make no mistake; this is what we're really fighting here. We're talking about the radical doctrines of Smith and Andrews. And if these dangerous thinkers are allowed to have their way, where will it end? Soon, they'll be advocating for the abolition of private property! The abolition of religion! Free lands, free love, and *free women*!'

He was thundering now, eyes bulging, his entire body shaking with the vehemence of his rhetoric. I was staring at him so intently that my mother had to nudge me twice to get my attention.

I looked over at her, and her gaze locked with mine. Her color was high, her lips pressed into a tight, straight line, her lower jaw shoved forward in that way she had. Her breath came so hard and fast her chest was jerking.

I understood, now, why my mother so often chose to sit at the back of the church. She gave me a barely perceptible nod, and we arose quietly to slip out the door into the hot, July sunshine.

She charged down the pathway to the street with such swift, long strides that I wondered if she feared being contaminated by the poisonous concepts spewing out of the church behind us. I had to run to catch up to her, grabbing her arm so that she swung around to face me.

'Is it true, what he's saying?' I demanded. 'That the Bible—'

'Amrie! No! That man is a pompous, self-righteous idiot. If you want to start reading it that way, the Bible also condones child sacrifice, the brutal extermination of entire societies, rape, and polygamy! What's next? Shall every man be permitted a dozen wives, simply because it was the custom of some primitive society that ceased to exist thousands of years ago? Good God!' She clenched her fists, and we heard a loud *crack* as the guardsticks of her fan snapped.

She opened her hand and stared down at the broken fan that lay across her palm. Then she startled me by going off into a loud peal of laughter.

I stared at her, puzzled and a bit frightened. In truth, a broken fan was nothing to laugh about. What might once have been a matter of no importance was now a real aggravation, for the worst of the summer heat was barreling down on us, and there would be no way to buy a new fan until the war ended and the blockade was lifted.

Her laughter died abruptly. 'I shouldn't have come,' she said. 'I should have realized he'd just make me angry if he decided to go off on this.'

'So why did we come?'

'"Know thine enemy", I suppose.'

I looked at her, at the familiar, determined tilt of her chin, the angry fire that lingered in her eyes. The golden morning sun poured down around us, the air already hot and humid with a breeze that blew a fine dust out of the road to powder the tombs around us. Yet in spite of the heat, I felt a sudden chill dance down my spine.

Perhaps the suspicion had been there before, unacknowledged. But it was only in that moment, as we stood beneath the spreading oaks of the quiet churchyard that held the graves of my brother Simon and another brother who had died just hours after his birth, that I first admitted to myself the truth: Hiram Tucker was not the only one who suspected that my mother was the intended recipient of the secret message that began, 'Dear Madam . . .'

Seventeen

What kind of unnatural child suspects her own mother of betraying her family, friends, and neighbors?

This was the question that now haunted my long days and sleepless nights. I told myself all sorts of reassuring lies, but I didn't really believe any of them. And then I started worrying; if even I could suspect my mother, was there any doubt of what would happen if the discovery of the drowned Federal and his undelivered message ever became known around town?

Yet it wasn't long before I had a new, more immediate concern. With the vast Union army now entrenched at Baton Rouge, we began seeing what they called foraging parties: troops of men who would descend on isolated farms to seize corn and hay, cattle and chickens, wagons and mules. But often, that wasn't all they'd take. It soon became obvious that as far as the invaders were concerned, everything we owned was theirs for the taking: gold and jewelry, silver and keepsakes, even silk dresses and children's toys.

We'd heard the same stories coming out of Tennessee and Virginia. At first, more cautious folks told themselves these must be isolated incidents, that American soldiers wouldn't ravage the homes of their own brethren, and American officers would never allow such behavior. But after the second house in our area was plundered, Mama and I hauled some empty barrels and oil cloth into the dining room, and spent one evening packing up our silver teapot and candlesticks, silverware and serving dishes. We sewed our jewelry into flannel pouches and stuck those in there, too, although we kept out a few pieces, because we'd heard that when raiding parties couldn't find any valuables to steal, they'd string up a woman by her thumbs and stick her with bayonets until she confessed to where she'd hidden her possessions.

We worked in a silence filled only with the rustle of the paper and old rags we used as wrappings. Finally, I said, 'Where we gonna bury this stuff?' The Federals were reputed to have an uncanny ability to know where to look – crawling under houses and kitchens, even digging under beehives.

She tucked a silver soup ladle down the side of the barrel. 'Priebus is going to dig a new privy over by the woodhouse.'

I stared at her. 'You're gonna put this stuff down the privy?'

'Not down the privy hole, no. He's going to bury it beneath the floor.'

I wasn't convinced that was going to work. I mean, if the Yankees were willing to crawl under porches and mess with bees, why not privies? But I couldn't come up with a better idea, so I kept still.

I settled back against the doorjamb, my hands resting slack as I let my gaze drift around the room. I looked at the gilt-framed oil portraits of my Grandfather Dunbar and my brother Simon; at the crystal glasses on the sideboard that had once belonged to Papa's grand-mère; at the delicately inlaid rosewood stand that Adelaide Dunbar's mother had brought with her from Boston and that had been in her family since before the Revolution. We couldn't bury everything. We could only hide the things that were most valuable and therefore most at risk, or that would at least fit in the barrels.

The Reverend Lewis was always talking about the vanity of material possessions. But I figured my attachment to the old ormolu clock on the mantel – or Grand-mère's delicate celery pitcher – had nothing to do with how much these things were worth. Their value to me was something intangible, something inside me, something that had to do with the bittersweet ache I felt when I chanced to look at Simon's portrait and the warm glow of belonging I got when I held my great-grandfather's worn letter opener in my hands. It was as if all these things both helped to define me and somehow *extended* me – into the past, where I could connect with forebears I'd never known, and into the future, to the grandchildren I'd always assumed would someday inherit these things from me.

The idea that someone could take all this from me – my sense of identity, my connection to ancestors I'd never known, the image of my dead brother – made me feel anxious and vulnerable in a way I'd never before realized I was. It also made me quietly, power-fully, and enduringly furious.

I said, 'I wish we could somehow hide it all – cast an enchant-ment on the whole house that would keep everything safe from any Yankees marching up the road.'

But such wishings came from the imagination of a child, and my childhood was rapidly slipping away from me.

August came, and with it rumors of vast troop movements. People said that the Confederate General John C. Breckenridge – once vice president of the United States – had come down from Mississippi with nearly four thousand men and was at Camp Moore, preparing to march against Baton Rouge. They said that the *Arkansas*, the mighty iron ram that had scattered the Federal fleet at Vicksburg, was on its way down the river, too. But I couldn't help thinking that if even I knew the Confederate plans, then surely the Federals at Baton Rouge must know about them, too?

No one could say exactly when the attack was expected to come. But one sticky, foggy morning, I awoke to a distant rumbling that went on and on and on. It could have been thunder. But I knew it wasn't.

Putting aside my mosquito bar, I crept from my bed to the open window. The blackness of the receding night still gripped the oaks and cedars below. But I could see the first rays of light creeping across the sky, streaks of gold and vermillion that spread like molten fingers across an aquamarine sky.

I wished I could see through the darkness, through the miles of swamp and woodland that separated us from Baton Rouge. A part of me felt a rush of excitement; *Finally* we were fighting back. But then I thought about all the women and children of Baton Rouge, awakened by the scream of shells and the *whump* of cannonballs, and I found myself trembling.

Finn and I had planned to spend the day scouting the woods for turkey roosts. But we had a hard time settling down to do much of anything. Sometimes the wind would drop, and we'd become aware of a stillness filled only with the chorus of birds in the treetops and the lowing of Queen Bee out in the pasture. But then the wind would shift and we'd hear it again: *boom, boom, boom.*

Finn was all for taking his mama's mule, Dander, and riding down to watch the battle himself. But she planted her fists on her hips and reared back her head and said, 'Sure then, you will not. Them Federals would as soon shoot you and steal your mule as look at you. And how'm I supposed to plow the fields with no mule?'

'Jimminy Cricket!' He slapped his hat against his thigh, eyes snapping in a red face. 'To hear you, a body'd think you care more about that mule than you do about me.'

She cuffed him on the side of his head and told him not to be a bleedin' fool. But frankly, I wondered. Mrs O'Reilly had three other children but only the one mule. And without a mule, how could she keep her family fed and alive?

Finally, along about midday, the cannons fell silent. Finn was ebullient, convinced we'd won. 'I reckon the *Arkansas* done for the Federal fleet, jist like she did up at Vicksburg. I bet the Yankees've run halfway to New Orleans by now.'

I wasn't so sure.

It was late in the evening, when the shadows were lengthening and a golden light spilled over the emerald rows of corn in the fields, that a tired, dust-covered rider appeared in St Francisville with the news that General Breckenridge had pulled his men back to the Comite River. Anyone with a wagon or carriage was asked to come help carry away the Confederate wounded, of which there were hundreds.

My mother set off at once with Avery in our farm wagon, the back loaded with everything from blankets and bandages to baskets of fruit and crocks of milk. Finn and I ran into town in search of more news.

We found a crowd gathered around a lean scarecrow of a man, his homespun butternut uniform hanging in tatters, so that the flesh of his scrawny torso showed through the rents. Red-rimmed eyes and swollen lips stood out stark against a face stained black from ripping open powder cartridges with his teeth. He sat perched on the edge of the boardwalk in front of the bank and was eating a plateful of red beans and rice that he shoveled into his mouth with a fist wrapped around the handle of a big pewter spoon. People kept saying, 'Let him eat! Let him eat!' But then somebody else would pipe up with a question, and the soldier would set down his spoon and answer them.

'I reckon we could've whooped 'em,' he was saying as we joined the back of the crowd, 'if the *Arkansas* had made it. But the Yanks had nearly twice the artillery we did. And without the *Arkansas* to occupy the fleet's guns, there weren't no hope.'

'What happened to the *Arkansas*?' Finn whispered to Mrs O'Sullivan, who was standing next to us.

'Engines failed,' she said grimly. 'It was shot up pretty bad in the battle for Vicksburg, and they're saying they didn't have time to fix it properly.'

I looked out over that sea of grim-faced women, children, and aging men. We all knew what the failure to retake Baton Rouge meant – not just for the nation and the war, but for us.

'How many men did we lose?' shouted Cyrus Pringle from the far side of the crowd.

'A couple hundred dead, maybe more,' said the exhausted soldier. 'There ain't no way to know for sure. General Breckenridge tried to negotiate a truce so's we could collect and bury our dead, but the Yanks wouldn't agree to it.'

A rumble of disgust spread through the crowd. Such arrangements were one of the accepted customs of civilized warfare. But lately, those customs seemed to be observed more in the breach, with wounded dying untended on battlefields and the dead left to putrefy unburied.

'One of the big problems,' said the soldier, 'is that General Williams was kilt. Shot by his own men, he was. Some of our boys seen it.'

Another murmur wafted through the crowd. It was no secret that the Union General Thomas Williams was powerfully unpopular with his men. Not only did he force them to drill in the heat, but he'd posted guards to prevent the troops from plundering the houses of Baton Rouge. Since far too many soldiers had come to view anything owned by a 'Secesh' as theirs, this denial of their right to steal without check had seriously enraged them. I had an uneasy feeling the death of General Williams was going to be a disaster for the people of Baton Rouge.

'Any chance Breckenridge might regroup and try again?' shouted someone.

The soldier shook his head. 'I reckon we're gonna fall back to Port Hudson and fortify that. It's more defensible than Baton Rouge, and the way the river turns there, any boat trying to steam up the

Mississippi has to come within reach of its guns. If we can hold Vicksburg and Port Hudson, we can at least keep the Red River open, and stop the Federals from controlling the whole dang Mississippi.'

I thought about old Mr Pierce Becnel, anxiously awaiting his sons' return from a rocking chair on the front porch of his tidy, whitewashed house on Port Hudson's main street. And I wondered if he knew that his small, sleepy town was about to become the focus of two nations' warring ambitions.

It was dark before my mother arrived back home. She brought with her three wounded men. One, a sergeant from Tennessee, had had his face shot off and died somewhere on the road. Another, a soldier from Kentucky, was gutshot and died the next morning. Mama kept him dosed up with her raw opium, so at least he didn't die screaming in agony. The third man, Corporal Eugene Price from Natchez, Mississippi, had a gunshot wound to his thigh. Mama was hopeful he might survive, if the wound didn't turn sepsis. I figured he had a better chance of living under my mother's care than in one of the crowded, makeshift army hospitals, where surgeons hacked off limbs while standing ankle deep in manure and muck, and sharpened their knives on the soles of their boots.

We put him in the guest bedroom on the ground floor, and Mahalia made him chicken soup and lemonade, and I sacrificed my last linen top sheet for his bandages. By afternoon he was running a fever so high he thought he was back in the fight for Baton Rouge. He kept thrashing about in his bed and yelling, 'They're over there!' and 'Look out!' along with a string of cuss words that made my ears turn pink. Then Mama gave him an infusion of yarrow, elderberry, and goldenseal, and he settled down.

Later that night, before I went to bed, I crept into the room to see how he was doing. Mama was sitting in a chair by the open window, her lap desk on her knee, an ink well and a candle on the table at her elbow. The only sounds in the room were the gentle stirring of the curtains in the breeze, the scratch of her pen across the paper, and the faint, slightly uneven breathing of the gaunt-faced man in the bed.

'How's he doin'?' I asked quietly.

She looked up. 'Better, I think.'

'You want me to sit with him? You look tired.'

She smiled but shook her head. 'Priebus is going to come stay with him in a little while.'

I stepped closer to the bed. The single tallow candle filled the room with only a dim yellow glow. In the flickering light, he reminded me a bit of Simon; the same wavy dark hair, the same slightly cleft chin.

I said, 'He doesn't look very old.'

'Most of them aren't.'

I glanced over at her. I'd assumed she was writing to Papa. But now I saw the unfamiliar tintype of a man and woman resting on the table beside her, and realized I was wrong.

I said, 'You're writing to the families of them two dead men?'

'*Those* two dead men,' she said. 'Yes.'

'What do you say? You don't know nothin' about either of them, 'cept that they're dead.'

'I tell them their loved one fought bravely, that he died easily with Christ's name on his lips, and that we wept when we laid him gently in his grave.'

'But that ain't – isn't true.' Both soldiers were still unburied. We had no idea if either man had fought bravely or not. The sergeant from Tennessee had slipped away in the back of the wagon before anyone even realized it, while the soldier from Kentucky had died in an opium-induced haze.

'There are times when what's true isn't what's important, Amrie. If I can say anything to help make these poor people's grief any easier, I will.'

I picked up the tintype. 'Which one'd this belong to?'

'The man from Tennessee.'

The photograph was of an older man and woman. The man was seated on a ladder-backed chair in the swept yard of a small, rustic log cabin; the woman stood beside him, one hand resting on his shoulder. The man had a bushy, salt-and-pepper mustache and what looked like a glass eye; the woman's cheeks were sunken, as if she didn't have many teeth left. Their clothes were worn and shabby; the woman's knit gloves were noticeably darned. They stared into the camera with an unsmiling intensity that answered none of the questions I wanted to ask them.

Had they thirsted for this war, I wondered, and proudly sent their son off to fight, cheering his patriotism and valor? Or had they listened to the talk of secession and war with growing dread, and choked back tears as they painstakingly gathered their son's uniform and filled his haversack? Was this an only child, or were there other children to help cushion the grief of having a son's face shot off in the fields outside Baton Rouge? Were there more sons still fighting in this cruel war, their lives also at risk?

I didn't know the answers to any of these questions, didn't know this earnest, hardworking, aging couple. But I found myself desperately hoping their other children were daughters.

All daughters.

Eighteen

Corporal Price's fever broke sometime during the night.

I came downstairs the next morning to find him sitting up in bed with our big black and white dog stretched out asleep beside him on my mother's best counterpane.

'Checkers!' I said in panic, although I had enough sense to keep my voice low. 'Bad dog! Get down! You know—'

'Hold on there,' said the corporal in a slow-as-molasses Mississippi drawl, one hand resting reassuringly on the dog's shoulders as Checkers raised his head and looked at me. 'I cain't rightly let you fuss at this here ole hound dog, seein' as how I'm the one coaxed him up here. Thing is, I got me a black and white pup named . . . well, named Dangit back home, and I miss him somethin' fierce.'

'Dangit?' I said with a laugh. 'You named your dog Dangit?'

'Well, to be perfectly honest, his name is somethin' a might more colorful, but after all your momma done for me, I wouldn't want to sully your ears with a word like that.' The corporal's smile widened. 'I was fixin' to give him a proper name, at first. But I was always yellin' at him, "Dang it, stop that infernal barkin'," and "Dang it, you done messed on the floor agin?" So in the end, I just give up and called him Dangit. That's what he answers to, and it seemed like what the Good Lord intended.'

Somehow, I doubted the Good Lord had anything to do with Eugene Price naming his dog what I suspected was actually 'Damnit'. But I was too polite to say so.

The Mississippian was a revelation to me. Folks around town

thought Finn O'Reilly was a bad influence on me. But Corporal Price had Finn beat all to flinders. He tried hard to keep from peppering his talk with colorful language. But when he got excited – like when he challenged me to a game of checkers, to which my mother reluctantly consented – he sometimes got carried away.

I carefully stored away each and every gem to share with Finn, later.

But it was more than just Corporal Price's language. He was so raw and uneducated, so ignorant he could take my breath away with the things he didn't know – or the crazy things he believed. He was also utterly lacking in all the refined niceties my mother worked so hard to impress upon me; he laughed when he busted wind, and his table manners were atrocious. Yet I liked him in spite of it all, because of his geniality and his unfailing good humor and his unblinking acceptance of the kind of vagaries and injustices of life that so often overset me.

I'd never met anyone like him. And it occurred to me, as I watched him laughingly protect Checkers from my mother's wrath when she found the dog up on the bed again, that the war was like some giant paddle stirring up the quiet, predictable rhythms and patterns of our lives. The result was mostly dislocation, trauma, hardship, disease, and death. But Corporal Price helped me realize that, sometimes, in some ways, stirring the pot can be a good thing.

'What you gots to remember about turkeys,' said Castile quietly, 'is that gobblers is interested in two things: food, and lady turkeys.'

Finn gave a soft chuckle, quickly stifled.

We were creeping through the woods toward a roost Finn had found that morning. The sun was hovering low over the tops of the oaks and pines, the air balmy and sweet with the scent of ripening muscadines, the light golden and mellow.

'This time of day,' said Castile, 'gobblers've mostly eat their fill of bugs and seeds and such, and they're startin' to get kinda lonesome, lookin' for company for the night. So what we gotta do is make a few hen yelps, and fool that ole tom into thinkin' he's gonna get somethin' very different from what we got waitin' for him.'

It seemed mean and unfair to me, to trick some poor lonesome turkey into thinking he was going to find a nice fat hen to snuggle with for the night, when he was really headed for our cookpot. But I kept those thoughts to myself as I hid behind the tall brush at the edge of the clearing, my bow and a couple of arrows in my sweaty hand.

Shooting at bales of hay had been fun, like pitching horseshoes or landing a fish or setting Magnolia to jump a log. But this was different. My throat felt dry, and I had to keep swallowing.

Castile positioned himself with his back to the thick trunk of a big old oak. Turkeys were smart birds, with keen eyesight and hearing, so it was important to stay still and quiet while we waited. From his pocket, he carefully eased a concave piece of slate and a reed. By scraping the reed over the stone, he produced a sound that was amazingly like that funny grating cluck of a wild turkey hen. Finn and I had both tried it, earlier, with godawful results. Sounding like a turkey takes more practice than you might think.

From behind his own bush, Finn whacked a tied bundle of turkey feathers through the air. It was meant to imitate the rush of a hen taking flight, and Finn had something of a knack for it. We did that for a time, alternating the hen yelps with the whirl of feathers, leaving plenty of minutes between each. Then I saw Castile nod ever so gently, his gaze on the far side of the clearing.

A big old tom strutted into view. He paused for a moment to scratch at the leaf litter, then came on. In the golden light of the fading day the black feathers on his back looked iridescent, a breathtaking shimmer of red and green, gold and bronze. As I watched, he fanned his tail in a proud flourish, puffing out the feathers on his back and dragging his wings so that he now looked twice his size.

Then, decked out in all his glory, he sailed toward us with the stately grace of a ballet dancer or a full-rigged ship gliding across the waters of an ocean. As he strutted, he ducked his head in time to his own secret music, his long beard swinging as he advanced with preening confidence toward what he thought was a willing lady turkey.

He was beautiful and grand and absurdly proud of his magnificence, and I had the impulse to leap from behind my bush, wave my arms, and holler, 'Run!'

But of course, I didn't.

Finn looked at me questioningly, as if to say, *You wanna shoot him?*

I shook my head.

He rose up with infinite slowness, an arrow already nocked in his bowstring. I watched him take aim, the turkey suddenly stilling, head lifting, eyes alert as if somehow sensing his own doom. I held my breath and heard the *whoosh* of Finn's arrow flying across the clearing.

The point struck the gobbler smack in the breast. He flopped over with a strange, almost human cry, then lay still.

'I hit it!' shrieked Finn with an exultant war whoop.

'You done good,' said Castile with a big grin, clapping him on the back hard enough to send Finn staggering. 'You done real good.'

Reluctantly, I followed my two fellow hunters across the meadow to where the gobbler lay tumbled and still in the dusty grass, its eyes already filming, the evening breeze faintly ruffling his feathers.

'I reckon he's a good twenty-pounder,' said Castile, easing his knife from its sheath. We didn't have far to go, but in this heat, it was always a good idea to field dress your bird.

'Look at them spurs!' said Finn. 'They must be nearly two inches long.'

'At least.'

I tried to say something, but couldn't.

I'd watched Mahalia wring the necks of more chickens than I could remember. But, somehow, killing this glorious wild bird seemed different, even if I couldn't exactly put my finger on why. It had something to do with his pride, and his beauty, and the treachery with which we had lured him to his death. It just didn't seem right for us to be boasting of his size or crowing over his killing. And while I knew it was being silly to mourn the death of a simple bird when our soldiers were dying horribly every day, I felt myself fill with a deep and powerful sadness that it would take me a long time to understand.

It rained the morning we buried the two soldiers from the Battle of Baton Rouge; a warm misty rain so soft it made not a sound on the leaves of the surrounding oaks or on the dark brown earth shoveled onto the crude pine boxes of the dead.

A number of the townspeople turned out, grim-faced in the defused light of the overcast day. Reverend Lewis's voice rolled over us, intoning the funeral prayer. None of us had known either of these men, but their deaths troubled me in a way I could not define. I kept my eyes squeezed tightly shut, as if somehow by concentrating on the rain and the thud of falling dirt and the reverend's time-hallowed

words I could ease the tragedy of their deaths or lighten the burden
of those unknown mothers and fathers who didn't yet know they
had a reason to grieve. Yet I couldn't shake the suspicion that I was
really there to make myself feel better, to fool myself into thinking
that I was doing something when there was actually nothing anyone
could do. The men were dead, and somewhere two mothers' lives
would never be the same again.

My own mother left after the service, but I lingered, wandering
between the simple wooden markers and moss-covered limestone
monuments. Mama thought I'd stayed because I wanted to visit
Simon's grave, and I did. But after that I found myself drawn to
the bare mound of earth covering the three Federal soldiers whose
own officers had simply tossed their bodies into the muddy waters
of the Mississippi. Surely, somewhere, their mothers also grieved.
Yet because their uniforms were blue and not gray, the tragedy of
their deaths had not touched me – not in this way, not *personally*.
I tried to let it touch me now. But when I closed my eyes all I could
see was the smile on the face of the golden-haired infantry captain
as he yanked my cross from around my neck.

I opened my eyes, and my gaze fell on a small bunch of soft
pink rosebuds that lay against the plain, unmarked wooden cross,
their delicate petals muddied by the rain that had now almost ceased.
I stared at it a moment, confused by its appearance. Who had left
it here, I wondered? Some secret Unionist? Or was it simply a quiet
tribute to the unknown dead, left by someone whose heart had a
greater capacity for compassion than my own, and a more profound
sense of the implications of our shared humanity?

I was still staring at those tattered flowers when I heard a peculiar,
high-pitched whistle that was like a loud, unnatural shriek. I lifted
my head, my gaze turning toward the river at the base of the bluff
as a thunderous explosion shook the ground beneath me.

The war had just come to us in a new and more horrible way.

Nineteen

A strange, loud hissing rent the air, followed by another explosion,
then another.

I threw myself flat beside the Yankees' grave, as if that low mound of loose earth could somehow protect me from the hot, tearing rounds of shot and shell exploding in the distance. My breath was coming so hard and fast I was shaking, my mouth dry, my hands clenched into tingling fists as I wrapped my arms over my ducked head. I could hear screams and shouts from below, smell the bitter stench of burnt gunpowder carried on the river breeze.

Then, as suddenly as it had begun, the firing ceased.

For the longest time, I didn't dare move. Finally, when I was pretty sure it was all over, I pushed to my knees. My pinafore was covered with dirt, crushed dry leaves, and bits of grass, and I brushed at it absently as I rose to my feet. I could see Reverend Lewis standing on the front porch of his rectory, an open book held absently in one hand, his spectacles pushed down to the end of his nose, as if he'd been interrupted in his reading by noisy children and stepped outside to discover the source of the commotion.

'What is it?' I called over to him. 'Can you see?'

He squinted down the hill to the river. 'From the looks of things, a Federal gunboat and troop transport simply dropped anchor off Bayou Sara and started shelling. Perhaps an opening artillery barrage has become their preferred version of a calling card?' He pushed his glasses back up onto the bridge of his nose. 'Now it looks as if they may be intending to land. You'd best head home, Amrie.'

I meant to go home. Only, first I thought I'd take a peak at what was going on down below.

I crept across the graveyard to the edge of the bluff, my breath catching at the sight of an ironclad ram tying up at Bayou Sara's wharves. It was the *Essex*, big and ugly and resembling nothing so much as a giant, malevolent water beetle bristling with death. Beside her, an old paddle-wheeled steamboat turned troop transport was disgorging a landing force of blue-coated men who poured onto the wharf the way ants swarm out of a nest when you poke at it with a stick.

As far as I could see, none of the houses or buildings down below had been hit; either the *Essex*'s gunners were lousy shots or they'd been more intent on scaring people than hitting anything.

In that, they'd succeeded. A throng of frantic, wild-eyed women, children, and aging men surged up the hill toward me, most bare-headed in the sun, their faces frozen masks of sweat-slicked terror as they slipped and slid helplessly in the mud. A half-grown boy in shirtsleeves and suspenders mounted bareback on a big roan thundered past me, a white-haired old woman clinging behind him on the horse's rump, the hem of her dress rucked up to show a froth of petticoats and bare, twisted feet.

The street that cut down the face of the bluff to the river was so steep that a heavily loaded wagon had to take the long way around; but in their panic, most people were coming straight up. I saw a woman trying to climb the slope with both a tiny infant and a two-year-old clutched in her arms, a slightly older child screamed as it clung frantically to her skirts. Behind her, a white-haired man staggered beneath the weight of a sick child wrapped in a blanket. Some carried bundles of their belongings, silverware and precious letters and photographs hastily tossed into everything from pillowcases to tablecloths, their contents spilling out to be crushed into the mud by the feet of those fleeing behind them.

I spotted Mr Bernard Henshaw laboring up the slope, his hat gone, his lank, graying hair plastered to his head with sweat, his mouth slack as he fought to suck in air. He caught sight of me and his eyes widened, his throat working as he sought to wet his mouth enough to speak. 'Amrie!' he said, his breath wheezing. 'They're sending out gangs to impress slaves and set them to loading the contents of the warehouses onto their boats. Does your mother still have that wounded soldier in your house?'

My heart squeezed in my chest with a new fear. 'Yes.'

'Then run, girl! *Run!*'

I ran.

By the time I turned in our gate, my breath was coming in long, painful gasps, the sweat stinging my eyes so I could barely see. I started hollering halfway up the drive. 'Mama? *Mama!*'

She'd been sitting in a rocker on the gallery, Corporal Price's worn gray uniform in her lap as she tried to darn the stained rent in the leg. At the sight of me, she rose, her sewing gripped in her hands. Sprawled at her feet, Checkers lifted his head and stared at me.

'Amrie? What is it? I heard what sounded like—'

'Yankees!' I drew up at the base of the steps and hunched over with my hands braced against my knees as I fought to draw wind. 'They done shelled Bayou Sara and now they're fixin' to send out press gangs. We gotta hide Avery and Corporal Price.'

For once, she didn't correct my grammar. While Mahalia and

Mama bustled around throwing bloody bandages into a water-filled, covered enameled pail and making the corporal's bed, a grim-faced, silent Priebus and Avery and I hustled Corporal Price and his uniform up into the attic. The movement busted open his wound and it was hot enough up there to cure a ham, but there wasn't anything else we could do with him. We left him and Avery with some water, hidden behind a pile of broken chairs and dusty old trunks. But we all knew that if the Federals took it into their heads to search the attic, they'd be found in an instant.

Mama wanted Priebus to hide up there, too, but he said there weren't no Yankee dumb enough to think he was worth much of anything, apart from which he figured they'd be less likely to search the place for able-bodied men if they saw him. So he took his hoe out into the garden and was chopping at weeds when a score or so soldiers led by a tall, ramrod-straight lieutenant turned in our gate.

Mama said to me, her voice low and strained, 'Amrie, take Checkers inside and stay there.'

I knew better than to try to argue with her, although I only went as far as the central hall, then ducked behind the open door. By peeking around the heavy panels, I could see my mother standing at the top of the front steps, her face tight but calm. The hand that smoothed her apron didn't even quiver.

I was shaking so hard it's a wonder the door wasn't rattling on its hinges.

The lieutenant drew up at the base of the steps. 'Sergeant,' he said to the lanky man beside him, 'tell the men to fall out under the trees.'

The men were all wearing dark-blue kersey wool frock coats and sky blue wool trousers, and sweating something fierce as a hot golden sun burnt away the last of the clouds and the wet earth steamed. I watched them flop down in the shade under our oaks and hoped they were lying on anthills.

The lieutenant himself looked about my mother's age or maybe a little younger, with a clean-shaven face and short-cropped dark hair and nice, clear gray eyes. But I barely noticed any of that. I was too busy staring at his corps badge.

Co. M, 4TH REG, WISC. VOL.

For a moment, all I could hear was the sound of my own ragged breathing. Only gradually did the Federal's voice begin to penetrate.

'. . . Lieutenant Lucas Beckham,' he was saying. 'We have orders from General Butler, requisitioning any hale young Negro men in your possession.'

My mother stared down at him, her voice dripping with scorn. 'So you're requisitioning human beings now, too, are you? The same way you requisition mules and corn and the family silver?'

I watched the lieutenant's jaw tighten, his nostrils flaring. But at the same time, a faint color showed on his cheeks. And I thought, He knows what he's doing is wrong and he doesn't like it.

'Ma'am, I'm sorry if you have suffered any previous injury. But you can either hand over any strong male slaves in your possession willingly, or my men will search for them and seize them. The choice is yours.'

Everyone knew that when soldiers 'searched' for anything or anyone, the results were usually heartbreaking.

My mother said, 'I *possess* none of my fellow men, Lieutenant. You will find no slaves here.'

The lieutenant squinted off across the yard to where Priebus had paused to lean on his hoe and was watching us, as if grateful for an opportunity to rest. 'What do you call him?' He nodded toward Mahalia, who stood a little ways behind my mother and off to one side. 'Or her?'

Mahalia took a hasty step forward, her upper lip curling with disdain. 'I's a free woman, thank you very much. And I got the papers to prove it!'

The Federal officer stared at her a moment, then brought his gaze back to my mother. 'You would have me believe you run this plantation with free labor?'

'This isn't a plantation. It's a small farm. My husband is a doctor.'

He gave her a faint smile that crinkled the skin beside his eyes. 'Off fighting with the rebs, is he?'

My mother locked her hands around her bent elbows and kept silent. The homes and possessions of the families of men fighting for the Confederacy were subject to confiscation.

The lieutenant readjusted his wide-brimmed, black felt campaign hat, his gaze drifting around our jumbled collection of outbuildings. 'Seems a strange thing to do – for someone with strong abolitionist beliefs to fight for the South in this war.'

'Robert E. Lee owns no slaves; can your own generals Grant and Sherman say the same?'

The lieutenant's eyes narrowed. 'General Grant freed his personal slave before the war started; those that remain belong to his wife.'

'Ah. That makes a difference, does it? You're suggesting he does not benefit from their labor—'

'And that's not true, what they say about Sherman.'

A contemptuous smile twisted my mother's lips. I'd never seen her looking so haughty or disdainful. 'You're certain of that?'

I watched a bead of sweat roll from beneath the officer's hat to leave a wet line down the side of his lean, sun-darkened cheek. He stared at my mother, and she glared back at him, and it occurred to me, watching them, that they might have been the only two people present.

The sergeant said, 'Should I take some men and search the house, sir?'

Without even looking at him, the lieutenant said, 'No. I'll take her at her word.' He tilted his head and brought one hand to his hat in a kind of salute. 'Good day to you, ma'am.'

He turned to his sergeant. 'Have the men fall in. We'll try the next place up the road.'

My mother stood where she was and watched the Federals march away, their rifles gleaming in the hot sun, their feet tramping on the hard-packed mud. I could hear a mockingbird singing from the top of a nearby live oak, his notes clear and melodious and heart-breakingly familiar, part of a simpler, safer time that should have no part in this sinister scene.

I crept from behind the door to go stand at my mother's side, one hand still holding Checkers.

After a moment, I said, 'How long do we need to leave Corporal Price in the attic?'

'At least until we see them heading back toward town again with their "requisitioned" laborers.'

'It's gotta be awful hot up there.'

'Yes.'

'You reckon they're gonna go to Bon Silence next?'

'Probably.'

'Miss Rowena won't like that.'

'If I know Rowena Walford, she'll smile and bat her eyelashes and ply the Federals with lemonade and peaches, and somehow convince them they only want half as many men as they'd planned to take.'

I went to wrap one arm around the post beside the steps, my gaze on the soldiers disappearing up the lane. 'Those men . . . They were from the Fourth Wisconsin Volunteers.'

'Yes.'

'That's the regiment they're saying killed their own general at Baton Rouge.'

'Yes.'

We'd been hearing increasingly disturbing tales about the Fourth Wisconsin. How they'd 'savaged' a woman in Kennertown – we all knew what that meant – and how General Williams had threatened to shoot a few of them if they didn't stop plundering houses in Baton Rouge. Of all the units under 'Spoons' Butler's command, they were generally acknowledged to be the worst. Which was really saying something.

I said, 'You reckon Corporal Price is fit enough to send up to Natchez yet?'

We'd talked about it, before – about moving him home in the buggy, with Avery driving.

She shook her head. 'Not quite yet. Perhaps in a couple of days – that is, if this afternoon in the attic doesn't kill him.'

The corporal descended from the attic weak and shaky, but alive. Hearing the Federals in the yard right below his hiding place had spooked him, and he was all for setting out right then and there for Mississippi. My mother told him not to be a fool and helped him back to bed.

But she changed her mind later that evening, when Mayor James Marks himself came out to tell us that the Federals had steamed away with the promise they'd be back.

'They claim they put into Bayou Sara looking for coal,' he said, easing himself into a worn armchair beside the empty parlor hearth. 'But then they saw the five hundred hogsheads of sugar and other stores in our warehouses, and I guess they got distracted.'

My mother poured Mr Marks a cup of coffee and handed it to him. It wasn't real coffee, of course; no one I knew had seen that for six months or more. Mama had tried a slew of recommended substitutes, from parched corn to roasted acorns, and finally settled on roasted okra seeds.

Mr Marks sipped his coffee without even a grimace. 'The captain of the *Essex* – Porter is his name – sent two of his men to haul me aboard. You should have seen him, sitting there behind his desk with his feet propped up on the blotter and the air of some mighty eastern potentate. He kept an unlit cigar clenched between his molars and looked me square in the eye while delivering all sorts of grandiose pronouncements about guaranteeing the safety of our inhabitants and respecting private property – except of course for the coal, which was being seized as contraband of war. I said, "And the sugar? Since when is sugar contraband of war?" But he just bit down harder on the butt of his cigar and said, "The sugar is for General Butler's brother."'

We all knew about General 'Spoons' Butler's brother, Andrew. Everything from capriciously confiscated merchandise to vast plantations worked by 'forced contract' black labor found their way into Andrew Butler's possession. Thanks to official passes provided by his brother the general, Andrew even shipped goods back and forth through enemy lines, banking huge profits. In just a few months, the two brothers had become millionaires many times over.

Mr Marks ran a shaky hand through his thinning hair. 'And then, while I'm still standing there and Porter is pontificating on about how grateful we should be that they're magnanimously *guaranteeing* our lives and property, I see them hauling Devon Gantry and Sean Gallagher aboard, too – in chains! Now, there's lots of folks in town has heard rumors about Gallagher being one of General Ruggles's observing officers, but what I want to know is, how the blazes did the Federals hear that?'

I glanced over at my mother, but she refused to meet my gaze.

I told myself that Sean Gallagher was Papa's friend, that she would never have betrayed him to what was most likely a firing squad. Only, why wasn't she looking at me?

Mr Marks said, 'Threw the two of them in the brig, they did, and carried them off to Baton Rouge as prisoners.' He leaned forward. 'But here's the thing: they filled their boats with so much sugar and stuff that they had to leave behind most of the coal and a bunch of other stores they're claiming. So while they've sailed away for now, they'll be back. I'm warning everyone who's been caring for any wounded from the fighting at Baton Rouge to consider moving them away from the river, if at all possible.'

My mother offered him another cup of coffee, but he politely refused, saying, 'If you ask me, the death of General Williams is going to be a disaster for folks around here. He was one of the few

Federal officers I've heard of who didn't see this war as a wholesale plundering expedition. The reports coming out of Baton Rouge these days are troublesome. Most troublesome. Without Williams to stop them, the troops are breaking into houses, smashing furniture, shredding whatever women's and children's clothes they can find. Who'd have thought our own former countrymen could behave like the worst Vandal hordes?'

'It's as if that's why they're fighting – for the opportunity to steal.'

'It does seem that way, does it not? And I'm afraid it's only just begun.' He set aside his teacup with a sigh and pushed to his feet. 'There was a civilian aboard the *Essex* – a dapper chap in a top hat and white silk waistcoat. I heard tell he's a factor for the Butler brothers. Before the *Essex* set sail, I saw him eyeing our wharfboat.'

Two stories tall and with outside steps leading to a gingerbread-draped second floor gallery, Bayou Sara's wharfboat was known as one of the grandest on the Mississippi. In the days before the war, the great paddle-wheelers plying up and down the river would land at the wharfboat rather than tying up directly at the pier. In addition to offices, a lounge, restaurant, bar, and vast freight storage area, it also contained dozens of small, elegant cabins where passengers awaiting a steamboat could spend the night.

'Surely they can't be planning to steal that?' said my mother, rising with him.

Mr Marks stood with his hat in his hands. 'If you'll steal a farmer's harvest and a woman's silver spoons and a little girl's necklace, why not a wharfboat?'

After he left, we stood in the yard. The light of day was fading rapidly from the sky, leaving it a shiny pewter backdrop to the dark shapes of the oaks shifting softly in the evening breeze. After a moment, my mother said, 'Is that what happened to your cross, Amrie, the day the *Katahdin* came? Did one of the Federals steal it from you?'

I couldn't figure out how she knew Mr Marks was talking about my necklace. But it was a relief to finally admit the truth to her. 'Yes,' I said in a small, strained voice.

She nodded, and rested her hand, ever so briefly on my shoulder as we turned back toward the house.

It would be a long time before I realized that she'd known the truth before that – that someone must have told her of the incident soon after it happened. It had simply taken her a while to figure out how to gently let me know it.

Twenty

We saw Corporal Price off to Mississippi at dawn the next morning, when a soft mist drifted through the oaks and the air smelled of wet trees and grass and the cabbage roses tumbling over the brick foundation of our cistern.

He paused with his weight leaning against the side of the buggy so that he could take my mother's hands in his. 'I don't reckon there's any way I can properly thank you, ma'am,' he said in his slow drawl. 'You saved my life.'

'You can thank me by taking good care of yourself,' she said.

He gave a throaty laugh. 'Reckon I'll try.'

Hunkering down awkwardly beside Checkers, he scratched behind the dog's ears and laughed again as Checkers's eyes closed with bliss. 'And y'all take good care of this here old hound. Don't let no Yankees at him, you hear?'

I nodded, one hand dropping to Checkers's head as we watched the corporal climb carefully up into the buggy's seat. Mahalia tucked a hamper of cornbread and ham, along with a crock of buttermilk, by his feet. Then we stood back as Avery danced the reins on Magnolia's rump and the buggy's big yellow wheels rolled forward, the spokes spinning round and round until they were only a blur.

Over the course of the coming weeks we were to become painfully familiar with the Federal fleet's gunboats.

On the thirteenth, the *Essex* returned, escorting a steam sloop, the *Anglo-American*. The *Essex* dropped anchor off Bayou Sara, her guns trained on the city, while the crew of the *Anglo-American* set about towing away our grand wharfboat.

The wharfboat's owner – a short, bandy-legged, red-headed old Scotsman named Alistair McDonald – tried to argue with them, citing Captain Porter's own 'guarantee' to respect private property. When the Federals just laughed at him, he stomped off home to fetch the old flintlock his daddy used in the great rebellion of 1810 when, for ninety glorious days, St Francisville was the capital of the independent Republic of West Florida.

By the time he made it back, the *Anglo-American* and the wharf-boat were pulling away fast. He stood on the levee, his thinning red hair flowing in the breeze, and started taking pot shots at the men on the steam sloop's deck.

'Take *that*, you thievin' varmints!' he yelled, ramming a new round home and raising the gun to his shoulder again. 'We mighta let yer dadburn President Monroe send his blue-backs in here fifty years ago and take down our Bonny Blue Flag. But we ain't gonna let you conquer us without a fight this time!'

He was too far away to hit anyone, the shots pinging off the sloop's hull. But a puff of smoke bloomed from the *Essex*'s ugly iron side. A geyser of mud and water shot up from the river bank as the *boom* of her cannons echoed over the surrounding countryside.

Alistair McDonald dove down behind the levee, losing his hat and ripping one trouser leg. By the time he dared raise his head again, the *Anglo-American* and his beautiful wharfboat were well out into the channel and steaming toward Baton Rouge. But he hauled himself back up to the top of the levee anyway and kept firing until the barrel of the old gun cracked and blew up, burning his face.

Folks said it was a stupid thing to have done, besides being a terrible waste of scarce ammunition. McDonald gruffly refused everyone's offers to put grease on his burns, and stomped off home to crack open the last of the whiskey he'd been saving since the start of the blockade. He made it halfway through the jug before he keeled over from a massive heart attack and died.

Everybody else waited anxiously to see what would happen next.

Commander Porter didn't take kindly to having part of his fleet fired on, even if it was by the angry owner of the wharfboat his men were stealing. The next day, the steam sloop USS *Sumter* appeared off Bayou Sara and just lay there, riding at anchor and watching us.

That's when some folks started packing up a few prized possessions and leaving the vulnerable port area. The lucky ones were able to move up the hill to relatives in St Francisville or further inland. But most folks had nowhere to go – or, even if they did, they were reluctant to leave their homes and businesses unprotected and vulnerable.

I walked into St Francisville a couple days later in a hunt for buttons for the new homespun dress Mama was sewing for me. I wasn't having much luck when I spotted Finn sitting on the edge of the boardwalk on Ferdinand Street, his gaze fixed on some workmen unloading freight from a wagon.

'Whatcha doin?' I asked, plopping down beside him.

Finn nodded across the street. 'See that?'

I stared at a workman on a ladder taking down a faded sign that read: J. RAFFERTY AND SONS, ATTORNEYS AT LAW. Once, these had been the law offices of Mr James Rafferty and his two sons, Joshua and Jeremy. But Joshua died of typhoid not long after Manassas, and Jeremy fell at Shiloh. Old Mr Rafferty just kinda withered away and died not long after that. The building had been sitting empty all summer.

Finn said, 'Guess who the Widow Rafferty done sold the place to?'

I shook my head in ignorance.

'Hilda Meyers!'

I could see her now, through the shop's dusty front window. She had her broom in hand, her gravely voice booming as she shouted at two workmen maneuvering a counter into place, 'Careful, you fools! *Mein Gott.*'

Finn said, 'Why you reckon she's movin' up here?'

I said, 'Folks is scared of staying too close to the river these days.'

All up and down the Mississippi, people were in motion, abandoning homes and farms, plantations and villages near the river and the marauding bands of Federal soldiers and seamen it brought. 'Refugeeing' they called it. The same thing was happening across Tennessee, Virginia, Arkansas, and Missouri; hundreds of thousands of old men, women, and children were fleeing – or being driven – from their homes, some with nothing more than the clothes on their backs.

Finn shook his head, 'When'd you ever know Hilda Meyers to be scared? Smart, yes; but scared?' He shook his head.

'What the heck you sayin', Finn?'

'I'm saying, maybe she ain't scared. Maybe she's smart. Maybe she knows somethin' about the Federal plans for Bayou Sara that the rest of us don't know.'

I kept quiet. I'd never told Finn about the drowned Federal they'd found down on Thompson's Creek. He didn't know I'd once suspected Hilda Meyers of being the intended recipient of the letter the dead man carried. For the last month or so, I'd swung to thinking maybe my own mother was the 'Dear Madam' to whom that letter was addressed. But now, as I watched the old German woman settle the diminished contents of her emporium into her new establishment, all my earlier doubts and suspicions came roaring back with palm-tingling intensity.

Finn pushed to his feet, saying there weren't no use in just watching Hilda Meyers, and we might as well go fishing down the bayou. But I told him I still needed to find those buttons for Mama and I'd catch up with him later.

It was only partially a lie.

The day was turning into one of those searing, breathlessly hot, energy-sucking furnaces that come to the Felicianas in late August. As I slipped and slid down the steep, dusty street that plunged down the face of the bluff to Bayou Sara, I could feel the hairs that had escaped from my untidy braids sticking to my face with sweat. The river was low now, the raging high flood waters of May and June just a memory. I could see the latest gunboat, the USS *Sumter*, riding silently in the water, its bare masts stark against a fierce blue sky.

The town looked funny with its long, grand wharfboat gone; diminished in a way the mere physical absence did not entirely explain. Once, the waterfront would have been alive with the shouts of men and the clatter of wagon wheels and the shrill whistles of paddle-wheelers jostling flatboats. Once, the wharves would have been piled with freight, barrels of flour and cornmeal, towering mounds of sacks filled with coffee and oats, rolls of bagging, and kegs of whiskey and cider whose scents permeated the town. But as I turned up Commercial, an eerie silence hung over the place. I heard only the distant pounding of a single hammer and the forlorn howl of an abandoned dog. Even folks who weren't leaving were obviously staying inside.

A wagon rattled past me, the back jumbled high with everything from chairs and rolled mattresses to pots and pans and a single cheval mirror that rocked back and forth with each jolt. The two women on the high seat, one youngish, the other old enough to be her mother or grandmother, kept their gazes fixed straight ahead, their faces stony and solemn. But in the back, perched atop a trunk, a tow-headed little girl clutched a fluffy gray kitten in her arms, her cheeks streaked with tears as she gazed at a white frame cottage receding into the distance.

The hammering grew louder as I walked up the street, and I realized it came from an elderly black man nailing boards across the empty windows of what was once Meyers Dry Goods Emporium and Grocery Store. I didn't see how a few boards could do much good against either exploding shells or looting soldiers, but maybe she just didn't feel right about going off and leaving it completely vulnerable.

I was standing at the edge of the boardwalk, my gaze on the shuttered storefront, when Castile Boudreau's son, Leo, came out of the livery stable and said, 'Hey there, Missy Amrie; how you doin' today?'

He looked much as I imagined Castile must have looked in his prime, big and strong, with a wide, toothy grin and a broad, flat nose. Only, unlike Castile, his skin had the golden tint of café au lait, and his eyes were a soft gray. I'd never heard what happened to Leo's mother, and I'd never felt compelled to ask. In my experience, when folks don't talk about something, it's because it's either too embarrassing or too painful to remember.

Leo had never been anything but cordial. Yet I always knew that at some fundamental level he really didn't like us much. I just couldn't figure out why.

I said, 'Hey, Leo. Castile around?'

Leo shook his head. 'We been movin' the horses up the creek.'

Castile possessed a small, weathered shack set high on the banks of the creek that fed into the bayou. Before the war, the town of Bayou Sara had been a big horse-trading center, with droves of horses brought down the river from Kentucky and Ohio. Men like Castile would buy the herds and then sell the stock to the various towns and plantations in the region. Once, Castile had pastured those herds up the creek. The knowledge that he was now moving all of his horses and mules out of town gave me a funny, panicky sensation.

It was as if my world were dissolving around me, like the sand-castles I'd built one summer when Grand-mère took me to the beach on Grand Isle. I wanted to be able to fling out my hands and yell, *Stop! Just, stop!* and put everything back the way it was before. I wanted to hear Castile's horses snorting and moving softly in their stalls, and see that heartbroken little girl and her kitten playing happily in the flower-spangled garden of their white frame cottage. I wanted to be able to walk home of an evening and see an oil lamp burning in the window of J. Rafferty and Sons, Attorneys at Law, and see the three Rafferty men, their dark heads bent over their law books as they worked together on a case. I wanted my papa home, alive and safe. I wanted shoes on my feet and something besides cornbread for breakfast. And I never, ever wanted to see a gunboat again.

Leo said, 'You want him for somethin'?'

I shook my head. 'No. I was just wonderin' if he knew why Hilda Meyers is movin' her stuff up the hill. But I guess more folks than I realized are gettin' out of Bayou Sara.'

'Them that can.'

The realization that Castile, too, feared a new, more serious Federal attack and was taking steps to minimize his losses seemed to suggest that Hilda Meyers had no special advance notice of the fleet's intentions.

But I wasn't sure if that made me feel better or worse.

I never did find any buttons.

In the end, Mama hauled out one of her old dresses and carefully snipped off the decorative row of buttons that ran down the front of the bodice. We were all used to this sort of thing, salvaging trims and ribbons from worn out dresses and hats; using rough homespun sheets on our beds and cutting up the linen of our old sheets for drawers and chemises. Some folks were even cutting up old saddles and leather chair seats for shoes.

That evening after dinner, Mama took her work out on the gallery and kept sewing as long as the last of the daylight lingered in the sky. Even tallow candles were getting expensive and hard to find, and we tried to use them as little as possible.

The night was hot and still, the horizon aflame with glorious streaks of orange and gold and blood red. Even as the purple shadows deepened beneath the oaks and a chorus of frogs started up from down along the creek, that glowing line of hellish orange continued to light up the night.

My mother finally rolled her sewing and tucked it into her workbox. Then she went to stand at the end of the gallery, one hand resting on the post beside her.

'What is it?' I asked, watching her.

'I was thinking the sunset is lasting an extraordinarily long time. But it can't be the sunset. It's more to the south than the west.'

I went to stand beside her, my gaze, like hers, on that unnatural fiery glow. 'So what is it?'

'I think Baton Rouge is burning.'

Twenty-One

A new wave of refugees straggled into town, bringing with them hellish tales, of women running screaming through the streets of Baton Rouge, their clothes aflame. Of lost children crying by the side of the road. Of the old and sick, alone and too weak to move, consumed by flames in their beds.

Even as the bloated, putrefying bodies of nearly a thousand dead men still lay unburied in the fields where they had fought over Baton Rouge, General Butler had decided that the city was indefensible and needed to be abandoned. But before the Federal forces moved out, they loaded their boats with the books from the state library and the paintings and statues from the capital and the governor's mansion. The gates to the penitentiary were thrown open, and some three hundred and fifty murderers, thieves, and rapists were set loose upon the people of Louisiana. Soldiers roved from house to house, looting anything that hadn't already been stolen or destroyed, piling their confiscated wagons high with rosewood armoires and mahogany desks and trunks of silken dresses.

And then they brought out the torches.

I watched my mother work tirelessly over the next several days, sewing up saber slashes and bandaging burns and holding the hand of a sobbing young girl with bruised wrists and a bloodstained dress, whose mother insisted she'd fallen and cut her leg – but not badly enough to require anyone to bandage it.

My mother's gaze met the older woman's ferociously determined stare, then turned away to prepare a bag of dried herbs from her garden. 'Use these to make an infusion and give it to her five times a day for the next three days. It will help her . . .' She paused, as if seeking the right words. 'Avoid any complications.'

The woman silently took the bag and led her daughter away.

It made no sense to me. Afterward, I said to my mother, 'Why wouldn't that woman admit what happened?'

My mother was sitting on the gallery with her head tipped back against the slats of her rocker, her eyes half-closed. But at my question, she raised her head and looked at me. 'Because she wants the girl to be able to marry some day, and if it becomes known she was raped by soldiers, that won't happen. That woman and her daughter would both rather die than admit the truth.'

'But it wasn't her fault!'

My mother stared up at a hawk circling lazily overhead, dark wings outstretched against a high, fluffy, white cloud. 'The thing of it is, Amrie, Southern men pride themselves on taking care of their womenfolk and children, providing them with food and a home, and protecting them. So when those Federal soldiers forced that girl, they weren't just shaming her. They were deliberately shaming her father and her brothers, too. It's probably the main reason they did that to her. So you see, if that girl were to admit her rape, she wouldn't simply be sacrificing her own honor, she'd become complicit in those Yankees' degradation of her family, her town . . . the South itself. That's why she'll never tell.'

'It don't seem fair.'

'*Doesn't* seem fair,' she corrected gently. 'And it's not. But what that girl is doing – hugging the secret of those soldiers' violation to herself – is incredibly brave and noble. And it's all the more admirable because no one will ever know of it.'

I couldn't quite wrap my head around it all, perhaps because I still clung to a child's fierce convictions of what is fair and right. How could that girl be held guilty of something that those soldiers had done to her against her will?

The concept that life is not fair still eluded me.

That afternoon brought us a new letter from Papa. This one was written on 2 July, which was a huge relief, for we'd been frantic ever since learning that the Louisiana Tigers had been heavily involved in a deadly series of battles in Virginia that became known as the Seven Days Battles. General Lee had managed to stop McClellan's attempt to capture Richmond, but at an awful cost. Papa said it was the worst fighting he'd ever seen, and that the Louisiana brigade had charged the Federals with 'Remember Beast Butler and the women of New Orleans!' as their battle cry.

He sounded awfully worried about us, but I was worried about him. There was a funny tone to his letter that I couldn't quite put my finger on, but that hadn't been there before.

And then, as if hearing from Papa hadn't been wonderful enough, a few days later we received another letter, this one from my Uncle Tate. Now, some might think that hearing from her brother would cheer my mother. But Mama's family was complicated.

My grandmother Adelaide Dunbar had given birth to ten babies. Two died as infants, and two more succumbed as children to swamp fever or Yellow Jack. They all lay in the walled, shadowy family cemetery at Misty Oaks, their graves marked by heartbreakingly small rectangular slabs of limestone that reminded me of tabletops missing their legs.

Sometimes when I went to visit my Grandmother Adelaide, I'd wander through the graveyard, trying to imagine all these dead Dunbars and McDougals that I'd never known. My Grandfather Dunbar was there beneath his own larger, cracked tabletop, as were Adelaide's blueblooded, Bostonian parents, the McDougals, who'd come down the Mississippi and died long before I was born. There was an empty tomb, too, dedicated to my great-uncle Justin McDougal, which always kinda gave me the creepies-jeepies.

But the grave that drew me with a powerful fascination was the monument that lay in a rare slice of sunshine just inside the cemetery gate, its tombstone half covered by a massive red rose that seemed perpetually in bloom. Heedless of the rose's wicked thorns, I'd always run my hand across the name inscribed there: *Hamish Dunbar*.

I'd never met Hamish, but I'd grown up hearing about him. Tall and handsome, with sparkling eyes full of mischief and good cheer, he was Adelaide's first born and everyone's favorite. I'd always thought of him as being an older version of Simon, although I'd seen his portrait hanging beside my grandmother's bed so I knew he was fairer than Simon, with a wide smile that looked like he was struggling to hold back a laugh. When Hamish was fifteen, my grandmother reluctantly allowed him to accompany her brother, Justin McDougal, on a buying trip down the river to New Orleans on the paddle-wheeler *Andrew Jackson*. As the steamboat pulled away from the wharf, man and boy were on deck, waving their hats to the crowd that had assembled to see them off.

My grandmother was just turning away, still faintly smiling at her son's obvious pride and pleasure, when the boat's boilers exploded in a concussion of steam and twisted, searing-hot metal.

The body of Adelaide's brother, Justin, was never recovered. But Adelaide's firstborn lived long enough to be carried back up the hill to Misty Oaks, his body lacerated and burned nearly beyond recognition. My grandmother nursed Hamish day and night for a week as he clung desperately, uselessly to life. His was a hideous death of unimaginable, writhing agony that his mother could only watch, helpless to alleviate in any meaningful way.

I asked Mahalia, once, if it was Hamish's death that had made Grandmother Adelaide such a hard woman.

'Mizz Adelaide always was a hard one. But there ain't no denying that watching Mister Hamish go through hell before he ever left this world hit her in a bad way. She weren't that way, before.'

Afterward, it occurred to me that Mahalia's statement could be read two ways. At the time, I thought she meant that Adelaide hadn't been as hard before Hamish's death as she was after it. But I eventually came to wonder if Mahalia meant something different, if she was saying that the horror of Hamish's dying had burned up something vital inside Adelaide, something that had made her vulnerable in a way she never intended to be again.

Hamish Dunbar's death had left Adelaide with three living sons and two daughters. My mother's younger sister, Aunt Em, married a merchant named Galen Middleton and moved up to Vicksburg. My Uncle Tate went to law school; Uncle Harley started a small plantation of his own near Donaldsonville; and Uncle Bo went off to West Point and shamed my Grandmother Adelaide for all eternity by refusing to resign his commission and return home to defend the land of his birth when war broke out.

Last we heard, Uncle Bo was an artillery captain, fighting with McClellan's Army of the Potomac in Virginia. It made my stomach hurt every time I thought about one of Uncle Bo's cannons maybe lobbing a shell into Papa's tent, so I tried not to think about it.

Of all my mother's brothers, Uncle Tate was my favorite, but Uncle Bo came a close second. His visits to us were rare but always precious. When I was little, he'd toss me high up onto his shoulders, or swing me round and round, his strong hands wrapped around my wrists, my feet flying through the air until I collapsed in dizzy delight. He taught Simon and me how to make moccasins and braid rawhide, and he'd regale us for hours with tales of buffalo-covered plains and Indian teepees and craggy, snow-covered peaks cut by clear, rocky streams bursting with trout and beaver.

Because he spent so much time out West, his skin was always sunbrowned, and he had a way of smiling that started slow, tugging at his lips and sparkling in his eyes before it engulfed his face in a paroxysm of delight. We laughed often when Uncle Bo was around. Things that ordinarily didn't seem funny at all suddenly became wildly hilarious. Papa said it was because Uncle Bo never made the mistake of taking anything too serious. I asked Papa once why all folks weren't that way, since it made life so much more pleasant. Papa said it was a gift. I wondered where Uncle Bo got his gift, because it sure wasn't from my Grandmother Adelaide.

We hadn't heard from Uncle Bo himself in over a year, but somehow news still managed to trickle through to us in ways I never quite understood, either from friends or from Uncle Bo's own two brothers. This time our news came through Uncle Tate.

Tate was my mother's youngest brother, just twenty-one years old. He'd still been studying to be a lawyer when the war came. I knew he was as unhappy about secession as Papa, because I'd once heard them talking late into the night. But like Papa, he'd felt honor bound to fight. He'd spent the better part of the last year in Tennessee. This was the first letter we'd had from him in a long time, and was dated the sixth of June. He wrote:

> Dear Sis and Amrie,
> Your letter of 22 April came to me just yesterday, after having been on the road for more than a month. It was a relief to hear that all is well with you, although I can't be entirely at ease because I know so much has happened in Louisiana since the letter was written. As for me, I'm writing to you from a pretty little village at the foot of a ridge of low hills. Yesterday was a day of hard marching, which hit the men sorely as they were already broken down and half-dead. We were dogged all night by the enemy's cavalry, and I fear they picked off many of our stragglers.
> Some of the land we passed through had been brutally used by the enemy, with hardly a house left unburned, the desolate

fields reeking with the putrefying carcasses of hogs, cattle, and
sheep, while dead dogs, geese and chickens littered the farm-
yards. We paused at one place, a small farm near a stream,
where they'd blown out the man's brains in front of his wife
and three small children, then drove the family from their door
and set fire to the house. The woman tried to go back in to
save some things, but they would not let her. When we came
upon her, she was sifting through the ashes of what had once
been her home, looking for her husband's bones, with her little
children sitting nearby, watching her. They are destitute, their
house, corncrib, and barns burned, their livestock slaughtered.
With no food or clothing or shelter, I wonder what will become
of them, especially as I fear the woman's sorrows have taken
her senses.

I would like to believe these horrors are the work of stragglers or deserters, but from what we are hearing it is not so.
There is a general here named Sherman who is said to scorn
the traditional rules of civilized warfare, who believes women
and children should be made to feel what he calls the 'hard
hand of war.' They say Lincoln is inclined to favor his approach
– a war waged not against armies of men, but against the
hapless, innocent populations of our cities and hamlets and
countryside, and against every living creature of our fields. If
that be true, I fear not only for our own fair land, but for the
future these men will bequeath to our world and generations
to come.

I can't tell you how hard it is for me to be here, fighting
so far from home while knowing the enemy has come to
Louisiana and could even now be marching against our own
homes. Since the fall of New Orleans, I have received but one
letter from Mother. She complains of disruptions of supplies
and the need to set torch to $20,000 worth of cotton she was
preparing to ship down the river. But otherwise she seems
undaunted.

Last I heard, Brother Harley was still plagued as are so
many by that malady which haunts our military camps. But
he was ever a hale fellow, so I doubt you need be made uneasy
by that fact. Two weeks ago, we captured several dozen of the
enemy, one of whom, when he heard my name, informed me
he has a brother in the Army of the Potomac with Bo. I gather

our brother is a favorite of both officers and men, for our prisoner spoke of him enthusiastically, and assured me he was well. I have not passed this tidbit of information on to Mother, as the last time I ventured to send her news of Bo, she threatened to throw my future letters unopened into the fire, should I ever again mention He Who is Dead to Her and Ought To Be Dead to Us All. So, be warned.

I'll restrain the impulse to add a bit here about how much I enjoy receiving letters. Scratch that and replace it with, I live for letters from home. I may covet the Yanks' good shoes and plentiful food and tents and blankets. But what I envy them far more than anything is their reliable mail service. There is no denying this country is pretty (at least, those parts the Yanks have yet to burn). But my heart aches for home.

Your loving brother and uncle,

Tate

After she finished reading Uncle Tate's letter, Mama went out in her herb garden and spent a couple of hours pulling weeds. I was beginning to realize that was her way of dealing with the sorrows and strains of life. I sat on the top rail of the pasture fence and watched Magnolia grazing lazily, one hip cocked. The morning sun slanted golden through the willows along the stream and the clear blue sky promised another hot day. I could hear the chatter of squirrels; smell the gentle hint of wood smoke from the kitchen. I thought about going to find Finn and maybe trying our hand at fishing, but I couldn't rustle up any enthusiasm for it.

My mind kept skittering like a shy colt, touching on first one aspect, then another of Uncle Tate's letter, as if afraid to alight anywhere too long. I tried to ponder how my Grandmother Adelaide could grieve so deeply for her dead firstborn and those other lost little ones, yet harden her heart against a living son because of a painful choice that had been thrust upon him.

But that made me feel so jittery and oddly vulnerable that I jerked my thoughts away, only to have them land on the raw image Uncle Tate had conjured for us, of a half-mad, desperate woman sifting through the ruins of her house, her husband's charred bones folded in her apron, while her small children – hungry, frightened, and surely doomed – watched. I thought of that general who had rated it a fine and just thing to wage war on helpless women and children, to send them naked and starving into the cold night, and I felt suddenly tired and sad and very much afraid.

Although I couldn't have articulated it at the time, I was nonetheless aware of a profound shift in this war we lived. Only, I'd no idea, then, just how bad it was about to get.

Twenty-Two

We awoke to a steamy wet morning of gray skies and a breeze that carried the stench of stale smoke and charred timbers. We thought at first that the smell came to us from the ruins of Baton Rouge.

We were wrong. It came from the USS *Sumter*.

Somehow, the *Sumter* had managed to run aground on a sand bar. Unable to free the sloop and feeling vulnerable to attack, the crew hastily abandoned the gunboat. What happened after that was never exactly clear.

Some folks said the crew set fire to the *Sumter* themselves to keep her from falling into enemy hands – which was standard tactics, really. But when Commodore Porter heard what had happened, he was furious. So the crew insisted they hadn't blown up their own ship; 'guerrillas' from Bayou Sara had done it. And then a couple of half-grown idiots from St Francisville named Ben Bradford and Taylor McGee went around town bragging about how they'd rowed out to the grounded ship and set her afire in the middle of the night. All we knew for certain was that someone also set fire to the coal and other stores the Federals were planning to come back for.

'Dadburn fools,' muttered Mahalia as she helped Finn and me clean a mess of catfish we'd caught. 'They think they're doin' somethin' grand? All they gonna do is get the lot of us kilt.'

'So what are you saying?' demanded Finn, green eyes snapping with indignation. 'That we should just stand back and let them gunboats steal our coal, knowin' they're gonna use it to steam back up to Vicksburg and kill the women and children there? How is that right? How is that honorable? How's that somethin' to be *proud* of?'

'Them Yankees is gonna go up to Vicksburg whether they gets

our coal or not. Only difference now is, what're they gonna stop and do to us, first?'

I kept silent, for I could see both sides of their argument. In a perfect world, men would ride out to do battle like the knights in some Sir Walter Scott novel, fighting brave, noble, and true. But there was nothing noble about this war of ours. Oh, there was plenty of grand language about liberty and independence on one side, and about the sanctity of the Union on the other. But there was something about the South's secession that reminded me of a bunch of spoiled, sulky boys angrily collecting their marbles and going home. While as for the righteous North, anytime you start killing women and children, burning their homes, and stealing their mules and jewelry, whatever moral justification you might think you had in the beginning is gone.

Yet while I knew it was cowardly of me, I still couldn't help but wish that Ben Bradford hadn't burned that danged coal.

Like an avenging demon torn from our worst nightmares, the USS *Essex* returned to us on a hot August morning, when the sun was a searing white disk in a cloudless sky. It had rained the night before, so that the heat leached the dampness from the earth and turned it into a heavy vapor that hung in the air like the rank miasma of an old graveyard.

We never knew for which of our sins we were to give penance, whether it was for the *Sumter* or the burned coal or maybe even Alistair McDonald's potshots at the men stealing his wharfboat. All would eventually be used as justifications for what they did to us.

Finn was down in Bayou Sara that day, trying to barter a bushel of his mama's corn for some molasses and other supplies. He told me later how he heard the clatter of the *Essex*'s engines in the distance; saw the white haze of her smoke drifting against the hard blue sky. But we'd become so accustomed to the endless passing of Federal boats that he paid it little heed. He was walking down Commercial when the first shell whistled over his head to smash into the side of a small white frame house, showering the street with jagged bits of charred wood and hot metal.

He was only dimly aware of the corn spilling across the dirt as the basket tumbled from his hands. This was no warning salvo, such as we'd suffered before. The *Essex* steamed in with all guns well aimed and blazing, a hail of shells and cannonballs screaming through the air to explode in thunderous geysers of dirt, shattered brick, and splintered wood.

He dove beneath the porch of what was once a tailor's shop but had been boarded up ever since Mr Bayer, the tailor, was drafted into the army. He found himself nose to nose with a wide-eyed, brown-skinned girl who looked maybe six or eight.

'Where's yor momma?' he asked as the *whomp, whomp* of exploding shells shook the earth beneath them and filled the air with fire and dust.

'I don't know,' she said in a scratchy whisper.

A cannonball landed in the street out front, and Finn clamped one crooked arm over his ducked head and threw the other around the girl's shivering shoulders. They huddled like that for the longest time, bodies jerking with each concussion, until he thought his eardrums would burst. He opened his mouth and swallowed, trying to pop them, and realized the bombardment had stopped.

Then he heard the tramp of heavy boots.

'What's that?' asked the little girl.

'Landing party, I 'spect.' Lifting his head, he edged forward so he could see. 'Looks like a shitpot load of 'em.'

Blue-coated men poured into the street, faces sweat-slicked, rifle barrels glistening in the harsh sunlight. They roved from shop to house, battering down any doors they found locked against them, laughing and jeering as they sent chairs crashing through windows and shredding drapes, bedding, and women and children's clothes with their bayonets. One seaman pranced out of Sylvia Higginbottom's millinery shop, a purple hat with ostrich feathers perched on his greasy red hair, one wrist limply cocked as he sashayed and cavorted to the cat calls and hoots of his comrades.

'Why are they doing that?' asked the little girl.

Finn just shook his head, because he didn't know what to tell her. From the looks of things, the officers had simply turned their men loose on the town. The air filled with shouts and screams, the crash of breaking glass and splintering wood. He saw one soldier run past clutching a bulging pillowcase from which poked the branches of a silver candelabra and the rounded dome of a mantle clock; another carried a massive, gilt-framed painting of an idyllic landscape with sheep grazing peacefully across verdant hills; another staggered beneath a keg of whiskey. Across the street, a sergeant had a woman backed up against the brick wall of the bank and was violently copulating with her, his trousers sagging down around his knees, the smooth café-au-lait skin of her fine-boned, heart-shaped face a mask of endurance. Finn dragged the little girl's head to his chest and whispered, 'Don't look.'

He didn't know how long they crouched there, hearts pounding, ragged breath mingling as heavy boots thumped the floorboards overhead and the shouts of the men grew rowdier. 'Sounds like they found the bars down by the Point,' said Finn.

He knew by the pinched expression on the little girl's face that she understood what that meant.

He saw two men disappear down an alley, dragging a woman by her arms between them. Her flaxen hair was a tumbled mess, her dress ripped, her face so contorted with terror that it took him a moment to recognize Eloisa Peyton, the woman who'd been running the butcher shop with the help of a half-blind, one-legged German ever since her husband Reuben went off to war.

And then he heard the crackle of flames, smelled the familiar aroma of burning wood.

'They done set fire to the town!' said the little girl, her voice a tight squeak. 'What we gonna do?'

Finn reached out and grabbed her hand. 'We gotta run. Come on!'

They slithered out from beneath the porch and took off toward the edge of town, where a green curtain of cypress and oak trees lined the bayou. He could see black cinders swirling toward the sky as if pulled by an unseen hand; the street became a dark canyon through towering walls of hot flames. He heard someone shout at them, but nobody was much interested in a couple of terrified children. When the little girl started flagging, he scooped her up in his arms and kept running, her skinny arms wrapped tight around his neck, her bare legs dangling. He was only dimly aware of the darkness of the trees closing in around him. He felt the earth turn cool and soft beneath his bare feet; heard his own breath rasping in his throat as he kept running, running.

The little girl said, 'When you gonna stop?'

He stopped.

She slid down to the ground. The shouts of the men, the crackle of the flames came to him as if from a distance or through a strangely compressed tunnel. He felt lightheaded, took a step, and stumbled, so that he had to sit down.

He sat with his elbows braced on his bent knees, his head hanging as he worked to draw in air. Then he heard a crackle of musketry in the distance. It came from above and to the right, and he realized that the Federals must be moving up the bluff to St Francisville. He thought of his mother and his younger brother and sisters left alone on their farm, and felt tears of frustration, fear, and rage sting his eyes.

The little girl said, 'What do we do now?'

He raised his head and looked at her – really looked at her – for the first time. He figured she was closer to six than eight, with a small-boned, heart-shaped face and big brown eyes that stared at him solemnly. 'What's yor name?'

'Calliope.'

'Yor momma belong to anybody, Calliope?'

She nodded her head up and down. 'Mizz Walford. We was down here gettin' some fish for dinner.' Her face crumpled. 'I wanna go *home*.'

Finn nodded, although he wasn't about to take her back to Bon Silence himself.

And so he brought her to us.

Finn told us all this while seated in a rocking chair on our front porch, a glass of Mahalia's lemonade in one hand. He was covered in dust and black streaks of soot, his bare legs and feet scratched and bitten, his face gray with exhaustion. The little girl was playing with Checkers nearby on the grass. Mama'd sent Priebus up the road to tell the Walfords where she was.

He'd come to us the long way around, by following the creek that curved north of the bluff, then cutting back up the slope. By the time he reached us, the Federals had already been driven back down the bluff from St Francisville by a dozen or so old men armed with muskets they'd carried in the Mexican War.

The *Essex* sailed away, vowing to return with reinforcements and burn St Francisville to the ground.

'Is there anything of Bayou Sara left?' I asked.

He shook his head. 'I dunno. Maybe a few buildings here and there.'

'What about Castile's livery stable?'

'I doubt it, Amrie.'

My heart felt as if it were swelling in my chest, so that it hurt.

'Reckon they'll really be back?' asked Mahalia from where she sat on the top step, her gaze on the child playing in the sun-spangled yard below.

'I suppose that depends on why they did this,' said Mama. 'If it was in revenge for the *Sumter*, surely they should be satisfied?'

We'd heard of other towns along the Mississippi destroyed in retaliation for some act of resistance in the area. Only two weeks before, Admiral Farragut had burned the city of Donaldsonville to the ground in retaliation for a nearby incident in which someone took a couple of shots at one of his gunboats. Once, Donaldsonville had been the capital of Louisiana; by the time the Federals were done, the only thing left standing was a walled orphanage run by an order of Catholic nuns. General Butler immediately evicted the children and sisters, and turned the building into the officers' quarters for the new fort he planned to erect on the ruins of the town.

But to my knowledge, St Francisville was the first town whose own inhabitants had taken up arms and fought back. They might have saved their city from the flames that consumed Bayou Sara today. But hadn't they just given the Federals another excuse for revenge?

'What happened to Calliope's mother?' asked Mama, her gaze, like Mahalia's, on the child.

'I don't know,' said Finn. But I saw the tightening of his jaw, the way his eyes drifted sideways when he said it.

And I knew he was lying.

Rowena Walford came herself to collect Calliope, driving a pretty, high-stepping chestnut hitched to a shiny buggy with red wheels.

Mama walked out to meet her and invited her inside. Miss Rowena smiled and shook her head.

'That's right kind of you, Kate. But I need to get this child home. Josephine – that's Calliope's mother – is frantic with worry.'

Priebus lifted the little girl up into the buggy, her eyes gleaming with the treat of a buggy ride – and in the exalted company of Rowena Walford, no less.

Mama said, 'Is Josephine going to be all right?'

I realized then that she'd seen that look on Finn's face, too.

Miss Rowena sucked her lower lip between her straight white teeth. 'We-ell,' she said, drawing the word out into two syllables.

'I'm sure I don't need to tell you what those Yankees did to her.'

'You want me to come take a look at her?'

'She says she's gonna be all right. I guess these things are different for them. I mean, it's not like they need to worry about their reputations or social standing.'

'Yet I've no doubt the fear and pain they experience are equally as intense,' said my mother dryly.

'At the time, yes; that stands to reason. It's just that the *consequences* aren't there.' Rowena Walford gathered her reins and said to the child, 'Tell Mrs St Pierre thank you, Calliope.'

And she drove off, the small dark child sitting bolt upright on the seat beside her, a wide grin splitting her face and one little hand clutching the dash rail before her.

Twenty-Three

It took me three days of pestering, but I finally convinced my mother to let me go see for myself what the Federals had done to Bayou Sara.

The morning had dawned hot and muggy, so that the stench of charred wood hung heavy in the air, along with a smell that reminded me of burned garbage. I made it as far as the edge of the bluff, then drew up, my breath catching in my throat as I looked down toward the river. I'd thought I was prepared for what I'd see. But nothing could have prepared me for this.

Bayou Sara didn't exist anymore. In its place stretched endless piles of rubble and charred timbers. Here and there, a blackened chimney poked up from the ruins, with an occasional stretch of brick wall, its gaping empty windows showing only more rubble beyond. I spotted maybe four or five structures that looked as if they'd escaped the worst of both the fire and the shelling.

'Sweet Mary,' I whispered.

A dozen or so women, children, and old men were sifting through the ashes and debris. They moved slowly, shoulders slumped, as if despairing of finding anything useful and yet feeling compelled to look nonetheless. One or two turned to stare at me, vacant-eyed, as I worked my way down the hill.

Without the familiar shops and houses to guide me, it wasn't easy navigating through the jumbled ruins. The only reason I was sure I'd found the site of Castile's livery stable was because he was sitting smack dab in the middle of the street in front of it, balancing precariously on a singed stool that looked as if it might collapse beneath his weight. His ragged trousers were streaked with black, and he had the sleeves of his homespun shirt rolled up to reveal a bandaged forearm.

'Hey, Castile,' I said softly.

He slewed around to look at me, his dark face splitting into a grin. 'Hey, Missy Amrie.'

I stared out over the ruins of his stables. 'I'm awfully sorry, Castile.'

He shrugged his big, strong shoulders. 'Leo and me can rebuild it, child. Don't fret about us. There's lots who're plenty worse off than me.'

At the far end of the street, I could see an old white woman with wild gray hair sitting on the brick steps of what had once been her home. She was just sitting there, her face blank, as if too stunned to even begin dealing with the ruins of her life.

'The amazing thing is, there weren't nobody killed,' said Castile. 'That's somethin' to be grateful for.'

I nodded to his arm. 'What happened?'

'Jist got singed a bit. I had a couple of mules still in their stalls when the place caught fire, and they were right stubborn about comin' out.'

'You should have Mama look at it.'

'I will, if'n it don't get no better. Right now, I'm puttin' the same salve on me and the mules, both.'

I laughed. Castile had all sorts of salves and liniments he mixed up for his mules and horses, and he was always using them on himself, too. 'Why you just sittin' on this here stool, lookin' at everythin'?'

'I'm trying to decide if I want to rebuild here, or move up the bluff to St Francisville.'

'You reckon the Federals are gonna come back?'

'Oh, they'll be back, child. Cain't say when, exactly. But they'll be back. Ain't no doubt about that.'

Late that afternoon, I was in the yard throwing a stick for Checkers when a man on a gray mule turned in our drive.

I sent the stick tumbling end-over-end through the air, Checkers barking joyously as he pelted across the grass to retrieve it. I returned my gaze to the man riding up the drive.

He wore a silk top hat and a rusty broadcloth coat, and had hitched his stirrups up so short he looked vaguely ridiculous. I knew only one man around these parts who rode like that: our school-master, Horst Fischer.

He reined in at the base of the steps and swung down with the sigh of a man for whom riding any distance is a discomfort. Checkers was frisking around me, trying to get my attention, first dropping the stick at my feet, then picking it up again in his mouth, wanting me to throw it.

'Just a minute, boy,' I said softly, dropping my hand to his head.

As I cut across the grass toward the house, I saw my mother come out onto the gallery. The two talked for a moment; then both turned to look at me.

I thought, *Now what've I done?* School wasn't set to resume for another week yet, so how could I be in trouble already?

With a lagging step, I trudged up the drive. To my surprise, Horst Fischer walked out to meet me. He held a slim blue book in his hands, and my gaze narrowed at the sight of it. It was my *Candide*.

'Miss St Pierre,' he said in his rough, gravelly voice. He always called the children in his class 'Miss' or 'Mister'. I think he had the idea it encouraged us to be better behaved. Or maybe he just thought calling us by our first names was too friendly.

Conscious of my mother watching from the porch, I dropped a small curtsy. 'Herr Fischer.' I was the only one who called him that – 'Herr' instead of 'Mr' – but I was no more certain of my own motives than I was of his.

'I have brought your book,' he said, and held it out.

I took the volume, more puzzled than grateful, although I'd wanted it back for nearly a year now. I should have said, 'Thank you'. Instead, I just shook my head in confusion and said, 'Why?'

He cleared his throat, uncomfortable. 'I am enlisting.'

I stared at him. '*You*? But . . . Whatever for?'

He tugged at the hem of his shabby waistcoat. 'It yoost seems the right thing to do.'

'But . . . You're Austrian! This isn't your fight. You've always said so.'

'*Ja*. But I have chosen to make my home here. After vhat happened to Bayou Sara, I cannot in all conscience sit at home like a – vhat do you call them? A fireside brave.'

It sorely pricked my conscience to remember that we'd once hoped this poor man would go off to war, simply so that we could get out of school. I said, 'No one with any sense will think less of you for not fighting. And those who do aren't worth worrying about.'

'This is not about vhat others think of me. Vhat matters is vhat I think of myself.'

I stared at his plain, ruddy face, so earnest and serious. I tried to imagine him as a soldier in a homespun butternut uniform, marching all day, sleeping on the cold, wet ground, and eating nothing but hardtack.

He wouldn't last a month.

But I also knew that he was beyond dissuading. I held the book out to him. 'Here. Keep it.'

I saw his eyes light up; then he shook his head. 'Thank you, but no; I cannot.'

'Please? I would like you to have it.'

In the end, he took the book. I'd heard of men going off to war with Bibles in their knapsacks. I didn't see any reason Horst Fischer couldn't take *Candide*.

After he left, I sat on the bottom step, my elbows propped on my knees, my chin resting in my cupped palms. Checkers finally gave up cavorting and trying to coax me into throwing the stick again, and plopped down panting in the dirt nearby. After a few minutes, my mother came to sit beside me.

I said, 'Horst Fischer is enlisting.'

'I know. He told me.'

I slid my hands down to wrap around my bare ankles. 'I don't understand it.'

'I think it has something to do with what society expects of men. They need to be seen as strong, and protective of women and children and the old.'

'But he said it isn't because of how other people might see him.'

'I doubt it is. I think it all comes down to how he views himself – his own sense of worthiness and self-respect.'

'But he's always been so contemptuous of anyone who ever said he should fight – for over a year now!'

'Yes. But this week the war suddenly became personal, didn't it?'

I stared out at the yard. The shadows were deepening beneath the moss-draped oaks, the sky streaked with purple and gold-tinged pink clouds against a robin's egg blue. I could see the darting flashes of fireflies, hear the droning croak of the frogs down by the creek. I said, 'I don't understand why they're doing this. The Federals, I mean. Burning our towns. Stealing our stuff. They say they want us back in the Union, only, they're acting like they hate us. And they're making sure we hate them.'

I heard my mother draw a deep breath, as if choosing her words carefully. 'I think in the beginning, they expected the war to be short – most people did, after all. They thought they'd win a few battles and march south, and people would greet them with rose petals and three cheers for the red, white, and blue. Only, that didn't happen. We're into our second year of war now. They're dying by the tens of thousands. And rather than greeting them as liberators, the people of the South see them as an invading army—'

'But that's what they are!'

'Yes. But I don't think they saw themselves that way, at first. I think they saw themselves as liberators. Heroes. Only, we treated them like cockroaches. So now they're angry.'

'I don't understand why they just won't go away and leave us alone.'

'Because they're stubborn, and proud, and they feel like their honor is on the line. And because they have a vision of the Unites States as growing ever bigger and stronger, and adding more and more territory, so they're not about to let a great, fertile, wealthy chunk of it slip away. They see this country as something ordained by God as a shining city on a hill – a noble beacon for the rest of the world to follow. But by seceding, the South has threatened to destroy what they believe is their sacred destiny. So it's no longer just about the flag. Now it's about God, too.'

Her words echoed something I'd heard Bernard Henshaw say last spring, the day the Federal fleet first sailed up the river. I wondered if he and Mrs Henshaw had still been in Bayou Sara when the men from the *Essex* rampaged through it. His untidy little book and stationery shop was now just a smoldering ruin. Although I doubted he'd been doing much business before the Federals came, anyway.

For some reason, I found myself blinking back tears. The sky was now dark except for a tiny red glow on the horizon. The air smelled of damp grass and jasmine, and the trees throbbed cheerfully with birds settling down for the night. Yet, for one moment I imagined I could taste the bitter remnants of smoke and charred wood in the air.

I said, 'Castile thinks they'll be back.'

There was a time I would have hoped my mother would contradict me; perhaps a part of me still did. But all she said was: 'We're going to make it through this, Amrie. If we keep our wits about us and stay strong, we can make it.'

Or die trying. She didn't say it, of course. But the echo of it was there, in the wind, nonetheless.

Twenty-Four

We all held our breath, waiting for the *Essex* to return.

But we just kept waiting.

September came, and the days began to grow shorter. In the woods, the sumac turned a brilliant scarlet, and the yellow leaves of the willow trembled in a blessedly cool breeze. With Horst Fischer now off to war, there was no school. At first I gloried in the freedom from the tedium and grinding boredom of daily lessons that moved at a snail's pace. But as September stretched into October, I came to realize that this wretched war was robbing me of something more ephemeral yet infinitely more valuable than the material goods the Federals helped themselves to so freely. And so I came to a decision: I might be scruffy and barefoot, but I refused to be ignorant, too. If I didn't have a schoolteacher, I was just going to have to educate myself.

And so, one rainy afternoon, I threw open the doors of the glass-fronted bookcases that flanked the fireplace in the parlor, and took stock. Some of the works, such as those by Virgil and Shakespeare, were old friends. But there were many that had always vaguely intimidated me, and these were the ones I forced myself to focus on – things like Herodotus and Plato, Cicero and Gibbons and Montesquieu. I drew up an ambitious list of books I intended to study and the order in which I would tackle them.

The problem was finding the time to actually read. Daylight hours were all too often swallowed by work, while our tallow candles were too precious to burn much at night. I tried reading by firelight, but it made my eyes sting, and the top of my head would get so hot, it hurt. But I kept at it.

And then, one afternoon when Finn and I were thrashing the branches of the pecan trees while Mahalia and Mama scooped the falling nuts into baskets, Trudi Easton came to see us.

She was a bony, thin woman with bulging eyes, a weakly receding chin, and big front teeth that all combined to make her look a bit like an angry rabbit. Her husband, a lawyer named Matt Easton, was a captain with a unit stationed over in Florida. She kept a coiled lock of his hair inside a heart-shaped crystal locket framed in gold that she wore always, and she had a habit of clutching it when she spoke, as if she drew confidence and reassurance from the tangible reminder of her absent spouse. She had five children, a couple of whom were around my age. Mama said to me once that she wondered how Miss Trudi was making ends meet, now that Mr Easton was off soldiering rather than lawyering. We'd heard she had to sell her horse and buggy, and when she came to visit us, she was walking. I saw her stop at the end of the drive, wipe off her feet with a rag she carried, and put on her shoes before continuing up to the house.

Mama set aside her pecan basket and went to invite her into the parlor. I tagged along out of vulgar curiosity. Trudi Easton had never been anything but polite to Mama – painfully, ruthlessly polite. I could not imagine what had brought her here.

'Why, thank you kindly,' she said when Mama handed her a cup of okra 'coffee'. 'Right cool today, isn't it?'

'Nice weather for working,' said Mama. 'And walking.'

A faint hint of color touched Trudi's cheeks. 'Yes, it is, isn't it?' She cleared her throat. 'I'm wondering if you might be interested in signing a petition some of us mothers have drawn up to send to Governor Moore.' She withdrew several folded pages from her tattered needlepoint reticule. I noticed they were actually pieces of cut up wallpaper; proper paper was getting increasingly hard to find.

She said, 'I'm sure that you, like so many of us, are concerned about the effect the continued lack of a schoolteacher is bound to have on our children's education. So we've written a petition asking the governor to assign one of the more learned members of our military to serve as St Francisville's schoolmaster. After all, the future of our young country is at stake. What sort of nation will we be able to build once this cruel war is over, if our children are ignorant?'

I looked at my mother. She said, 'I'll sign it, of course. But . . . Why don't you do it, Trudi? Teach school, I mean. You know you could do it.'

I wanted to throw something at my mother. Horst Fischer had been bad enough; I could not imagine Trudi Easton as our schoolmistress.

'Me?' Trudi Easton stared at Mama as if she'd just suggested she take up can-can dancing in an Irish barroom. 'I hope you don't mean to suggest that I *need the money*?'

'No, of course not,' lied my mother. 'It's just that, while I commend your initiative, I fear this petition may not work. The war has closed schoolrooms all over the South; I don't see how any governor could agree to spare enough soldiers to man all of them – however much he might wish to do so. So while we hope he will agree to your proposal, why not consider alternatives if he does not? I know you attended a prestigious academy in Philadelphia—'

'Hampton Hall,' said Miss Trudi with no small amount of pride.

'You could even teach the older children Latin, and—'

'No.' Miss Trudi pulled her chin back into her neck in a way that thrust out her top teeth even more than usual.

My mother said, 'It's become quite common in the North, you know, for ladies to serve as schoolmistresses.'

'Not *ladies*, surely?'

'Oh, yes.'

'Really? Well, we all know what the North is like.'

My mother set aside her cup. I could tell she was choosing her words carefully. 'While I understand – and applaud – the sensibilities that in the past have prevented Southern wives and daughters from venturing into public employment, surely the exigencies of war must take precedence over such constraints? We are talking about our children's future.'

For one moment, Miss Trudi looked tempted. Then she said, 'No,' her fist coming up to tighten around her locket with such fierceness I wondered she didn't snap the chain. 'Even if I were willing to do it, Mr Easton would never agree to such a thing. For his wife to be seen working outside the home would be an unconscionable affront to his pride.'

'Understandable, perhaps,' said my mother smoothly, 'if you were doing it because you needed the money. But we all know that's not true.'

'No. Of course not.' Miss Trudi did not meet my mother's gaze. 'But . . . Mr Easton would still never allow it.'

'Perhaps you could write and ask him – in case the petition to the governor should fail.'

'I suppose I could, yes.' She sat up a little straighter, a half smile flirting with her crimped lips. 'As you say, the future of our nation and our children is at stake. Why shouldn't we women fight for the South here at home in our own way? We've rolled bandages and scraped lint and sewed uniforms; why not pick up the tasks our men are unable to do now that they are off to war?'

'Why not, indeed?'

It suddenly occurred to me that here might lie part of the explanation for our community's continuing hostility to my mother, despite all that she'd done for them. It was one thing for a woman to tend to the ills of her own family – both her 'white family' and her 'black family', as plantation owners called the slaves who lived in their quarters. But my mother had gone beyond that. She *worked* as a doctor the same way Papa had, and people paid her. Not usually in money, which had become scarce since the war, but in things like chickens and hams. Just the other day, Cyrus Pringle had reshod Magnolia after Mama lanced a boil on his wife's leg.

Miss Trudi tucked her signed petition back into her reticule and rose to her feet. 'I thank you for the coffee. Roasted okra seed, was it?'

'Yes.'

'Hmm. You have a lovely way with it. I've been using parched corn, but I'll have to try this. Of all the items that have become so scarce, I can't decide which I miss most: coffee, wheat flour, or salt.'

'Oh, definitely the salt,' said Mama, walking with her to the door. 'There is no substitute for it. I don't know how we're to cure our bacon and hams for the coming winter.'

'True. I suppose since I don't raise hogs, I don't notice it as much. Rowena Walford was telling me that they're digging up the dirt floor of their smoke house and separating out all the salt that's dripped on it over the years. It's quite a laborious process . . .'

I slipped quietly out the back door. In my experience, women could talk forever about shortages and substitutes. I figured Mama and Trudi Eason were about as different as two women could be. But the war had taught them they had more in common than they might otherwise have realized. They both loved their children and feared for their future.

And they both really, really missed coffee.

That fall, the news of the war grew increasingly worrisome. Yes, Lee had managed to stop the Federals' latest attempt to take Richmond. But when he tried to take the fight into Federal-held territory, the result was a hideously bloody battle that left tens of thousands wounded or dead. Some folks were calling Sharpsburg; others called it Antietam. Officially it was said to be a draw, but it halted Lee's advance, and rumor had it the battle also put a stop to the British and French plans to recognize the Confederacy. So it sorta sounded like a defeat to me. These days, it seemed like all we heard was bad news.

Winter came early that year.

There were some years when the hand of winter laid gently upon the Felicianas, when the grass stayed green in the meadows and the last of the leaves fell from the trees only as the new shoots of spring began to show. But not that year.

By November, we had a fire every night and most days, too. We were lucky; we had acres of woodland, and Avery had been busy for months sawing logs and chopping kindling and stacking it in the woodhouse. But I worried about the poor folk in all the towns and cities across the South; what were they doing? How could a soldier's wife already struggling to feed her hungry children ever afford to buy enough fuel to keep them alive through a cold winter?

And then I awoke one morning to find a light dusting of snow covering the grass and surrounding fields, and ice crystals sparkling in the cold, clear air. It wasn't unheard of for St Francisville to have snow. But we never had it this early. I was still tugging on a pair of Simon's old boots when a snowball splatted against my window. I went to throw up the sash and leaned out to find Finn waiting down below.

'Come on, sleepy head!' he called up. 'Me and Castile is fixin' to go deer huntin'. You want to come, don't you?'

For a moment, my stomach heaved. But somehow I managed to plaster a sick smile on my face and holler, 'I'll be right down.'

We hadn't been hunting since the *Essex*'s last, disastrous visit, for Castile had been busy rebuilding his livery stable and putting up a new house. He and Leo had decided to move their establishment up the hill to St Francisville, and bought a stretch of land to the north of Ferdinand Street. But I guess he figured he needed a break.

The snow had brought an unnatural hush to our world and scrubbed the sky a crisp, clear blue. I wore the gloves Mama had knit for my birthday, but the hand gripping my bow soon grew numb, and Finn laughed at me and said my nose was red. I followed behind him and Castile, the powdery snow crunching and squeaking beneath the heavy soles of Simon's old boots.

I was hoping we wouldn't find anything, but it wasn't long before Castile spotted tracks that showed clearly in the fresh snow. We traced them down a ravine and up the other side to an open, snow-filled meadow so beautiful it took my breath. At the edge of a clearing stood a big buck, his head held high, his attention fatally focused on something deep in the wood.

Run, I thought, watching him. *Oh, please, please run.*

Finn quietly nocked an arrow and then threw me a hard, intense stare. We'd agreed that if we found a deer, Finn and I would both shoot at it. Hunting was becoming serious business; people were already going hungry, and a long, hard winter stretched ahead of us.

I told myself, *You have to do this*, and eased an arrow from the quiver I wore slung across my back. Yet at the same time, I was still quietly praying, *Please run!*

I saw Castile nod, and forced myself to hold steady and focus. Finn and I lifted our arrows, eased back our bowstrings, and released them simultaneously.

The two arrows flew across the clearing with a lethal hiss. Finn's went wide. But mine struck home. The magnificent animal crumpled with a groan.

I guess maybe Finn and Castile could tell how I was feeling, because neither one of them whooped or hollered in triumph the way they would have done if Finn had been the one to bring down the buck. I walked across the meadow to where the deer lay, his hot blood staining and melting the white snow beneath him.

He was beautiful, his eyes a soft, gentle brown, his body sleek and strong. I couldn't believe I had killed something so grand and noble.

Castile came to stand beside me, his voice quiet. 'What you do, Amrie, is say a prayer to the deer's spirit. You thank him for his noble sacrifice, you honor him for his grandeur and his courage, and you wish his soul a speedy journey into a better future.'

I nodded gratefully, unable to speak. My heart felt like someone was searing it with a fiery poker, and tears stung my eyes. But I didn't cry. Not then.

I saved my tears for my pillow, when I lay alone in the darkness of the night, with a lone wolf howling somewhere in the distance, and soft flakes of new snow whispering against my windowpane.

Twenty-Five

In the middle of December, my Grandmother Dunbar came to stay with us.

It had long been Adelaide Dunbar's practice every Christmas to descend on one of her surviving children for a visit that lasted until after the first of January. This year, it was our turn. I'd thought for a while she might not come, since we'd all grown leery of leaving our houses empty. When Federal raiding parties came upon an uninhabited house, they were more likely to strip it or burn it. So folks had taken to staying home as much as possible.

But early in December came the news that my Uncle Harley's new house near Donaldsonville had been torched by the Federals. Harley's wife, Mandy, and their young son, Wills, had taken refuge with Adelaide at Misty Oaks. Now, most folks might expect Adelaide to decide to spend that Christmas at home with her traumatized daughter-in-law and only surviving grandson. But no; this was supposed to be our year, and Adelaide wasn't about to let little things like a war and Yankee raiding parties interfere with her schedule.

She came to us on a cold, sunny morning, when the dead brown grass in the fields lay in stiffly frozen tufts, and the sky was a clear, crisp blue. She brought along her own servant, a plump, good-natured woman named Chesney. I could never figure out how Chesney had managed to live with my grandmother for more than sixty years

and still stay cheerful. Chesney had belonged to Adelaide literally
since the day she was born.

It was the practice amongst plantation families to 'gift' a slave
baby to a young child at birth. The two children would play together
while young. Then, slowly, the relationship would shift. The result
was a strange dynamic that involved varying degrees of genuine,
lifelong affection and carefully hidden resentment. I guess, like
anything else, it depended on the personalities of the two people
involved. If I'd been Chesney, I'd probably have been tempted to
smother Adelaide with a pillow.

But Adelaide was my grandmother, and my affection for her was
as real as it was wary and muted. I just didn't like having her around
too long. She always made me feel fidgety and awkward and wanting
in ways she never failed to innumerate.

'Anne-Marie, are those *boy's* boots on your feet?' she demanded
as I dutifully reached up to plant the required welcoming peck on
her cool cheek.

We were still standing in the central hall, and she'd yet to even
remove her bonnet and gloves. Usually she waited until Avery had
at least carried her trunks into the guest bedroom before she started
in on me. 'Yes, ma'am,' I said bleakly. I'd grown so much that my
dress was also shamefully short, but at least she didn't comment
on that.

'They were Simon's,' said Mama. 'We're lucky they fit her. You
know how impossible shoes are to get. And while she could go
barefoot in the summer, it's too cold now.'

At the mention of Simon, a faint shadow of grief darkened
Adelaide's features before being quickly tucked away out of sight.
Simon had been Adelaide's first grandchild, and she had loved him
with a fierceness that always surprised me. Perhaps he'd reminded
her, as he reminded me, of the scalded boy who'd died in agony in
her arms so many years ago.

'Really, Katherine?' she said, her lips tightening. 'Barefoot? If
you're not careful, someone might mistake her for the grubby little
sister of that rude Irish boy in whose company she spends so much
of her time.'

I opened my mouth to rush to Finn's defense, but my mother
knew me well enough to dig her fingers into my arm and stop me,
just in time.

Adelaide Dunbar was a sparse woman, lean and wiry and hard

in body and mind. She always seemed tall to me, but I don't think she really was. She had thick, iron-gray hair that was always meticulously coiffed, and small dark eyes that could bore right through you. By the time war came, she was well into her sixties, but she had a vigor and energy that in some ways reminded me of Hilda Meyers. She'd never been sick a day in her life, or so she claimed, and she certainly never had sympathy for anyone who was ill, regarding a tendency toward sickness as a symptom of both moral weakness and inferior breeding. Her father had been a colonel in the Revolution, and it was her one vanity. She mentioned it constantly.

In addition to Chesney, Adelaide also brought along her aged, white-haired coachman, Uncle Kashi. 'Uncle' like 'Aunt' was a term of affection applied to aged servants. But Kashi was different from any black man I'd ever known, for he bore a strange pattern of spirals and dots tattooed across his wrinkled forehead and cheeks that had scared me when I was little. He also spoke with a strange guttural accent that reminded one that English was not his first language, for he'd come to our shores long ago directly from Africa.

I'd always regarded him with awe. He was a link to that strange, dark continent about which I knew little, but which was always presented to us as a dangerous, frightening, benighted place, a place of witchcraft and superstition, of fearful pagan rituals and cookpots kept boiling in preparation for any stray, ill-fated European explorers who happened along.

Most of the slaves who moved through the background of my days had always been slaves, as had their parents and their parents before them. Their grammar and diction might at times be torturous, but English was nevertheless their native tongue, and they didn't sound all that different from the poorest of the white 'plain' folk we knew. They baptized their children and packed the galleries of our churches, they wore familiar calico dresses or sturdy trousers, and in every way seemed to fit naturally into our world.

But Kashi gave the lie to that comfortably reassuring assumption. He was a living, startling reminder of a distant, unknown land with alien ways, and of a harsh, brutal passage and violent dislocation that our preachers might reassure us was benevolent, but which when confronted directly tended to cause discomfort and fear amongst the apologists for the institution my parents had long ago rejected.

I asked Priebus, once, if Uncle Kashi remembered Africa. He gave me a funny look and said, 'I reckon he remembers his memories.'

Sometimes, I tried to look at our world through Kashi's eyes, tried to see us as he must see us. But I knew it was impossible to accurately do so.

I didn't have that good of an imagination.

Adelaide fit far better into St Francisville's social life than Mama ever had. In fact, in a sense, she revived it, for lately folks had taken to hunkering down in their homes as if afraid to live. They were just enduring, waiting for the war and all its shortages and terrors and heartaches to finally go away.

Two days after she arrived, Adelaide invited a bunch of the area's ladies over for a 'recipe party'. Recipe parties were becoming popular across the South. Women would get together and read their favorite recipes out loud. Most of the ingredients hadn't been available for the better part of a year, so the women would just sit around and imagine what the dish or dessert would taste like. I thought whoever came up with the idea must be sick in the head, but the concept spread like the chicken pox.

I tried to duck out of it, saying I'd planned to go hunting with Finn. I hadn't been hunting again since I'd shot the deer, but I figured anything was better than spending an afternoon with a bunch of ladies sighing over imaginary apple pies and biscuits. But Adelaide gave me a stern look and said, 'Anne-Marie, it is high time you learned to comport yourself as befits a lady of your station, rather than tramping through the woods with some Irish no-account.'

I felt my hackles rise. 'He's my friend.'

'I know. That's the problem.'

I'd heard Adelaide complaining to Mama just the day before about all the time I spent with Finn. 'It's not right, Katherine. It was bad enough when she was simply tagging along with Simon. But Simon's dead, and she's not exactly a child anymore.'

'Yes she is. And she misses Simon and her father enough without me trying to separate her from her best friend.'

'*Her best friend*? A scruffy little Irish boy? And that's not to mention the time the two of them spend with Castile.'

'Finn and Castile are both extraordinary people, each in his own way. I can't believe they're a bad influence on her.'

'Do you even hear what you're saying, Katherine?'

There was a tense silence.

Then, inevitably, Adelaide said, 'And to think that child's great-grandfather was a colonel in the army of Washington himself.'

And so that Friday I found myself sitting on a straight-backed chair in the parlor. Our house was so small that the ladies were spread out around both the parlor and the dining room, with the wide pocket doors between them thrown open. As usual, everyone was talking at once, a dozen different conversations hopelessly entwining in my head.

'—what you think of this new general they've sent to replace Butler? At least the Beast is gone! I hear he needed ten ships to haul away his loot—'

'—Federals moved back into Baton Rouge – or what's left of it. Just sailed right in and reoccupied it, with no one there to stop them. I ask you, what was the point in leaving? They can't seem to make up their minds what they're doing. Folks say they're going to try to take Vicksburg again. How many times—'

'—hoping maybe they were so busy plundering and pillaging their way up the Bayou Lafourche that they'd at least leave us alone for a time. But I had a letter from my sister just two days ago, and she says—'

'—I tell you we've received a response to our petition? The Governor was most gracious, but he says it's impossible to grant our request.'

I recognized Trudi Easton's voice and slewed around so that I could hear better. This was a conversation I had a vested interest in.

'Oh, Trudi; I'm so sorry,' said my mother, although I knew she'd understood from the beginning that Miss Trudi's scheme would never succeed. 'Did you ever write to Mr Easton about the possibility of teaching school yourself?'

If I leaned sideways, I could see Miss Trudi, dressed in pink homespun, one fist wrapped tight around her silly locket. 'I did, yes. I was most hopeful that he might find my arguments persuasive. Unfortunately, he insists that he simply cannot allow it.'

I squirmed in my chair. If any husband of mine ever tried to tell me what I was and wasn't 'allowed' to do, I reckoned I'd wallop him a good one. Then I became aware of Adelaide frowning at me, and quickly straightened up again.

'—overseer told me just this morning we've had another half dozen men walk away from the quarters,' said a voice I recognized as belonging to Rowena Walford. 'Off to the contraband camps, no doubt. The fools. I try not to worry about them, but I can't help it, even if I am as mad as all get out. I hear they're dying like flies there, from all sorts of dreadful diseases. And of course the Federals aren't giving them enough to eat. At least when the Yankees first came, they were returning runaways to their masters. But that's obviously a thing of the past.'

'Of course it is,' said Adelaide in that calm, assured way of hers. 'They've figured out there's no better way to bring us to our knees than to entice away our workforce. You've heard about this "Emancipation Proclamation" Lincoln is planning to issue in January?'

Rowena Walford gave a loud, ringing laugh. 'Pricelessly hypocritical, is it not? It only applies to those states in rebellion! And if we meekly return to their precious Union, we'll be allowed to keep our slaves.'

I was aware of Mama looking at me. I met her gaze, and she ever so slightly shook her head at me in warning.

'Naturally,' Miss Rowena was saying, 'all thirteen of the parishes around New Orleans are as exempt as New Hampshire and Kentucky.'

'Naturally,' echoed Jane Gastrell. 'You don't expect them to free the slaves working the cotton and sugar cane plantations taken over by all those Yankee speculators, now do you? You have to laugh at how they show their sympathy for the slaves by emancipating those they cannot reach, and yet keep enslaved those they could set free.'

'Well, I've heard that some Union regiments are threatening to mutiny, saying they're not fighting this war to free the slaves so they can go North and take their jobs back home.'

'Old Mr Mason says it's a military maneuver,' said Margaret Mason. 'And a clever diplomatic tactic. He doubts the French or the British will recognize us now.'

This pronouncement was met with a sudden, oppressive silence. Recognition was the one thing everyone had been hoping for; now it seemed more unlikely than ever.

'Enough of all this,' said Adelaide. 'Who would like to give us the first recipe?'

'Oh, I will, I will,' said Trudi Easton, squirming in her seat with one hand raised like an eager child in school.

My grandmother gave her a benevolent smile. 'Mrs Easton; please.' It amazed me how my grandmother had managed to learn the names of all the women present, despite having just met them.

Trudi Easton stood up and cleared her throat. 'This is the recipe for Mr Easton's favorite banana cream pie. You take ripe bananas and—'

I couldn't remember the last time I'd had a banana. With a stifled groan, I slid down in my seat and prepared to endure.

Later, when the last of the ladies had finally taken themselves off and Adelaide retired to her room to rest, I said to my mother, 'Do you think Lincoln would really withdraw this Emancipation Proclamation if all the Confederate states agreed to return to the Union by the first of January?'

'I think he'd try. But it would never work. Things have gone too far now. You heard Rowena; the slaves are emancipating themselves and have been for months. I think eventually Lincoln will be forced to extend his proclamation to all states, North and South – whether he wants to or not.'

'That's a good thing, isn't it? It's what you and Papa always wanted.'

To my surprise, my mother rolled her lower lip between her teeth and looked troubled. 'It is, yes. But . . . I try looking ahead, and I can't help but worry about what sort of future we're making. This war has caused so much grief and loss, and stirred up so much anger and resentment. How can we ever live together again? North and South, black and white?'

'The other day, I heard Reverend Lewis saying to Mr Marks that the United States government could have bought every slave in their country and ours, and given them a mule and a hundred acres of land out West, all for less than what the first year of this war has cost, and with no lives lost. So why didn't they do that – or at least try?'

'Because that's not what they really want. What they want is to keep the West for *whites*, and whites only. And because they're proud, and reckless, and unutterably stupid,' she said, her face so hard that for an instant she reminded me of Adelaide.

'You mean, Lincoln and the Federals?'

'I mean the leaders of both sides. They've led us all into hell.'

* * *

That night before going to bed, I let Checkers out for a run. It was cold but calm, a universe of brittle stars blinking at me from out of a midnight blue sky. The air smelled of wood smoke and frosted fields, and I went to sit at the top of the steps of the back gallery, my arms wrapped around my bent knees for warmth as I watched Checkers frisk happily about the yard, loping from one ghostly tree trunk to the next. Tipping back my head, I exhaled a long breath and watched it crystallize in a white cloud around me. But as I blew out another, I became aware of a soft murmur of voices.

Uncle Kashi said, 'That Massa Abe, he done promised freedom to any slave what walks into a Yankee camp.'

I could see them now, Priebus and Uncle Kashi, sitting on the porch of Priebus's cabin, the red coals of their clay pipes faint glows in the darkness.

Priebus gave a derisive snort. 'I hear all this talk 'bout Massa Abe, and it make me think of my pappy. He used to tell 'bout how black folks said the same things about Ole King George, back in the day – how he was gonna deliver them and make them all free. 'Cept he didn't. It was all just talk. In the end, he got on his boat and sailed away.'

Kashi stretched slowly to his feet, then bent down to knock out the coals from his pipe against the edge of the porch. He was small and withered, and must have been seventy-five years old, although his movements were still supple and strong. 'You got no cock in dis fight; you's already free, you. But I been prayin' for this day my whole life, and I ain't gonna live much longer. I'd like to die free.'

Checkers came back to me then, hind end wiggling, nose cold when he thrust his face up against mine. I rose and quietly opened the back door. But Uncle Kashi's words haunted me as I climbed the stairs to bed. I wasn't surprised when we awoke the next morning to find the old man gone.

At first, Adelaide refused to believe he'd run away; she was convinced something must have happened to him. She set us all to searching the barns and fields, thinking he'd gone for a walk and had his heart give out. She kept saying, 'He was happy and contented; why would he leave? I've never had him whipped – I treated him like a member of my family. How could he do this to me?'

But Kashi was definitely gone.

He could easily have stolen one of the mules or horses, but he didn't. He just walked off into the night, an old man with a tattooed face and memories of distant drums echoing in his heart.

Twenty-Six

Two days before Christmas, I was down cutting holly from the bushes along the drive when I heard a woman's voice, loud and tight with anxiety, carrying from my mother's doctor's office.

'But there must be something I can do!'

I froze, embarrassed to be hearing something I obviously wasn't meant to hear, but afraid to be noticed if I tried to move away.

My mother's answer was a soothing murmur. 'If only you had come to me right away, Eloisa. But it's too dangerous, now. Anything I gave you could kill you, too.'

'You think I care? Don't you understand? I can't have this! What do you think it would do to Reuben, if he knew that while he was off fighting for our independence, *this* happened to me? Or, what – what if he doesn't believe I wasn't willing? I mean, I never told anyone about it. Now it won't be long before everyone in town knows that I – that those seamen—'

'Eloisa—'

She gave a wild, hysterical laugh. 'What kind of merciful God would let this happen? I must do something!'

'You can't. Don't you understand? It's too late. And I don't say that because of the new laws, but because it's too dangerous at this stage.'

'No. Those men may have burned Reuben's butcher shop and looted our house, but I'm not going to allow them to take what's left of my pride and use me as an instrument to shame my husband and my country. I'd rather die first.'

'Eloisa—'

I heard the door yank open and barely managed to duck down behind the holly before Eloisa Peyton came hurtling down the path to the gate. Her face was contorted with a horrible mixture of rage and grief and pain; her hands curled into fists she held tight to her sides. To my relief, she didn't even glance in my direction, but took off toward town with long, determined strides.

I was aware of my mother coming to stand on the low, shallow porch. Then she turned her head, and her gaze met mine.

'You didn't hear that,' she said.

'No, ma'am.'

That Christmas was the coldest anyone could remember. A soft white layer of snow blanketed our world in a deceptively peaceful and heart-breakingly beautiful hush, and icicles formed on the edges of roofs. I'd never seen icicles before.

We decorated the hall, windows, and mantels with holly, pine boughs, and mistletoe. Avery hauled in a small pine tree from our woods, and we set it up on the round table in the parlor. Adelaide and I spent hours making strings of popcorn and red berries, and hung them on the tree along with pinecones and stray bits of ribbon from Mama's workbox. In the past, we'd always made cornucopias of colored paper and silver foil, and filled them with hard candies. But not this year. We had no paper, foil, or candies. Even dried fruit was too precious to hang.

There was no money to buy gifts, and nothing in the shops to purchase anyway. I unraveled an old pink shawl that had been mine when I was a little girl and that had been so precious to me that I'd refused to let my mother throw it away. It had languished, forgotten, on a shelf. Now I rolled the wool into balls and used it to knit scarves for Mama, Mahalia, and my grandmother. I was better at knitting than sewing seams, although I did tend to drop a stitch now and then, and I could never keep my tension even, so the rows were kinda wavy, going from tight to loose and back again, depending on whether I was feeling tense or relaxed when I worked on them.

For Castile, Priebus, and Avery, I made corncob pipes, although I wasn't sure they'd get much use out of them. Some folks in the area grew tobacco, but it was getting pretty scarce these days.

At least we still had chickens for eggs, and milk from Queen Bee, and Mama had been carefully hoarding the last of her rum. On Christmas Eve, she whipped up a batch of eggnog, and we sat around the fire in the parlor and exchanged our presents. Adelaide gave me a gold thimble nestled in the crown of a tiny, fairy-sized hat knit of fine blue thread and lined with cotton, with a flap closed tight by a pearl button.

'I know you loath sewing even more than you dislike going to school or church,' she said to me with a rare smile lighting her eyes. 'But it belonged to my mother, and I wanted you to have it.'

I slipped the thimble over my finger, more touched than I could begin to explain. It had a delicate pattern of ivy incised around the rim, and I could see where the edges had been worn thin by the labors of generations of McDougal-Dunbar women.

It was a sign of our times that my first thought was, *Where can I hide this so the Yankees won't find it if they come?*

Adelaide pretended to be pleased with the scarf I gave her, although it looked more pitifully uneven than I'd realized when she held it up. Mama gave me a pair of warm wool socks the exact shade of blue of *her* favorite shawl, and Mahalia had plaited me a new palmetto hat bleached white. 'For when it gets hot again – if it ever does,' she said, and we all laughed.

After a dinner of ham and sweet potatoes and squash, Finn came over. I gave him the arrows I'd made for him, and he grinned and gave me the arrows he had made for me. Then we all stood around the piano in the parlor while Adelaide played Christmas carols. We sang 'O Come, All Yee Faithful' and 'Jingle Bells'. Then she started on 'Silent Night', and I felt my throat close up and tears prick the back of my nose.

I glanced over at Mama. She had her fingers curled around the carved back of Papa's favorite reading chair, and I knew by the stricken look on her face that she was thinking the same thing I was: that somewhere far, far away, Papa was sitting beside a fire, missing us, just like we were missing him – and Uncle Tate, and Uncle Harley, and Uncle Bo. So many friends and loved ones, all alone this Christmas and far from home.

'. . . *all is calm, all is bright . . .*'

I tried to swallow, tried to keep singing, but I couldn't. A howling wind drove the snow against the windowpanes; the tallow candles dipped and wavered in a cold draft, and I felt a welling of such hopelessness and despair and fear that for a moment, it almost crushed me.

Then Adelaide looked up from her keys and sent me a fierce look that said more clearly than words ever could, *You are my grand-daughter, and McDougal-Dunbars do not crumble.*

And so, somehow, I found my voice and managed to warble along with everyone else, '*Sleep in heavenly peace. Sleep in heavenly peace.*'

Two days later, Reverend Lewis sent for Mama. One of the wharfmen had just pulled Eloisa Peyton from the ice-rimmed bayou.

Twenty-Seven

Chesney and I were taking down the swags of holly and pine boughs in the wide central hall – with Adelaide directing and criticizing – when Mama walked in the front door and shut it behind her with a snap.

'How's Miss Eloisa?' I asked, craning around to look at her.

She tugged so hard at the frayed ribbons of her bonnet that they broke. She stared at the tattered fragments almost stupidly a moment, then tore off the bonnet and threw it on a nearby chair. 'She's dead.'

She walked into her room.

My grandmother and I looked at each other.

'Well, go on,' she said, giving me a nudge.

I handed Chesney my armload of greenery and went to the bedroom's open door. My mother was sitting in the chair by the fire, staring at the dancing flames.

I said, 'Did she do it deliberately?'

'I think I managed to convince Reverend Lewis she did not.'

'So maybe she didn't.'

Mama looked up at me, her face drawn with anguish. 'Her pockets were loaded with brickbat.'

There didn't seem to be anything to say to that. I went to sit cross-legged on the hearthrug beside her, my gaze, like hers, on the fire.

After a moment, my mother said, 'I should have given her something.'

Giving a woman 'something' had been technically illegal in Louisiana for some six years now. But it was still done all the time, as long as it was before quickening.

I watched her bring up one splayed hand to rub her forehead. 'If only she'd come to me sooner,' she said. 'Or if I'd have realized what she intended. I should have known. I should have listened to what she was saying and realized she'd rather die than have her husband and the entire town know what happened to her.'

'How could you have known?' I asked.

Her hand dropped to her lap, revealing features pulled tight by the intensity of her emotions. 'It happens all the time, Amrie. When women are desperate and have no choice . . .'

We sat together in silence for a moment, listening to the crackle and hiss of the flames. I felt a heavy weight of sadness pressing down on me, along with a powerful sense of wrong, although I could not have articulated it at the time. All I knew was that none of it was my mother's fault.

And it occurred to me that this was why my mother had taken me to see Sarah Knox Davis's grave, because I was always thinking I should be able to control everything that happened around me, and blaming myself when I couldn't. It was disconcerting to realize it was a trait I'd inherited from my mother.

I said, 'If you had given her the herbs she wanted, and they'd killed her because she was too far along, how would you be feeling now?'

She looked over at me. 'Responsible,' she said.

Then she reached out to take my hand and squeeze it tight, and I saw a faint, ironic smile lighten her haunted eyes.

Grandmother Adelaide left just after the New Year, when a hard freeze turned the rutted, muddy roads to stone, and a thick fog lay heavy and oppressive upon the land. Goodbyes were sobering occasions these days, as all our uncertainties and fears about the future hung over us, unsaid. With Uncle Kashi gone, Avery volunteered to drive her. I can still see him sitting up on the carriage's high seat, the reins in his hands, a big grin spreading across his face as she shouted up at him, 'Now, don't you drive too fast, you hear?'

'Yes, ma'am.'

'And while I understand the roads are atrocious, you can at least try to avoid hitting every rut and bump between here and Misty Oaks.'

His grin widened. 'Yes, ma'am.'

'And I have my pistol with me, in case any Yankees try to mess with us.'

My mother said, 'The Yankees are all up at Vicksburg, Mama. They're saying Lincoln himself is now taken with the idea of moving the Mississippi away from the city's bluffs. He's set some new general named Grant to widening and deepening their old canal.'

'Fools,' said Adelaide.

'As long as it keeps them busy and away from us.'

Adelaide turned her cheek for us to kiss. Chesney helped her up the steps into the carriage and tucked a warm lap robe around her, with a couple of hot bricks for her feet. Then she climbed up herself.

Mama said, 'Give Mandy and Wills my love.'

Avery cracked his whip and the carriage jerked forward. We stood at the base of the gallery steps and watched them bowl away up the foggy drive. As he turned into the lane, Avery lifted his hat and waved it at us, a dark, misty figure in a blurry white landscape.

We never saw him again.

We didn't start worrying about Avery until some weeks later. We figured lots of things could have happened on the journey to Livingston Parish and back. Our roads had always been awful. But with the war, they'd become even worse. Broken wheels and snapped axels were all too common, and these days they weren't easy to get fixed. Even without any mishaps, they'd have needed to travel by easy stages, stopping often to rest the horses. And we all knew just how demanding and critical Adelaide could be.

But at the end of January came a chatty letter from my Uncle Harley's wife, Mandy. She talked about Adelaide and Chesney's return to Misty Oaks, and about how they'd insisted Avery rest up for a few days before they sent him off again on one of their mules.

'Oh, Gawd,' said Priebus when he heard. 'Yankees done got him.'

'Priebus, we don't know that,' said Mama calmly, although I'd noticed her hands weren't quite steady when she refolded the letter.

Priebus thrust out his jaw. 'They took twenty field hands off Belle View just last week – and a couple dozen from Pointe Coupee a few days before that. They be diggin' that danged cut-off again. Grant's Canal I hear they callin' it now.'

'Could've been paddyrollers,' said Mahalia.

Mama shook her head. 'He had his papers. He could easily prove he's free.'

'Maybe somebody stole his papers.'

'He could have sent word to us somehow.'

'If the paddyrollers nabbed him, yes. But not if the Yankees got him.'

We kept hoping. But as one day rolled into the next, and then the next, a sick certainty began to settle into our souls. Avery wasn't coming back.

Along with our worry and grief for Avery came an understanding of the many ways in which his loss was going to affect us. Priebus was getting old and increasingly unwell. It was Avery who would have plowed our fields that spring, Avery who had filled our wood-house for the winter, Avery who did a hundred and one different things around the place. In a sense, Avery had shielded us from the hardships faced by so many women whose men had gone off to war.

Now, all that was changed.

The winter dragged on without any sign of letting up. Old folks said they'd never seen such a hard winter in the Felicianas. Orange trees died. Gaunt-faced, sad-eyed women and children could be seen along the rutted, icy roads pushing baby carriages piled with pine cones and dead branches to take home and burn. Every Sunday, Reverend Lewis begged his parishioners to dig deep and give to the poor. The problem was, we were all poor, and real money had just about disappeared. Shop-owners needing to give change started handing out little promissory notes – 'Good for fifty cents at Meyers Emporium' – and folks used those amongst themselves as money. Barter had always been common amongst the plain folk; now, everybody did it.

One icy morning in mid-February, Finn and I loaded a couple bags of his mama's potatoes onto their mule, Dander, and headed into town to trade them. The day was clear but frigid, with a cutting wind out of the north that froze my ears and made my cheeks hurt. Finn had wrapped rags around his ankles for warmth, but the soles of his feet were bare. I said, 'Why didn't you wrap them rags all the way around your feet, too?'

He looked at me like I was an idiot. 'How long you think these rags'd last, if I was walkin' on 'em?'

I guessed he had a point. Only, I didn't know how he stood it. I had Simon's boots, and although they were starting to fall apart, they were still boots. Yet I was still so cold I felt like I was dying.

'What you lookin' to trade these potatoes for?' I asked as we walked along. The weak sun was only beginning to melt the frost off the fields, and in the cold air, every bird call, every rustle in the brown, dry grass seemed unnaturally loud.

'Just about anything we can get,' he said. 'I'd be hard pressed to think of somethin' we don't need.'

In the end, he managed to swap the potatoes with Cyrus Pringle for a repaired spade they could use for the spring planting, and an old child's coat Finn figured would fit one of his little sisters.

Finn was wriggling up onto Dander's back when Mr Pringle said, 'D'you hear one of them danged Yankee press gangs got Castile's son, Leo?'

I felt my stomach seize up in a vicious twist so intense I could only stare at him.

I guess Mr Pringle took our stunned silence as evidence of ignorance, because he said, 'Mmm. Yesterday. He was fishing off the levee when a longboat come ashore from the *Brooklyn*. Nabbed him and carried him off along with some of Serenity's field hands.'

Finn and I looked at each other. Without a word, he leaned down to haul me up onto Dander's broad back behind him, and we pounded around to Castile's new livery stable.

'Castile?' we called, slipping off Dander's back.

Silence.

We searched the paddocks and the stables, where horses and mules moved restlessly in the cold, steam rising from their backs. No Castile.

Finn's feet were turning blue. I said, 'Why don't you go on home, Finn? I can keep looking.'

'Nah.' He bent down to readjust his rags. 'I'll be all right. Hear that?'

'No.'

I followed Finn around the side of the stables and down the slope to where Leo and Castile were building a new shotgun-style house. I could see him now, his arms rising and falling as he chopped firewood with vicious concentration. I could feel the vapor of my own breath freezing on my eyelashes, hear Finn's teeth chattering. But Castile had stripped down to his flannel shirt, his bald head and tense, set face glistening with sweat, his massive shoulders flexing savagely each time he drew back his heavy axe and then let it fall.

He didn't miss a beat or even look up as we walked over to stand well back from the flying logs and chips. But after a moment, he said, 'I reckon you heard about my boy, Leo?'

I could only nod. What was I supposed to say? *I'm awful sorry, Castile?* What had seemed appropriate when the Federals burned his old livery stable didn't begin to fit this situation.

Finn said, 'Maybe they'll let him go once they realize he's free.'

Castile glanced over at him, then let his axe fly again. 'They didn't take him because they thought he was a slave. They took him because his skin is black. White folks is white folks, whether they live in the North or the South or on the moon. To them, if a man's skin is dark, it means they can use him as if he's a mule or an old hound dog. Like he ain't got no wants or feelings or dreams that they gotta respect. Like he ain't nothing. *Nothing*.'

He'd stopped chopping wood now, his chest heaving, his eyes wide and bloodshot. He said, 'My boy, Leo, he was always talkin' about how he was gonna go North, like it's the land of milk and honey. Me, I know better. I done been north. You know how they treated me? Like I was a freak – 'cept when they was treatin' me like I was dirt or some kinda halfwit. I met this fine, fancy lady and her husband. She was an abolitionist, and she was right proud of it. Talked to me like I was a little bitty chile, like because I got black skin I ain't got a brain in my head. And all the while she insultin' me, she's feeling so proud, because she congratulatin' herself on being better than anybody livin' south of the Mason-Dixon line. Reminded me of all them dumb white crackers in the piney woods here about, so ignorant and poor that all they owns is themselves. But they's happy, long as they can convince themselves they better'n anybody with black skin.'

Finn and I exchanged glances. I said, 'Reckon they'll let Leo go once they finish their canal.' It was meant as a reassurance, but I wished I hadn't said it, because we all knew Leo. He was so fiercely proud, and headstrong to the point of being foolhardy. If he tried to escape or even mouthed off too much, they'd shoot him. I didn't need to see the pinched look around Castile's nostrils to know he feared that even more than he feared the hardship and exposure of the labor itself.

Then his gaze fell to Finn's feet, and he slung his axe to bury the head deep into his chopping block. 'Y'all come inside,' he said and scooped up a load of kindling in his arms.

We followed him into an unfinished frame house still smelling of freshly hewn lumber and sparsely furnished with whatever Castile and Leo had been able to collect or build since the fire. The house was stone cold, colder even than it was outside, and I wondered when he'd last lit a fire in here. It was as if the walls had absorbed the brutal temperatures of the darkest hours of the night and now threw the cold back at us.

Castile thrust kindling and chunks of wood into the rusty old stove that stood on a platform of bricks in one corner, then set about starting a fire. We'd all run out of matches long ago, which is why most folks were careful to leave a fire banked, even on the hottest days. But Castile easily coaxed a spark from an old tinderbox, the flame licking and spreading rapidly as the wood caught and flared up.

Finn sat as close to the stove as he could and stuck out his hands and feet. Wordlessly, Castile sat down beside him and drew Finn's frozen feet under his own shirt to hold them against his bare stomach.

The soles of those feet must have been like the blocks of ice they used to float down the river from the north in the days before the war. But Castile didn't flinch. He just sat there, warming Finn's feet with the heat of his own body. After a time, he said, 'I gots me an old, worn-out saddle ain't doin' nobody no good. Reckon we could make a couple soles for shoes outa one of the flaps, and sew 'em to some sturdy canvas. Might last you till spring. You not careful, you gonna lose you some of these here toes, you.'

I stared at him, both humbled and oddly troubled by the way Castile had turned from his own anguish and worry over his son to concern for a boy who was no kin of his. It had never occurred to me to wonder why Castile had befriended Finn, Simon, and me; I had simply accepted his presence in our lives, the way children accept so many things without question or analysis. But as the old stove slowly banished the cold from the inside of that unfinished house, as my ears and cheeks stopped stinging and I watched Castile selflessly work to bring life back to Finn's frozen feet, I realized to what extent I had taken his friendship, his patient tutorials and gentle mentoring, all for granted. And the more I studied on it, the more I realized just how inexplicable it was.

Then Finn said, 'How'd you know the Federals got Leo?'

Castile rubbed his hands briskly over Finn's feet, which were now red rather than blue. 'He had Josephine and her little girl with him. That's why they caught him. He told Josephine and Calliope to run, and then just stood there to give 'em time to get away.'

I thought about the beautiful, long-necked woman I'd seen in the parlor of Bon Silence, and the little girl who'd played with Checkers on our sun-spangled lawn.

Castile said, 'Leo's sweet on Josephine. He been wantin' to buy her and Calliope for years. Only, Mizz Walford, she won't sell.'

'Why not?'

'I don't know. Ask me, she just being mean.'

I stared at him. This was a new idea to me. I'd always thought of Rowena Walford as smiling, exquisitely mannered, sugarcoated steel. But it had never before occurred to me to see her as mean.

He said, 'I still got the money we been saving. Maybe Mizz Walford'll sell 'em to me.'

But I knew by the way he said it that he wasn't holding out much hope. And it occurred to me that maybe it wasn't Leo she was punishing. Maybe it was Josephine.

What I didn't understand, yet, was why.

Twenty-Eight

Even the longest and fiercest of winters must eventually give way to spring.

The cold loosed its hold on the Felicianas that year in lurches and gasps, with warm days that lured over-eager farmers to plow and plant their fields, only to watch the seedlings die when the temperatures again plunged.

But gradually the threat of unexpected late freezes passed, and the bitterness of winter faded into a wretched memory. Yet spring had come to mean more to us than just balmy days and fields cloaked with breeze-rippled emerald green new growth. We'd learned by now to dread the arrival of good weather, for it was in spring that armies moved out of their winter quarters, generals plotted offensives and counteroffensives, and our husbands, sons, and fathers started dying again.

Near the end of March, we heard that the Federals had once again given up on their canal across De Soto Peninsula. After digging a trench sixty feet wide and more than seven feet deep, they let the water break through, only to have the canal collapse and backfill while the mighty Mississippi just rolled on the way it always had. We started hoping maybe Leo would be coming home. Then word trickled through that a bunch of laborers from Grant's Canal had been set to building a brutal, seventy-mile long corduroy road through the swamps and bayous to Hard Times, Louisiana.

Castile spent a lot of time chopping wood.

With Avery gone, Priebus had to take over the plowing. And when his back gave out, Mama finished it herself. We all worked together – Mahalia, Priebus, Mama, and I – putting in Irish potatoes and cabbages, eggplants and tomatoes, beets and spinach, and we planned to keep planting new rows every couple of weeks through the summer until it got too hot. Up the road, Rowena Walford experimented with growing rice and tried to convince everyone else to do the same. Mama took one look at the elaborate network of canals and dams required, and went on planting her corn.

And then one night in mid-March, I awoke unexpectedly to a dark room. I lay for a moment, confused. I knew I couldn't have been asleep more than an hour or two; so why had I awakened?

Then I heard the low, distant rumble of a coming storm.

Slipping from my bed, I crossed to the window. The moon was still well up, the sky sparkling clear and filled with stars. Feeling oddly tense and short of breath, I threw up the sash and leaned out into the cool night air.

A restless wind stirred the branches of the oaks and brought me the scent of damp earth and green growing things. But from far to the south came an unmistakable, *boom, boom, boom.*

It wasn't thunder.

My heart beating fast, I pulled on my night-robe and I felt my way down to the central hall to find the front door open. Mama was standing out on the gallery, her gaze fixed toward the south.

'What do you think it is?' I asked, my toes curling away from the cold boards underfoot as I went to stand beside her.

'Sounds like the Federals are attacking Port Hudson.'

By that spring of 1863, the South controlled only two strongholds on the Mississippi: Vicksburg, to the north of us, and Port Hudson, which lay just ten miles to our south. Together, they were enough to keep the Federal fleet from dominating the river. They also kept open the Red River, a crucial conduit for the cattle, horses, and supplies coming out of Texas and Mexico. So everybody with any sense had figured out that both towns would be targeted this year.

We lay right between them.

I wrapped my arms across my chest against the cold night air, my gaze, like my mother's, on the south. We stood side by side, watching the flashes on the horizon and listening to the endless *whomp, whomp, whomp* of artillery. Then the flashes turned to a warm glow that lit up the dark sky.

I said, 'Looks like a fire. You think they could've captured Port Hudson that quickly?'

She shook her head. 'You can still hear the cannons firing.' She surprised me by slipping her arm around my shoulders and drawing me close. 'We should go back to bed. There's no point in standing out here. Come on, honey.'

I knew she was right. But it's one thing to go to bed, and something else again to sleep.

I laid awake most of the night, listening to the artillery barrage roar on and on and on, until I wanted to scream. Them, as a hint of dawn lightened the sky and the cold morning air filled with a chorus of birdsong, the firing ceased.

I was just slipping into a deep sleep when a roaring explosion shook the house and sent startled flocks of doves and sparrows shrieking from the treetops.

It wasn't until later we learned what had happened, how General Banks had marched from Baton Rouge with twelve thousand troops, while Admiral Farragut gathered his fleet for what was supposed to be a mighty joint assault on the fortifications of Port Hudson. Except that Banks's army spent so much time plundering the farms and villages between Baton Rouge and Port Hudson that Farragut grew impatient and launched his attack without them.

He paid heavily for his arrogance and overconfidence. The great fires we'd seen that night had been kindled by an outpost on the western bank of the Mississippi. With the dark outlines of Farragut's ships silhouetted against the flames, the batteries at Port Hudson were able to savage the Federal fleet. Only two ships, the *Albatross* and the *Hartford,* had managed to slip through. The rest had been severely damaged, while the spectacular explosion we'd heard at dawn was the USS *Mississippi* blowing up.

Without Farragut's fleet to back him up, General Banks called off the land assault on the fortress.

We all cheered when we heard, relieved to know that for now, at least, Port Hudson was safe. We didn't stop to think that an army of thousands lay just a few miles to the south of us, angry, frustrated, and eager to wreck havoc before returning to their camps.

Early that afternoon, Mahalia and I were weeding the vegetable garden while Mama was off tending Margaret Mason's aged father-in-law, who was dying. A thick bank of clouds hung on the horizon, turning from purple to green as they bunched and rolled. But the rest of the sky was a clear, balmy blue of a color that reminded me of a little girl's satin sash. I straightened for a moment to stretch my back, a soft breeze feathering the loose hair around my face and carrying with it the scents of plowed earth and the sweet perfume of the jasmine blooming in a sunlit white cascade over the garden fence.

It was the kind of day when the earth seems bursting with joy and the energy of renewal, when the pulse of life throbs at peace with the serenity of a natural beauty so rich and pure that it aches. I was just reaching for another tuft of sedge grass when I heard Finn holler, *'Amrie!'*

I straightened again with a jerk.

I could see him now, pelting down the lane toward us, one elbow cocked skyward as he held his straw hat clamped to his head. 'Amrie! Federals comin'! A whole passel of 'em! They're rounding up everybody's livestock. You gotta hide your animals, quick!'

'Oh, Gawd,' said Mahalia, dropping her hoe in the dirt.

We took off running for the pasture. Finn got there first. He scooped up our goat, Flower, and threw her over the withers of one of the mules. Mahalia ran to open the gate as he scrambled up behind the bleating goat bareback and sent the mule cantering into the canebrakes. Checkers raced, barking, beside him, while I grabbed Queen Bee's halter.

But the big black and white cow wasn't having any of it. She'd already been milked that morning and wasn't due to be milked again until evening, and she knew it. Digging in her heels, she threw her weight onto her hindquarters and let out a loud bawl.

'Queen Bee, *please*,' I said, tugging harder.

Mahalia came to flatten her hands on the cow's hindquarters and push.

Queen Bee wouldn't budge.

I could hear the heavy tramp of marching feet drawing closer; see the dust lifting from the lane to hang like a golden curtain in the sunlight.

My gaze met Mahalia's, and I saw my own carefully checked hysteria mirrored in her tight face. I thought of all the things we'd talked about hiding if the Federals came: the personal letters and journals the soldiers stole to use for toilet paper; the seeds we were saving for our later sowings; the small bag of salt Sophie Gantry had given Mama for saving her little girl when she was so sick. Nothing was more vital to our survival than the mules that pulled our plow, the sheep that gave us wool and meat, the cow and goat that gave us milk. But how do you keep animals hidden from an army that can descend without warning at any moment?

Mahalia picked up a rotten branch that had fallen from a nearby oak and whacked Queen Bee across the rump. With a loud bellow, the cow jerked the halter from my grasp and bolted across the pasture.

'Oh, Gawd,' said Mahalia. 'Now I done gone and done it.'

Men in blue uniforms were already spilling across the pasture, laughing and shouting like schoolboys on a lark as they set about rounding up our mules and sheep.

A beefy corporal with sunburnt, freckled skin and red hair walked over to snag Queen Bee's halter. When she bawled and hung back, he pulled a pistol out of his belt and pressed the muzzle to her forehead.

'*No!*' I screamed.

The booming report echoed across the pasture. Queen Bee's legs crumpled slowly and awkwardly beneath her.

'Amrie!' Mahalia tried to grab my arm, but I jerked away from her.

The redheaded corporal was already turning away when I sank to my knees beside Queen Bee. I could feel the warmth of her familiar body radiating up to me, her soft black and white hide glossy in the sunlight. But I knew even before I rested my hand against her neck that she was dead.

With a sob, I looked up.

Some of the men were chasing our chickens around the yard, laughing dementedly, wringing the necks of those they caught and tossing their bodies into the air. I watched in helpless, useless rage as they hitched four of our mules to our heavy farm wagon and set to work filling it with the hams and sides of bacon from our smokehouse, the butter and cheese and crocks of milk from the cool brick dairy beneath our cistern. Others were stripping the boards from the fence that protected our vegetable garden.

I thought at first they were simply taking the fence boards for firewood. Then I saw them drive our sheep into the field, arms waving as they shouted, '*Hah! Hah,*' the panicked sheep's small sharp hooves sending up clumps of earth and newly sprouted vegetables high into the air.

Shaking now, I pushed to my feet and walked with pounding heart to where a lanky, brown-haired soldier with bad skin was slipping a halter onto my mother's aged bay gelding.

I said, 'Hennessey – this horse – is old. He won't be of any use to you. Why can't you leave him for us?'

He looked over at me, his pimply face splitting into a jeering grin as he tongued a bulging wad of chewing tobacco from one side of his mouth to the other. 'Aw. Looky here. The little Secesh baby is cryin' 'cause we takin' her hoss. Maybe you shoulda thought 'bout that before you started hurrahing for ole Jeff Davis, God rot his soul in hell.'

Somehow I managed to swallow the retort that sprang naturally to my lips. But inside, I was thinking, *I hope you die. I hope you die gutshot and screaming in pain and begging for mercy, and abandoned by the God whose strictures you flout even as you claim to honor him.*

Then I heard a shout, 'Form up, men!'

I'd thought this a group of stragglers rampaging without direction. But in that, I realized I had given them too much credit. An unshaven, weather-browned sergeant was working to assemble his giddy, jubilant party of vandals and thieves in order again, all beneath the amused gaze of a tall lieutenant with flowing, greasy black curls who sat astride a big, rangy chestnut.

'Sergeant,' he said, stretching up in his stirrups before settling more comfortably and gathering his reins. 'Move the men out.'

I was aware of Mahalia coming to stand beside me, a dead white chicken in her arms. Together, we watched the Federal troops march down the drive to the lane, the rattle of our wagon's wheels and the plaintiff *baa-baa* of our sheep mingling with the raucous laughter of the men to drift back to us on the warm, gentle breeze.

'I guess we should be grateful they didn't burn the house,' I said, although I didn't feel grateful. I was trembling with rage and a corrosive sense of powerlessness, all combined with a child's outrage at the unfairness and the naked *bullying* of it all.

Mahalia said, 'At least they didn't get Magnolia.'

A new fear reared within me. 'As long as Mama and Priebus don't run into them.'

She shifted her grip on the dead chicken in her arms. 'Looks like we got us a heap of work to do.'

I stared out over the ruined vegetable garden and swallowed hard.

She said, 'I jist don't get why they done this. I mean, I can see takin' the stock. But why kill the chickens and jist leave 'em? Why drive the sheep through our garden? Why?'

'Because they're evil.'

Mahalia was quiet for a moment, her gaze troubled and focused inward. Then she said softly, 'No, child; they just men.'

But I would have none of it.

I had seen what the Federals had done to Bayou Sara, heard the tales of their devastation of Baton Rouge and Donaldsonville and Grand Gulf, and of hundreds of such towns across the South. But there was something about watching the joy with which those men had sat about willfully destroying our lives – something about the naked hatred I had seen in their sweat-sheened faces – that shocked and troubled me more than I could have explained. But beyond that, it had awakened something in me that hadn't been there before.

I, too, had learned to hate.

Twenty-Nine

Mama and Priebus came home just as the sun was slipping below the line of oaks and willows along the creek. The yard was cool and blue with shadow, and a soft, sweet-smelling breeze blew out of the east. By then, Mahalia had finished gutting the slaughtered chickens and was helping Finn and me replant as many of the uprooted seedlings in the vegetable garden as we could salvage. Priebus immediately set to work butchering Queen Bee.

But I noticed he had tears streaming down his cheeks as he did it.

Thankfully, Finn had collared Checkers and kept him from rushing the Federal troops, for which I was inexpressibly grateful. The Federals were always shooting folks' dogs. In addition to our goat, Flower, he'd also managed to save three mules. Mama insisted he take one, for the Federals had stolen Dander. A half-dozen or so of our hens had survived by scattering beneath the kitchen and other outbuildings. Our pigs had been rooting in the woods and were still there, along with three sheep that had somehow managed to evade the soldiers. But our corncribs, smoke house, and dairy had been stripped bare. And without Queen Bee, we would now have only the milk from Flower.

Some of the soldiers had also rampaged through the house, leaving their muddy boot prints across the floorboards and simple mats. But they'd taken relatively little – a silver-backed hairbrush and mirror from Mama's dresser; Papa's collection of carved, wooden pipes; a small bronze horse that had stood on a chest in the hall. The truth was, we'd been lucky. It could have been so much worse, and we knew it.

And yet, I was aware of having lost more than our livestock and food stores, more even than my mother's beloved old gelding and the placid, black and white cow that had been a part of my life for as long as I could remember. I couldn't have explained it, then. But I knew those soldiers had taken from me something substantial and vital, for I had wished pain, death, and everlasting damnation on a fellow being. And though I knew I should ask God's forgiveness for my unbridled rage and the wickedness of my thoughts, I could not. The problem was, I wished it still – not only on the pimply soldier stealing Hennessey, but on the freckle-faced corporal who so coldly and senselessly sent a bullet smashing into Queen Bee's brain, and his curly-headed lieutenant, and every one of the laughing, jeering soldiers who'd rampaged through my world.

That night, my mother climbed the stairs to my room. I'd changed into my nightgown – now wretchedly thin and so short it barely covered my knees – and was standing at the open dormer window, my gaze on the moonlit treetops dancing softly against a misty, midnight blue sky. She set her tin candlestick on my bedside table and said, 'I'm sorry you had to face what happened today alone, with only Mahalia and Finn.'

I shrugged. After all, if she'd been home, we'd have lost Magnolia and the buggy, too.

She said, 'You can't let things like what happened today harden your heart, Amrie. If you do, they win.'

I twisted around to look at her over my shoulder. The dim, smudgy glow from the tallow candle was kind to her, making her look soft and pretty – more like the mother I remembered. In the past year, she'd aged so much. She wasn't just thinner; she was also more drawn, shadowed always by worry and a bone weariness that had etched lines deep into her face.

I said, 'Our men would never do what those Federals did today.'

'I'd like to think so. But . . . There are always some.'

'Seems to me, the Federals have more'n their fair share.'

'Perhaps. The thing is, Amrie . . . War brings out the worst in people. But it can also bring out the best. I know it's hard, but that's what we need to stay focused on.'

I'd seen a heap of bad brought out in people by the war, but not so much of what anyone could call 'good'. I couldn't say what I knew my mother wanted to hear, so I just kept still. But I did shake my head, and then I wished I hadn't when I saw her lips part and her chest rise on a painfully indrawn breath.

I knew she worried a lot about the 'effect' the war was having on me, for I'd heard her talking about it when she thought I wasn't around – not just with my Grandmother Adelaide, but with Mahalia and even Castile. 'It can't be good,' she was always saying, 'to come of age surrounded by so much bitterness and brutality and fear. What sort of future are we raising? Where will it all end?'

'Amrie . . .' She reached out her hand to take mine and squeeze it, tight. 'I wish . . . Oh, *God,* how I wish this would all be over.'

'Folks are saying there's a peace movement up North. That Ohio and Illinois and California are talkin' about seceding, too. That Lincoln is gonna start up a draft, and lots of folks are real mad about it. Maybe he'll be forced to make peace.'

'Maybe,' she said.

But I knew she didn't believe it. And the truth was, I didn't believe it myself.

We lost Priebus a few days later. Mama said his heart gave out and he just slipped away peacefully in his sleep. I figured that sounded like a good way to go. I was becoming only too familiar with how horrible death could be.

It seemed as if every day brought us new nightmarish tales of senseless cruelties and unimaginable horrors. Of puppies torn from the arms of screaming children, their heads bashed in with rifle butts. Of a four-year-old girl dragged from her home and savaged by a band of marauding soldiers. Of villages like Ponchatoula, ravaged by a two-day orgy of pillage and plunder that sounded like something out of the darkest Middle Ages. We lived in a vortex of mounting terror, of atrocity followed by atrocity, until a kind of numbness set in. I suppose the only way to cope with a world gone mad is to pretend that madness is normal. The problem is, when that happens, your world tilts, distorts. And I'm not sure you can ever make it right again.

Rather than spillikins and hopscotch, children now played 'military hospital'. They wrapped 'bandages' around their eyes and strapped up one bent leg so that they could hobble around on a crutch like a crippled soldier. They held mock court-martials and executed dolls by firing squad, then buried the 'dead' with military honors. They played 'run the blockade', and built stick towns, only to demolish them with a fierce artillery fire of pinecones and dirt clods that left nothing but a pile of rubble.

But these days, only the youngest children had time to play. Even if Horst Fischer had never gone off to enlist, I doubt many would have been able to attend school. My days were filled with weeding the fields and helping Mahalia wash, or splitting kindling and hauling water now that Priebus was gone. Sometimes I still managed to steal an hour or two to curl up on my window seat with the likes of Apollonius or Rousseau. But those occasions were becoming more and more rare.

And then, in May, came the news that the Federals under General Grant were encircling and laying siege to Vicksburg. Shelled night and day, the women and children of the town took refuge in caves they dug out of the earth of the hillside. When food grew scarce, they started eating mules and dandelions. And when even those disappeared, they turned to rats, pets, and, it was whispered, their own dead.

Those of us with loved ones trapped in the city could only wait. And pray.

Thirty

So much had happened in our lives lately that I rarely thought of the golden-haired infantry captain who had taken my necklace that long ago spring day on the sunlit levees of Bayou Sara. But in that May of 1863, he rode back into my world once more. And this time, the results would be more horrible than I could ever have imagined.

With all the menfolk off to war, there weren't many babies being born around St Francisville any more. Plenty of folks were dying, though. Mama said the war was killing them, that grief, worry, and fear can be as deadly in their own way as bullets and shells. It didn't make much sense to me, but there was no denying that most every day brought word of someone dying – not just soldiers, but the wives, children, sisters, and aged parents they'd left behind, too. Once, we'd looked forward to letters. Now, I noticed Mama would tense every time she opened one, for they always seemed to contain news of another cousin or dear friend lost. These days, everyone we knew was in mourning.

So when Amelia Ferguson gave birth to a baby boy that May, it put a rare smile on the face of most everybody in town. Her husband, Micajah, had been home the previous year on a long medical furlough after almost losing an arm at Shiloh, and she named the boy Theodore, because she said he was a gift from God. Just a few days after the child was born, we heard Micajah Ferguson had been shot and killed while on sentry duty up at Vicksburg. Folks shook their heads and sighed, and agreed it was a sad thing, although at least Miss Amelia had her dear sweet babe to comfort her.

Problem was, Micajah Ferguson's death devastated his young wife. Her milk dried up, and little Theodore, who'd once been so hale and rosy-cheeked, turned pale and sickly and failed to thrive. Mama said she thought Theodore's tummy might not like the cow's milk Amelia Ferguson was now feeding him. I figured Miss Amelia was lucky she still had her cow. But Mama suggested Miss Amelia try feeding her little boy with Flower's milk, and he started getting better.

It became my job to carry a crock of goat's milk to the Ferguson place every morning and evening. The Fergusons farmed a small spread some three miles up the road from our house, which meant I was doing a lot of walking. I asked my mother why we couldn't just let Amelia Ferguson keep Flower for a few months. But Mama said if we did, Miss Amelia'd need to do the milking herself, and she wasn't sure she was up to that.

I had to agree Flower wasn't easy to milk. But I figured Miss Amelia could get the hang of it soon enough if she tried. I'd yet to learn just how paralyzing grief can sometimes be.

But it didn't take me more than a few days to realize that something was seriously wrong with Miss Amelia. Not in her body, but in her mind and her heart. Often times I'd come and find her sitting in a dark room, her hands resting palm up in her lap, her gaze fixed on nothing in particular.

She wouldn't even get up out of her chair, just say, 'Set it over there, Amrie. Thank you kindly.'

The empty crock from my last visit would be unwashed. And as the days passed, I noticed the dust thickening on her tabletops, the weeds growing up beneath the azaleas and gardenias in her garden beds. Once, she'd been a plump, pretty little thing, with fine black hair and merry blue eyes. Now her hair hung in a matted mess down her back, and she grew thinner and thinner until I began to wonder if she was even eating. But what scared me even more were her eyes. It was like they were dead.

I worried for a time that maybe she was neglecting her baby the same way she was neglecting her house and herself. Then I realized the little boy was the only thing she was taking care of – almost obsessively so.

I didn't particularly mind the trek out there on fine mornings, when the sun shone golden and birds sang in the misty willows and moss-draped oaks. But I hated the driving rains that came this time of year. And as May wore on, the afternoons got increasingly hot. Miss Amelia never invited me to sit and rest, or offered me anything to drink before I headed home again, so I often found myself dragging before I made it back to our house.

Halfway between the Ferguson place and ours lay Belle Grove, a fine, white-pillared Greek revival plantation house that belonged to Winston and Gussie Holt. Mr Winston, like Papa, was off with the army in Virginia, leaving Miss Gussie alone with some one hundred and ninety slaves. I knew Miss Gussie was nervous about it, because one time when I was in St Francisville, I'd heard her talking about it with Rowena Walford.

'I just can't rest easy at night, knowing they're *out there*,' Miss Gussie said in a low voice as the two women walked slowly through the churchyard. 'The slaves, I mean. Every time I see a shadow on my bedroom wall or hear the creak of the house settling around me, I think it's *them*, coming to murder me in my bed. Just like those Frenchmen they killed down at German Coast.'

It had been more than fifty years since the German Coast slave uprising killed two white men down by New Orleans. But it still haunted folks, reminding them that the horrors of Nat Turner's far bloodier rampage or John Brown's more recent raid could also happen here. And in places like the Felicianas, where slaves outnumbered whites and free people of color by more than four to one, a lot of womenfolk were nervous about all the men going off to war.

Rowena Walford said calmly, 'I don't think you need to be afraid, Gussie.'

Gussie Holt glanced over at her, her fine-boned features pinched into an expression somewhere between admiration and disbelief.

Miss Gussie was a striking woman in her late twenties, tall and slender, with pretty hair the color of peaches and lovely pale skin faintly dusted with cinnamon across the high bridge of her nose. She said, 'You mean to say you're not? Afraid, I mean.'

'No, I'm not.' A slight frown knit Miss Rowena's normally smooth forehead. 'Well, to be sure, I do sometimes worry about roving bands of runaways from *other* plantations. But I don't have any concerns about our own black family, if that's what you mean. They're happy.'

I thought it a funny thing for her to say, given that I'd heard Bon Silence was losing field hands nearly every week.

But that argument obviously didn't occur to Gussie Holt. She gnawed one side of her lower lip between her teeth. 'But do you think they're *really* happy, Rowena?'

Miss Rowena gave a merry, tinkling laugh that showed her dimples. 'Of course they're happy, Gussie! Why wouldn't they be? They're well fed and clothed, with a snug roof over their heads. And Lord knows they don't work very hard. We call the doctor for them when they're sick, and when they get too old to work, we keep taking care of them until they die. I've no doubt there's many a poor Irish immigrant who'd be more than happy to trade places with them.'

'You think so, Rowena?'

Miss Rowena gave another laugh, although this one was more scornful than merry. 'For a full belly and a warm place to eat? I know so.'

Miss Gussie shook her head. 'Not me. I'd rather starve in a ditch than be a slave. I can't even imagine it. And if someone did enslave me, I think I'd want to slit their throat and gouge out their eyes.'

Miss Rowena screwed up her face in a grimace of mock horror.

'Well, that's your problem right there, Gussie. The thing of it is, you've got to understand that the Irish and the Africans are different from us. They don't have the same wants, needs, or feelings we do. They're happy just to go along to get along.'

Miss Gussie kept quiet. But I could tell by the troubled look on her face that she was still unconvinced. After a moment she said, her voice throbbing with barely suppression emotion, 'I wish that abominable, "peculiar institution" had never been brought to this land.'

Miss Rowena looked unperturbed. 'Slavery is as old as the Bible, Gussie. It was instituted by God for the good of His weaker creatures.'

By 'His weaker creatures', I guessed Miss Rowena meant the men and women who toiled in her cotton and sugar cane fields, and in her house. People like Josephine and Calliope. That made me think about Leo, and how Rowena Walford had refused to sell him Josephine, and I wondered how I could have been so wrong about someone I'd once thought nice and charming.

'And really, Anne-Marie,' said Miss Rowena without changing the level of her voice or even looking up, 'didn't your mama teach you not to eavesdrop on other people's conversations?'

I gave a guilty start and felt my cheeks flame hot. It went against everything I'd been taught about proper manners, not to answer her with a politely murmured, *Yes, ma'am*. But if I did, I'd be admitting that I was listening to them.

So I just ducked my head like a guilty coward and walked away.

I was aware of Miss Rowena's softly melodic laughter, following me. But when I threw a quick, surreptitious glance back at them, I saw Miss Gussie looking after me, an indescribable expression on her pale, lovely face.

It was one afternoon when I was walking home from Miss Amelia's house, my empty crock tucked awkwardly under one arm, that I spotted Miss Gussie standing in the small walled graveyard that lay not far from Belle Grove's gateway. She had her head bowed, her thoughts obviously far, far away. I'd heard that she'd birthed three babes. But they were all buried in that shady plot, and as I drew closer, I could see the small bouquets of fresh pink rosebuds and white lilies that rested against each simple limestone marker.

Then she looked up, her face softening into a smile when she saw me. I would have kept walking, but she waved and called out to me, so I stopped.

'Amrie,' she said, walking toward me, 'I've seen you passing a few times. Tell me, how is Amelia's little boy?'

I turned into the drive to meet her, awkwardly aware of the time I'd been caught eavesdropping on her conversation with Rowena Walford. 'He's perkin' up right fine,' I said. 'Reckon the goat's milk was what he needed all along.'

She nodded and looked pleased, although there was a wistful quality to her smile that made me think of the three small graves behind her. She said, 'You look hot, child. Come on up to the house and I'll get Aunt Selma to fetch you a nice cool glass of lemonade.'

I shifted the smelly empty crock to my other arm. 'Thank you kindly, ma'am. But I can't impose on you like that.'

'Nonsense. I won't take no for an answer. You must come up to the house every afternoon on your way home and get a drink. I insist on it.'

And so I did. Not just because I was almost always thirsty, but because it didn't take me long to figure out that Miss Gussie was as lonely as all get out. She lived all by herself in that great, big house, just her and a couple hundred people whose dark skin – and the seething hatred she imagined it hid – terrified her. She always came and sat with me on the gallery while I drank my lemonade, and we'd talk about the weather, and the riot of brilliantly colored roses blooming in her garden, and the latest news from the war.

But never once did she broach the subject I'd heard her discussing with Rowena Walford that day.

'Have you heard anything from your Papa since Chancellorville?' she asked one glorious, sunlit afternoon, when the watermelons were ripening in the fields, and wild flox and primroses splashed the meadows with muted shades of blue and yellow.

I shook my head, trying to ignore the painful twist in my stomach. By then, we'd all heard of the great battle that had raged for over a week in Virginia, between General Lee and a Federal army twice his size. It was a sorely needed victory for our side, and everyone was still jubilant about it. But we knew Papa's battalion had been involved and that the casualties had been high. Until we heard he was safe, it was hard to join in the celebrations.

She said, 'Rumor is, Stonewall Jackson has been wounded –

grievously so. If he dies, I fear this triumph may prove a hollow one.'

'He can't die,' I said sharply – more sharply than I'd intended. And I realized I was doing it again – imagining that I could somehow control the march of fate by the things I said or even thought.

The shadows were already deepening beneath the trees, the heat bleeding slowly from the day. I drained my glass and carefully set it on the wickerwork table beside my chair. 'Thank you kindly for the lemonade, Miss Gussie.'

She came with me to the top of the steps, then stood there watching me, still vaguely smiling, as I skipped down the drive to the lane. For some reason I could not have explained, I stopped at the long, sweeping curve flanked by a row of brilliant red rambling roses, and looked back to give her a wave.

Still smiling, she raised one hand in farewell. I try hard to remember her like that.

Rather than the way I found her the following morning.

Thirty-One

The next day dawned gray and cloudy, with wispy skeins of mist that drifted through the oak and willow trees lining the lane. I kept the heavy, full milk crock tucked up under one arm as I walked, my gaze on the lightning veining the dark, swollen storm bank that hung over the river. By the time I reached the Ferguson place, a fierce wind was whipping the branches of the trees overhead, and the first drops of rain had begun to fall, striking the giant leaves of the magnolias that flanked the front walk and pattering in the dust.

I found Miss Amelia in the front parlor, sitting in the same chair beside the empty hearth where I'd left her the afternoon before, her dark eyes hauntingly vacant as she stared at the thrashing shadows on the far wall. Lately I'd started wondering if she slept in that chair.

'Mornin', Miss Amelia,' I said gaily, going to change out the crocks. Little Theodore was in his basket by the front window. I stopped to coo at him, and he wiggled with what I fancied was delight. He always had on fresh clothes, so I guessed him mama must get up out of her chair at some point to take care of him. But there was a sour smell about the place that I figured couldn't be good for either of them.

I said, 'How 'bout I help you 'round the place a bit this mornin', Miss Amelia? It's fixin' to rain something fierce out there, so I may as well do something while I'm waitin' for it to blow over.'

She didn't say anything. But she didn't tell me not to, either. So I swept the dried leaves out of the central hall and threw open all the doors to the drumming rain, letting the warm, fresh wind blow through the house. I picked up things as best I could, and found a rag to dust. Then I dashed out to the kitchen and found some food I brought to her on a plate I washed. The kitchen made me gag, for Miss Amelia's Jenny had run off late in February, and it didn't look to me as if Miss Amelia had done anything out there since word came of Micajah Ferguson's death. I wondered what she'd been eating – or if she even was.

'Here you go, Miss Amelia,' I said, putting the plate on the small pie-shaped table beside her. 'You need to eat up now, you hear?' I knew I was talking to her as if she were a small child or an old woman who'd lost her wits, but I didn't know what else to do. 'I'll be back this evening. You take care.'

By now, the rain had slowed to a soft drizzle. I carefully closed all the doors I'd opened and headed for home.

I walked quickly, even though the worst of the storm had passed. I couldn't have said if it was the oppressive weather or the disturbing vibrations of near madness in the house I'd just left, but I felt uncharacteristically jittery. The clouds still pressed low upon the countryside, the air heavy with the smell of wet trees and mud, the sky filled with the dark bodies of birds on the wing. I kept throwing glances over my shoulder, my gaze raking every dripping, dark-green stand of cypress and the deep shadows of the gulley that fell away to the north.

I'd almost reached Belle Grove when I heard the pounding hooves of horses ridden fast, coming toward me. I instinctively drew back against a dripping willow thicket, my mouth dry, my heart pounding wildly as I watched two magnificent, long-legged dapple grays come thundering around the bend.

And I saw him the second time in my life.

He wore the same dark-blue frock coat and black felt hat that I remembered from that day on the levee of Bayou Sara in what now seemed like a different lifetime. His golden hair was longer, and he had a bloody, crescent-shaped cut on one cheek that he kept dabbing at with the back of his wrist. But I would have recognized him anywhere A silver bread basket tied to the pommel of his saddle bounced up and down with the horse's gait, and he had what I realized was a bulging pair of women's linen drawers, with the legs tied off to form a kind of double sack, thrown across his horse's neck. I could hear the clatter and rattle of its contents as he drew abreast of me. I'd never seen the stocky sergeant who rode with him, his long, dark brown hair stringy with rain and sweat, his full cheeks unshaven.

I knew if either man glanced sideways, they'd see me, for I wasn't exactly hidden. I held myself very still, the sour milk crock clutched against me so tightly the edge of the bottom rim bit into my ribs. They cantered past, saddle leather creaking, horses' hooves splattering in the muddy lane, so close I could smell their sweat and the warm hides of their horses.

But they didn't look at me, didn't slow. Their gazes fixed straight ahead, they disappeared around the distant bend.

The crock tumbled unheeded from my grasp, and I found my legs suddenly so weak I sank to my knees. My breath came hard and fast, and my head felt as if it were swelling. I could feel the muddy wet grass soaking through my dress and petticoat, imagined I could still feel the vibration of their horses' powerful hooves trembling the earth beneath me.

And then it occurred to me to wonder whose home they'd just looted.

I pushed to my feet and took off at a run. I could see a brown smudge of smoke billowing above the treetops and realized it came from Belle Grove.

By the time I turned up the long, rose-lined drive toward the big house, I was gasping for air. Smoke still boiled from the elegant pedimented porch of the west wing, but some of the field hands were beating at the fire with rugs and blankets, and almost had it out.

Miss Gussie's housekeeper was standing on the shell drive, her apron up over her face, her shoulders heaving with her sobs. But when I approached her and said, 'Aunt Selma?' she let her apron fall to show a face ravaged by fear and horror and a raw kind of grief that made my stomach twist with foreboding.

'Oh, Gawd, child. What you doin' here?'

'Where's Miss Gussie?' I asked hoarsely.

Aunt Selma nodded toward the house. 'She in there.'

I started toward the front steps.

Aunt Selma said, 'Child, don't go in there!'

But I kept walking, and I guess she didn't feel it was her place to stop me.

The front door stood wide open, the elegant central hall beyond in shadow. 'Miss Gussie,' I called.

The house was cool, the smell of smoke mingling with the sweet scent of roses and lilies from the big vases Miss Gussie always filled every morning. Even in the dim light of the cloudy day, the fine European furniture gleamed with beeswax and orange oil, the rich citrus scent mingling with the clove-like aroma of the roses.

'Miss Gussie?'

I took another step forward and saw her. She lay sprawled on her back on the far side of the large round satinwood table that stood in the center of the hall's long expanse of gleaming wood flooring, the lacy white scarf that normally topped it crumpled beside her as if she'd grabbed it as she fell. The broken fragments of a smashed crystal oil lamp crunched beneath my feet as I approached her. She had her arms flung up on either side of her head, and even in the dim, smoky light I could see the purple bruises on the pale flesh of her slim wrists.

'Miss Gussie?' I said again, although a part of me knew she couldn't answer me.

I crept forward, my heart pounding in my chest, and for a moment my vision went out of focus and I felt dizzy. Her skirts and petticoats were rucked up to her waist, her drawers torn, so that it seemed an obscene intrusion to come upon her like this. I snatched up the muddied, lace-trimmed scarf from the floor to spread it awkwardly over her nakedness, my hands shaking badly. Then I made the mistake of looking up into her face. Her eyes were wide and staring, the flesh of one temple hideously bruised, the skin pulpy and bloody. A small rivulet of dark blood had trickled from one ear to darken the hair at the nape of her neck.

I shoved my fist in my mouth and squeezed my eyes shut. For a moment, all I could hear was my own breath rasping in and out.

Then I heard Aunt Selma say softly, 'Miss Amrie? Come away, child.'

I opened my eyes and turned. The aged housekeeper stood in the doorway, her face wet and swollen, her fists twisting in her tear-stained apron. I stared at her. All I could think was how much Miss Gussie had feared this woman and her fellow slaves, yet it was white men who'd killed her.

'What happened?' I asked, my voice a whisper.

'Two Yankees. They come poundin' on the door, saying they was after guerrillas. Only, they was really after anything they could find to steal. They even got the gold coins out the secret drawer of Mr Holt's desk and the jewelry Miss Gussie done hid behind a loose brick in her bedroom fireplace. Then one of them – the good lookin' one with the pretty blue eyes and golden curls – he say Miss Gussie's a fine woman, and he guesses he'll have a taste of what she been given her Secesh husband all these years. Had his sergeant hold her down while he went at her. Only, she kept fighting him – even bit his cheek, she did. So he took out his pistol and bashed her in the side of the head. She lay still after that.'

I shook my head no, as if by denying her words I could somehow make the reality of it all go away. Then I realized I was crying, my chest jerking, great tears welling up to chase each other down my cheeks, although I made not a sound.

Aunt Selma said, 'Come away, child, do. Let me send my boy, Jasper, with you to see you home. There be Yankees crawlin' all over today.'

I looked at her. But I still couldn't seem to find my voice.

'Miss Amrie? You all right, child? Oh, Gawd. What this world comin' to? A child, seeing somethin' like this!' Then she said it again, as if answering her own question with the same query. 'What this world coming to?'

I arrived home to find a cool, damp wind ruffling the feathers of dead chickens scattered around our muddy, dripping yard. I stumbled over a leather-bound book lying face down in the mud and reached stupidly to pick it up, smoothing the crumpled, stained pages with a shaky hand. I could see the gate to our pasture hanging open, the wet green expanse empty except for Mama and Mahalia, who were staring down at a still, small white lump at their feet.

It took me a moment to realize the lump was Flower.

Then my mother looked up and saw me. 'Amrie.'

She came to hug me to her with a crushing fierceness. 'Thank

God, honey. You were so long, I was afraid something must have happened to you, that the soldiers . . .' She drew back, her hands bracketing my cheeks, her eyebrows puckering as she anxiously scanned my face. 'Are you all right?'

I nodded.

It was Aunt Selma's son, Jasper, who said, 'Yankees done hit Belle Grove, Mizz Kate.'

She glanced over at him. 'And Augusta Holt? Is she all right?'

Jasper stared down at his muddy feet.

My mother looked from Jasper to me. 'Amrie? Is Miss Gussie all right?'

The wind dropped suddenly, so that the air hung thick and foul with the smell of mud and drowned earthworms and death. My throat swelled up, so that I found I couldn't say anything. But I guess at that point I didn't need to.

My mother knew.

She set off for Belle Grove at once – on foot, since the soldiers had taken Magnolia and our remaining mules. I didn't want her to go, but she said she had to. I guess she wanted to make sure Miss Gussie really was dead. Or maybe she figured somebody needed to take charge of Gussie Holt's burial.

It was Mahalia who told me what had happened, about the dozen Federal soldiers who'd romped through our house, saying they were looking for guerrillas even as they helped themselves to anything that struck their fancy. About how they'd laughed as they overturned mattresses and broke open work boxes and drawers, saying, 'Got any Rebs hiding in here? How about over here?'

I walked slowly through the ransacked rooms, my footsteps echoing hollowly on the mud- and debris-strewn floorboards. Drawers had been wrenched from chests, their contents scattered and crushed; the splintered doors of armoires hung open on broken hinges. I felt oddly dead inside, my arms and legs so weighted it seemed more than I was capable of doing to lift the overturned chairs or pick up the precious books they'd knocked off the shelves, or sweep up the fragments of my great-grandmother's crystal glasses that sparkled on the hearth. And it occurred to me to wonder if this crushing grief was a faint version of the way Amelia Ferguson felt, if this was why she just sat in her chair all day, staring at the wall. And I felt a flash of guilt for judging her and finding her lacking because of it.

Mahalia came to stand in the parlor doorway, her arms wrapped across her full breasts, hugging herself as she watched me pick my way through the litter. 'I jist don't understand why they kilt that goat,' she said. 'Your momma begged 'em not to do it, sayin' there was a poor little babe needed that goat's milk to survive. But they just laughed and shot Flower anyway. What kind of men would do something like that?'

It was a good thing she didn't expect an answer, because I had none that I could give her. If we hadn't wanted to live in the same country with these people, before, I couldn't figure out how they thought we'd be any more willing now, after all they'd done to us. I guess they didn't care whether we were willing or not.

But they were so bent on punishing us and forcing us to their will that it seemed to me they'd lost the whole point.

I was helping Mahalia sweep up the broken crockery in the kitchen when Finn came over. The Federals had hit the O'Reilly place, too, stealing the mule Mama had given him after the last raid, and breaking their plow.

'Did it out of pure meanness, I guess,' said Finn, going to right a barrel the raiders had overturned. ''Cause we didn't have much for them to steal. But we already been cleaned out once already, so what'd they expect?'

Mama came home not long after that, and we all sat on the gallery and watched the evening sky turn a light blue ribbed with thick strips of pink and gold-tinged clouds. The breeze was warm and wet, and smelled of night-blooming flowers and stale smoke, the atmosphere oppressive with a sense of fear and despair that seemed almost palpable.

After she left Belle Grove, Mama went to check on Amelia Ferguson, too. She said a raiding party had taken Miss Amelia's cow and horses, but otherwise they'd left her alone. I guess maybe she spooked them as much as she did me. Mama said when she told Miss Amelia that Flower was dead, she'd sunk to the floor in a faint.

Finn stared out at the oak and pecan trees still glistening and heavy with rain, their trunks black in the gloom. 'There's a farmer named Skate Mooney outside of Clinton who keeps a big herd of goats. He might be willin' to sell us one – that is, if the Federals ain't stole them all already.'

The town of Clinton lay some twenty-five miles to the east of us, on the far side of Jackson, Louisiana. It seemed a risky thing to do – to travel so far when the roads were crawling with Federal raiding parties.

But Mama said, 'That's a good idea, Finn. I'll leave first thing in the morning.'

Finn shook his head. 'Let me go, Miss Kate. It'd be better.'

'No,' she said in that voice I'd learned long ago meant, *Don't even think about arguing with me*. 'I can't ask you to do something like that.'

'But you aint' askin' me, ma'am; Hells bells – it was my idea!'

'No, Finn.'

He argued with her for what seemed like forever, growing red in the face and saying he should never have said anything – should've just gone without telling her what he intended. But Mama stood firm.

In the end, though, Finn got his way, for a message came that night from Reverend Lewis, saying he was afraid old Hypolite Brewster's heart was giving out. So Mama had to hurry into town.

I sometimes wonder what might have happened had old Mr Brewster not chosen that night to die. Useless imaginings, I know. But it is on such randomly timed events that the entire course of our lives can hinge and turn, for good or for ill.

Finn left for Clinton early the next morning, carrying a hundred dollars that folks in town collected when they heard what'd happened to Flower.

Finn could've walked to Clinton and back in a couple of days, if he'd been traveling by himself. The problem was, he wouldn't be by himself on the way back; he'd be leading a goat.

'How far you reckon a goat walks in a day?' I asked Mahalia while we were scrubbing the muddy mess the Federals had made of our parlor.

She screwed up her face with thought. 'Well, I reckon a she goat *could* walk a fair ways, if'n she had a mind to. But a goat ain't like a horse or a dog; they can be downright ornery and contrary. I reckon if we're lucky, we might see that boy again in four or five days. Or maybe a week.'

We both fell silent. We weren't sure how long little Theo could last.

About the only cow in the area the Federals had missed killing or stealing belonged to Mrs Mumford. I'd always thought her a mean, crotchety thing. But as soon as she heard what'd happened to Flower, she not only contributed five dollars to the collection to buy one of Skate Mooney's goats, but started sending some milk over to Miss Amelia every day, too.

Problem was, little Theodore couldn't stomach cow's milk any better now than he could before.

I said, 'Maybe Skate Mooney'll lend Finn a mule and cart.' But even as I said it, I knew how unlikely that was. All we could hope was that he sold Finn a very cooperative she goat.

Two nights later, we awoke in the dark hours before dawn to a strange rumble that grew louder and louder, a cacophony of lumbering wagon wheels, men shouting, horses neighing, and the heavy tramp of tens of thousands of marching boots.

We'd become accustomed over the past week or so to the distant boom and crash of the Federals' regular nightly bombardment of Port Hudson. But this wasn't five miles away. This was *here*, in St Francisville.

'What is it?' I asked, tumbling down the stairs to find Mama in the hall. 'What's happening?'

She shook her head. 'I don't know.'

But we soon found out. General Nathaniel Banks had just landed an army at Bayou Sara's old wharves and was marching them through St Francisville on his way south to Port Hudson.

All twenty-one thousand of them.

Thirty-Two

The Federal army churned through St Francisville like a raucous plague of locusts sweeping across a cornfield. By the time the dust raised by the last rattling caisson, the last lumbering supply wagon and party of stragglers had settled, virtually anything the earlier raiding parties had missed was gone – including Mrs Mumford's brown milk cow.

Even though I didn't have any milk to bring her, I still went morning and evening to help Miss Amelia, who spent most of her time walking up and down with little Theo in her arms, his thin, reedy wail gradually growing fainter and fainter. We looked for Finn every day, but he didn't come. I spent hours mentally recalculating times and distances, as if I could somehow come to a different conclusion from the obvious one: that Finn had run smack dab into the Federal army and something awful had happened to him.

Mama tried everything she could think of, including thinning mashed potatoes with water and feeding Theo that. But Miss Amelia's little baby boy was failing fast.

By the end of the week, he was dead.

A grim-faced Cyrus Pringle built the small, whitewashed coffin, and Devon Gantry's widow, Sophie, lined it with white silk she cut up from the wedding dress she'd been saving for her daughter's First Communion dress. Mahalia dressed the babe in his christening gown, and I gathered white rosebuds from Miss Amelia's overgrown garden and tied them up with a white satin ribbon donated by Laura Winthrop.

The coffin rested on a dining-room chair set up by the front window of the parlor. Miss Amelia sat in a chair beside it, her hands clenched together in her lap, her gaze on her sweet baby's pale, waxen face. Mahalia had coaxed her into putting on a fresh dress and letting Mahalia brush her hair, but she still looked awful. Her once shiny blue eyes were dull and lifeless, and she'd grown so thin and wan a body'd be hard put to recognize her as the plump, pretty woman she'd once been.

I was in the yard drawing water for her when I heard the clatter of hoof beats coming fast. There'd been a steady stream of folks stopping by to pay their respects that morning, but they'd all arrived on foot. These days, the only horses around here belonged to either Federal raiders or Confederate cavalry patrols.

My breath catching, I dropped the bucket and pelted around the side of the house in time to see a single rider on a big, lathered bay rein in beside the steps, a bleating, hogtied goat held slung across his horse's withers.

'Finn!'

He leapt from the saddle, hauled down the goat, and turned toward the house, as if he were planning to run right up the steps with it.

'Finn!' I cried again.

He swung to face me, the goat gripped tightly in his arms, his face taut with determination and a coiled, wiry kind of desperation. 'Tell me I'm not too late.'

I skidded to a halt. 'My God, Finn; we've been so worried about you! What happened?'

'Never mind that. Just tell me I'm not too late.'

I shook my head, tears stinging my eyes.

He sat down on the bottom step. The goat bleated and bucked against him, and he ducked his head to loose the bindings on the goat's legs and let her go. She scampered some feet away, then stopped. He just sat there, watching the goat pull at the long, over-grown grass, his gaze fixed on it with an intensity that suggested the answers to life's cruelest ironies and heartaches could somehow be found in that simple scene.

I went to catch his horse's reins. It was a magnificent animal, at least sixteen hands high, its hide dark and shiny with sweat. I studied the black, high-backed dragoon saddle, the US stamped on the bridle bit, the dark red stain on the saddlecloth. Then I looked over at Finn.

His gaze met mine. And I saw the shifting shadows and ghostly echoes of the kind of events that twist souls and will forever bring their survivors shaking and screaming from sleep in the dark bowels of the night. Whatever had occurred on the long road to Clinton and back had changed him profoundly and irrevocably. This was not the same laughing, light-hearted boy with whom I'd once caught tadpoles and schemed to unmask Hilda Meyers as a witch. That boy was gone forever.

'Finn,' I said quietly. 'What happened?'

His answer was terse and vague in details. All I ever knew was that he'd almost made it back to St Francisville with a goat when he ran into General Banks's army. A troop of New Yorkers took him captive, tied him up, and promised to shoot him as a spy – once they'd killed and roasted the goat and finished the keg of whiskey they'd found in a farmer's cellar.

His eyes slid sideways when he got to that part of his tale, and I knew that he was omitting something vital. All he'd tell me was that the New Yorkers got so drunk they passed out, so that Finn was able to free himself and steal one of their horses. Then he rode back to Skate Mooney in Clinton and talked him into giving Finn another goat.

It made a good story, but it didn't explain all the missing days, or why he moved so stiffly, or where he got the good Wellington boots he wore.

'When did the babe die?' he asked.

'Last night.'

'So I almost made it.'

'Yes.'

He pushed silently to his feet and walked into the house, one hand slapping his palmetto hat against his thigh as he went to stand for a long time looking down at the tiny, rose-draped coffin. As if oblivious to his presence, Miss Amelia rocked back and forth, humming what I realized with a chill was a lullaby. Finn pressed her hand and told her he was sorry, but she just stared at him as if she hadn't understood a word he said. Then he turned and walked back out to the gallery, his new boots clattering on the floorboards.

I followed him, wondering when he'd grown taller than me. There was a new slimness to his body, a definition to his jaw line and the bridge of his nose that I suppose had been slowly evolving, but that I only now noticed. At the top of the steps he paused, still slapping his hat against his thigh. He stared up at the great, creamy-white cups of the magnolia blossoms shifted by a warm wind against the blue sky.

'I'm joining the Partisan Rangers, Amrie. I'll stop by to tell Ma and the children goodbye, then I'm off.'

He was fourteen now – had been for a couple of weeks. Time was, they'd have turned away a boy that young. Not any more.

I felt my mouth go dry, my heartbeat slow to a heavy, painful thump. I could think of nothing to say that wouldn't shame us both.

He looked at me then, and I could see the new hardness in his face, feel the heat of fury and determination that thrummed through him. But there was something else there, too – something alien to me, something I suspected was uniquely male and a part of that masculine cult of honor that was all tied up with Southern concepts of worthiness and self-respect and the nobility of the soul.

I wanted to scream, *No! Not you, too!* Instead, I blinked back the tears that threatened to spill over and said, 'You will write?'

He nodded, and I saw his jaw tense, his throat work as he swallowed. The breeze gusted up harder, lifting the moss on the oaks and dappling his face with shifting patterns of light and shadow. I smelled honeysuckle and the four o'clocks just beginning to open

along the walkway; then the wind dropped and in the silence I could
hear him breathing.

He looked directly into my face, and I felt a stirring of something
I suppose had always been there, unrecognized and unacknowledged.
I put my hands on his shoulders and reached up to kiss his cheek.
His skin was cool and dry against my lips, and I felt him tremble
slightly beneath my touch. Then I dropped my hands and took a
step back.

It was one of those moments in life when something shifts, when
you realize that your world – that *you* – will never be the same
again. I'd had so many such moments over the past two years, I
suppose I should have been used to them. But I wasn't.

Once upon a time, we'd been the Three Musketeers: Simon, Finn,
and me. We'd fought mock duels with wooden swords, turned our
hay barn into the bastion of St Gervais, dreamt of noble causes and
heroic deeds. Now those days seemed as unreal to me as the marve-
lous adventures we'd once read and hoped with passion and joy to
emulate. Simon was long dead, Finn was going off to war, and the
last remnants of our childhoods and lost innocence were like cold
ashes scattered by a whirlwind.

I knew what was expected of me; every woman in the South
knew it. Somehow, I kept a brave smile plastered on my face as
Finn gathered his bay's reins, swung into the saddle, and rode away.
He almost caught me when, at the end of the drive, he wheeled
suddenly, the bay cavorting beneath him with gracefully arched
neck as Finn lifted one hand, palm outward, in a last farewell. Then
he tightened his knees and the big horse whirled and leapt forward,
carrying him away from us.

I waited until he was lost from my sight, until the last echo of
his horse's hooves had died away. Then I sat down on the step and
cried until I wondered if I'd ever stop.

Word came that Papa had been lightly wounded at Chancellorville,
but he was all right now.

May bled into June, and the nightly bombardment of Port Hudson
continued, a nerve-wracking rumble of distant death that filled my
dreams with images of bomb-cratered muddy fields and dead, bloated
horses and the shattered, maggot-infested bodies of long dead men.
A vast Federal army now encircled the fortified bluffs to the south
of us, forming an impenetrable wall of troops and artillery that

squeezed the starving garrison within while feeding itself on the surrounding countryside. It seemed as if every day a raiding party descended on some hapless farm or small hamlet in the area, stealing food, fodder, and cotton, ripping up fences and chopping up furniture to carry away for firewood and sleeping boards. We learned to chart their progress by the columns of dirty smoke smudging the sky.

And then a Federal gunboat, the USS *Albatross*, appeared to hover off St Francisville. A screw steamer rigged as a three-masted schooner, she was one of the two Union boats that'd managed to slip past Port Hudson's defenses in that massive firefight last March, and had spent the past months ravaging the banks of the Mississippi between Port Hudson and Vicksburg. Silently tacking back and forth before the ruins of Bayou Sara, she kept the deadly mouths of her guns trained upon us, an ominous portent of things to come.

'What I want to know is, why the Sam Hill are they here?' Castile muttered one morning when I brought him some of the extra seeds Mama had saved for heat-tolerant vegetables like collards, sweet potatoes, and pumpkins. 'Bayou Sara ain't nothin' more'n a heap of blackened rubble these days, and St Francisville is full of scared women and children. So why them Yankees send that boat up here to watch us?'

'Maybe they're planning to try to land more troops from across the river,' I suggested.

'*More* troops? What they need more troops for? They already squeezin' Vicksburg and Port Hudson so tight there ain't a rat left alive to squeak in either one. What they need more troops for?'

I knew he didn't expect an answer, so I didn't even try to come up with one. I wanted to ask him about Leo, but I figured if he'd heard anything, he'd have told me. So I said, 'You hear anything about Finn?'

He shook his big, bald head. 'Nope. But they say some guerrillas kilt three Federal raiders up by Woodville. Don't know if Finn had anything to do with that or not. All I know is, the Federals dragged an old man and his twelve-year-old grandson outta a house near where it happened and hanged them both because of it. Then they burned the house to the ground, leaving that poor widow woman and her five younger children with nothin'.'

Such tales had become commonplace. One Federal general boasted he'd hanged five civilians for each stretch of telegraph wire he found cut; another ordered every building in a five-mile radius

burned, every animal killed, in retaliation for the death of one of
his aides. I stared at him. 'What you sayin'? That what them guerrillas did was wrong? That we should just let the Federals burn our
towns and steal anything they want from us, *kill us*, and not fight
back?'

Castile blew out a harsh breath. 'I don't know what I'm sayin'.
All I know is, that old man and his grandson is dead.'

Yet in spite of everything, I still somehow clung to a child's notion
that things happen for a reason, that God protects the good and
punishes the bad, and that going to church and Sunday school
should somehow protect me and others like me from the kind of
evil that can come suddenly, irrevocably into one's life without
warning.

All that was about to change.

I arose early the next morning to go out looking for turkeys.
Hunting was serious business these days, for what had begun as
an adventure and a test I'd once failed miserably had now become
a pressing necessity. Every time I brought down a buck or a bird,
I still said a silent prayer of thanks to the spirit of the dead animal.
But it was hard for me to remember the time I'd shrunk from
killing. I wished I could see that as something good, but I didn't.
As far as I was concerned, my aversion to killing animals in the
wild was just one more precious thing this war had ripped from
me.

It was still only mid-morning when I headed for home again, but
a gusty wind was kicking up, shifting the leafy branches overhead
and scuttling puffs of white clouds across the sun. I followed a
narrow trail deep in pine needles that led through the stand of
shadowy cypress and oak in the gully behind our house, then broke
suddenly out of the shade into a hot sun smelling of baked earth
and the wood smoke that curled away from our kitchen chimney.
Mahalia was in the yard chopping kindling, but when she saw me,
she paused with one hand on her hip and called out, 'Jist look at
that gobbler! Mm-mm; we gonna have us a good supper tonight.
You leave him on the bench there, and I'll take care of him, honey.'

'Where's Mama?' I asked, thankfully dumping the heavy fifteen-
pounder beside the kitchen door.

'Last I seen her, she was lookin' for where Cassie done hid her
eggs this time. Stupid bird. Anyone ever wonder where that saying

"birdbrained" come from ain't never met Cassie.' Cassie was the only chicken to have survived the two Federal raids – a nasty-tempered black and white spotted hen that Mahalia kept threatening to dump in a stew pot if she didn't mend her ways.

Smiling faintly to myself, I unstrung my bow as I climbed the steps to the back gallery. I propped the bow and my quiver of arrows in the corner just inside the door, even though I knew Mahalia would complain about it. She was always saying, 'Anybody see this hall, they'd swear trash lives here. Just 'cause there be a war on, ain't no excuse to forget who and what you is.' But the war had given me a new understanding of the motivations for the behavior of those my class had always stigmatized as 'trash'. I figured most of them were just too tired or downhearted to attach much importance to the effort required to keep up appearances.

I went back outside to draw a bucket of water from the cistern and hauled it up the steep stairs to my room to wash my hands and face. I was reaching for my threadbare towel when a clatter of hooves drew me to the dormer window.

Carefully parting the lace curtains, I saw two Federals cantering up the drive on a pair of magnificent dapple-grays doubtless stolen from some local planter. One of the men, a sergeant, was dark and stocky, with several days' worth of beard shadowing his face. But it was his golden-haired companion who captured my attention. He cavorted his horse on the shell sweep before the front steps, the sun glinting on his rows of brass buttons, his head falling back as his blue gaze raked the roofline as if he somehow knew someone was watching him.

I stood perfectly still, my heart beating so hard it hurt. And it seemed in that moment as if I'd always known that someday he'd come back into my life, that our fates were entwined in a way that was no less real for being beyond my comprehension.

Then I saw his head turn, his gaze shifting as the *thwunk-thwunk* of Mahalia's axe echoed through the stillness. The two men exchanged a silent glance, and spurred their horses into a trot toward the back yard.

I threw the towel toward the washstand and bolted for the stairs.

Thirty-Three

Softly humming to herself, Mahalia was halfway to the kitchen with an armload of kindling when the Federals came upon her. She drew up abruptly, the pale sticks of newly chopped firewood clutched to her chest, her face bland with the glaze-eyed starkness of one who knows she is staring into a dark and terrible future, yet sees no way to avoid it.

The two men pranced their horses around her, the sun-glossed hides of the animal's powerful hindquarters bunching and shifting threateningly with each step, the smiles on the men's faces showing the fixed, emotionless concentration of an alligator lying half-submerged in a murky bayou. There was a time I would have burst out of the house to confront them, full of righteousness and fury and heedless of the reality of my inability to do more than complicate an already desperate situation. But something – Wisdom? Fear? Experience? – checked my forward rush.

I drew up in the shadows just inside the open back door, my knees weak and trembling, one hand clutching the smooth painted wood of the jamb as if it might not only steady me but also help me to think.

'Hey, you a good-lookin'gal,' I heard the stocky, dark-haired sergeant say to her, his broad face flushed with heat and primitive arousal. ''Specially for a darkie. You got white in you, gal? I always did like a touch of cream in my coffee.' His pig-like eyes squinted with merriment and he laughed at what he fancied was his own cleverness, his gaze cutting from Mahalia to his captain, as if desirous of sharing the mirth.

The Wisconsin captain sat tall in the saddle, his spine straight but limber, his broad shoulders squared, his blue eyes hooded with something I could not name but that made me squirm with revulsion. I could see the half moon-shaped scar on his cheek where Gussie Holt had bit him, white now against his sun-browned skin.

'Get her,' he said quietly.

Mahalia dropped the load of kindling with a clatter and took off toward the tree-lined gully at the base of the yard, her hands clenched in the skirts of her worn homespun dress, the soles of her dusty bare feet flashing in the sun. With a laugh, the sergeant spurred his horse to cut her off, whirling the big gray first one way, then the other, as she tried to dart around him.

I wanted to close my eyes and cover my ears, wanted not to hear Mahalia's terrified scream, wanted not to see the feral tautness in the man's face as he leapt from his saddle.

She tried to duck around him, toward the house. But he caught her by the arm and pulled her back around. The raucous guffaws of his laughter carried to me on the warm, scented breeze. But the captain remained oddly grim-faced as he swung out of his saddle.

'Ooh, I like a gal with spirit,' said the sergeant, laughing again. 'But the captain here, he gets riled when they fight. You best—'

'Let her go.'

I'd been so intently focused on Mahalia and the two men that I hadn't noticed my mother striding across the open stretch of grass from the corncrib, a clutch of Cassie's eggs cradled in one corner of her apron.

They swung to face her with the fixed intent of a pair of vicious dogs scenting fresh prey. I could feel my mouth going dry, and it was as if all my past terrors had combined with the fresh horror of that moment to warp around my chest and stop my breath.

The wind gusted up stronger, blowing a strand of honey-colored hair across my mother's face. She put up a hand to brush it back, the gesture unconsciously lifting her breasts and silhouetting her form against the sunlit pasture beyond. The war might have aged and worn my mother, but she was still an attractive woman, with high-boned cheeks and a generous mouth and fine gray eyes.

But if she noticed the taut hunger in the men's faces or the coiled, aggressive purposefulness of their hard bodies, she gave no indication of it. She strode toward them with her head up, anger whitening the edges of her nostrils with each breath. 'I said, let her go.'

The tall captain glanced at his companion. 'You heard the lady, Boyle.' It was said in the same deep, preacher-like voice I remembered from the banks of the river, a voice smooth with self-satisfied righteousness and a confident assumption of divine favor. 'Let her woman go.' He rested his thumbs on his belt, his thin lips tightening into a smile that did not match his eyes as he brought them back to my mother's face. 'Personally, I never did care much for blackberry jelly. Are you offering me a taste of marmalade, instead?'

My mother stumbled to a halt. I saw the hand that was holding up the corner of her apron fall, the nest of eggs tumbling to smash against the hard earth at her feet.

Moving slowly so as not to draw anyone's attention, I picked up the bow leaning in the corner and carefully eased the string into its nock.

'Grab her,' I heard the captain say.

My head jerked up. I saw my mother whirl to run. But the dark, stocky sergeant was on her instantly, dragging her down, his laughter low and husky as her nails raked his cheeks and he had to rear back his head to keep her from gouging his eyes.

Standing above her, the captain slammed the toe of his boot into her ribs hard enough that I heard the impact. 'Try that on me, and I'll bash your brains out.'

A broken sob ripped from me, tearing my throat. Throwing the quiver over my shoulder, I ran across the gallery and down the steps, feet pounding on the boards. I didn't care anymore who saw me.

But no one was looking in my direction. They had my mother on her back, the stocky sergeant jerking her arms over her head while the golden-haired captain shoved her legs apart, raked up the froth of her petticoats. I skidded to a halt, yanked an arrow from my quiver, fit its nock onto the bowstring and drew it back.

My heart was pounding so hard I was shaking. I watched the Federal rear back to fumble with the flap of his trousers, saw him shove them down on his hips, his buttocks smooth and white in the sun. I wanted to scream, *Stop! Stop, or I'll shoot!* But the raw sexuality of the moment, the sight of such unimagined ugly, violent lust directed at my own mother brought a burn of nausea to my chest. I swallowed, fighting to slow my breathing, trying desperately to force the words – any words – out of my mouth.

Then I saw my mother jerk her knee up, hard, into the Federal captain's groin. I heard his guttural curse, saw his hand scrabble for the butt of his pistol.

His hair was the color of spun gold touched with fire, his blue-coated back broad and sun warmed. I squinted against the glare of the fierce midday light, opened my fingers and let the arrow fly.

It cut through the air with a lethal *whoosh* to strike between the captain's shoulder blades, burying the fine point deep into sinew and muscle and tender organs. I saw him tense, arms flinging out to his sides as if in surprise, his body turning as he surged halfway to his feet. He hovered there for a moment, his gaze meeting mine across the sun-spangled yard, his arms stretched out against the Southern sky, his mouth open as if in a silent scream.

Then he pitched forward and lay still.

I stared at him, oddly aware of the clouds moving across the sun, the dust lifting in billows off the fields.

'Why you—'

The angry snarl jerked my gaze to the sergeant. He lurched up, his homely, sunburned features twisted with rage, his pig-like eyes narrow and dark as he snatched his bowie knife from its sheath at his waist. I was only dimly aware of my mother scrambling to her feet, her face a white blur.

She screamed, 'Amrie. You've got to shoot him, too! Amrie!'

I fumbled for another arrow. Dropped it. Grabbed another. I was trembling all over now, the arrow's point swinging wildly as I drew back the bowstring and let it fly.

It soared some two feet over the man's head.

'You goddamned little bitch,' he roared, his naked knife blade gleaming in the hot sun. He filled my vision, his sweat-streaked face red and shaking, so close now that I could smell the foul stench of his body odor and the reek of sweat-dampened wool. 'I'm gonna kill you, you hear? I'm gonna gut you like a fish and—'

He stopped suddenly, his face going almost ludicrously slack, his eyes widening until I could see the blood-shot whites rimming his smoky-brown irises. I stared at him, not understanding. He took a step forward and stumbled, the look of wonder on his face turning into horror and then something else, something dark and terrible that I knew would haunt my dreams forever.

He took one more step, then pitched forward at my feet, his body slamming into the ground, a dark red stain blooming around the bloody blade of the axe buried deep in his back.

My breath was coming so fast it was like a roaring in my ears. Somehow, I dragged my gaze away from the blood-drenched dead man at my feet to where Mahalia stood, her hands now pressed flat to her thighs, her gaze fixed on the man she'd just killed. I could see the pulse beating in her throat, the strange tick that pulled a muscle beside her mouth. Then she swallowed hard and raised her gaze to mine, and we shared a quiet, intense moment of horror oddly mixed with exultant triumph.

A movement drew my gaze to my mother. She was kneeling now beside the officer. He lay crumpled on his side, my arrow still sticking out of his back, one hand flung out as if reaching for something that would remain forever beyond his grasp. 'Is he dead?' I asked, my voice such a broken whisper I wasn't sure she'd heard me.

She looked up. Her hair was coming down, curtaining her face, the bodice of her dress torn and dusty. 'Yes,' she said simply.

She rose and came to crouch beside the sergeant. I stared down at his beard-shadowed face, twisted sideways. His eyes were wide and staring, and a pool of blood darkened the earth beneath his slack, open mouth. 'And him?'

She nodded, and all I felt was relief.

I watched her sit back in the dirt, her hands draped limply over her bent knees and stained now with the dead men's blood. The sky had darkened, the wind gusting up cool and smelling of the stagnant water in the nearly gulley and a fresher scent that told of coming rain. The air filled with a chorus of birdsong from the high branches of the oak and pecan trees. Then, just as suddenly, all was quiet, as if the world waited with bated breath.

'What we gonna do wit them?' said Mahalia, giving voice to the thought that was on all our minds. 'Two dead Yankees, both kilt from behind. What we gonna do?'

Thirty-Four

I walked across the yard to where the golden-haired captain still lay sprawled awkwardly on his side, his blood soaking the warm clay beneath him, his head tipped sideways as if he were only sleeping. I stared down at him, waiting to experience an exponentially heightened version of the horror and revulsion I'd felt the first time I killed a deer.

Instead, I felt . . . nothing.

A hawk circled overhead. I could see distant rain falling in a shaft of sunlight to the south like an isolated phenomenon outside our reality. I sucked in a deep breath and heard Mahalia say, 'Maybe we can drag 'em out into the road. Make it look like partisan rangers done got them.'

'No,' said my mother after only a brief moment's thought. 'We can't risk having the Federals' retaliation for this fall on our neighbors.'

'So what we gonna do? We sure as heck can't just leave 'em lyin' here in the yard. More Federal troops could come ridin' by any minute. They see what we done, they hang us, for sure.'

'We can hide them in the barn for now,' said my mother, 'while we figure out what to do with them more permanently. Amrie, grab their horses and tether them down in the gully. Mahalia, you take this one's other arm and help me drag him out of sight.'

My mother's words seemed to wash over me as if from a great distance. I was intensely, inexplicably focused on the limbs of the live oaks thrashing in the growing wind and the white curve of the half moon-shaped scar Gussie Holt had left on the sun-reddened cheek of the man who'd killed her.

The man I'd killed.

'*Amrie*. Get the horses.'

Tearing my gaze from the dead man at my feet, I whirled to catch the reins of the two dapple-grays and sprinted with them toward the coulee. The clouds were bunching heavier, the rain on the horizon a glimmering curtain advancing slowly toward us. I could smell the horses' warm hides and the dampness carried by the wind, hear the creak of empty saddle leather and my own frightened breath rasping in my throat as I ran. The sun had become a red ball behind the clouds. I never knew if it was some eerie trick of the coming storm or a figment of my own imagination, but the day's light had taken on a strange hue, more crimson than golden, that drenched the world in a hellish glow.

I led the horses deep into the tangle of brush edging the stream that trickled at the base of the gully. They were magnificent animals, with long graceful necks and legs, high withers, and deep chests. As I loosened their girths, I noticed the V hanging S brand clearly visible on their near hips. It was a brand familiar to everyone in these parts as belonging to Virgil Slaughter, an old Kentucky native who raised some of the best racehorses in Louisiana. I'd heard the Federals had raided his place, killing his octogenarian mother, burning his house, and emptying his stables. Now, as I traced the outline of that telltale brand, it occurred to me that these horses could be as dangerous to us in their own way as the two dead bodies.

By the time I climbed back up to the yard, the wind was kicking up whirlwinds of dust and the two dead men were gone.

But I could see quite clearly where their heavy bodies had been drug through the fragile grass, and the earth where they had lain was stained dark with their blood.

'We should have thrown their bodies over the horses and moved them that way,' said my mother, later. 'It was stupid of me not to realize that dragging them would leave traces anyone could come along and see.'

We were huddled together around the fire in the kitchen, although it was not really cold. The door stood open to the storm, the rain drumming on the roof and sluicing off the eaves in a roaring torrent.

'Don't make no difference, now,' said Mahalia, stoking the fire higher. 'Ain't nobody gonna be able to see nothin' after this storm.'

My mother remained silent, her gaze on the dancing flames, her lips pressed into a flat line. To my mother, the fact that her error would have no consequences was immaterial. She couldn't get past the realization that she had allowed the pressure and emotions of the moment to overset the clarity of her thinking, and she was both mortified and deeply furious with herself for what she saw as an unforgivable failing.

She sat on a low stool, a collection of the personal items she had gathered from the men's pockets in her lap. I watched her sift through them: letters; a gold pocket watch; an ivory toothpick holder; a heavy purse that clinked with coins. But what caught my attention was the tintype of two children, a fair-headed girl who looked about my age and a boy a few years younger. They stared silently out at us, two nameless strangers connected to us in a way they hopefully would never know.

'You think that's his children?' I asked. 'The captain, I mean.'

My mother nodded. 'According to his papers, he was Captain Gabriel Dupont, from Racine, Wisconsin.'

Gabriel. It was a name that had always been associated in my mind with archangels and joyous messengers from God. Not with violence, greed, and murder.

She started to toss the photo onto the fire, but I put out a hand, stopping her. 'Can I see it?'

She handed it to me.

I held the small, cardboard-mounted photograph cupped in my

palm and stared down at the faces of his children. I kept waiting to feel something – guilt, horror, compassion. But that strange, dislocated sense of numbness remained.

My mother drew one of the letters from its envelope and scanned it quickly. I watched her face harden, her breath blowing out in harsh incredulity. 'Listen to this,' she said, and read aloud. '"The blue silk dress you sent arrived last Thursday. It is by far the grandest thing I have ever owned, and I was the envy of everyone when I wore it to church yesterday. I couldn't help but smile, thinking of the Sesech woman you took it from and how furious she would be to see me peacocking about in her finery. Jenna loves the books and the newest necklace you sent her, and the silver looking glass. She says Maddie's father sent her a piano he took off a Reb in Virginia, and she'd like that next. I told her that until we get the Mississippi opened up, you might have a hard time shipping one home . . ."'

She paused for a moment, her features suddenly, oddly pinched. Watching her, my chest felt tight, my skin cold from the damp wind gusting through the open door. 'What?' I asked.

'Oh, God,' she whispered. 'Who could do this to a child?'

'What?' I asked again.

She read on. '"Michael has continued to cause me problems, even more than Jenna. He's so contrary and naughty. What he needs is a good, hard licking, and though I try to give him one, he laughs at my feeble attempts. I said what you suggested, that he needs to be good for your sake. I told him that you live always with the danger of being killed, but that if he is a good boy and Jenna is a good girl, God will take care of you and protect you from harm. I explained how they must be good children, and mind me always, for when they are naughty and disobedient, God removes his protective shield from around you. I believe they finally listened to me. Hopefully fear has achieved what threats had heretofore failed to do."'

She fell silent, the letter crushed in her hand. In a swift gesture of revulsion, she threw the pages in the fire and sat watching the lines of flowing script darken and curl before flaring up hot and bright.

Mahalia rubbed her forehead with her hand. 'Oh, Gawd. And now that poor little boy and his sister is gonna go through the rest of their lives thinking it's their fault their daddy done got hisself kilt.'

Mama quickly skimmed the second letter, then consigned it, too, to the flames.

'What was the other man's name?' I asked. 'The sergeant?'

'Jules Boyle. That letter was from his mother.'

Mahalia pushed to her feet. 'Well, I ain't gonna waste no pity on her. She done raised a mean son, and the world's better off without him.'

I stared down at the tintype in my hand.

'Throw it on the fire, Amrie.'

'But—'

'We can't risk being found with any of this. Do it.'

I hesitated a moment longer, then tossed the photo toward the flames.

It fell short, fluttering to land on the hearth. I watched it begin to smoke, the face of the little girl seeming almost to glow. Then Mahalia picked up the poker and shoved the photograph deep into the fire.

I looked up. 'What we gonna do with them bodies?'

'Those bodies,' said my mother in a distracted, automatic way. She and Mahalia had hidden the two dead men beneath a thin covering of hay so old and moldy the Federals hadn't bothered to rake it up and steal it. But we couldn't leave them there.

Mahalia said, 'I reckon we could feed 'em to the hogs. I heard tell about a farmer over in Mississippi who went down to feed his hogs one night and fell and hit his head. By the time they found him in the morning, the only thing left was his wooden teeth and his belt buckle.'

'Good Lord,' I said, staring at her in horror.

I expected my mother to reject the idea out of hand; the sanctity of human remains was important to her because of both her religion and her medical training. But to my surprise, she seriously considered Mahalia's suggestion before shaking her head. 'No; it's too risky. I've heard of instances where hogs ate part of a body but there was still enough left to identify. Besides . . . however despicable those men may have been, they were God's children and they deserve a burial.' She hesitated, then added. 'Of some sort.'

'So where we gonna plant 'em?' said Mahalia. 'Down by the creek?'

'No. That's too dangerous, as well,' said Mama, and Mahalia nodded, her chest rising on a long, indrawn breath.

The problem was, Federal troops seemed to have a genius for spotting recently disturbed earth. And it wouldn't do any good to try to make the graves look like those of our own kin. We'd all heard tales of raiders digging up any new graves they found, convinced they contained not the dead but stashes of gold and silver. It hadn't been more than a month since Irene Irvinel's cook had gone mad at the sight of her three-year-old little girl's gruesome, half-decayed corpse dug up by a band of Federals.

'We need to bury them someplace they won't be found,' said Mama.

'How about down by Cat Island?' I suggested.

Mama turned to look at me. I expected her to dismiss the suggestion out of hand. Instead, she said, 'How well do you know it?'

'Finn knows it better'n me. But we've fished the area a lot.' I sat forward. 'There's one place near the bayou where an old oak fell over, and its roots left a big hole. I reckon we could hide them in there and cave the sides of it in on top of them.'

Mama rose and went to the open doorway to stare out at the storm.

In the silence, the kitchen filled with the roar of cascading water and the clean, fresh scent of the driving rain. Mahalia and I exchanged glances.

'We'll need to move them tonight,' said Mama, as if coming to a decision. 'We can load the bodies on their horses.' She turned to look at me, her face set in tense lines. 'Can you find your way there in the dark?'

'I think so.'

The storm raged around us, drowning out all other sounds and obscuring our vision of the world more than twenty or thirty feet beyond the kitchen. I was painfully aware of both our isolation and our vulnerability. *If only Finn were here,* I found myself thinking. *Or Avery. Or if Simon were still alive, or Priebus . . .* If only there were *someone* who could help us cope with what we were now called upon to do.

But the men in our lives were all either off to war, or dead.

Something of my thoughts must have shown on my face, because my mother said, 'We can do this, Amrie. We can.'

But I wasn't sure if her words were intended to convince me, or herself.

Thirty-Five

That night, the sky went black long before sunset as the storm continued to bear down in a swirling fury of wind and rain and jagged flashes of lightning that lit up the roiling underbelly of the heavens.

'At least we don't need to worry about anyone seeing us,' said my mother as we slogged through the flooded yard toward the barn. 'No one with any sense is going to be out in this. And even if they are, it's too dark.'

She was wearing a pair of Papa's boots along with one of his broad-brimmed felt hats, and had pulled on his old oilcloth jacket over her dress. She'd shaken her head when I suggested she borrow a pair of his trousers, too, but told me to go ahead and wear a pair of Simon's, if I wanted. I hadn't taken two steps away from the house before I was soaked, Simon's flannel shirt sticking to my skin and my hair plastered down around my head.

'Except for the lightning,' I said as an electric sizzle lit up the yard in a pale, ghostly glow. I'd retrieved the two dapple-grays from the coulee as the last of the light was fading from the day, and now led them behind me, their big hooves making sucking sounds in the mud.

'What I wanna know is, how *we* gonna see?' muttered Mahalia, her hands shaking as she drew back the bolt on the barn door. 'You tell me that. I hear tell there's sinkholes and sandbars down around Cat Island that can swallow a big old black bear.'

The soft golden light from my mother's tin lantern illuminated the barn's dusty interior, empty except for the small pile of moldy hay hastily raked into the center to cover the bodies of the dead Federals. She hung the lantern on a hook near the door, where it swayed, casting macabre shadows over the rough plank walls and dark, cobweb-draped rafters overhead.

I led the two horses into the barn, my step faltering as the heavy stench of urine, excrement, and blood hit me. 'Oh, Gawd,' I whispered.

My mother eased the coiled length of rope she'd brought off her shoulder as calmly as if she were a field hand going out to lasso a cow. She was a woman who was no stranger to death, who'd worked unflinchingly with hideously mangled bodies in need of care. And I knew from the distant, cold manner she'd now assumed that she'd slid naturally into the same frame of mind in which she dealt with those crises. 'Mahalia, shut the door. Amrie, help me uncover them.'

I stood where I was, the bile rising in my throat, my gaze fixed on that musty pile of hay. I willed my legs to move, but it didn't seem to work.

I expected my mother to holler at me. Instead, she came to stand before me and rest her hands on my shoulders. I realized with a vague, detached sense of surprise that she must now be only a few inches taller than me, because she essentially looked me in the eye.

'Amrie,' she said, squeezing her hands with enough force to rock me back and forth. 'I know this is hard. If Mahalia and I could do it without you, we would. But we can't. We need your help. This war has forced us all to do so many things we thought we'd never need to do. It's horrible and it's brutal but it just . . . is. Try to remember one thing: these men brought violence to us. All we did was protect ourselves and each other. And now we have to protect ourselves from the consequences. *You can't freeze up.*'

I drew in a breath of the damp, foul air and nodded.

She gave me another gentle shake. 'Come on, then.'

We went to work, the only sounds the rush of the rain and the soft shifting of the old hay. Not long after we'd decided to move the men to Cat Island, Mama had gone out to the barn to – as she put it – 'bend them'. At the time, it hadn't made much sense to me. But as we worked to brush away the last wisps of the moldy hay covering the dead Federals, I understood why she had taken care to position them on their sides, with their bodies curled at the waist and their arms extended straight over their heads, like swimmers about to dive into an unseen lake.

Rigor mortis had almost fully set in, making the dead men as stiff and unyielding as if they'd been carved from wood. If my mother hadn't had the forethought to keep them from hardening straight, I don't know what we'd have done.

'How we gonna get them over the horses?' I asked, settling back on my haunches, my wrists resting on my knees, my hands dangling limply. I was glad the man I uncovered had turned out to be the dark, scruffy sergeant and not the golden-haired captain I'd killed.

I didn't want to look at him; I certainly didn't want to have to touch
him.

My mother shook out the length of rope she'd brought and stooped
to tie one end around the waist of Sergeant Jules Boyles. 'Leverage,'
she said, and threw the other end over the shadowy beam overhead.
'Bring up one of the horses, Amrie, and hold him steady while
Mahalia and I lift the sergeant.'

Sometimes in my dreams I still see that scene, wrapped always
in the golden light of the lantern, dust motes shimmering in the
close damp air. The storm raged on around us, thrashing the limbs
of the unseen live oaks and pecans of the yard and banging a loose
board somewhere in the night. The rain hammered on the roof
and shot off the eaves with a force that swaddled us in a deafening
roar.

'Easy boy. Easy,' I whispered, bringing the first horse up, the
shuffle of his hooves muffled by the loose hay. 'There.'

The big gray shivered nervously, spooked by the smell of blood
and death. His ears flickered, nostrils distending on a panicked
snort as a streak of lightning lit up the shadowy interior of the
barn in a blinding flash. I watched my mother and Mahalia wrap
the other end of the rope around their fists, legs braced, the muscles
of their backs tightening and bunching.

Both had always been strong women. But they were even stronger
now, their bodies honed and hardened by years of the kind of work
that had once been the province of only men. The dead Federal rose
slowly into the air, his body frozen in the bizarre U-shape into
which my mother had positioned it before death hardened muscles
and joints in a fixed lock. The rope creaked, and he spun in a slow,
graceless pivot, arms and legs suspended downward in a way that
sent spindly, nightmarish shadows dancing across the barn's dirt
floor and rough walls.

'Amrie,' said my mother, jerking my attention to her again. 'Back
the horse up beneath him now. Quickly.'

'Back, boy,' I said softly, pressing the horse's heavy left shoulder.
'Atta boy. Whoa.'

Mama and Mahalia let the dead man's weight settle face down
across the saddle. The horse shuddered, head jerking up.

'Easy boy. Easy,' I said as my mother moved quickly to lash the
Federal's extended arms and legs together.

'Don't you think maybe we oughta cover him with an old blanket or something?' asked Mahalia, hugging herself against the cold, her face a mask of terror.

My mother looked up from testing her knots, a lock of wet hair falling over one eye. 'Even with a blanket over him, he'd still look like a dead man. And I frankly don't have any blankets to spare. If anyone sees us, they're going to know what we're hauling – blanket or no blanket.'

'Maybe. But at least it wouldn't be obvious we're hauling dead Federals.'

Mama just grunted and went to untie the rope from the sergeant's waist. Then she hunkered down beside the golden-haired captain.

Like the sergeant, he lay on his side, bent at the waist, arms extended over his head as my mother had positioned him. She'd also removed my arrow from his back and hitched up his trousers. The cold calculation of all this wise premeditation troubled me, even as I had reason to be grateful for the wisdom and fortitude that had inspired it.

I hadn't wanted to look at his face again, but I couldn't help it. His lower jaw had sagged in death and was now locked open, as were his eyes. But there was no doubt in my mind that these were the eyes of a dead man. They were sunken into his head and glassy, like the eyes of the lifeless bass Finn and I used to string on a line and leave cooling in the water while we kept fishing.

'Amrie,' said my mother gently. 'The other horse.'

Afterward, I would look back on that dreadful night and marvel at the ruthless single-mindedness with which two women and a girl could go about disposing of the corpses of the men they'd killed. The war had taught us so many things: how to spin wool and weave cloth; how to fashion our own shoes from old saddle leather and sturdy canvas; how to plow fields and mend fences.

Now it had taught us to kill, and how to protect ourselves from the consequences of those killings with a grim purposefulness that would have been unimaginable even a year before.

What we called Cat Island wasn't really an island at all, but a low area of bottomland and swamp that stretched along the Mississippi to the northwest of St Francisville. A tangle of bald cypress and tupelo, oak and sweetgum, sugarberry and wild azalea, it had once been riverbed but was now marshland cut by sluggish bayous and shadowy lakes rimmed with rushes and cane that thrashed and bent with the wind.

Here lived black bear and white-tailed deer, bobcat and mink, river otter and deadly water moccasins that slithered through the thick undergrowth of dewberry and wood sorrel and dark green, feathery ferns. No one had ever bothered to build levees here, so the land flooded every spring when the river rose with the northern thaws. Normally much of the area would still have been inundated in June. But this year, the high water had peaked early, with long stretches of dry land already emerging from the festering muck.

Even in daylight, it was a forbidding place. At night, with lightning flashing on the underbelly of thickly bunching clouds and silhouetting the tops of the wind-thrashed trees against a ghastly white glow, it was terrifying. I could hear night-feeding bass flopping in some unseen stretch of bayou and a furtive rustling in the dark wet tangle of thick saplings and underbrush up ahead. I tried to tell myself it was just a possum or a raccoon. But my heart pounded in my chest, and my mouth went dry.

We cut down the bluff to the bottomland, then followed a narrow trail that snaked along the side of a low ridge. The wet humus underfoot was slippery and treacherous, the air heavy with the stench of dank vegetation, sour mud, and decay. I led the first horse, with Mama and Mahalia following. No one spoke, although whether it was from fear or respect for the dead, I couldn't have said. I tried not to focus on the muffled thump of the horses' hooves, tried not to think about the two dead men tied face down across their saddles and growing colder with each step.

Then a sizzle of lightning showed a streak of white just ahead, a ghostly gleam against a darkly sullen stretch of water that appeared for only an instant and then was gone.

'There it is,' I said.

The path opened up into a grassy stretch along the bank of the bayou. A massive felled oak tree, its bark long ago eaten away by beetles, the smooth inner wood bleached by the action of sun and rain, lay with its rotting root mass raised to the sky, its broken top thrusting out over a motionless expanse of water that brooded dark and unknowable in the night. The gaping yaw left when some forgotten hurricane toppled the tree and tore its roots from the earth had half filled over time with silt and dead leaves and debris. But it was still deep and wide enough to form a tomb.

My mother paused beside me. Her face glistened with rain, her hair hung in dark wet clumps, her chest rose and fell with a combination of exertion and what I realized with shock was a rare agitation she was trying desperately not to show. Then her gaze met mine, her eyes fierce with a determination that was at once tortured and vulnerable. And in that one, unforgettable moment I felt closer to her than I ever had before, even as I was simultaneously aware of all the many aspects of my mother that I did not know, that I had never known and that would probably always elude me – the parts of herself that she kept hidden away from me, or perhaps that I had simply never bothered to try to understand. And it came to me that, for the first time, I was looking at her as a woman with her own needs and fears and wants, rather than simply as my mother.

She said, 'I wish it was farther from town.'

'I know,' I said. 'But I'm afraid I'll get lost if we try to go much further.'

'It's far enough for me,' said Mahalia.

My mother nodded and turned to untie the shovel we'd lashed to one of the saddles.

We took turns scooping out the sodden leaf litter and loose dirt. I tried not to think about the beetles and spiders that could be lurking there.

'That's good,' said my mother at last.

I looked up at her. Lightning forked across the sky, a quick slither that reminded me of the darting strike of a snake's tongue. The rain had eased up by now, but the wind still blew showers of droplets out of the leaves of the nearby stand of willows to pepper our faces with a cold sting and dimple the dark water beside us.

I saw her throat work as she swallowed. Then she turned to fumble with the knots at the captain's wrists.

Her fingers were clumsy with cold and exhaustion and fear. The wind whipped and flattened her sodden skirts against her legs and flapped the hem of my father's oilcloth coat. I sank the blade of the shovel deep into the soft earth and went to help her.

We brought the horse to the edge of the hollow and shoved the body off the saddle. He flopped back into the hole, arms still extended stiffly over his head, his face turned up to the moonlight that peeked unexpectedly from the shifting clouds overhead. His skin was pale and puckered now with gooseflesh as if he were cold. For one hideous moment, shadows from a fingerlike wisp of cloud moving across the surface of the moon made it look as if he breathed.

'Amrie,' said my mother, touching my arm. I turned away.

The sergeant fell half in, half out of the cradle of roots, so that my mother had to clamber down into the muddy hole with the two dead men and arrange them better. I told myself that once you've dissected a week-old cadaver pulled from the warm waters of the Mississippi, death must surely lose some of its horror. But I noticed a pinched look about her nostrils when she climbed out of the hollow, and decided maybe there were limits to the callousness that sort of experience imparts.

We stripped the saddles and blankets from the horses and threw them in on top of the men, along with their knives and pistols, their cartridge boxes and canteens, the pocket watch and other personal items we had found. There was much that we could have used, for materials of any kind were rare and precious these days. But Mama said it was too dangerous to keep anything – and the truth was, we wanted no part of any of it, anyway.

We worked silently to cover them with the soil and leaf litter we'd shoveled out. I could hear an owl hooting in the distance and, nearer, the soft plop of some night creature hitting the water of the bayou. Now that it had quit raining, a swarm of insects descended upon us. The wind had died, and the air was thick and breathless, like steam rising from a boiling pot of spinach.

My mother straightened slowly. 'I think that's the best we can do.'

We stood at the edge of what was now only a shallow depression. Mahalia cleared her throat. 'I reckon we ought to say some words over them. Seems like the Christian thing to do.'

I looked at my mother. She still held the shovel clenched in her muddy hands. In the moonlight, her face shone so pale and hard it might have been carved from alabaster, and her eyes were focused on some bleak, inner place. But she nodded and swiped one crooked elbow across her wet face.

'In the midst of life we are in death,' she said solemnly. 'Oh Lord, Almighty Savior whom our sins justly displease, deliver us not unto the bitter pains of eternal death. Thou knowest, oh Lord, the secrets of our hearts. Shut not thy eyes to our prayers, but spare us Lord most holy. Amen.'

'Amen,' murmured Mahalia and I together.

It was only later that I would come to wonder precisely which sinners my mother was praying for: the dead men, or the women who had killed them.

Thirty-Six

By the time I awoke late the next morning, the sky was a clear, hard blue baked by a golden sun that dried the mud in the lane and shimmered in the fresh green grass of our empty pasture.

I came downstairs to find Mahalia sweeping the leaves and twigs blown by the storm onto the gallery. 'Where's Mama?' I asked.

'She done gone to give them horses to the Underwoods. Hear tell they refugeeing to Texas.'

I nodded. As rare and precious as horses had become around here, it seemed almost crazy to be giving away such beautiful animals. But it was simply too dangerous to keep the two distinctive thoroughbreds anywhere in the area. Texas sounded like a good place for them.

Checkers was lying in a patch of sunlight at the top of the steps, and I went to sit beside him. He spent a lot of time sleeping in the sun these days. I wrapped my arms around his neck and pressed my cheek to his sun-warmed back. For some reason, I had expected the world to look different today. But it didn't. I could hear a mockingbird singing from the branches of a nearby live oak; a small yellow butterfly hovered over the bright red flowers of the salvia that grew along the walkway, wings fluttering in the breeze. The air smelled fresh and clean from last night's rain, and the sun on my skin felt warm and good. I didn't understand how everything could be so much the same, when I was so different.

'You all right, child?' Mahalia asked, looking over at me.

'Yes,' I lied.

That afternoon, I found my mother seated in a chair beside the parlor's cold hearth. She wore a homespun dress of saffron yellow, with her hair washed and neatly drawn back into a graceful chignon. She looked nothing at all like the kind of woman who could carefully position a dead man's body in anticipation of rigor mortis or bury him in a hollow hidden deep in the swamps.

She had a gold chain wrapped around one clenched fist, and when

I asked, 'What's that?' she opened her hand to show me the trinket that lay against her palm.

It was a large locket formed of two halves of heart-shaped, clear crystal rimmed in gold and hinged to hold a familiar curl of hair.

I said, 'That's Trudi Easton's locket, isn't? What're you doin' with it?'

'I found it in Captain Dupont's pocket.'

I wondered why she hadn't shown it to me yesterday. I said, 'What're you gonna do with it?'

'I can't decide.' She held it up so that the locket swung gently on its chain, twisting first one way, then the other. 'What do you think I should do?'

I was both startled and flattered that she would ask my opinion. 'Well, it seems almost mean not to give it back to her, when we know she must be grieving at its loss. But—'

I broke off.

My mother finished the sentence for me. 'But if I give it to her, she'll realize I know how she lost it. And I'm not convinced that wouldn't be even worse.'

'You could lie,' I suggested. 'Tell her you found it.'

The heart was twirling faster now, the crystal winking in the sunlight.

'Well, I can hardly tell her the truth, can I?' She closed her fist around the spinning locket.

I stared out the window, to where Checkers had bestirred himself enough to half-heartedly chase a squirrel up a tree. I said, 'Did I do wrong? Was it wrong of me to shoot that man . . . To kill him?'

Her features contorted in a look of pinched horror. 'Oh, Amrie . . . No.' She rose from her chair and came to wrap her arms around me, hugging me close. 'You saved my life. You saved all our lives – and the lives of who knows how many other women and children those men might have gone on to kill.'

'Does that make it right?'

She drew back, her hands sill clutching my shoulders. 'Of course it does, honey. Sometimes we need to do things that otherwise would be wrong because the consequences of doing nothing are worse.'

It seemed to me that kind of argument could be used to justify a heap of awful things, including this dreadful war. I felt tears sting my eyes, and tightened the muscles of my face to keep them from falling.

She cupped my cheek with her hand, and I saw that her eyes were as wet as mine. She said, 'I wish to God you'd never been thrust into the situation those men put you in, Amrie. But I'm proud of you for what you did. It took quick thinking and courage and a fierce determination to do what needs to be done – to overcome doubts and hesitancy and react calmly in a moment of intense pressure.'

'I wasn't calm. I was shaking so hard I missed that sergeant by a good two feet when he came at me.'

'Honey, you can't feel bad about that. I . . . I'm sorry I've been so caught up in other things that I haven't taken the time I should have to talk to you about what happened. About how you're feeling.'

'But that's just it. When I shot him, I didn't feel anything. The first time I killed a deer, I cried all night. Yet I killed that Federal captain, and I didn't feel nothing.'

Her brows twitched together, and I thought she must be horrified to discover that she'd raised such a daughter. But all she said was, 'Maybe it's because that deer didn't do anything wrong. He was just living his life, being a deer in the wood. But those men . . . They came to us, Amrie. They came intending to do us terrible harm. We stopped them. No one – not God, not anyone – can say that stopping them was wrong.'

I wanted to believe her.

But I couldn't.

Only two tangible remnants of the dead Federals' disastrous intrusion into our lives now remained: Trudi Easton's locket and the leather pouch heavy with gold coins.

'We should've buried that money with them two down by the bayou,' said Mahalia as we sat on the front gallery, trying to decide what to do with our unwanted wealth. The sky was still blue overhead, the afternoon hot and airless, the Spanish moss hanging gray and still from the spreading limbs of the live oaks in the yard. Mahalia's pretty round face shimmered with perspiration, and her features were troubled. 'It be bad luck, keepin' it here.'

Mama stared out over the gallery's railing to where Checkers was rolling in the dust. 'Yet it seems wrong to simply throw it away when so many are in want.' Specie had disappeared early in the war, making the contents of that purse precious indeed.

'That be blood money,' said Mahalia. 'How you reckon that

golden-haired Federal got his hands on all that gold? He stole it, that's how – and likely killed whatever poor man or woman he took it from. I'm tellin' you, ain't no good gonna come of that money.'

'We could give it to Reverend Lewis,' I said.

They both turned to look at me.

'Well, we could, couldn't we?' I said.

'I reckon we could,' Mahalia said slowly. 'If anybody can overcome the evil attached to that gold, it's the good Lord himself.'

So Mama tied the pile of twenty dollar gold pieces up in one of Papa's plain old linen handkerchiefs, and burned the leather pouch. We decided to tell the reverend the coins had been dropped by a band of Federal raiders. Mahalia said it didn't seem right, lying to a man of the Lord that way. But Mama said the less Reverend Lewis knew about the true history of the money, the better for him, which made sense to me.

Mahalia suggested I should be the one to take it to him, because I lied better'n Mama – which is exactly the sort of thing Mahalia would say. I stuck out my tongue at her, but she only laughed, and so did Mama, and after a moment's hesitation, I joined in.

The afternoon sun was already slipping in the sky by the time I headed into town. The live oaks lining the lane throbbed with birdsong, and a warm breeze rippled the tall, vivid grass of the verge.

Most of the fields on either side of me lay abandoned and were already growing up thick with saplings and brambles. The rows of neat fences that had once lined the road were gone, torn down by Federal troops and burned for firewood or just in spite. When I reached the old Jenkins' place, I started to quicken my pace, for the house had stood empty ever since the Federals wrecked it last September. Its windows and doors were now just gaping black holes, and it always gave me the jitters, passing it. Then I spotted Ira Jenkins's skinny old orange cat, Juicy, peering at me from a thicket of rambling rose, and paused to try to coax her to come to me. But she shot away, tail flicking as she disappeared into the underbrush. The only two people she'd ever really warmed to were the Widow Jenkins and her son, Eddie. But Eddie died of measles at Camp Moore back in '61, and after the Federals destroyed her house, Ira Jenkins just kinda shriveled up and died the way so many folks seemed to be doing.

I walked on, conscious of a heavy weight of sadness settling in my chest. Too many were dead, too much of what we'd spent years building up had been destroyed, too much anger and bitterness and hate had seeped into the fabric of our being to ever be rooted out. And I was filled with a sudden rage – at the obscenely rich planters and land speculators and arrogant politicians who'd dragged us into secession, and at all those North and South who'd arrogantly, stupidly believed war could be quick and easy and glorious. But most of all, I was filled with rage at God, for allowing all this to happen.

I clutched the bundle of coins to me, my breath coming shallow and quick, the heat of the day slicking my face with sweat, and walked on.

As bad as the countryside looked these days, St Francisville was almost worse. The *Albatross* and the *Hartford* had been tacking up and down our stretch of the river for months now, periodically lobbing shells at us. Reverend Lewis told me once he thought they used his church for target practice, sighting on the bell tower to see how close they could come to hitting it. If that was true, they were lousy shots. Most of their shells seemed to fall on the nearby houses, or slam into the new domed courthouse across the street, or plow through the tombs and graves of the churchyard to churn up bones and bits of scorched coffin.

As I walked down Ferdinand Street, I wondered if they'd just had another shelling, because there seemed to be a heap of folks milling about, and the crowds grew thicker as I neared the church. A cluster of men wearing the tattered gray shell jackets, slouch hats, and black boots of Confederate cavalry had gathered in front of the white clapboard Masonic lodge that stood just across the street from the battered courthouse. As I drew closer, I recognized the tall, lean man in a silk officer's sash as William Leake. My mother had delivered Margaret Leake's last baby, and I called out, 'Hey, Cap'n Leake,' as I turned into the churchyard. He smiled and raised his hand to me.

Confederate soldiers lucky enough to be serving nearby could sometimes make it home for a short leave. It was dangerous, of course, since they had to be careful not to be caught by one of the Federal raiding parties that were always sweeping through the area. But as I cut across the shell-ravaged cemetery, I couldn't help wishing Papa hadn't been sent all the way to Virginia so he could come home sometimes, too.

There were more folks gathered about the graveyard, and I started

worrying maybe I'd stumbled onto a funeral, although I hadn't heard
of anyone dying lately. I cautiously pushed open the door to the church,
figuring it was as good a place as any to start looking for the reverend,
and was relieved to see him sitting alone in one of the pews near the
back. He didn't look like he was praying; just had his head tipped
back against the rear of the pew like a man who was feeling tired.

I hesitated, the door closing softly behind me with a snick. He
lowered his head and turned to see me.

'Ah, Amrie,' he said, pushing to his feet and coming toward me.
The church must have taken another hit from the *Albatross*, because
new cracks showed in the plaster ceiling and a couple more stained-
glass windows had been shattered and were now boarded over. 'This
is a pleasant surprise. Is there something I can do for you?'

It was one thing to sit on our gallery with Mama and Mahalia
and talk about lying to Reverend Lewis, but something else entirely
to actually stand in the church and do it. I tried to tell myself I had
a good reason for lying, but it didn't make any difference. I still
felt dishonest.

I set the bundle of gold on the table that stood behind the last
pew and had once held church bulletins, back in the day when there
was paper for such things. The coins clinked heavily, and I saw
surprise and puzzlement pucker the reverend's heavy gray eyebrows.

I said, 'We found this. Some . . . some Federal soldiers dropped
it. We didn't want to keep it so we figured the best thing to do
would be to give it to you, to . . . to help the poor soldiers' wives
and widows in the area.'

Still faintly frowning, he reached to untie the knots in the handkerchief. The crumpled linen fell open, and even in the dim light
of the half-boarded-up church, the gold gleamed. He stared at it as
if not quite comprehending what he was seeing.

'Good heavens, Amrie.' His gaze shifted to me. 'Are you certain?
This looks like a lot of money.'

'Yes, sir. I mean . . . Yes, sir; we're certain.'

I heard a shout from the street outside, followed by another.
'What's goin' on out there, anyway?' I asked. 'Did somebody die?'

'Not one of my parishioners.'

I shook my head. 'I don't understand.'

He scooped up the coins. 'Wait here while I put this someplace
safe, and I'll tell you about it. I think this is something you ought
to see.'

Thirty-Seven

What happened that day would, in time, become a part of the lore of St Francisville; a single, heart-wrenching moment of humanity that glowed all the brighter in our collective memory because of the dark horror of the years that surrounded it.

It actually began the previous afternoon, when the USS *Albatross* once again dropped anchor off the ruins of Bayou Sara and the people of St Francisville braced themselves for another round of random, senseless shelling. What they didn't know was that the *Albatross*'s commander, John Hart – a man, ironically, from the same New York town as our own Reverend Lewis – lay in his quarters wracked by swamp fever. As his delirium mounted, he seized his revolver, thumbed back the hammer with a trembling hand, put the muzzle to his head, and squeezed the trigger.

'Did you know him?' I asked Reverend Lewis as we walked across the churchyard toward the street. A hush had fallen over the crowd; the only sound the swish-swish of the ladies' fans.

'No,' he said, squinting up at the hot sun. 'But then, it's been many years since I was in Schenectady. I'm told he leaves behind a widow and two young children. It's tragic. Very tragic.'

'Why'd he do it?'

'Who knows? They say he was in great pain from some other, long-standing malady. Perhaps it simply proved too much for his fevered mind.'

I stared down the bluff toward the river, where a longboat flying a white flag rocked gently against Bayou Sara's dilapidated old wharf. A warm wind kicked up choppy white caps on the water and brought us the smell of fish mingling with the pinch of old charred wood from the burned-out town below.

It seemed that before his death, Commander Hart had expressed a wish that he be given a Masonic burial rather than having his body consigned to the muddy waters of the Mississippi. And so his fellow officers had put ashore early that morning under the same white flag to ask if there were any Masons in the area.

In fact, St Francisville was home to Louisiana's oldest Masonic lodge. Not only that, but the Senior Warden, Captain William Leake of the 1st Louisiana Cavalry, just happened to be in town on furlough. He met with the Federal Navy men and assured them that as a soldier he was duty-bound to cooperate in the burial of his enemy's dead, and as a Mason he would be honored to perform the service for a fallen brother.

And so, standing beside Reverend Lewis at the edge of a cemetery plowed by the *Albatross*'s shells, I watched three blue-uniformed ship's officers step ashore, followed by sailors and a squad of Marines at trail arms. The sun glistened on their brass buttons and brought a sheen of sweat to their faces. They loaded the plain wooden coffin of the *Albatross*'s commander onto a simple cart drawn by a black mule and started up the hill, a snare drum beating a slow, mournful dirge.

'Them Yankees is luckier'n they know. Where the blazes did Leake find anyone hereabouts with a mule and cart?' muttered someone, and a few people nearby tittered softly.

As the funeral cortege neared the top of the bluff where Captain Leake and his fellow Confederate Masons waited, I drew back. I didn't want to be anywhere near any Federals, alive or dead. But I didn't feel like I could leave, either. And so I watched through the silent, moss-draped oaks and lichen-covered tombstones as the men in blue and gray uniforms, together, lifted the simple coffin to their shoulders and carried it through the bomb-ravaged churchyard.

I stayed well back from the others, wandering the churchyard as I listened to the two funeral services, Episcopal and Masonic, drift on the warm breeze.

'. . . through our belief in the mercy of God, may we confidently hope that our souls will bloom in eternal spring . . .'

The solemnly intoned words seemed to echo off the shattered belfry above us. I stared down at the bits of blue and red glass at my feet, fragments from the broken stained-glass windows that sparkled in the late afternoon sunlight. And I found myself wondering how anyone who believed in a Christian God could use one of His churches for target practice, or how men truly dedicated to His teachings could lob shells into a town filled with nothing but terrified women and children.

'Most glorious God, Author of all good and giver of all mercy . . .'

I realized my steps had led me without conscious thought to

Simon's grave, and I sank down into the grass. Drawing my bare feet up under my dress, I wrapped my arms around my bent knees and listened to the voices drone on and on.

Then, finally, I heard a clink of arms and a guttural shout. 'Ready. Aim. *Fire*.'

I jerked, the boom of the discharging rifles startling the sparrows from the leafy oak overhead so that they rose up shrieking into the clear blue sky.

'Ready. Aim. *Fire*.'

I flinched again, and then tensed in expectation of the third volley.

'Ready. Aim. *Fire*.'

The pungent odor of burnt gunpowder carried on the breeze, followed by the melancholy sound of a bugle that floated over the churchyard. The haunting call swelled, one clear, piercing note following the other. I felt the poignant melody of the piece wash over me, pure and sweet and so mournful it was like a physical ache inside me. I pressed my face against my knees, the worn homespun cloth of my dress rough against my skin.

How could men who considered each other deadly enemies also see themselves as brothers, I wondered? Why could they stop a war for a day to cooperate in the burial of one man, yet not find a way to end that war and save the lives of hundreds of thousands?

The last of the bugle call faded away. I heard the tramp of marching feet, the tap-tap of the drum, the soft murmur of voices. I stayed where I was.

It was some time later when a shadow fell over the sun-spangled grass beside me, and I looked up to find Reverend Lewis watching me.

He said, 'It was a fine thing, was it not?'

The afternoon heat had brought a warm flush to his cheeks, and he had a faint smile on his face. I noticed for the first time just how rusty and threadbare his cassock was, and where his surplice was singed from when the vestry took a hit in one of the Federals' recent shellings.

I wanted to say, *Was it really, Reverend?* Instead, I said, 'Are they gone?'

He nodded. 'They invited Captain Leake and his men aboard the *Albatross* for refreshments, but the captain declined.'

'Reckon maybe he thought the Yankees would arrest them.'

'Oh, Amrie . . . I don't think so.'

I stared out across the churchyard to where the aged sexton was shoveling dirt into the Federal commander's grave, the scrape of the metal against earth carrying clearly through the trees. 'Seems funny, him lying here amongst our own dead. After all the *Albatross* has done to us.'

'We are all the same unto the angels and are all the children of God, being the children of the resurrection,' said the reverend softly.

I thought about the two Federals that Mahalia and I had killed, lying now in unhallowed ground deep in the swamps below the bluff. And I felt the urge to blurt out the truth of it all to Reverend Lewis, to seek his gentle wisdom and guidance, or maybe simply to ask for his forgiveness and God's absolution.

But I didn't.

He said, 'We can't let this war harden our hearts and poison our souls, Amrie. That is why what happened here today is something to be cherished, because it shows that even in the midst of war, some shreds of our common humanity remain.'

'And if that Commander Hart hadn't been a Mason, Reverend? Would this have happened? Seems to me, people can't stop dividing the world into folks they think are like them, and everybody else. The only thing that changes is how they decide which folks are like them and which folks aren't.'

He looked troubled, and I wished I hadn't said anything.

I pushed to my feet, conscious of the lengthening shadows and the fierceness easing out of the tea-colored light as the day stretched into evening.

He said, 'It's a start, Amrie. When this war is over, it's memories like this – sentiments like these – that will help us begin to heal and learn to live together again.'

His words shocked me, for it was the first time I'd heard anyone suggest out loud that the South wouldn't eventually prevail, that peace might come not with a begrudging coexistence and hard-won independence but with our ultimate, crushing defeat.

In the deepening shadows, the tombstones around us looked cool and gray and achingly peaceful. I smelled the tang of dank old stone and the mustiness of freshly turned earth mingling with the sweet perfume of a rambling pink rose tumbling over the palings of a nearby rusty iron fence. 'We can't lose,' I said, my voice husky. 'We can't have gone through all of this only to lose in the end.'

The reverend's mouth flexed soundlessly, his gaze not meeting mine, his features wan and sad.

'We can't,' I said again.

But I'd learned by then that saying something and making it happen are two very different things.

Thirty-Eight

That night I lay awake with my heart pounding, my thoughts leaping from one alarming scenario to the next. All my life, Mahalia had been telling me, 'Child, you borrow trouble worse'n anybody I ever knowed. You spend so much time frettin' about what might happen tomorrow that you forget to just enjoy today.'

But I couldn't help it. It had occurred to me that if the *Albatross*'s officers would go to such lengths to give their commander a Masonic burial, then what would Gabriel Dupont's comrades do when they realized he was missing? How long, I wondered, would it take them to become alarmed when the captain and his sergeant failed to return to camp? A day? Two? How long before they realized that something more serious than a lame horse must have befallen the two men?

How long before they sent out search parties to scour the countryside?

I tried to tell myself that no one could possibly have known the two men had come here to our house. But was that true? What if they'd told someone their intended destination? What if some passerby had chanced to see them riding up our drive? Or what if . . . What if someone had seen us leading the two heavily burdened horses deep into the swamp that dreadful night?

I told myself I was being foolish, that there was nothing to tie us to the dead men. But as I watched the shadows of the wind-tossed live oaks move on my wall and listened to the whine of the insects buzzing against my mosquito bar, my imagination conjured for me a dozen hideous scenarios.

It was a long time before I slept.

The next morning, Mahalia and I were washing our swamp-stained clothes in big kettles set over slow fires in the yard when we heard a distant rumble start up and then go on and on and on.

Over the past few weeks, we'd grown accustomed to the Federals' relentless nightly bombardments of Port Hudson. But this was something both more intense and ominously different. I lifted the three-pronged stick I was using to stir the clothes in the steamy, soapy water and tapped it against the side of the kettle. A warm breeze was shifting the willows and persimmons that grew along the gulley, and carrying the sweet fragrance of the honeysuckle scrambling over the ruins of an old nearby shed.

'What you reckon's happenin'?' Mahalia asked, eyes wide in a slack, heat-sheened face as she stared toward the south.

I shook my head. 'I don't know.'

An hour later, the bombardment stilled, and the air filled with a chorus of birdsong, as if all of nature had been holding its breath along with us.

But it wasn't long before we heard the relentless crash and roar begin all over again and continue the rest of the day and on into the night. Then, just before dawn, the wind picked up harder, blowing out of the south and bringing us the pinching reek of gunpowder and burned timbers and a foul, indefinable odor that we knew now to recognize as the stench of battle.

'I guess them Yankees got tired of waiting for their siege of Port Hudson to work and decided to launch an all-out assault,' said Mr Marks later that morning when he stopped by to sit on our front gallery and drink some of Mama's okra coffee. 'I don't rightly see how a few thousand starving men can hold out against an army of thirty-five thousand, but there's a heap of folks think they'll do it.'

'They're very determined,' said Mama.

I sat at the top of the steps with Checkers while he and Mama talked for a time about the siege and what it would mean for Vicksburg if Port Hudson fell. But after a while, Mr Marks scratched his chin and worked around to the real reason he'd walked out to see us.

'We got a letter yesterday from my Mary's young cousin, Ned, from Richmond. He was taken prisoner at Fredericksburg, you know, but they paroled him after he lost one of his legs in a Yankee hospital. He says to tell you he saw your brother, Bo, while he was there.'

A vast, informal web of communication existed, spreading throughout the South to carry news of sick, wounded, and captured loved ones to those with no other way of hearing what they so desperately wanted to know. But I'd noticed that folks were always hesitant and embarrassed when they brought us word of Bo. When the loved one was fighting for the Federals, things got a bit awkward.

I glanced over at Mama and saw her face go pale. She said, 'Bo has been hurt?'

'Oh, no, ma'am! Didn't mean to make you think that. Bo was at the hospital visiting a sick friend. But he recognized Ned and come over and talked to him. Helped get Ned released, he did. Bo's a lieutenant colonel now, you know.'

'No, I didn't know,' said Mama. 'And how is Ned?'

'Well, you know Ned. He's frettin' that no girl will want to marry him, now that he can't dance.'

'I'm sure he has no cause to worry,' said Mama, smiling. Then her smile slipped a bit. The truth was, so many men were dying that the South was full of girls and young widows who were never going to have husbands.

Mr Marks set aside his empty cup and rose to his feet with a grimace. 'There is one other thing I wanted to tell you about. Word is, a bunch of Federals was ranging along Plank Road yesterday afternoon. Seems they're looking for a couple of their men who've gone missing. I doubt we'll hear much more about it as long as things are heating up down at Port Hudson. But it doesn't hurt to be on your guard.'

'Missing men?' said Mama, as calmly as if they were discussing a couple of straying cows.

'Mmm. A captain and his sergeant. I'll let you know if I hear anything more.'

Mama walked with him to the steps, then stood beside me while Mr Marks headed back down the drive. The wind rustled the Spanish moss and cast shifting patterns of light and shadow over his shoulders and bowed head.

I waited until he was almost to the lane, then said, 'What do we do if the Federals come here asking about those men?'

'We act as if we're the most weak, foolish, and hopelessly incapable females they ever met,' said my mother, and turned toward the house.

Her idea might have worked – if the Union officer who rode into our yard two weeks later hadn't already tangled with my mother once before.

His name was Lieutenant Lucas Beckham, and he came back into our lives the day after my thirteenth birthday.

It had rained that morning, a light sun shower that left the air balmy and the grass fresh and green in the fields. I'd been in the woods gathering blackberries, and was coming up out of the gully when I saw half a dozen blue-coated men turn their horses in through our gate.

The pail slipped from my fingers, the fat ripe berries spilling in the long grass as I ran across the yard and up the steps to the back gallery.

The central hall was still dark and cool with morning shadows, and the front door stood open to catch the breeze. When I'd left to go blackberrying, Mama had been taking the whalebone out of her fraying old stays so that she could reuse it in a new garment she was making of homespun. But she must have heard the approaching horses because she was now standing on the front gallery, her bent elbows cradled in her palms, her spine straight as she watched the Federals ride up to the house.

Once before, I'd hidden in the hall while she confronted a group of soldiers. Not this time. I shut Checkers inside and went to stand beside her at the top of the steps. She cast me a quick, sideways glance. But she didn't tell me to go back inside.

They were near enough that I could see them now: an officer, his sergeant, and four troopers, all from the 4th Wisconsin Volunteers, which had recently become a mounted infantry regiment. I heard Mama suck in her breath and knew that she, too, had recognized the young, dark-haired lieutenant at their head. It was the same lieutenant who had ridden into our yard looking to impress slaves after the Battle of Baton Rouge.

They reined in at the base of the stairs, horses sidling and tossing their heads as if sensing the agitation of their riders. We could see no bundles of loot tied to their saddles, but that didn't mean anything. Maybe they were just getting started.

The lieutenant tipped his hat, his features lean and browned by the hot Southern sun. 'Mornin', ma'am,' he said. He let his gaze wander over the house and yard. The past year had been hard on our place.

'Lieutenant,' said my mother, staring coldly down at him.

'We're looking for two of our men. A Captain Gabriel Dupont and Sergeant Jules Boyle. We think they may have come through here several weeks ago.'

'What's the matter, Lieutenant?' said my mother, her voice dripping with amused condescension. 'Have you misplaced them?'

I threw her a frowning glance. If this was her idea of acting like a weak and stupid female, she needed to take lessons from the likes of Jettie Irvinel or Mary LeBlanc. The problem was, there was something about this particular lieutenant that affected my mother in an indefinable but significant way. But I wasn't old enough yet to figure out what it was.

He stared at her, his gaze steady and unreadable and yet vaguely unsettling. 'In a manner of speaking, ma'am; yes.'

She said, 'The last group of Union soldiers we had through here rounded up what was left of our livestock and stole or destroyed much of value in the house. I don't know if your missing men were amongst them or not. What do they look like?'

He kept his features carefully composed, although his horse moved restlessly beneath him. 'Captain Dupont is of above average size and frame, with long gold curls and blue eyes, while his sergeant is shorter, heavier, and dark.'

'I don't believe I have seen them,' she said. 'Perhaps they deserted. It does happen, does it not?'

The lieutenant had his hands draped over the pommel of his saddle, and he studied the backs of them as if he found the subject of their conversation distasteful. And I thought, *He might be out searching for Gabriel Dupont, but he doesn't like the man. He doesn't like him at all.*

He said, 'Captain Dupont wouldn't desert.'

'So certain?'

He raised his gaze to her face. 'Yes.'

'Then perhaps he was taken prisoner by one of the cavalry patrols out of Camp Moore.'

'There've been no reports of it.'

The breeze gusted up, warm and sweet and billowing the leaves of the live oaks against the soft blue sky. 'Is he a good friend of yours?' asked my mother.

'A friend? No. But he is a fellow officer.' The lieutenant gathered his reins. 'He's also the nephew of the Governor of Wisconsin.'

Oh, God, oh, God, I thought in a rush of panic. I forced myself to focus on the smooth coolness of the gallery's floorboards beneath my bare feet and the wet odor of dew-dampened vegetation and earth rising from the tangle of salvia and indigo that grew across the front of the house.

'Ah,' said my mother with an assumption of calm indifference that filled me with both awe and admiration. 'An important personage.'

'Yes.'

'Then I hope you find him. Quickly.'

His gaze met hers, and something passed between them, something no less real for being unspoken. He said, 'If we don't, I'll be back.' Then he wheeled his horse with a curt order to the sergeant beside him.

We watched the horses' hooves churn up the damp earth of our drive as they thundered toward the gate. Then I sank down on the top step, my arms wrapped around my knees. 'Oh, Jesus,' I said softly. 'They ain't never gonna stop lookin' for him. Not if his uncle is the Governor of Wisconsin.'

'Don't say "ain't",' murmured my mother. But she said it half-heartedly, and I knew her thoughts were with the Federal lieutenant she was watching turn down the sunlit lane toward town.

Thirty-Nine

A cool, misty morning a few days later brought an unexpected letter from Finn.

> Hey Amri,
>
> I said I'd write, so here tis. I'm with Kernel Parker now. We been harryin the Fedrals camped out around Port Hudson. It weren't easy at first, livin in the saddle, but I've got to where I don't mind it atall. Got shot once already, but it weren't bad, and I'm fine now.
>
> You mite be interested to know Hiram Tucker was ridin with us, but he run off last week. I heard tell he joined some bushwhackers down by New Iberia, but I don't know for sure. He was a good fighter but a mean, nasty varmit for all that. I know you never did like him, and I gotta say I'm glad he's gone.

Tell yer momma, Mahalia, and Castile hey for me, and maybe go tell Ma I'm all right? I know she worries, but she cain't read so there ain't no use me tryin to write her. I'd make this longer but I always did find writin a chore.

Yer friend,

Finn

A few days later I walked into St Francisville to take a package of Mama's herbs to Mrs Caine, whose boy, Spencer, was feeling poorly. While I was there, I stopped by to tell Castile about Finn.

Castile had lost most of his stock back in May, when General Banks's three divisions swept through Bayou Sara and St Francisville on their way to lay siege to Port Hudson. All he had left were the half-dozen mules and few horses he'd kept pastured down by the creek, and he'd decided to just leave them there and hope the Yankees never found them.

These days he spent most of his time hunting and fishing, selling or trading the meat to anyone in town able to afford it and giving what he could to those poor families who'd starve without it.

He was in his front yard filleting a mess of catfish when I walked up to him. 'Hey, Amrie,' he said, his eyes crinkling into a smile when he looked up at me. 'How you doin', child? Mahalia told me y'all had them Federals to yor house, lookin' for them two missing men.'

I studied his face as he reached for the next fish. But if Mahalia had told him of the part we'd played in the two Federals' disappearance, I saw no sign of it.

I perched on a nearby log, the sun warm on my shoulders, a soft breeze billowing the pale green leaves of the nearby willows against a clear blue sky. 'That lieutenant, he says one of the missing men is the nephew of the Governor of Wisconsin.'

Castile clicked his tongue against the roof of his mouth and shook his head. 'That ain't good. No, siree. That mean they ain't ever gonna stop lookin' for him.'

I watched Castile run his knife up the belly of the catfish, then hook his thumb in its lower jaw. 'You still ain't heard nothin' about Leo?'

He stilled for a moment, then tossed the fish guts away in a quick, jerky motion.

I said, 'You have heard something, haven't you?'

He nodded, the muscles of his jaw bunching. 'Ain't nothin' I want gettin' out, Amrie, but Leo done joined the Union army.'

I stared at him. In the first, heady days of the war, the *gens de couleur libres* of New Orleans had formed the 1st Louisiana Native Guard, with over fifteen hundred free blacks signing up to fight for the Confederacy. They'd served for a year before being disbanded when the Federals overran New Orleans. We'd heard that some of those soldiers and their officers had now joined the Union Army to form the nucleus of the Federals' own 1st Louisiana Native Guard. I knew lots of folks felt hurt and betrayed by the whole idea of it, and I had to admit, the thought of Leo fighting against us when we were struggling so hard just to survive hit me like a fist in my stomach.

'Is he down at Port Hudson, Castile?' I asked.

He nodded. 'With the Corps d'Afrique, they're callin' it.'

I'd heard that when the Federals first started enlisting freed slaves in their army, folks in other parts of the South had laughed, convinced that Africans were by nature cowards. Folks said that's why they were slaves, because they lacked the kind of courage that had driven the Indian tribes to fight to extinction rather than allow themselves to be subjugated by the white men. But free men of color had served in the militias of Louisiana for decades and fought bravely against the British at the Battle of New Orleans. No one I knew was surprised by the news that the black Federal units besieging Port Hudson were fighting with a tenacity and valor that was changing the thinking and attitudes of many of the Northern men fighting beside them.

I said, 'My Uncle Bo is fighting for the Union, Castile.'

'I know, Amrie. Reckon I wouldn't have told you, if'n he wasn't.' He looked over at me, and we shared a wry smile.

Then a shout went up out in the street, followed by another and another, and the sound of running feet.

We saw the widow Carlyle's Tom dashing past, and Castile hollered at him, 'What is it? What's happening?'

Tom swung around to look at us, eyes wide, a big grin I'll never forget sliding across his face. It told me all I needed to know about where Tom's sympathies lay in that long, dreadful war. 'Vicksburg done surrendered!'

'When?'

'Three days ago. On the fourth of July!'

We were still reeling from the news when, less than twenty-four hours later, word came of General Lee's awful, massive defeat at someplace up in Pennsylvania called Gettysburg. The day after that, the starving garrison of Port Hudson surrendered.

The Federals were now in complete control of the entire Mississippi River. The Confederacy had been split in two.

It was at dusk that Monday when Mama looked up from tending her herb garden to see a barefoot skeleton of a man in butternut rags stumbling up the lane. The breeze was cool and sweet, and the setting sun had painted pink and purple streaks across the fading sky. He paused and wavered for a moment, his face gray, his eyes rolling back in his head.

She ran to catch him as he fell. 'Amrie!' she called. 'Mahalia! Come help me! Quick.'

His name was Private Beni Toggard, and he'd somehow managed to walk the ten miles from Port Hudson before his strength gave out on him. He said he was only twenty-two, but he looked like an old man, his skin sunken and sagging against bones so prominent it hurt to look at him. I didn't know a body could get that skinny and still live.

'He won't be alive much longer if we don't get food into him,' said Mama.

She nursed the emaciated, half-dead soldier with turkey broth and teas brewed from the herbs in her garden. A couple of days later he was well enough to sit up in bed and talk. In a soft Mississippi drawl, he said the Federals had carried off the officers from Port Hudson to prison, but paroled most of the enlisted men. He'd been on his way home when he collapsed at our gate.

'Where's home?' Mama asked, dipping another spoonful of turkey broth and holding it to his lips. He was still too weak to be of much use feeding himself.

He swallowed and said, 'Natchez.'

'Ah.' She dipped more broth from the bowl in her hand. 'Do you know Corporal Eugene Price?'

'I did, yes, ma'am.'

Did.

She froze, her gaze locking with mine.

I said hoarsely, 'Is he all right?'

Private Toggard glanced over at me, then back at Mama, his young-old features even more pinched than they'd been before. 'I'm sorry, ma'am; I reckon y'all don't know?'

'Know what?'

'He was blown to smithereens down at Port Hudson almost a month ago. A Yankee shell hit his bunker.'

I was sitting on a straight-backed chair near the bed, my hands curling around the wooden front edge of the seat to grip it hard. I said, 'You're sure?'

He nodded slowly.

'Amrie,' said my mother as I jumped up so fast I sent the chair skittering backward across the floor. '*Amrie!*'

I kept running, out the door and down the steps and across the yard. I was aware of Checkers barking as he tried to keep up, but I didn't stop. I ran until the cool shadows of the trees closed in around me and the earth grew soft with leaf litter beneath my feet.

I could not have said why the death of Corporal Eugene Price affected me so profoundly. True, I'd grown fond of him in the short time his life had crossed with ours, but I'd lost so many who were much dearer to me. Perhaps it was what struck me as the senselessness of it all. Why would any benevolent God save a man from a painful brush with death after the Battle of Baton Rouge, only to blow him to pieces in the defense of a bastion that was fated to fall anyway?

I suppose that at some level and despite all that I had witnessed, I still clung to a child's naïve belief that life should be fair, and that the events of our days should make sense.

I was yet to learn just how wrong I could be.

Forty

The black-edged letter from Adelaide came a week later.

Uncle Henley was dead, she wrote, felled not by a Federal bullet or cannon ball but by a typhoid epidemic that swept through his camp in Mississippi. Also dead was Chesney, the woman who had been with Adelaide from the day she was born; her heart had given out on her one rainy morning. She'd died in Adelaide's arms. But all Adelaide said was, 'I know it's odd, but for some reason I always thought that, of the two of us, I'd go first.'

The letter was tersely written, its words carefully parsed to betray not a hint of the emotion or grief its author was surely feeling. Only the shaky penmanship gave her away. Then she added a postscript: 'The Federal raiding parties in the area grow more vicious every day. If Mandy had her way, she'd take Wills and refugee to Texas. I told her Dunbars are made of sterner stuff.'

I found it hard to believe that Uncle Henley was dead – had been dead for weeks by the time we received the letter. Sometimes reports of deaths were wrong, so I held out hope for a while. But then word filtered through to us from a friend's cousin who'd been with Uncle Henley when he died, so we knew it had to be true.

For some reason, Uncle Henley's death made Papa, Uncle Bo, Uncle Tate – everyone we knew who was away at war – seem that much more vulnerable. I tried to tell myself that kind of thinking was irrational, but it really wasn't. As bad as this war had been before, it was now getting worse. For everyone.

The first week in August, I went with my mother to Jackson, a college town nestled in the rich, rolling farmland to the east of St Francisville. Many of the sick and wounded paroled from Port Hudson had made their way to the military hospitals there and at Clinton. They'd always been short of medicines, but word had reached us that their situation was now desperate. So Mama decided to do what she could to help.

I watched her agonize over the carefully hoarded glass vials of liquids and pills in the cupboard of what had once been Papa's office, but that I now thought of as hers. Some, like the castor oil, balsam of wild cherry, and spirits of lavender, she could concoct herself from her own herb garden or the wild plants of the surrounding woods and marshlands. But stuff like the Peruvian bark, the Dove's powders, and the basilicon salve would be irreplaceable.

'If you give it all away, whatcha gonna do when folks around here get sick or hurt?' I asked as she packed her selections into a basket.

She looked up at me, her features solemn with the gravity of the choices she was being forced to make. 'Men are dying, Amrie. I have to give what I can.'

We left early the next morning, when the air was still heavy with mist and the sun no more than a pink glow on the murky horizon. The breeze was gentle and sweet, the oaks and magnolias that lined the lane heavily in leaf and pulsing with birdsong, and I found myself giving a little skip as I walked. Part of my unexpected lightheartedness came, I suppose, from the natural relief of moving away from the river and its ever-looming threat of Federal gunboats, of temporarily leaving behind all the pressures and endless fears that had come to constrict our days. But part of it came from the mist itself, which not only hid the untended fields and burned farmhouses from my sight, but also seemed to wrap us in a protective cocoon that was utterly illusory but comforting nonetheless.

I said to my mother, 'Remember the time Papa gave a guest lecture at the college in Jackson, and we all went with him?' Simon had been alive then. Normally I didn't like to talk about memories that included Simon. But for some reason I found the ache of it a little more bearable today.

She glanced over at me. She held the handle of her basket looped over her arm, its weight balanced against one hip. In the soft light of dawn, she looked relaxed, almost happy, and I wondered if she felt it, too – that feeling of brief escape from a brutal reality that had been grinding us down too long. 'You mean the time you both ate so many cream puffs you got sick – and Checkers, too, because you fed some to him?' She laughed, the sound ringing out lighthearted and clear. And I felt for a moment as if I were spinning back in time.

When I was a little girl, my mother would take me for walks in the woods. She'd tell me the names of the yellow and purple wildflowers that splashed the meadows in autumn, and the jays, larks, and cardinals that flickered through the woods in flashes of blue and yellow and scarlet. Even as I grew older, we'd sometimes go for a stroll to the top of the bluff and watch the big, white, gingerbread-draped steamboats, the flatboats and cotton-laden barges spinning away down the river toward New Orleans.

But I couldn't remember when we'd last spent time alone together like this, just the two of us, walking and talking. I'd always blamed the war and my mother herself for the loss of such moments. But it occurred to me now to wonder if maybe I'd been the one pushing her away, if this was all just a part of growing up. And I felt a melancholy rush of yearning for a past that was forever lost to me.

By the time we reached the outskirts of Jackson, the sun was well up, sucking the last of the coolness from the morning and drenching the gently rolling hills in a fierce light. Once, Jackson had been a prosperous town, its graceful streets shaded by leafy oaks, its venerable brick and frame buildings adorned with balconies and white-columned porches and slate roofs softened by gray-green lichen. The presence here of Centenary College and so many prestigious preparatory and finishing schools had led folks to call it the 'Athens of the South'. But the college and the other schools were all closed now, students and faculty alike gone off to war. We walked down rutted, nearly deserted streets, where white paint peeled from cracked columns and weeds choked the pink and yellow roses running rampant over rusting iron fences. Jackson might lie beyond the reach of the Federal gunboats, but the hand of war lay heavy here, too.

What had been one of the grandest colleges outside of New England was now a bedraggled military hospital. It stood on a hill on the northeastern edge of the town, with a magnificent domed and pillared academic building that soared four stories high and was flanked by long, red brick dormitories fronted with rows of fat white columns. When we'd come here before, with Papa, young men had been playing baseball on the green, their shouts and laughter drifting gently through the moss-draped oaks. Now, the long grass rippled forlornly in the breeze, the only sound the tap-tap of a ragged, one-legged soldier hobbling up the rutted, overgrown drive on a single crutch.

He was hunched over and moving slow, like an old man. But when he turned at our approach, I saw that he wasn't a man at all, but a boy not much older than Finn, only gaunt and sandy-haired, with a scattering of freckles that stood out stark against his pale skin.

He listened while Mama explained the purpose of our errand, then said, 'I reckon the one you ought to see is Dr Arnaud Seauvais. 'Cept, he's over in Clinton right now. His assistant surgeon is here, though – Captain Lamar Crowley. Heard tell he was fixing to cut off the rest of Jeb Odom's leg this morning, so he's prob'ly up at the academic building. They use one of the debate rooms there for surgeries, you know. Here, I'll show you.'

'Please, I don't want you to have to put yourself out for us.'

'No trouble at all, ma'am.' He swung the crutch carefully over the uneven ground. 'I was heading up there anyway.'

I found it hard not to stare at the pinned-up leg of his trousers.

I should have been used to such sights by now – the empty sleeves and missing feet, the maimed faces and blind, milky eyes. But it still made my stomach hurt. I said, 'You were wounded at Port Hudson?'

He nodded. 'Caught a Minié ball just below the knee. But Major Seauvais says things are looking good.'

He didn't look too good to me. But I kept the observation to myself and shifted my gaze to the soaring portico before us.

They said this was the biggest academic building in the country. Finished just before the war started, it housed a three-thousand-book library, an observatory, a gymnasium, and a vast auditorium as well as classrooms, science laboratories, and offices. Now it was just a half-abandoned hospital.

We entered one of the high arched doors to find a small, lithe man hurrying across the dusty, marble-tiled vestibule. He was younger than I'd expected, probably still in his mid-twenties, with a clean-shaven face and short, honey-colored hair and eyes of such an intense blue as to be startling.

'Captain Crowley,' called the one-legged soldier. 'These here ladies was looking to talk to you.'

The surgeon pivoted to face us, his open military frock coat flaring. It looked relatively new, of good English cloth and well tailored, although liberally splashed with bright red blood mingled with older, darker stains. His gaze shifted from the soldier to my mother, and an ill-disguised expression of impatience flitted across his even features. 'Yes?'

'I'm Katherine St Pierre,' she said. 'My husband, Anton St Pierre, is a surgeon with the Army of Virginia.'

'Yes?'

I glanced at my mother to see a faint stain of color riding high on her cheekbones. She held the basket out to him. 'We'd heard the hospitals here and in Clinton are dangerously short of medicines, so I brought a selection of supplies I thought you could use.'

Crowley's frown deepened as he took the basket. 'Anton St Pierre, did you say? He's the Creole abolitionist, isn't he?'

'He is.'

The surgeon grunted, the glass vials clinking together as he sorted through the basket's contents. 'Mmmm. Yes; these will be most useful. Tell your husband thank you.'

He started to turn away.

My mother said, 'I have considerable experience with . . .' She paused, then changed what I knew she'd been about to say. 'Nursing. If I could be of assist—'

He swung to look at her again, his upper lip pursed and quivering as if he'd just smelled something foul. 'In my opinion, females have no place in hospitals. Not only do they lack the strength and stamina to be of any real use, but they're utterly deficient in the emotional fortitude one requires when dealing with the horrors of war wounds.'

'Really?' said my mother with a tight smile. 'Yet I presume you have heard of Florence Nightingale? There are even places – such as Paris – where women are allowed to become physicians themselves.'

'*France*,' he said scornfully. 'Not here, thankfully. I fear the rigorous demands of medical study are utterly beyond the limited mental and physical capabilities of the fair sex, while the thought of a woman – a *lady* – actually seeing and touching the male physique must be repugnant to any gentleman worthy of the name.'

'Repugnant,' said my mother, her smile never slipping. 'An interesting word choice, given how succinctly it sums up my opinion of such primitive thinking. Good day to you, Captain Crowley.'

Lifting her dusty homespun skirts with all the grace and dignity of a debutante maneuvering a silk ball gown, she left him standing there, his features puckering with confusion as he struggled to understand how someone of a sex he scorned could have just succeeded in making him feel so small.

'Do you think it will ever change?' I asked my mother later, as we dined on cornbread and thin mutton stew at an inn opposite the college.

'Will what change, honey?' she asked, looking up at me.

I stared out the window at the sun-drenched brick walls and massive columns of the grand buildings across the street. I'd always known that only men were allowed to attend places like Centenary College. But for some reason, today's reminder that I would never be allowed to study here just because I was a girl filled me with an outrage so profound and visceral that I was practically shaking with it. 'The idea that women are too frail – and stupid – to go to a real college. To become doctors or lawyers or – or anything.'

'It might change. If women are willing to push for it, hard. Otherwise . . . probably not.'

'Push for it how?'

'By refusing to believe that we really are weak and stupid, simply because we've always been told that we are. By loudly and repeatedly demanding that men treat us like adults rather than simple-minded children who never grow up. And by demanding that if we're required to pay taxes, we should also have the right to vote and sit on juries and represent ourselves in government.'

I was silent for a moment. The thought that women ought to be able to vote had never occurred to me. 'I'd like to vote someday,' I said quietly.

'There's talk in Washington of making Negro men citizens and giving them the right to vote. Why not women?'

I threw a quick glance around to make sure I wouldn't be over-heard, then leaned forward and lowered my voice. 'But there are white men out there fighting for the Negroes. I can't see men ever fighting for women.'

'Some might.'

'You mean, *really* fight? With guns?'

'No. But it's not this war that is winning the Negroes their freedom and citizenship. It's not even Lincoln – although I've no doubt he'll get both the credit and the blame for it.'

'So what is?'

'It's the black people themselves who are refusing to be slaves any longer, who are educating themselves and showing the world what they're capable of. That and the realization by right-minded people that the force of history and justice demands it.'

I sat back in my chair. One of the many painful lessons I'd absorbed from this war was that people's ideas of what justice and history and God demand were usually self-serving and narrow.

We'd been planning to leave for home that afternoon, once the westering sun took the worst of the heat from the day. But it was just a few hours later, when Mama was adjusting her hat before the long pier glass in the inn's shadowy parlor, that we heard the sound of running feet and panicked shouts mingling with the thunder of scores of horses' hooves, the rattle of caissons, the all-too-familiar tramp of marching soldiers.

Her gaze met mine in the mirror. 'I hope to God that's a patrol from Camp Moore.'

Kneeling on the tufted velvet settee beside the window, I carefully parted the lace curtains to see the street filled with soldiers in dark-blue coats and kelpies. Some were white men, their faces sweat-slicked and freshly sunburned. But most were black, the long barrels of their rifles gleaming in the golden light of the waning day.

Forty-One

'Folks are saying there's a hundred or more cavalry,' the innkeeper told us in a hushed voice as the Federal troops settled into the business of occupying the town. 'Along with some artillery and maybe a hundred infantry from the New York Volunteers. But the rest is all Corps d'Afrique. Hundreds of 'em. That's why they're here – they're recruitin' whatever slaves is willin' and impressin' them that ain't.'

The innkeeper was a stout, full-bosomed Irishwoman named Maggie Dwyer, with blunt features and iron-gray hair and almost no teeth. I'd seen her ten-year-old son, Jesse, out in the street, darting through the troops, his sharp-featured face alert and watchful.

'My Jesse says they're gonna make the college their headquarters. Turned out all the sick and wounded what was there, they did.'

I thought about the young, one-legged soldier who reminded me of Finn. 'But . . . what are they gonna do?'

'I'm putting up as many of 'em as I can here. But don't you worry; I'm saving you and your momma a room. Ain't nobody gettin' out of Jackson as long as that lot is here. Jesse says they've posted pickets on all the roads.'

My mother's face took on the bleak-eyed starkness of someone confronting a disastrous but unavoidable march of events. 'I have patients depending on me. I need to get home.'

'We-ell,' said Mrs Dwyer, turning the word into two syllables. 'I reckon you could try appealing to the major what's leadin' them – he's one of the Woodville, Mississippi Hanhams, if you can credit it. But if I were you, I'd stay safe indoors till they're long gone. Pretty thing like yourself, you—' She broke off, her gaze drifting to me, then grimaced and shrugged. 'You know.'

'But what if they don't leave?' I said.

Mama just looked at me.

By late the following afternoon, it was obvious the Federals were settling in for a prolonged stay. I came inside after watching them from the gallery to find my mother once more positioning her hat before the pier glass. I didn't need to be told where she was going.

'I'm coming with you,' I said.

She looked over at me. 'It's not safe, honey.'

'I'm still coming with you. You'll be safer with me than alone.'

I expected her to argue with me, but she didn't. Something was shifting between us, a subtle alteration in how we dealt with each other that had begun perhaps earlier, but had accelerated with the killing of Gabriel Dupont and his sergeant. I could sense that she was beginning to see me less as a child, more as someone she could rely on as our world became increasingly dangerous.

It didn't occur to me until later that a similar shift was taking place in the way I saw myself.

We pushed our way across a raucous street boiling with shouting men and heavy wagons and balking mules, the air thick with the reek of manure and sweat and dusty cotton. It was obvious the Federals weren't here simply to recruit new troops; they were also stealing cotton from the farms and plantations in the area. Piled high on confiscated wagons, the big bales would be hauled to Port Hudson and then floated down to New Orleans to be loaded on steamers destined for New York and the mills of New England.

The fences that had until yesterday surrounded the college grounds were mostly gone, torn down for firewood and bedding boards to lift the sleeping soldiers out of the mud. Herds of cavalry horses grazed on the overgrown green, the hot August sun gleaming on their hides. Off to one side stood two big brass artillery pieces, their bores black and deadly. And it came to me that I was looking at the inevitable result of the fall of Port Hudson and Vicksburg; the massive forces that had once been focused on overrunning those two strongholds were now free to roam roughshod over us.

'Hey there, gorgeous,' called a man in a low, sultry voice. 'Got somethin' yer lookin' to sell?'

A group of men bunched beside one of the dormitory's pillars laughed.

Mama and I kept walking, our gazes fixed straight ahead.

'What the hell you talkin' about, Meacham?' said another man.

'I don't buy nothin' from no Secesh. I see somethin' I want, I take it.'

A hand reached out to close around my mother's arm, jerking her around. The cluster of leering men shifted, encircling us. My vision filled with sun-reddened, whiskered faces, bloodshot eyes, and mouths full of rotting teeth. I sucked in a quick breath so fouled with the stench of rancid hair oil and hot male sweat that I wanted to retch.

'Take your hands off that woman,' someone ordered in a soft Mississippi drawl.

I craned around to see a small, incredibly dapper young major descending on us, the brass buttons on his dark-blue frock coat gleaming in the sun, the sword at his side swinging with his quick step. He didn't look as if he could be more than twenty-three or -four, with a neatly trimmed square beard and high cheekbones and a long, patrician nose.

'Good God,' he said. 'What sorts of mothers raised you men? You're a disgrace to your uniform, your nation, and your sex.'

The men melted away as the officer drew up before us with a short, punctilious bow. 'My apologies, ladies. I am Major James Moore Hanham.' He gestured with an extended hand. 'Please; may I escort you to my office? If it were up to me,' he continued as he led us to what looked as if it might once have been a professor's study, 'men like that would be horsewhipped. Unfortunately my superiors don't agree with me.'

'Yet you fight for them,' said my mother, drawing up just inside the office door.

The major went to stand behind the broad mahogany desk as if it were his own. 'I fight for my country.'

'A country that no longer exists.'

'It will again. And soon. Although not, I fear, soon enough to prevent the part of it that you and I both love from being left in such shambles that one wonders if it will ever be set right again.' He removed one of the absent professor's cigars from a box on the desktop, bit off the end, and clenched it between his molars without making any move to light it. 'Please, won't you sit down? I assume you were on your way to see me for a reason?'

My mother stayed where she was. 'My daughter and I wish to return to our home in St Francisville. I'm told we require your permission to leave town.'

The major rested his knuckles on the desk's surface and leaned into them. 'You would, yes. Unfortunately, I'm afraid I can't give it to you. You see, ma'am, the pickets we've posted around town are not there simply to warn us of the enemy's approach. They are also intended to prevent any of the town's traitorous citizens from slipping out and alerting the enemy to our presence.'

'Yet your presence will surely in time become known.'

'In time, yes. But we don't intend to remain long. We're here recruiting slaves for the Corps d'Afrique.'

'Recruiting or impressing?'

A musket popped in the distance, but he didn't even look around. We'd been hearing occasional gunfire ever since the Federals arrived. It seemed as if they were always shooting at something: squirrels, ducks, chickens, cats, dogs, shadows.

'Most enlist willingly,' he said. 'Eagerly, in fact. But those who don't are impressed, yes, just like the Irish immigrants on the streets of New York City. The Democrats made them all citizens, and now they're rioting because they can't afford the three hundred dollars to keep from being drafted.'

'And because, ironically, the Negroes on the streets of New York are not being drafted since they're not considered citizens.'

Another sputter of distant rifle fire sounded.

He pointed the unlit cigar at her and grinned. 'Very true. Tell me: do you play chess?'

'No.'

I glanced over at her in surprise. She was always trouncing Papa at chess.

'Pity,' he murmured. 'The thing is, the Negroes are a wonderful untapped source of manpower. If the South had enlisted them two years ago as some suggested, this war might be turning out very differently. But you and I both know the terror kindled in the Southern breast by the very thought of Africans with guns.'

A shout went up on the far side of the green, then another.

'A not unreasonable fear, under the circumstances,' said my mother.

'Perhaps. Are you certain you don't—'

He broke off as a bugle call cut through the air; from the open window came the distant thunder of hooves. I could see troopers running, horses sidling nervously as saddles were thrown on their backs.

'What the— Excuse me, ladies.'

He hurried to the door just as a dusty, hot soldier smelling of saddle leather and horse sweat appeared. 'Force of rebel cavalry, sir,' he said, panting hard. 'Must be five hundred of 'em or more, comin' in fast.'

'Form up a battle line parallel to the street,' shouted the major, throwing away his unlit cigar. 'We'll—' He paused to turn and shout back at us, 'For God's sake, you women stay here. And keep away from that window!'

Forty-Two

The Confederate cavalry swept through the streets of Jackson, the fierce golden light of the setting sun at their backs, their horses' hooves pounding on the hard earth. I watched frozen with fascination as they thundered down on the hastily drawn up line of Federal infantry. The silken colors of battle flags unfurled against the sky; drums rolled and bugles shrilled, and from hundreds of rebel throats came a high-pitched, ululating yell like a cross between an Indian war whoop and the scream of a cougar. An oddly mingled shiver of excitement and fear ran up my spine. I could not tear my gaze away.

'Amrie. Please, get down.'

'Hold your line,' I heard someone shout. 'Fire!'

The splintering crack of hundreds of rifles cut through the air. I ducked down, my back to the wall, my hands splaying out at my sides.

'Fire!'

I could smell the drifting powder smoke, hear wood splintering from the oaks and strange thwunking thumps I realized must be the sound of hot bullets burying themselves deep into the trunks of trees.

Or the bodies of men.

I turned my head to meet my mother's gaze. We had lived through more than two years of war, endured constant raiding parties and the shelling of Federal gunboats. But this was the closest we had ever been to an actual battle. I could feel the earth tremble with the pounding of hundreds of hooves. Then the reverberating boom of a cannon sent a shell whistling through the air to explode with a roar.

The din was deafening, a confused tumult of men shouting orders, cheering, cursing, screaming. Horses neighed and squealed; men cried out in agony. Then a clash of steel joined the endless cough and crack of musketry. The gunpowder grew so thick it pinched my nostrils and stung my eyes. One of the windowpanes shattered beside us, spraying shards of glass across the bare floorboards, and I bit down hard on my lip to choke back a startled scream.

I could not understand how anyone could survive such a maelstrom of tearing, exploding, ripping death. And it struck me that battle was a kind of infectious madness, a brutal, primitive, socially sanctioned excess of brutality and savagery that defied logic and required a rejection of everything truly good and noble about humanity.

My mother said, 'It sounds like some of our cavalry is sweeping around behind the building.'

I realized the yelling was now coming from two directions. I heard someone shout, 'Hold your line!' Then: 'Back! Back!'

I said, 'Does this mean we're winning?' How could anyone tell who was winning or losing in such a wild, smoke-billowed confusion? How could you know who was companion and who was enemy? Or did you just fire and hack and scream your way forward in a frenzy of terror-driven bloodlust and rage?

Yet even I, blinded by smoke and crouching behind thick brick walls, could sense that the line of battle was shifting, that the Federals must be falling back toward Pine Street and Asylum Branch Bridge, their artillery now silent, the sustained crackle of rifle fire becoming more ragged and distant.

Beside me, my mother shifted ever so slightly, her hand reaching out to clutch mine. And my world narrowed down to the mingled panting of our shallow breaths and an unnatural awareness of the blood coursing through my veins and the reassuring pressure of my mother's living flesh against mine.

We emerged into a hellish world of shredded leaves, splintered branches, and jagged chunks of bullet-torn wood that covered a hillside littered with the dark bodies of men and downed horses and every imaginable kind of debris. Wounded horses thrashed and screamed; someone somewhere was crying over and over again, '*Momma!* Oh, God; Momma . . .' Someone else screamed in agony. The air was thick with the smell of blood and offal and a stench that reminded me of burning cane fields.

'Jesus,' whispered my mother beside me.

We could still hear desultory rifle shots in the distance. Yet already the people of Jackson were emerging to spread out over the battlefield. I watched a boy of eight or ten yank the boots off a dead Federal who lay with his head thrown back, flies already circling his open mouth and the bloody pulp of his chest, his outflung hands curling into claws. Nearby a woman was shoving everything from cartridge boxes to knapsacks into a bulging old flour sack. To a people starved by two years of brutal blockade and stripped of the barest essentials by succeeding waves of raiding parties, every blanket roll and bowie knife, every canteen, every button or spent bullet was precious.

A familiar, one-legged boy on a crutch was hobbling from one screaming downed horse to the next, systematically putting them out of their misery with a rifle. I saw one sobbing woman – slim, fair-haired, still relatively young – kneel beside a moaning, writhing soldier whose face ended in a bloody, bubbling mess, his lower jaw shot away. She eased the pistol from his belt, pressed the muzzle to his temple, and put up one crooked arm to shield her face from the splatter as she pulled the trigger. The report echoed through the foul, smoky air of the coming evening, and I jerked. I might have thought it an act of cold revenge had I not seen the fierce compassion that pinched her face. Nearby, a middle-aged man in a bowler hat and broadcloth coat was hunched over retching uncontrollably, the sour stench of his vomit making my own stomach heave.

'Amrie,' called my mother. 'Grab some of those canteens and start taking water to the wounded. And you there,' she called to the vomiting banker, 'help carry this man inside.'

Her face pale and set, she worked unflinching to separate the wounded from the hideously mangled dead, then corralled strong women and some of the less aged men to help carry the living up the hill to the dormitories. I kept expecting Captain Lamar Crowley to appear and start braying about the weakness of the fair sex. But someone said he'd hightailed it into the woods yesterday at the first sign of the Yankees.

'Reckon he's in Clinton by now,' said Jesse Dwyer, sporting a new bowie knife on his belt and a fine pair of boots.

I saw perhaps half a dozen dead and wounded men wearing ragged, patched uniforms of gray and butternut. But a hundred or more Federals lay sprawled over the college green and the surrounding streets. I moved from one moaning man to the next, their hands clutching my wrist as I held the canteen up so they could drink, the water running down their chins to wash clean rivulets through the grime and powder and blood. I recognized one of the dead as the man who had grabbed my mother. He lay with one leg bent, his head thrown back, eyes wide and staring, his belly a torn, bloody tangle of exposed entrails.

I passed him by without another glance.

My mother worked through most of the night, sawing off shattered limbs and sewing up saber slashes. At one point, the commander of the Confederate cavalry, a dark-haired, dark-eyed, intense colonel from Arkansas named John L. Logan, appeared and started to question her competency. She looked up at him, her face streaked and splattered with blood, and said calmly, 'Do you care to take over, Colonel?'

He backed from the room, hands splayed out to his sides.

I found her just before dawn, slumped asleep beside a fair-haired boy whose bandage-wrapped chest jerked painfully with each breath. Her basket of medicines, which we'd found untouched in one of the debate rooms, rested at her side. It was now nearly empty.

I started to creep away, but she awoke, a faint smile lighting her eyes when she saw me. 'Why are you up, honey? You must be exhausted.'

'I came to see how you're doin'.'

She glanced at the boy on the cot beside her. 'I'm not sure he's going to make it.'

'Where's he from?'

'Vermont.'

'So why do you care?'

'Oh, Amrie . . . They're just men – good, loyal men, like Papa and Uncle Tate and all the others – risking their lives for what they believe in.'

'No, they're not. If they were good men, they wouldn't be down here burning our houses and shooting our cows and stealing anything and everything they can get their hands on.'

'Amrie—'

I ran from the room, my bare feet slapping against the cool brick of the walkway. The soft pink glow of the rising sun warmed the long row of tall white columns beside me, turning them a rich pastel hue. The damp air smelled of grass and wood smoke. I could see the dark, bullet-shattered branches of the live oaks silhouetted against the lightening sky, hear a cavalry horse nickering in the distance, the sound clear and disembodied by the morning mist.

I ran on, following the path that led across the overgrown, abandoned railroad tracks to the burial ground that had been set up when Centenary College became a hospital. The bare earth of the new Southern graves showed dark and stark against the grass and, beyond that, I could see the trench that had been dug off to one side for the Federal soldiers, in case they ever chose to reclaim their dead.

I could not have said why I'd come here. But I sat in the grass with my arms looped around my bent knees, the graves of the Confederate dead on one side, the Federals on the other, and watched the sun rise like a shimmering ball of fire over moss-draped limbs alive with the glorious song of larks.

Captain Lamar Crowley returned late the following morning, his oiled locks flowing, his mustache carefully trimmed, his vivid blue eyes snapping with indignation.

I knew my mother was reluctant to turn her patients over to his care, but she really had no choice. Maggie Dwyer had two mules and a cart that Jesse had managed to snag in the confusion after the battle, and she offered to have her boy drive us back to St Francisville. Mama was tired enough to accept.

We left shortly after midday, when the air was blistering hot and breathless, and dark clouds bunched on the horizon. The mules plodded along, dust rising from their heavy hooves to shimmer in the fierce sunlight. Every once and a while we'd hear the crackle of musketry somewhere in the distance. Colonel Logan had some of his men out scouring the countryside for Federal soldiers who'd become separated from their units in the fighting and were now trying to work their way through the woods back to Port Hudson. Some of the stragglers had attacked a couple of farmsteads outside of Jackson, which spurred the aging men who formed Jackson's Home Guard to join the hunt. We'd heard the militia wasn't too keen on taking prisoners, especially black prisoners. The idea had taken hold that any ex-slaves found under arms were traitors and spies and should be treated as such. But I tried not to think about that as the road wound through a stand of big old live oaks and magnolias, their spreading branches meeting overhead to form a cool, shadowy green tunnel.

'I can't believe we left home only three days ago,' I said.

Mama brought up one hand to rub her tired eyes with a splayed thumb and forefinger. 'Mahalia must be frantic with worry.'

'Reckon she'll have heard about the Federals?'

'I hope not. It would only worry her more.'

I thought about Avery, who'd driven off to Livingston Parish and never returned. So many people had simply vanished in the last couple of years, victims not only of the marauding Federal armies, stragglers, and deserters, but of our own home-grown thieves and murderers – the kind of men who had always lived amongst us but were normally held in check by civilian forces of order that had now ceased to exist. And I wondered, How does a society ever come back from this kind of chaos and brutality? What happens when violence becomes an everyday way of life? When hatred festers and twists and distorts a people's soul? When brutality and horror have become so commonplace that a young woman in a calico dress and flaxen braids can press a revolver against a dying man's temple and calmly pull the trigger? I'd shot a man in the back, but I wasn't sure I could do that.

I glanced at my mother. She had her head tipped back as she dozed beside me on the cart's hard bench, the sunlight flickering down through the leafy canopy overhead to cast shifting patterns of shadow across her face. I wanted to say these things to her, to have her tell me I was wrong, that everything would be all right, someday. But I knew that was only childish wishful thinking on my part, that even if she mouthed comforting words they would fail to reassure me.

'Oh, Gawd,' whispered Jesse Dwyer, sawing back suddenly on the mules' reins, his eyes widening with stark horror as he brought the cart to a shuddering halt.

Even before I turned to see what he was staring at, I heard the telltale buzzing of flies, smelled the stench of recent death.

Two bodies hung suspended from a stout branch of a big old magnolia that grew at the side of the road. The taut ropes had furrowed deep into the men's necks, and in the deep shade of the grove their navy blue coats looked almost black. The violent compression of their deaths had swelled their faces, so that their eyes bulged hideously and their tongues thrust grotesquely from between curled lips.

The man on the left was unknown to me, a tall, ebony-skinned soldier of perhaps thirty or more. But even with the distortion of his features, I recognized his sergeant, recognized the smooth golden tone of his skin and the broad shoulders and strong chest that were so like those of his father, Castile.

It was Leo Boudreau.

Forty-Three

I wish I could forget the look on Castile's face when he saw the body of his dead son, but I know I never will.

He was up on a ladder, patching a hole left in the side of his stables by the latest shelling from the Federal gunboats when we pulled up out front. He hollered and scrambled down to meet us, teeth flashing in a broad smile that slid away when he saw the still, covered form in the back of our cart. I didn't understand at the time how he knew who it was even before he got close enough to see properly, but he did. Later I figured he must have seen the truth written on my face.

He stumbled to a halt, his body shuddering like a man who's just taken a bullet in his chest, his face contorting with the savagery of his grief. 'Oh Lordy, Lordy, Lordy,' he wailed, his head swinging wildly back and forth in hopeless, desperate denial. 'Tell me that's not my boy. Leo? Oh, child; what they done to you?'

He clambered up into the back of the cart and gathered the stiffening, blue-clad body in his arms. He sobbed openly and without restraint, eyes squeezing shut, tears glistening on his dark, scarred cheeks. And I knew a deep and powerful shame, as if I were somehow personally responsible for what had happened.

For the truth was, my kind had done this. Those I'd considered good and noble and true had brutally murdered a vital young man for the sin of having been born with darker skin.

Two days after Leo's burying, my grandmother, Adelaide Dunbar, came to stay with us.

She arrived without warning in a rattling old cane wagon drawn by two mules and driven by a one-armed boy about my age whose skin was so dark it had almost a purple sheen to it. Between the boy and my grandmother sat a fair-haired, sun-browned little girl in a ragged dress who looked maybe four or five.

Mama and I were shucking corn, and I heard her breath catch when she looked up and recognized the diminutive, straight-backed woman on the high seat. 'Mother?' she said, walking out to meet them.

Adelaide clambered down from her high perch without assistance. She wore a palmetto hat and a lilac silk gown that was charred along one side of the hem, and her skirts made a faint clinking sound when she brushed against the wagon's massive front wheel. 'Katherine,' she said, turning her head so that first my mother, then I, could plant our perfunctory kisses on her dry cheek.

I accidentally knocked her hat brim askew, and when she reached to straighten it, I saw that her hands were bare. It was the first time I'd ever seen Adelaide out of doors without gloves in my life, and I felt my stomach twist. Adelaide would never have driven bare-handed all the way from Livingston Parish to St Francisville in an open farm wagon unless something awful had happened.

She looked beyond us toward the front gallery, and I saw the faintest shadow of some emotion pass over her features. 'I was hoping to find your sister and little Hannah here. I was told that worthless husband of hers has been trying to bribe their way out of Natchez.'

There was nothing really wrong with Aunt Em's husband, Galen Middleton; in fact, I liked him. But my grandmother didn't hold a high opinion of any of her offsprings' spouses.

Mama said, 'We've heard nothing from Emma. But . . . For God's sake, Mother; what has happened?'

'I'll thank you not to take the Lord's name in vain, Katherine. It's the influence of that Catholic husband of yours, no doubt.' She smoothed her rumpled, dusty skirts. 'I am refugeeing, of course.'

I felt my insides give another ugly lurch. 'Misty Oaks?'

'Burned to the ground. The house, the sugar mill, the quarters, the barns and stables. Everything. All gone. Even the land, for some speculator from New York is claiming that.'

I started to cry, but Adelaide snapped at me, 'Anne-Marie; cease that blubbering this instant. You are allowed to weep – in private – for the loss of a person or a noble cause. But never for a mere possession.' Without altering her voice, she continued, 'There's a basket of my things in the back of the wagon; you may get that while your mother tells the boy Dibbie where to go.'

Then she sailed toward the house, her head held high, the singed train of her gown trailing in the dust.

She never would tell us much about the day the Federals descended on Misty Oaks. All we learned was that afterward, she, Aunt Mandy, and Wills had taken refuge with a neighbor named Silas Babcock, who'd also sold her the wagon and mules. They'd saved nothing from Misty Oaks except the bag of clinking coins Adelaide had tied to the hoops under her skirt. Lots of Southern women had given up wearing crinolines with the coming of the war. But Adelaide always said they were too useful to be abandoned.

'Mandy and Wills have gone to New Orleans to stay with some of her people there,' Adelaide explained after she'd had something to eat and was drinking a cup of ersatz coffee on the gallery. 'Had to take the Oath, of course. But she said she'd rather live under Yankee rule than risk having a third roof burned down on top of her.'

I was outraged at the thought that Uncle Harley's widow had agreed to take the hated Oath of Allegiance to the government that had killed her own husband. It seemed a repudiation of everything for which he'd fought and died. But Adelaide said she wasn't the least surprised. 'Girl has no grit, I'm afraid.'

I said, 'Was Dibbie hers?' The one-armed boy confused me, for I didn't recollect having seen him or the fair-haired little girl at Misty Oaks.

Adelaide shook her head and took another sip of her coffee. 'He says he belonged to some Quaker up the river before his mother ran off with him last spring. But he doesn't know what happened to her; one morning he simply woke up and she was gone. If you ask me, she ran off and left him, too. Silas Babcock was telling me one of his field hands ran off and abandoned a babe in her cradle.'

'But . . . what are you doing with him?' asked Mama.

Adelaide looked oddly flustered, almost embarrassed. 'I needed someone to drive the wagon, didn't I? He agreed to work for ten dollars a month, plus food.'

It was only later I discovered she'd taken in the children after finding them half-starved by the side of the road, and that the little girl was no relation to Dibbie at all. In fact, she was probably white, for where the sun hadn't browned her skin, she was paler than me. Dibbie said he'd stumbled across her in a burned out homestead where he was rummaging for food. He'd backed out of there in a hurry when he came upon the flyblown corpses of a woman and another older girl who'd had 'terrible things done to 'em.' He called the little girl Althea because he'd found her under an althea bush, but he'd no notion of her real name. She was certainly old enough to tell us herself, but she hadn't uttered a word in all the time since he'd found her.

'Reckon she seen some things no child oughta ever see,' said Mahalia that evening while giving the little girl a bath in a big round tub we'd hauled out so the sun could warm the water.

I watched her gently soap the child's hair, and somehow I summoned up the courage to ask something that had always puzzled me. 'How come you never had any children, Mahalia?'

She looked over at me. The hot August sun was bright on her face, her arms slippery with soapy water as she stilled momentarily at her task. 'What makes you think I never did? I birthed two babes. Only, they both come at the same time and was too tiny to live.'

I stared at her, a strange sensation crawling over my skin, almost like gooseflesh. I could not believe I'd gone my whole life without knowing something so vital about one of the central people in my existence. True, I'd never actually asked. But how could she have kept something so important to herself?

I said, 'You never tried to have more?'

She lifted a gourd full of water and let it run down over Althea's soapy back. The child simply sat there, a disconcertingly blank expression on her serious, young-old face. 'I reckon you's old enough to know that a woman needs a man to be making babies.'

'So what happened to him?'

She lifted Althea from the tub and wrapped her in one of our few remaining towels. 'He was a free man of color. Fine lookin' fella – an undertaker, from Springfield. Tall and lean, he was, with a neat little black moustache and flashing brown eyes and the prettiest straight white teeth you ever did see. Swept me off my feet, he did, and I fell real hard. Told me he loved me and that he was gonna buy me from your Grandma Adelaide and marry me, and I believed every word of it.'

'He didn't even try?'

She shook her head, her lips pressed into a flat line, her pretty turquoise eyes going out of focus, as if she were looking far into the past. 'Come to find out he was courtin' the high-yeller daughter of a woman owned a plantation up Cane River way. When I confronted him about it, he said, he had *ambitions*, and those ambitions didn't include marrying someone who was born a slave.'

'But you could've found someone else.'

'I coulda. But why would I wanna let myself in for that again? Ask me, most men's more trouble'n they worth.' She scooped Althea up in her arms and turned toward her cabin.

I fell into step beside her. 'You reckon Althea will ever talk again?'

'She might. I 'spect the best we can do is give her lots of lovin' and make her feel safe.'

But I didn't see how anyone could ever feel safe in a world flying apart.

It quickly became apparent that Mahalia intended to take the orphans under her wing, and she set about mothering them with a passion that left me feeling a bit jealous, although I would never have admitted it.

We were all having to make some adjustments. Truth be told, I don't think things were running all too smoothly between my mother and Adelaide, either. It was one thing for my grandmother to come for an extended visit that had a definite end in sight. But this was different. There was no knowing when she'd be able to go home again – if ever.

Adelaide allowed herself one day of rest, then she set off with Dibbie for town, where she sold the cane wagon and mules to Hilda Meyers.

When I found out, I was scandalized. 'But . . . she's just gonna turn around and use them to haul in stuff she buys from the Federals.'

My mother cast me a warning frown. 'Amrie, you don't know that.'

'Don't I? Why, I heard just last week that—'

Mama trod on my bare toes, hard, and said evenly, 'Mother, why don't you show us what you bought?'

Adelaide had come back from St Francisville with four bolts of muslin, a bolt of gray foulard, and a supply of scarce needles, pins, and thread. I'd no doubt Hilda Meyers had bought the lot from the speculators that were becoming more and more active in the area since the fall of Port Hudson, but Mama wouldn't let me whisper a word of it. Adelaide was such an ardent patriot that she'd have thrown it all away and gone naked if she thought the goods came through the Federals.

She and Mama set to work at once with scissors and thread, and before the week was out Adelaide had a new set of underclothes, two nightdresses, and a new gown with an elegant gored skirt and a high, plain bodice embellished with rows of neat, narrow pleats from neck to waist. They also made me a new chemise, petticoat, and set of drawers, which I sorely needed, for I'd already grown out of the ones we'd made from the last of our linen sheets. I tried to tell myself I didn't know for certain that the muslin had come through the speculators, but the suspicion was strong enough that it spoiled my pleasure in the new underthings.

Time was, I'd never have given a thought to stuff like chemises and drawers. But I'd long ago stopped taking even the simplest of things for granted.

As soon as she was outfitted respectably, Adelaide set out on a round of social calls in the neighborhood, becoming reacquainted with all the old residents and meeting whatever friends and relatives were now refugeeing with them. Then she invited everyone who was anyone for what she called a 'musical evening'.

I didn't think they'd come. It had been less than a year since Adelaide's last social, but so much had happened since then. There wasn't a woman in town – except maybe Hilda Meyers – who hadn't lost someone dear, and not just the husbands, fathers, sons, brothers, cousins, uncles, and friends who'd marched off to war. So many others had died, too. Aged parents. Sisters. Children. Seemed like every day brought word of *someone* dying. Lately we'd all taken to focusing on just surviving. I couldn't see many folks wanting to come for a 'musical evening'.

But the need for human companionship and comradeship was obviously stronger than I'd realized, and the lure of music irresistible. My grandmother was wiser than I knew.

Singly, in pairs, or in groups of three or more, the women came walking up our drive in the golden light of the long August evening, past salvias abloom in a last blaze of glory and mockingbirds singing sweetly from the branches of the live oaks. Most were barefoot, although some clutched precious shoes and a cloth they used to wipe the dust from their feet. Many wore homespun dresses that hung limply with nothing except a single ragged petticoat beneath. But a few had dragged out silk dresses in rich jewel tones that smelled strongly of camphor and often sagged on their owners' now gaunt frames.

'I figured, what am I saving it for?' said Delia Stocking, smoothing one hand down over the folds of a magnificent Garibaldi striped silk with rows and rows of flounces. 'So the Yankees will have something to steal next time they come a'calling? Time was, I figured I'd wear it to celebrate when the war ended, but . . .'

Her voice trailed away, but I knew what she'd been about to say. Lately more and more folks were despairing of ever living to see the war's end. And even those who held out hope that peace might still come with independence knew it would never be greeted with celebrations. Not now. There'd been too much suffering, too many deaths for peace to be greeted with joyous fetes.

We gathered in the parlor and dining room, everyone talking at once, although for some reason I didn't seem to mind it anymore. Mahalia and I walked around with pitchers of blackberry tea we'd cooled in the old dairy beneath the cistern. Most of the ladies had brought their own tin cups or gourds, because we all knew the Yankees took a fiendish delight in breaking glasses, china, and crockery. Few folks had enough left to serve a crowd.

I heard Trudi Easton say to Mama, 'I wrote to Captain Easton again, trying to impress upon him the importance of not allowing a second year to pass without a teacher for the area's children. But he still refuses to countenance the thought of allowing me to take up the position.'

I glanced over at her. These days, Miss Trudi was practically as skinny as that soldier we'd taken in after Port Hudson. She wore a faded brown homespun dress darned at the hem and patched at the elbows, and as she talked, I saw her put up one hand to her throat, still reflexively trying to touch the heart-shaped crystal containing the lock of Captain Easton's hair. Then she must have remembered it was gone, because her hand slid away to grip the arm of her chair.

Mama had decided in the end that it was better not to return the locket to her. I still thought it was cruel, but I acknowledged Mama probably understood a woman like Miss Trudi better'n me. Personally, I couldn't begin to fathom how any woman could remain so attached to a man who'd rather see his wife and children starve than have her shame him by working outside the home.

'Did you hear about Charlotte Salinger's husband, Bayard?' Rowena Walford was saying. Like Miss Trudi, Miss Rowena was wearing homespun, but her dress looked almost new and was beautifully made, with mandarin sleeves and a double skirt. Miss Rowena always contrived to look elegant, even in homespun.

'Oh, no,' said the Widow Carlyle. 'Don't tell me Bayard is dead, too.' Charlotte Salinger had already lost three brothers and two sons to the war.

Miss Rowena nodded, her pretty face puckering with empathy. 'At Manassas Gap. I was with her when Bayard's boy, Jeremiah, came home. Brought her Bayard's sword and his bloody, ripped uniform, all folded up. Handed them to her along with the letter Bayard had written the night before he was killed, and a note from one of Bayard's comrades. And then you know what he did? He just turned around and walked off without so much as a by-your-leave.'

I thought it an incredibly noble, selfless thing for Jeremiah to have done, to have hazarded the long journey from Virginia to Louisiana simply to return a dead man's effects to his widow. He could so easily have thrown them away and headed north to freedom. But I guess Rowena Walford didn't look at it that way.

'Shall we begin?' said Adelaide, rising to her feet. 'Who'd like to play first?'

'Well, I guess I'll do it,' said Rowena, her dimples peeping as she rose to her feet with a clutch of sheet music she'd brought along. 'Y'all know I'm not the deftest hand, but I'll try to make up with enthusiasm for what I lack in technical skill.'

She was being modest, of course; Rowena Walford played the pianoforte with the same exquisite grace she did everything. Her daughter Laura was with her, looking unusually quiet and subdued, and went to sit beside her mother and turn the pages for her. I'd found these days that I didn't mind Laura the way I once had. In fact, I almost felt sorry for her, although I couldn't quite figure out why. I think it had something to do with her mother, who I was learning wasn't nearly as charming or sweet as I'd once thought.

Rowena started out with songs that made us laugh, like 'Goober Peas' and 'Mister, Where's Your Mule?' But it wasn't long before we veered toward the sentimental favorites, like 'Lorena' and 'Aura Lee', the songs that seemed to open our hearts and bleed out the pain and loss and yearning we all felt. We sang 'The Vacant Chair' and I heard voices catch, saw the glint of silent tears quickly wiped away.

Margaret Mason had brought along her guitar, and Delia Stocking came clutching her flute, even though it was a bit bent from having been tossed out an upstairs window in the last Yankee raid. A few of the other women took their turns at the piano. Then Adelaide settled on the bench, her back straight, her own eyes enviably dry, her still agile fingers gliding over the keys as she began to play 'There's a Good Time Coming, Boys'.

I realized Laura Walford was standing next to me and felt her hand reach out to clutch mine as we sang, "*War in all men's eyes shall be a monster of iniquity, in the good time coming . . .*"

We sang as if by our voices we could somehow lift each other up and carry each other forward into the increasingly harsh and terrifying future that loomed before us.

"*Nations shall not quarrel then, to prove which is the stronger . . .*"

I wanted so desperately to believe it was possible, to believe that no women or children anywhere would ever again suffer what we were enduring.

"*Nor slaughter men for glory's sake . . .*"

Was it possible? In that one moment, I fervently believed it could be.

"*Wait a little longer.*"

Forty-Four

Early one morning in mid-September, I awoke to the soft thump of what I groggily realized were cautious footsteps on the gallery below.

I lay still for a moment, listening to someone's quick retreat back down the front steps. When he hit the drive, he broke into a run.

I slipped from my bed, the cool damp air nipping at my bare legs and feet as I crossed to the dormer window. The moss draped live oaks and pecans in the yard were hazy with mist turned a glowing pink by the rising sun. All looked still and quiet. But I knew I hadn't imagined it.

Someone had been there.

I threw on my clothes and crept downstairs to open the front door. A grubby, battered envelope slipped from where it had been thrust into the crack of the door to land at my feet.

My breath caught in my throat. I bent to pick up the message, my mind leaping back to another, half-forgotten morning when someone had hung a banner crudely lettered with the words Traitors Live Here beside our front gate. Had that unknown enemy returned? Then I saw the familiar, bold hand of the address.

It was a letter from Uncle Bo.

I peered uselessly into the drifting white mist. But whoever had brought the letter was long gone. I understood, now, why they hadn't wanted to be seen and recognized.

I heard my mother's door open. 'What is it, Amrie?' she whispered.

I held the letter out to her, and she read it aloud.

My dearest Kate and Amrie,

I've found a way I may be able to get this to you, so I'm seizing the chance.

I think of y'all constantly, worrying about what must be happening now that Port Hudson and Vicksburg have fallen. I've tried to get word of Em, Hannah, and Galen, but to no avail. The stories coming out of Louisiana these days remind me of the tales I read as a boy about the Thirty Years War. Who would have thought we'd come to this in our supposedly enlightened age? Lately, I've started thinking about requesting a transfer out West someplace. Not good for the career, I know. But . . .

I understand you've heard about Henley. I still find it hard to believe he's gone. I always thought he was the finest of us Dunbar boys – tall and handsome, kind-hearted, brilliant at everything he ever turned his hand to. And now he's just . . . dead. I've had no news of Tate for months, but I did run into a prisoner from Alabama the other day who told me Anton was well, at least as of early August.

I'll spare you the usual soldiers' complaints about the food and weather. I haven't tried to write Mother, for I know she doesn't want to hear from me. I just wish there was some way for me to tell her that I love her. I hope that someday the breach between us can be healed.

Your ever-loving brother and uncle,

Bo

Mama had just reached the letter's end when Adelaide appeared. 'Who is that from?' she demanded with a sharpness that told me she already had a pretty good idea of the answer.

'It's from Bo.' Mama hesitated, then held out the closely covered pages. 'He's well and sends you his love.'

'Bo Dunbar has been dead to me for over two years now,' said Adelaide, and walked back into her room to close the door behind her with a snap.

I didn't understand how any mother could so repudiate her own son simply because of a difficult choice he'd been forced to make. But Adelaide Dunbar was a hard woman – far harder than I figured I could ever be. I veered back and forth between thinking that was a good thing and worrying that maybe it was just another of my many failings.

Some hours later I was in the garden, cutting a bouquet of late-blooming roses and white chrysanthemums when I came upon her sitting on a weathered bench in the shade of the peach tree. I drew up awkwardly, not knowing what to say, that morning's incident still oppressively heavy on my heart.

But my grandmother had always dealt with familial unpleasant-nesses by acting as if they did not exist. She looked at me from under the wide brim of her palmetto hat and said, 'Good afternoon, Anne-Marie. That's a lovely bouquet.'

'Thank you, ma'am,' I mumbled.

'Don't mumble, Anne-Marie. It's a most unattractive habit.' She nodded to the flowers in my hand. 'Who are they for?'

'I thought maybe I'd put 'em on Leo's grave.'

She looked at me steadily for a moment, her brows twitching together into a frown. 'You mean, Leo Boudreau? I didn't know he'd died.'

I thought about telling her how Leo had died, then decided that was not a good idea. So I just said, 'Yes, ma'am.'

She gazed off across the sunlit garden to where a squirrel was scampering along the low branch of a pecan tree. 'He was always a clever boy. But stubborn and sullen, even as a small child.'

I stared at her, not understanding, or maybe simply not wanting to understand what she was saying. 'You knew Leo when he was little? How?'

She brought her gaze back to my face. 'He was born at Misty Oaks. I'm surprised no one ever told you. He was part of your mother's inheritance.'

I could hear my ears ringing, so that my own voice sounded as if it were coming from a long ways off when I said, 'And Castile? You owned Castile?'

A breeze had kicked up, shifting the branches of the peach tree overhead and slanting a palm-patterned speckling of sunlight across her aged face. 'Yes.'

AD. I should have known, of course. Should have been able to put it all together long ago. But I hadn't.

Understanding slammed into me, and I felt a rage explode within me, entwined with a horror that churned my stomach and stole my breath. 'The initials on Castile's cheeks . . . They're yours, aren't they? Adelaide Dunbar. You *branded* him. My God, how could you do that?' I backed away from her, shaking my head, not wanting to believe that someone I loved, my own grandmother, could have perpetrated a cruelty that had repulsed and enraged me for as long as I had been old enough to comprehend it.

She rose calmly to her feet, her face devoid of all expression. 'Don't you presume to judge me, young lady.'

'How could you?' I cried. The roses tumbled from my grasp as I whirled to run blindly, my tears transforming my world into a blur of blue and green and brown.

'Anne-Marie, you come back here. Anne-Marie? *Anne-Marie.*'

When Simon and I were little, a nasty September storm brought down a big old oak tree in the gully behind our house, partially damming the shallow stream and causing enough of an eddy that it hollowed out what we fancied we could turn into something far grander. Hauling in buckets of old bricks from the crumbling foundation of an abandoned mill, we did our best to supplement nature. The resulting pool was never very deep or wide, but when the stream was running well, it was enough to sit in and cool off after a hard day's work or play, surrounded by a thicket of wild grapes and enchanter's nightshade and native azalea.

These days, I mostly came here to sit on the log and watch the water trickle its way through our old brick dam. The light that afternoon was soft and golden in a way that told of the coming end of summer. And for one, intense moment, I missed Simon so much it hurt. Then I heard a soft rustle and felt a wet nose pushing against my hand.

'Hey, Checkers.' I looped my arm around his neck and drew his sun-warmed body close. 'How'd you find me? Hmmm?'

'I suspect he knows you better than any of us,' said my mother, inching her way down the steep path into the gully.

I stared out over the sun-dappled water. 'I won't apologize to her, if that's why you're here.'

She came to settle beside me on the log. She was silent for a moment, her gaze, like mine, on the softly rippling water. 'We should have told you long ago. I realize that now. I'm sorry.'

I couldn't look at her. 'I can't believe you kept it from me all these years. All of you! You and Papa. Castile and Leo. Even Mahalia and Priebus. Why?'

'It wasn't deliberate, at first. But we knew how you felt about the brands, and once we realized you didn't know who Castile had belonged to . . . It just seemed best.'

'Best? How could you ever have believed that?'

She pressed her lips together and shook her head, as if the answer now eluded her, too.

I picked at the pealing bark beside me. 'Why did she tell me herself, now?'

'She didn't realize we'd kept the truth from you. But you know what she's like. She would never have kept silent, anyway. She blames me for keeping it from you all these years, and to tell the truth, I think now that she's right.'

Checkers nudged me again, and I let my hand trail down his back. 'I don't understand how she could do something so cruel. So . . . evil.'

My mother eased out a long, heavy breath. 'We like to think of evil as something that exists outside of us – an entity the church personifies as the devil. But I've never been able to believe that. I think the potential for evil is *inside* of us – inside all of us. Our lives are a constant struggle not to give way to it.'

I turned my head to look at her. 'You would never do something like that!'

'I like to think I wouldn't. But do I know that? No. I don't think anyone ever really knows what they're capable of – good or bad – until life thrusts them into a situation where they need to make hard choices. Even then, I suspect most folks are very good at justifying the evil they do, convincing themselves it either wasn't that bad, or they had a good reason for doing the awful things they did. That's why Lincoln and his generals and soldiers can destroy entire cities and still flatter themselves they're serving a noble cause. How else can anyone unblinkingly kill half a million people and still think they're doing God's work?' she huffed a soft, bitter laugh. '"His truth is marching on."'

'You say that as if it somehow excuses what Grandma did. Well, it doesn't.'

'I didn't mean to imply that it does, Amrie. Only that I don't think there's a person alive who hasn't at some point done something reprehensible, something despicable, something they'd be amongst the first to condemn in another. It's one of the most pernicious aspects of slavery and war; both institutions remove the restraints under which we normally operate. I don't think there are many who can be trusted not to abuse that kind of situation.'

'She *branded* him!'

I saw my mother's nostrils flare on an indrawn breath. 'Amrie . . . She is today the same person you've always known and loved: stubborn and opinionated, strong-willed and caustic, judgmental and unforgiving, and at times ruthless and intolerant. You said this morning you couldn't understand how she turned away from Uncle Bo when he chose to fight for the Union. Yet isn't that what you're doing now? Turning away from her for a choice she made?'

'They're not the same at all! Uncle Bo thinks what he is doing is right and honorable. What she did was just mean and nasty!'

My mother rested one hand on Checker's back. 'Those dark impulses lurk within all of us, Amrie. All of us. For one hideous, irretrievable moment, she gave way to them. That doesn't mean she is evil.'

I started to say, *Not in me! That kind of capacity for darkness doesn't live within me!* Then I remembered the murderous rage that had thrummed through me as I eased back my bowstring and sent an arrow flying into Gabriel Dupont's blue-uniformed back. And I knew then that I was my grandmother's granddaughter, after all.

Adelaide Dunbar might have cruelly branded a man. But I had killed one. Without hesitation or remorse.

I was kneeling beside Leo's grave when Castile found me.

The raw, bare earth was only just beginning to settle, beaten down by the late-summer rains and the inexorable passage of time. Soon the dirt would sink, the grass would grow, and it would be as if Leo had never lived. Or died.

Castile settled cross-legged in the grass opposite me, and I was reminded of a time when Finn had sat thus on the far side of Simon's grave.

He said, 'I done talked to yor momma.'

I pulled aimlessly at the grass beside me with one hand. I didn't say anything, and after a moment, he went on.

'Most folks, they keeps their heads down and goes along to get along. Whatever life hands them, they just accepts it and tries to make the best of whatever bad lot they been dealt. But some of us, we're always kickin' against reality, even when it hurts us way more'n it hurts anybody else. That's just the way we is made and we can't be no different.'

I shook my head, not understanding. 'What're you sayin', Castile?'

'I was born a slave, just like my momma and daddy. But I wasn't gonna be like them – I wasn't gonna just *accept* it. I was thirteen years old the first time I run away. Made it maybe ten miles before they caught me and brung me back. I had no idea where I was goin'. I was just goin' away.

'That's when I realized it ain't enough to run, you gots to know where you running to. You gots to have a plan. Next time I lit out, I went to this old Choctaw feller traded along the river in the summertime and spent his winters up with what was left of his people.'

I stared at him. I'd always known Castile had lived with the Indians. That was how he'd learned to make bird traps, and to fashion his own bows and arrows, and to imitate the call of a wild turkey well enough to fool an old tom. But I'd never put any of it together.

'How many times did you run away, Castile?'

'Half a dozen, maybe more. Made it as far as Ohio, once. Was there nearly nine months when a big Scotsman named McIntire came up from Livingston Parish to buy cattle. He seen me and hauled me back to Louisiana. I reckon that was the hardest. I thought I'd rather die than be a slave again.' He paused. 'That was in '39.'

I felt a chill corkscrew up my spine. That was the year Hamish Dunbar had been scalded to death in a steamboat explosion.

Castile said, 'All them times I'd run away, yor grandma never done nothin' to me. She was always threatin' to sell me down the river to New Orleans, but she never done it. I sure didn't think she was really gonna brand me. But she did.' He was silent for a moment, his gaze hazy, unfocused, as if looking into the past. 'I hated her for a long time after that. But hate is like a poison. You nourish it within you like it's something precious, like you punishin' whoever done you wrong by hatin' them, as if the power of yor hate can somehow hurt them and pay them back. But you just bein' foolish, because the only person yor hate hurt is yor self.'

I shook my head. 'I don't understand how you can be my friend, when my grandmother . . .' My voice cracked, and I had to swallow hard. 'When every time you look in the mirror, you're reminded of what we did to you.'

'Child,' he said softly, 'you ain't never done me nothin'. And I don't need no mirror to remind me of them days. But I'm free now, and that's because of yor momma. I'll forever be grateful to her for that.'

Seemed to me, my parents had only done what was right, had simply given up what was not theirs to possess. My gaze shifted to the clutch of crimson roses I had laid on the bare earth between us. 'That's why Leo never liked us, wasn't it? He never said anything, but I could always tell.'

Castile was silent for a moment, and I knew the loss of his son lay grievously heavy on his heart. There was a slump to his shoulders, a heaviness to his movements lately that hadn't been there before and that betrayed his age. 'I reckon maybe it's easier to forgive the wrongs done to us than the wrongs done to those we love.'

'I'll never forgive her.'

Castile rested his wrists on his knees, his big, work-calloused hands hanging limp, his bullet-like head tilted to one side as if he were struggling to see his way forward. 'Leo . . . He had a heap of anger in him, not just toward y'all, but toward me, too. The last couple times I run, I run away from him and his momma, Fiona, too. You never knowed Fiona, but she was a pretty little thing, with skin the color of the palest hickory and the prettiest smile God ever give a woman. She never forgave me for just up and leavin' her like that, twice, with no warnin'. When yor momma set us all free, Fiona done left me and went up north.'

'But Leo stayed?'

'Fiona didn't give him no choice. Said he would just remind her of me and of the past, and she didn't want no reminders. Leo blamed me for that, too. And I reckon he was right.'

For a moment, I could only stare at him, at his high ebony forehead and familiar scarred cheeks. And I found myself wondering how well we can actually know the people in our lives, even those who are the closest to us.

I wasn't ready, yet, to ponder too hard on how well we ever really know ourselves.

Forty-Five

'How long do you intend to keep treating your grandmother like this?'

I tugged at the chickweed crowding a patch of comfrey. The day was overcast and sultry, and I was helping my mother weed the herb garden down by the front gate. 'You can't accuse me of being rude to her.'

'No; you're being painfully polite. Amrie—' she began, then broke off, her grip tightening on her hoe, her gaze fixed on the tattered buggy drawn by a bangtailed bay coming down the lane.

The driver was unknown to me, an extraordinarily big man, tall and fleshy, with a long, untrimmed gray beard and no mustache. As he drew nearer, I saw his collar and knew him for a preacher of some sort. A woman sat on the bench beside him, her arm around a small child who huddled against her. Both the woman and the child were painfully thin, their faces hollow and stark, their clothes grubby rags. But I felt my heart begin to thump with hope.

'Whoa, thar,' called the preacher, sawing back on the reins as he drew abreast of the gate. 'This it?' he asked the woman, then turned his head to shoot a glob of tobacco juice into the dirt.

'Yes; thank you.'

'Emma!' said my mother, her hoe tumbling to the ground. 'Oh, thank God.'

The woman climbed stiffly down from the buggy's seat, then reached up for the child. 'Thank you,' she said again to the man, although her voice was flat and perfunctory.

He danced his reins on the bay's rump and rattled off toward town without a backward glance.

'Emma!' cried my mother, laughing and crying at the same time as she hugged her younger sister to her. 'Oh, Emma.'

Emma Middleton was the youngest of Adelaide Dunbar's surviving children. She was less than twelve years older than me, although she'd been married for five years. What Adelaide called her 'worthless husband', Galen, had managed to bribe his wife and daughter's way out of Vicksburg, after all. But it was hard to recognize this skeletal, worn-down, shattered woman as the beautiful, gay, vibrant young aunt I'd always known.

'I had a trunk full of clothes and things,' she said as we turned up the drive, Mama carrying Hannah on her hip. 'But the soldiers at the checkpoint stole it all – despite the fact I had a pass signed by General Grant himself.'

Mama looked over at her, the breeze fluttering wisps of Hannah's soft brown hair across her face. 'You took the Oath?'

'I had to. They wouldn't let us out otherwise.'

'Mother is here,' said Mama. It wasn't quite the non sequitur it seemed.

Aunt Em nodded. 'I know. Mandy wrote to me from New Orleans.' She stared out over the empty pasture and overgrown fields, and I saw her throat work as she swallowed. 'I still can't bear to think of Misty Oaks . . . not there anymore.'

'Grandma ain't gonna like it, you taking the Oath of Allegiance,' I said.

'Don't say "ain't",' chorused my mother and Aunt Em together.

I was wrong about my grandmother. It seemed Adelaide's outrage was an elastic thing. An action deemed unforgivable when committed by a daughter-in-law was perfectly understandable in her own child.

The truth was, Aunt Em had been so desperate to get away from Vicksburg that I think she'd have sold her soul if that's what it took to escape. Her little girl, Hannah, was so ill that Aunt Em was afraid she might die.

They tucked the child up in Adelaide's bed, with a hot brick at her feet and the covers piled high. And still the child shivered, although the day was warm and sultry.

'Do you think it's intermittent fever?' Aunt Em asked Mama as she tried to coax the child to drink a warm infusion of wormwood and willow bark.

I stood in the doorway, a sick feeling laying heavy in my stomach. Some folks called it intermittent fever; to others, it was swamp fever, ague, marsh fever, or bilious fever. The Sicilians who before the war used to sell oysters and crabs up and down river called it *mala aria:* bad air. It was caused by a dangerous miasma that arose from damp earth – or so they said. Folks in Louisiana were always sickening from it, particularly in late summer and early fall. Sickening and dying.

Mama held the cup to Hannah's lips again. 'How long has she been sick?'

'Weeks.' Aunt Em sat perched on the other side of the bed, one of Hannah's tiny hands between her own. 'A Federal doctor kindly gave me some quinine before we left Vicksburg, but the soldiers at the checkpoint took it along with everything else.'

'I have some left,' said Mama. 'And this should help with her chills and fever.'

'What kind of monsters steal medicine and clothes from a woman and her sick child?' said Adelaide. She had moved her things up to Simon's old room and now sat in the low sewing rocker beside the empty hearth, her gaze fixed on Hannah's wan, pinched face with a fierceness that was almost palpable. Of the ten children Adelaide had birthed, only four still lived – three if you didn't count Uncle Bo. And three grandchildren.

'The same kind who will starve and shell a city full of women and children, forcing them to eat rats and live like animals in holes grubbed into the sides of hills,' said Aunt Em. 'It's a wonder any of us survived.'

I still couldn't wrap my head around the idea of pretty, delicate Aunt Em living in a cave with a dirt ceiling and walls while listening to the interminable whistle and shriek of shells. Knowing every time she ventured out for food or water that she risked a hideous, searing, agonizing death. But I guess people do what they have to do to survive.

After Hannah fell asleep, Aunt Em talked to us about the caves that took direct hits from massive mortar shells and collapsed on their inhabitants, and about the stray red-hot pieces of shrapnel that could slice through a cave entrance to cut a child at play in half.

'It's no wonder Em's nerves are shattered,' I heard Adelaide say to Mama in the parlor later that night, her voice low so as not to awaken the mother and child now sleeping across the hall. Adelaide was already busy sewing new underthings for both Aunt Em and Hannah from the remnants of the bolts of muslin she'd bought, her needle flashing in and out of the cloth. She looked up, her face a tense mask as she stared at Mama. 'Do you think the child will live?'

Mama brushed a stray wisp of hair off her forehead. 'I honestly don't know. She's so thin. All those weeks of not having enough to eat and living in a damp cave . . .' She thrust up from her chair and went to stare out the window. It had come on to rain just before dark, and we could still see flickers of lightning flashing on the horizon. 'Damn this war. Damn Abraham Lincoln and every hotheaded Southerner who pushed for secession and every sancti-monious Northern abolitionist who ever thought that one sin justifies another. Damn them, damn them, damn them.'

I tensed, waiting for my grandmother to jump all over her for using a word like 'damn'. Adelaide normally had no tolerance for swearing of any kind. But all she said was, 'How much quinine is left?'

'Enough to see her through this bout. But if it comes back . . .' She left the thought unfinished.

Adelaide worked her needle in and out of the small nightdress she was making. Thunder rumbled in the distance, a long, low roll that sounded enough like cannon fire to make me shiver. 'We must pray,' she said.

I wanted to scream at her, *Praying doesn't do any good!* Folks were always praying, but their loved ones still died. The graveyards of the South were so full they kept having to open up new ones. Seemed to me, if God really cared, he wouldn't have let this wretched war start in the first place.

'Pray for quinine,' said my mother.

But God had other ideas.

Aunt Em refused to leave her daughter's side.

She barely ate and only half-slept, curled up beside the alternately shivering and sweating child, watching anxiously for any sign of change, for better or worse.

'She's ill herself,' said Adelaide the next afternoon as Aunt Em's wracking cough carried down the hall to the parlor where both Adelaide and Mama were sewing.

'I know.' Mama looked up from pinning the hem in a tiny pair of drawers. 'And she's not taking care of herself.'

Dibbie was off fishing, while Althea was just sitting at Mama's feet, staring into space in that way she had. Because my own needle skills were still considered substandard, no one had asked for my help with the sewing. Instead, Mahalia and I were working our way around the house, hanging the heavy curtains that would block the cold drafts in the coming winter. It had long been a ritual in the South: in the spring, heavy damask and velvet drapes came down and wool carpets were rolled up, to be replaced by light linen or muslin curtains and rush matting. Our own carpets were long gone, of course. And this year, only the parlor and the bedrooms would get winter drapes, because Mama and Adelaide were going to cut up the cloth from the dining room's dusky blue velvet drapes to make dresses for Hannah and Aunt Em.

'Amrie,' said Mahalia from the top of a stepladder beside the parlor's French door. 'Pass me the next panel.'

She had the curtain half hung, her arms stretched high over her head, when we heard the beat of a dozen or more cantering horses and the yelps and coarse jeers of rowdy men.

'Mother of God,' Mahalia said softly, leaving the curtain half hung as she scrambled down the ladder to scoop Althea protectively into her arms. 'Not again.'

I stood with my back pressed against the wall, the next panel still clutched in my arms, as blue-coated men swarmed over the yard and pounded up the front steps.

Mama rose to her feet as the first of the men – a big, dark-haired sergeant – burst through the parlor doorway. 'What do you want?'

I dropped the drapes and ran to where Checkers sleepily raised his head from beside the empty dining-room hearth to growl. Crouching beside him, I looped my arms around his neck, shielding his body with my own. '*Shh*, boy,' I whispered frantically. '*Shhh.*'

The sergeant sauntered up to Mama, his thumbs hooked in his belt, his smooth, startlingly young face alive with merriment mixed with something else – something hard and malicious. 'What ya gonna give me?' he asked, one cheek distended from a wad of tobacco that dribbled thin brown juice down the side of his chin.

When she simply stared silently back at him, he pursed his lips and spit a stream of tobacco juice that landed with a splat on the polished floorboards at her feet.

'Come on, boys,' he shouted, clapping his hands as he turned away. 'Let's make 'em some Yankee stew!'

A dozen howling, whooping men rampaged through the house, bringing with them the smell of sun-warmed horses and half-masticated tobacco and unwashed, sweaty bodies. 'We can start with these,' said one of them, seizing the pile of neatly ironed drapes and tossing them into the center of the room.

'Here's another one!' The sergeant closed his fist around the curtain Mahalia had only half hung. His yank pulled the rod out of the wall and brought it crashing down. He threw the curtain on top of the others, then grabbed the rod like a club to sweep the ormolu clock, English porcelain vases, and brass candlesticks from the mantelpiece. 'Aw,' he said in mock contrition. 'Look what I done.'

A slim corporal with bad teeth and swelling red mosquito bites covering his face nodded to the oil portrait of Simon hanging over the sideboard. 'That yer boy?' he asked Mama.

'Yes.'

'Bet he's a Johnny Reb, ain't he?'

'No.'

'Sure he is.' His grin widened. 'Watch this.' Still grinning, he brought up his bayonet and thrust the point into the canvas. 'See? Got him right through the heart.'

'No!' I cried as he jerked the bayonet down, ripping the canvas.

'Amrie,' said my mother softly.

I tightened my hold on Checkers and buried my face in his black and white coat.

My world narrowed down to an endless nightmare of pounding boots, ripping cloth, breaking glass. They brought in armloads of bedding from Mama's room and threw them into the center of the room with the curtains and the precious, beloved books they swept from our glass-fronted cabinets; they tore engravings off the walls and smashed them over chair backs before tossing the pieces onto the growing pile. Someone seized the glass-based kerosene lamp, long since dry, from a side table and hurled it into the mirror over the parlor mantel; a delicate alabaster carving of a long-necked

Egyptian goddess shattered into pieces against the fireplace grate beside me.

'*Oh, no,*' I heard Mahalia whisper beneath her breath as a big, red-headed Scotsman came charging into the room, the axe we used to chop wood in his hands. He swung it first at the piano, the blade sinking deep with a discordant jangle, before turning toward the long rosewood table that my great-grandmother McDougal had brought all the way from Boston.

From the other side of the hall I heard Aunt Em scream, 'Oh, please; no! There's a sick child in here.'

One of the men growled, 'Get her outta that bed.'

'For God's sake; can't you see she's dangerously ill?'

'Ya got money hid under the mattress, don't ya? Well, ya can either get the brat outta that bed, or I'm gonna dump her out.'

'No, don't! I'll get her.'

A moment later, Aunt Em burst through the parlor door, Hannah's frail body clutched in her arms. Mama went to take the child from her, but Aunt Em shook her head and hugged Hannah close.

Through it all, Adelaide hadn't moved. She sat stoically with her workbox on the cushion beside her, the half-sewn nightdress gripped tightly in her lap.

Then a stocky, flaxen-haired soldier picked up the intricately lacquered workbox and yanked the nightdress from her hands. 'Here, gimme that,' he snarled as he threw them on the pile that now covered most of the floor between the parlor and the dining room.

'You ought to be ashamed of yourselves,' said Adelaide evenly. 'All of you. You are behaving like heathens.'

'You shut up, old woman,' snarled the soldier, pressing the muzzle of his pistol against the side of her head. 'Shut your jaw, or I swear, I'm gonna blow your damned brains out.'

'Don't,' said the sergeant, knocking up the barrel of the pistol.

The charge exploded, filling the room with smoke and the stench of burned powder. A shower of pulverized ceiling plaster crashed down around them, and the young sergeant laughed uproariously, as if he were drunk. Or mad.

'Look what I found,' shouted one of the men, staggering into the room beneath a barrel of molasses.

'Now we can make us some real Yankee stew!' howled the sergeant.

I'd vaguely assumed that they were making the pile of clothes and bedcovers and books to set them alight and burn the house down around us. Perhaps that had been their intent, if they hadn't found the molasses. Instead, they poured the thick, dark, sticky syrup over the pile, then splashed it liberally over the walls and furniture.

'Here; let me stir it up for you,' said the mosquito-bit corporal, raking his bayonet through the molasses-drenched heap of clothes, bedding, broken china, shredded paintings and torn books.

'Yankee stew!' shouted another, attacking the pile with his sword.

I sat back on my rump, my arms still locked around Checkers' neck, angry tears blurring my eyes. I felt like I had a Yankee bullet lodged in my throat, so that it hurt to swallow.

'There; that oughta do it,' said the sergeant. He leaned in close enough to my mother that his breath disturbed the fine wisps of honey-colored hair that lay against her cheek. 'You like our cookin', you be sure to send the recipe to Ole Jeff Davis. You hear?'

She stood as still as someone posing for a daguerreotype, her gaze fixed straight ahead.

After a moment, he gave an unnaturally loud laugh and turned away. 'All right then, boys. Mount up!'

Elbowing and backslapping each other like unruly schoolboys, they tramped out the house and down the steps, leaving a sticky trail of molasses behind them. We heard the creak of saddle leather, more shouts; then the clatter of hooves receded into the distance.

None of us moved.

'Are they all gone?' asked Aunt Em, clutching Hannah's trembling body to her so tightly the little girl murmured in protest.

Mama walked to the broken front window, one hand coming up to touch the shredded linen curtain that hung beside it. 'Yes.'

Mahalia stared out over the molasses-drenched shambles of our house. 'The saints preserve us. Where do we even start?'

The four of us exchanged silent glances.

Then Mama let out a muffled exclamation and took off at a run toward the back of the house.

Confused, I pelted after her, Checkers barking at my heels. At the doorway to the spare bedroom, I drew up.

The mattress had been overturned and slit open, scattering feathers everywhere. The graceful round table that had stood at the bedside lay upside down; the mosquito bar was a torn tangle mixed with fragments from the shattered cheval mirror and the white ironstone pitcher and basin that had been swept from the washstand.

I was aware of Aunt Em and my grandmother coming up behind me. Hannah had begun to cry softly, her arms clinging to her mother's neck.

'What are you looking for?' Adelaide asked as Mama picked up the ripped coverlet and threw it aside.

'The quinine bottle.'

'There,' said Aunt Em in a strained, hollow voice.

Mama straightened slowly, her gaze following her sister's.

The bottle lay shattered on the hearth, the label still clinging to the broken, amber colored fragments, the bricks beneath stained dark where the precious, life-giving tincture had seeped away.

Forty-Six

There'd been a time when the senseless, deliberate destruction of so much that I held dear would have filled me with a heartsick rage. But I felt deadened inside, my world focused on one little girl who alternately shivered and sweated beneath a hastily mended coverlet on a patched mattress, the sickness within her raging beyond my mother's ability to control it.

Mahalia and I spent days sweeping and scrubbing and separating what was salvageable from what was hopelessly ruined. Sometimes Adelaide or Mama would come help. But they mostly took turns sitting with Aunt Em at Hannah's bedside. No one said anything, but it didn't take me long to figure out they wanted someone to be with Aunt Em when Hannah died.

I kept thinking about what Adelaide had said when I cried about Misty Oaks, that you're allowed to weep for the loss of a person or a noble cause, but never for a possession that can be replaced, maybe, someday, somehow. And I found myself making a silent bargain with the Lord: Just let those I love live through this war, God, and I promise I won't doubt you ever again.

But I was about to learn that bargains don't work any better than prayers.

Hannah died early on a Saturday evening, when the trees were throbbing with joyous birdsong, and the sky was a soft pastel pink the color of the last roses of summer that tumbled over the gallery railing.

I'd been fishing in the bayou and was walking back toward the house, lost for one brief, stolen interlude in the joy of the moment. The cool, sweetly scented breeze felt good on my face, and I was proud of the string of bass I was bringing home for supper. I'd almost reached the kitchen when I heard a low, keening wail that made my stomach twist and my step falter.

I looked over to see Mahalia standing in the kitchen doorway, her hands fisted in her apron, her eyes swollen and red-rimmed. 'Here; let me take them fish, child,' she said, reaching for them.

I shook my head back and forth in hopeless denial. 'Tell me she's not dead,' I said, as if I still believed, even then, that I could somehow make reality bend to my will, just by wishing it.

'She went easy, when the time come. That poor baby is with the Lord now.'

'She doesn't belong with the Lord,' I screamed, practically throwing the fish at Mahalia. 'She belongs here, with her mother, with *us*. She was supposed to grow up and go to school, and learn to ride a horse and play the piano and dance and . . . and a thousand different things she'll never get a chance to do. Never.'

'Amrie—'

'I hate this damned war! I hate Abraham Lincoln, and General Sherman, and every damned Yankee who ever set foot down here where he don't belong. But you know who I hate more'n anything? God. I hate God.'

'Don't say that, child.' She reached for me, but I jerked away.

'Why? You think he's listening? Haven't you figured it out yet? He never listens to anybody! He doesn't punish the wicked or reward the good. He just flat out *doesn't care*.'

'Amrie!'

I hurled my fishing pole away from me, the cane bouncing on the hard, sunbaked ground. I could hear the distant hoot of an unseen owl, smell the bite of wood smoke on the cooling air as the last of the day's sunlight bled away. Once, I might have run off to sob out my fear and anger and pain alone in the barn or within the sheltering branches of my favorite live oak. The urge to do so was still strong.

Instead, I swiped one crooked elbow across my wet face and walked into the house to wrap my arms around my sobbing aunt's trembling shoulders and whisper, 'I'm sorry, Aunt Em. I'm so, so sorry.'

Castile fashioned a small coffin of boards salvaged from our ruined rosewood dining table. We rested the coffin, as was the custom, on two straight-backed chairs we positioned in front of the parlor windows. The curtains hung in tatters, and the room still smelled of molasses, although we'd scrubbed and scrubbed. Mahalia said she reckoned some of it had seeped down between the floorboards where we couldn't get at it. But everyone who came to pay their respects already knew what had happened to us.

That night, long after the last of our friends and neighbors had come and gone, Aunt Em still sat on a stool pulled up beside the coffin. She'd been sitting there forever, just gazing at her dead child's face as if desperate to etch every line, every beloved feature in her memory for all time.

Finally, Mama came to rest her hand on her younger sister's shoulder. 'Emma . . . I know it feels unbearable, now. I know . . .' Her voice cracked, and she had to hesitate and start over again. 'I know you feel like you can't go on, like you don't want to go on. But in time it will get better. It won't ever go away. But it will get better, I promise.'

'How did you live through it, Kate? *Twice*? And Mama . . . she lost so many. Hannah was my joy; she lit up my life. And now she's gone, I . . . I just want to die.'

'Oh, honey . . . no.'

I stood in the shadows, holding myself very still, feeling like I was intruding on something I wasn't supposed to hear.

Aunt Em said, 'One night in Vicksburg, during the siege, a mortar shell hit a cave just a few hundred feet from ours. A little girl was killed. One minute she was just sleeping in her bed, and the next instant, she was dead. She was only three or four – Hannah's age. It could so easily have been Hannah. I remember sitting in the moonlight in front of our cave and listening to that poor bereaved mother. She cried all night, sometimes wailing and screaming, sometimes sobbing, sometimes moaning so softly I could only just hear her. And I kept thinking, How can she stand it? How could I stand it, if . . .' A ragged sob stole her breath, her face crumpling, and she put up a hand to cover her grief-contorted mouth.

Mama knelt beside her to take Emma's other hand between hers.

'You need to sleep, Em. You'll make yourself deathly ill.'

'What do I have to live for, now?'

'You need to live for yourself, Em. For yourself, and for Galen, and all the future children you will have together. At least you still have a husband.'

Emma shook her head. 'I just can't care anymore. I don't think there's anything that compares to the love a mother feels for her own child. It's . . . it's all-consuming and selfless and . . . and . . .' She paused, her body wracked by a wet, tearing cough. 'I just don't know how I can go on without her.'

'But you will, Em. I know you can't see it, now. But you will. We go on because we must. We take one breath after another, live one day after another, and eventually that unbearably painful pressure of sadness in our hearts eases. It never entirely goes away, but it eases.'

'I just miss her so much,' Emma cried, her body convulsing with her sobs. 'I think about never seeing her again and I feel like I'm being torn in two.'

Mama put her arms around her sister's shaking shoulders and held her close. But she didn't say anything, I suppose because in the end there was really nothing to say. How do you comfort the mother of a dead child?

The truth is, you can't.

The next morning dawned overcast and unseasonably cold, with a biting wind that scuttled dried leaves down the weed-choked drive.

Cyrus Pringle came out from St Francisville with a handcart, and Castile brought a hammer and a handful of precious nails he'd salvaged from a burned-out building down in Bayou Sara. But Aunt Em couldn't bear to let them close the tiny coffin's lid or load it on Mr Pringle's cart.

'Em, it's time,' said Mama softly.

'I know. Just one more minute . . .'

The faint clip-clop of horses' hooves carried above the thrashing of the limbs of the live oaks and pecans in the yard.

'Who's that?' asked Adelaide sharply. These days, horses almost always meant trouble.

Cyrus went to peer out the ruined curtains. 'Two Yankees; a lieutenant and his sergeant. I seen him before. It's that Lieutenant

Beckham what was around early in the summer, asking after them two Wisconsin fellers who disappeared.'

For one brief instant, my mother's warning gaze met mine. I was careful not to even glance toward Mahalia. But I could feel my heart racing in my chest so hard and fast that my fingers were tingling.

Adelaide – who knew nothing of what the three of us had done – said, 'What now? Haven't they done enough?'

'Maybe I'll jist go ask them that,' said Castile, walking out onto the porch. 'There's a dead child in here,' we heard him say, his voice carrying clearly. 'Can't y'all leave these poor womenfolk to mourn in peace?'

'I'm sorry,' said the lieutenant, the shells of the drive crunching under his boot heels as he swung out of the saddle. 'But I have my orders.'

He left his sergeant with the horses and came into the house with his hat in his hands, which I suppose was an improvement over the last lot of his compatriots we'd had. He drew up just inside the entrance to the parlor, his gaze fixed on Hannah's tiny coffin, and I knew from the expression on his face that he hadn't actually expected to find a dead child, that he'd assumed it was just another Southern strategy to avoid the ravages folks tended to associate with visits from anyone wearing a blue uniform.

His gaze shifted to the torn curtains, to the axe-chopped piano, to the bayonet-slashed portrait of Simon that still hung over the sideboard. 'Who did this?' he asked.

'Unfortunately, they failed to leave a proper calling card,' said Adelaide tartly. 'But they obviously learned their manners from your General Sherman.'

He brought his gaze back to Hannah's pale, waxen face. 'And the child? Did they kill the child?'

It was my mother who answered. 'Did they bayonet her, the way they did the cushions of the sofa or our bonnets? No. But they broke the bottle of quinine that was keeping her alive. So I'd say, yes; they killed her.' Her features contorted with a raw upswelling of the anger and hatred she normally managed to suppress. 'He's a fine man, your President Abraham Lincoln, is he not? Making war on women and children in the hopes that their suffering and death will draw their menfolk away from the battlefields, thus achieving what your mighty armies cannot.'

The lieutenant's gaze drifted again around the ruined room, lingering on the empty bookshelves, his eyebrows twitching together in a troubled frown. 'He is a great president. That's not to say he hasn't listened to some bad advisors.'

'Great presidents don't listen to bad advisers.'

'There are those who say that desperate times call for desperate measures.'

'So I've heard. Is that not the argument always used to justify the worst kinds of evil? I'd say the genuine measure of a man – of a nation – is to be found in how true they remain to their principles in times of duress. Under that test, I'd say your president – and your nation – have failed miserably. Although I've no doubt that, should you prove victorious, these barbarities will be justified by future generations. That is, if they are acknowledged and remembered at all.'

I looked from my mother to the young lieutenant, and back again. And I knew the same odd sensation I'd experienced the first time this man rode into our lives – the sense that he and my mother might have been the only two people in the room, for they spoke solely to each other.

He looked again at the coffin that rested before the front windows. A muscle worked along his tightly held jaw. 'I am sincerely sorry for your loss. But I'm afraid I must ask you some questions. Last June, two men from the 4th Wisconsin disappeared while in this area: a Captain Gabriel Dupont and a Sergeant Boyle.'

He paused, but when no one said anything, he continued, 'Captain Dupont and his sergeant were riding two rather conspicuous racehorses taken from the stables of Virgil Slaughter: Dance Away and Rainstorm. One of the horses – Dance Away – recently turned up near Pointe Coupee in the possession of a man named Cato Quincy.'

I saw my mother suck in a quick breath, her eyes widening almost imperceptibly with shock and fear. It was subtle enough that I hoped the lieutenant didn't notice. I was glad he wasn't looking at me because my own horror and guilt were surely written all over my face.

'Quincy claims he bought the horse in Texas, from one Peyton Underwood, who refugeed there early last summer. He says Underwood told him he was given the horses by a woman from St Francisville.'

'And did he tell you the identity of this woman?' asked my

mother, her voice so clear and strong – even vaguely scornful – that I was in awe.

'No.'

I risked throwing a quick glance at Mahalia, but she'd assumed the look of bland innocence perfected early by anyone who'd ever been enslaved. Aunt Em was quietly weeping on Adelaide's shoulder, while Cyrus Pringle and Castile stood with their hands loose at their sides, their faces set in angry helplessness.

'So you're . . . what?' asked my mother. 'Visiting every woman in St Francisville to ask if she gave away two racehorses? This is why you've interrupted my niece's funeral?'

A faint tinge of color darkened the lieutenant's face. 'I have my orders, ma'am.'

'Then you may tell your superiors that I haven't seen Dance Away since he ran in the Governor's Cup in 1861.'

For a long, breathless moment, the Federal lieutenant stared at my mother. I had the uncomfortable sensation that beneath his careful manners and seeming nobility of spirit, this man was no fool, and he knew my mother was perfectly capable of lying with calm composure.

But he simply shifted his grip on his hat's brim and sketched a short bow. 'My apologies, again, and my condolences.'

Then he swept from the room.

No one moved or spoke. We listened to the hollow clatter of his boot tread descending the wooden front steps, to his curt orders to his sergeant, and the rhythm of their horses trotting back toward the gate.

Cyrus Pringle blew out a long, quavering breath and said, 'This ain't good. This ain't good at all.'

Adelaide looked up from comforting Aunt Em. 'Since when is the Union Army so interested in the fates of two men?'

'Since one of them is the nephew of the Governor of Wisconsin,' said Mama.

For one brief, stolen moment, Mahalia, Mama, and I exchanged glances. Somehow in the course of all that had happened over the past few months, I'd almost convinced myself that Captain Dupont and Sergeant Boyle had been forgotten by the Federals. I could sometimes go nearly a whole day at a time without thinking of them myself – until, maybe, the wind blew hot and sour out of the bayou, or the rain teemed down in hard, blinding sheets that would forever bring back that night in shivering, vivid detail.

But Captain Gabriel Dupont had not been forgotten. And I found myself obsessing over the other breadcrumb trails that could conceivably lead back to us, the gold coins we'd given to Reverend Lewis and a certain crystal, heart-shaped locket preserving an absent husband's sandy-colored curl.

It never occurred to me that the two dead men themselves could yet betray us.

Forty-Seven

The one-armed boy, Dibbie, left us soon after that, taking up with the itinerant preacher who'd given Aunt Em a ride from Vicksburg.

As the last of the summer heat died and autumn settled over the Felicianas, the hair grew thick on the backs of the creatures of the woods and swamp, and thunder rolled often in the distance. Folks started muttering about the early migration of the geese and ducks, about the numerous, heavy fogs we'd had in August, about the frequent halos visible around the moon. All were signs of another harsh winter.

Mama said, 'It's rank nonsense. Squirrels gather lots of nuts every year. And don't get me started on the wisdom of woolly worms.'

I hoped she was right. Last year's winter had killed folks all over the South. And this year our situation was a whole lot worse. Nobody anywhere within reach of a Union army had any livestock left, and the salt needed to preserve even wild game was impossible to find. Rampaging soldiers had emptied our corncribs and raided our pantries; they'd broken our windows, stolen or destroyed our blankets and warm clothes. Even when folks had real money, there was nothing to buy. And Confederate script was practically worthless. 'Confederate' had become an adjective used to describe anything that was rough, crude, or improvised. Thus, Confederate silver was a tin cup; Confederate gas was a pine torch, and a Confederate carriage was an old wagon drawn by mules – although these days we saw precious few of those, too.

So I was surprised when I took a slab of venison to Mrs O'Reilly one day in early October to see a mule grazing in the long grass near the cottage's broken front stoop. The Federals had burned all her fence rails, so she had the mule tethered to a sycamore tree. As I drew nearer, I could see the US branded on its flank.

'Finn give him to me,' she said, bustling about to put a battered kettle on to boil.

'How is he?' I asked, settling on one of the benches drawn up to their trestle table. I knew Finn dropped in to see his mother from time to time when the Partisan Rangers were in the area, and it kinda hurt that he'd never once come to see me. But Mrs O'Reilly said it was because he didn't want to put us in any danger. The Federals were known to wreck a special kind of vengeance on the homes of anyone related to or suspected of helping the Rangers.

I saw the shadow of some emotion I couldn't name pass over her sharp features. 'He's fit and healthy. And he's grown so, I reckon he's bigger'n his da ever was.'

'He's with Banyon now?'

She nodded, her lips pressed into a tight line. Folks told troublesome stories about Colonel Banyon – the kind of tales repeated in whispers and likely to leave you feeling a bit queasy.

I looked out the window to where Finn's younger brother and sisters were engaged in a mock battle, with long sticks standing in for rifles and a big fat log pressed into duty as a cannon. As I watched, the younger sister, Annie, pantomimed a direct hit, clamping her hands to her thin chest and falling over in an artistic heap.

'You'd think they'd get enough of this damned war without needin' to play at it, too,' said Mrs O'Reilly, following my gaze. 'Now I've got my Benjamin mad to go off to war, and him only ten.'

I didn't know what to say. Christian LeBlanc had run off that spring to be a drummer boy at the age of twelve. His mother just heard he'd died of diphtheria in a hospital in Georgia.

'How's your aunt doing?' asked Mrs O'Reilly, setting a chipped cup of blackberry tea in front of me.

'She ain't never been well since living all them weeks in that cave in Vicksburg. She keeps coughing something awful. And she's grieving bad for Hannah.'

'Poor woman,' said Mrs O'Reilly, settling on the opposite bench. 'She needs another baby to take her mind off the one she lost.'

In the mock battle taking place outside, the older girl, Jessica, was the next to die, hands flung out dramatically. The boy, Benjamin, let out a victorious war whoop and beat his fists against his chest in triumph.

'Ireland was bad, but this . . . this is worse,' said Mrs O'Reilly, her gaze, again, on the children. 'It alters a body, all this hardship and anger and death. Twists and stunts them, and turns 'em mean and hard. There must've been a better way – you ain't never gonna convince me otherwise. But that's men for you, ain't it? Always so full of bluster, so eager to fight, so cocksure they can win the day. And there's my Benjamin, wantin' to have at it and worryin' the war'll be over before he gets a chance to fight.'

'Maybe it will be,' I said.

But she just looked at me, her face pinched with worries and sorrows the nature of which I could only guess.

Two days later, another letter was found thrust into our door at dawn. But this one wasn't written by Uncle Bo.

15 October 1863

Dear Mrs St Pierre,

It is with deepest sorrow and the most sincere condolences that I write to tell you of the death of your brother, Lieutenant Colonel Bo Dunbar. He died bravely and heroically, rallying the men at Auburn. I hope it brings you comfort to know that his death was quick, and that he died with Our Lord's name on his lips.

He spoke of you often, and I know you don't need me to tell you what an extraordinary man he was: cheerful, honest, brave, always ready to sacrifice for a friend or comrade. He will be dreadfully missed by his regiment and all who knew him.

He will be buried at the new cemetery at Arlington. Let us pray for a happier time when you will be able to visit him there.

Sincerely,
Colonel Harrison Henley

Mama read the letter aloud to Aunt Em and me while standing at Aunt Em's bedside. A hard autumn rain pounded on the roof and clattered on the trembling leaves of the live oaks barely visible out in the yard through the downpour. Her voice cracked at one point, but she kept going. At the end, she looked up to find Adelaide standing motionless in the hallway just outside the door.

'Well,' said my mother, her glittering gaze meeting Adelaide's from across the room. 'You always said he was dead to you. Now he truly is.'

And with that she walked into her own room and closed the door behind her with a snap.

That night I lay awake thinking about Uncle Bo and listening to Aunt Em's wet cough echoing through the house.

I knew Mama was dreadfully worried about her. She'd tried bleeding her and dosing her with lemon and honey. But what she really needed was the kind of medicines denied to us by the Federal blockade, things like Dover's powder and sulfur.

I'd never understood before how a body could die of grief. But I was afraid that was what was going to happen to Aunt Em now. Technically I supposed the inflammation in her lungs was killing her. But she'd lost the will to fight it off and live.

How many more? I wanted to scream at the dark ceiling above me. *How many more of the people I love are you going to take? What'd Aunt Em ever do to you?* I was pretty sure she'd never screamed, *I hate God!* Yet I was still alive and healthy, and she was down there hacking her lungs out.

And then I became aware of another sound, a sound so faint, so unexpected that I slipped from my bed to make sure I was hearing it right. I stepped carefully to avoid any betraying creaks, my toes curling away from the cold floorboards as I crept across the room, hardly daring to breathe when I paused beside the wall that separated my room from what was now my grandmother's.

Adelaide had always prided herself on her ability to fall asleep quickly and stay asleep. She considered habitual or even occasional bouts of wakefulness a self-indulgence and a weakness to which she claimed never to succumb. Yet in the dark silence of the night, I could hear the quiet shifting of Simon's old bed, and something more.

I stood disbelieving in the frigid darkness, hot tears stinging my eyes, a nearly unbearable weight of sadness pressing my chest as I listened to the quiet, muffled sounds of an old woman's sobbing,

her voice choked and torn with the ferocity of a grief carefully kept
hidden all day long.

'Oh, Bo,' whispered Adelaide. 'My son, my son . . .'

Forty-Eight

The folks who'd said we were in for another hard winter were right.

The first snows fell in October, sweeping down out of the north
on a vicious, bitter wind. 'Ain't it enough that God sends all them
blue-coated Yankees down here to torment us?' grumbled Cyrus
Pringle one day when I took in a scythe for him to mend. 'Did he
haveta send us their dadburned weather, too?'

The problem was, our houses were built for hot weather, not cold,
with high ceilings that sucked up the warmth from our fires and wide
eaves that kept out any feeble sunshine that might have helped. Many
of us also had to contend with what folks called 'Yankee ventilation';
windows broken by the Federal raiding parties that seemed to swarm
over us nearly every week. Glass was now even harder to come by
than salt. All we could do was cover the empty panes with scraps of
oil cloth, which made our houses dark and depressing.

By late November, the ice froze so hard and thick on the bayou
that those children who had shoes could go sliding down it, arms
windmilling wildly, their shouts and laughter carrying on the cold,
clear air. That's when we started hearing tales of people freezing
to death. Old folks or those too sick and infirm to go out and collect
wood were found stiff as boards in their beds.

And on top of it all, everybody was hungry. Not only had the
Federals emptied our larders and corncribs, and driven off or
killed our livestock; but fishing hooks were becoming as scarce
as needles and hairpins, and no one had powder or even a gun
anymore. Castile collected a group of ten- and twelve-year-old
boys, taught them how to make bows and arrows, and took them
out hunting. Game was scarce, for the animals were having as
hard of a time as we were. But I don't know how the town
would've made it through that winter without Castile and the
skills he'd learned hiding out as a fugitive slave with a now-
vanished tribe of Choctaw.

Still, folks kept dying. We lost Aunt Em three weeks before Christmas and buried her next to Hannah, although the ground was so hard that Castile, Cyrus Pringle, and Reverend Lewis himself had to take turns hacking at the frozen earth. I still remember standing at her graveside, listening to the reverend's words washing over me, my nose and cheeks burning from the cold wind, my toes numb. My heart must've been numb by then, too, because I didn't cry. Neither did Adelaide. There was a time I'd have faulted her for it, but now I understood. Of the ten babies she'd birthed, only two remained alive. I guess she was numb, too.

But I still couldn't find it within myself to forgive her for what she'd done to Castile. Truth was, I wasn't trying. Seemed to me, some things were unforgivable, and that kind of cruelty – whether to a fellow human being or an animal – was one of them. I'd always seen her as a hard woman, although I'd loved her anyway. But I realized now that I'd never really known her, never known the woman that lived inside her.

I refused to believe that all I had glimpsed was something that lived inside each of us.

About a week after Aunt Em's funeral, we received a letter from Uncle Tate telling us he'd been captured at Chattanooga and was now in a prison camp up in Chicago. He tried to make light of it, but the conditions sounded awful enough to make me think he was more in danger of dying now than he'd been in battle. And I started wondering if this was how the war was going to end – with all of us dead.

It was not too long before Christmas, when the sky was frosty white and the air glittered with ice crystals, that Adelaide came back from town one day with a ragged woman and her two pinch-faced children in tow.

The woman's name was Rhoda Magruder, and she looked well over forty years old, although I later found out she wasn't even thirty. She was a small, ferociously skinny thing with a riot of red hair and the ghost of freckles across her high cheekbones. Her husband was with the army in Tennessee, and as far as she knew he was still alive, although she hadn't heard from him in nearly a year. They'd had a farm near Liberty, Mississippi, until a raiding party burned the farmhouse and all the outbuildings. And so she'd walked down to St Francisville, hoping to find a room or even just a shed to shelter her family through the winter. She didn't have a cent to her name, and neither she nor the children had eaten any proper food for a week, so they were pretty near dead when Adelaide brought them home.

I never could understand why she did it. Adelaide had never had much use for philanthropy. And what made her rare gesture of generosity all the more surprising was that Rhoda Magruder was exactly the kind of illiterate, unwashed, ignorant pineywoods plain folk that Adelaide normally abominated. Not only was Rhoda superstitious and quick-tempered, but her twangy accent was enough to make Checkers howl in agony, and her grasp of the complexities of English grammar was faulty to the point of nonexistence.

That first frigid afternoon, she and her children huddled in front of our kitchen fire with their fists clenched crudely around spoons as they shoved corn mash into their mouths. They all had rags tied around their bare feet, and their eyes were like sunken purple smudges in their pale, bony faces.

'We can put them in the room next to Anne-Marie,' Adelaide told Mama. After Aunt Em died, Adelaide had moved back down to the first-floor bedroom. She would never have admitted it, but the truth was that climbing those steep steps had been hard on her.

I saw the look on Mama's face, although she quickly hid it. We were having a hard enough time finding food for ourselves. Now we had three more mouths to feed. But she never said anything. We'd all just need to eat a bit less.

I hadn't expected to like Rhoda Magruder – I guess I'd inherited more of my grandmother's prejudices than I liked to admit. But it didn't take me long to realize just how wrong I was. She was funny and warmhearted and honest, jaw-droppingly blunt and pragmatic, and fiercely brave. The only thing she owned besides the filthy rags on her back was an Allen and Wheelock revolver with four precious bullets she kept with her always. She said she'd taken it off a Federal soldier she'd found dead along the road between Liberty and St Francisville. But Mahalia reckoned that was a story.

'What makes you think that?' I asked her later that night, when Rhoda Magruder and her children were tucked up for the night in Simon's old room. We were sitting in front of the fire in the parlor with Mama; Adelaide had already gone to bed. I'd noticed she went to bed real early these days.

'Because if that woman really found a dead Yankee,' said Mahalia, 'she'd have stripped him of everything he had – clothes, boots, haversack, knapsack. Everything. So where's the rest of his gear?'

'Maybe she sold it,' I said.

Mahalia shook her head. 'Your grandma was there when the three of 'em come limping into St Francisville. They didn't have time to sell nothin'. And they didn't sell it on the way, neither, because you can tell they ain't been eatin' nothin' but bark and whatever old berries they could find. I reckon maybe she did take that pistol off a dead Yankee, but I'd say it's been a while.'

'Why would she lie?'

Mama looked up from working at altering Hannah's dress to fit Rhoda's little girl, Lisette. Lisette was maybe five and had the same wild hair as her mama. The boy, Hatch, was a couple years older and dark. 'I've no doubt she has her reasons,' said Mama.

At her words, the room suddenly got so quiet that I could hear the ash falling on the grate. I suspected we were all thinking the same thing, and I knew it when Mahalia said, 'You reckon that Lieutenant Beckham will be back?'

We'd never spoken of the lieutenant's appearance on the morning of Hannah's funeral or the implications of the disastrous return to the area of Virgil Slaughter's famous racehorse. In fact, we never talked about Gabriel Dupont and his sergeant at all.

We didn't talk about them now.

'He'll be back,' said Mama, and that was that.

Lately, a new menace had appeared in the area to threaten us.

In addition to the Federal raiding parties, the countryside was becoming increasingly infested with all sorts of dangerous men. Deserters from both armies, men avoiding conscription, paroled prisoners, ex-slaves, and bushwhackers and jayhawkers from places like Missouri and Arkansas had joined up with the kind of rough local elements that in times of peace were usually locked up in our parish jail.

They roved the countryside, as rapacious as the Federals at their worst and engaging in the same kinds of mindless cruelties and senseless destruction. Some claimed sympathy for one side or the other, but in practice they owed allegiance to nothing and no one. Mama said she thought most of them belonged in a lunatic asylum, but as far as Adelaide was concerned, the only thing you could do with men like that was shoot them.

I tended to agree with Adelaide. The problem was, we lived in a no man's land between two warring armies, and all civilian authority in the state of Louisiana had virtually ceased to function. With our menfolk off fighting, we were a vulnerable population of women, children, and aging or mutilated men. Most of what few guns we'd once possessed had been seized by the Federals, leaving us essentially defenseless.

As the tales of theft, murder, torture, and rape grew increasingly frequent, I found more and more comfort in the existence of Rhoda Magruder's revolver – however she'd happened to come by it.

Two days before Christmas, it got so cold the mercury dropped below zero. I don't think it'd ever got that cold in the Felicianas before. Birds fell frozen dead out of the live oaks, and everything from lemon trees to camellias and gardenias shriveled up and turned brown. It was as if God had forgotten us.

Or hated us.

Lots of folks quietly decided not to observe Christmas that year. There wasn't any food to eat, nobody felt much like celebrating anything, and few people even had stockings, let alone the where-withal to fill them. Most mothers told their children Santa Claus couldn't get through the Federal blockade. Others just flat out said the Yankees had shot him.

But Mama decided we were going to give Lisette and Hatch Magruder and little Althea a real Christmas – or at least, as good of a one as we could manage. She cut down a three-foot pine tree that we set up on the ruined piano and decorated with pine cones and holly berries. Adelaide sewed rag dolls for Lisette and Althea, and Mahalia traded some onions for an old snare drum. You could still sorta see where someone had scratched off the US to replace it with CSA, and there weren't any sticks, but like most boys his age, Hatch was army-mad. Come Christmas morning he pretty near drove us all crazy by marching around the house and rapping on his new drum with his knuckles until his mother finally took it away from him, saying, 'Soldier-boy, you keep bangin' on that-there drum, somebody's gonna stand you up agin a wall and shoot you daid.'

I'd gone out early that morning and shot a big, twenty-pound tom that Mahalia roasted with a pile of potatoes and carrots. I was just helping her carry it all into the house when a band of half a dozen bushwhackers descended on the yard, whooping like Indians and laughing like the demented demons of hell.

They rode around us in an ever-tightening circle, their breath forming white clouds in the frosty air. 'Whatcha got there, girl?' asked one of them, an appallingly filthy, brown-haired, bearded man who leaned sideways in his saddle and made a play out of inhaling the hot turkey's aroma. 'Mmm-mm, that smells mighty good.'

He was built long and skinny, with a big hooked nose and hair so matted and greasy that it glistened. He wore nearly new, sky-blue Federal trousers with a yellow stripe up the sides, a grubby shirt made out of mattress ticking, and a gray Confederate officer's frock coat festooned on the sleeves with golden Hungarian knots and showing a charred hole in the breast that suggested how its previous owner had met his end.

I edged closer to Mahalia, the dish of precious carrots and potatoes gripped tightly against me. I could feel my mouth going dry, my heart seizing up so that it hurt.

'Looks mighty good, too,' said another man with an ugly laugh. These were no Yankees, for their accents were as broad and twangy as Rhoda's. 'That was right thoughtful of y'all to fix us Christmas dinner. But you ain't invited us in to eat yet. You don't expect us to sit out here in the yard, now do ya? We ain't niggers.'

All the other men laughed uproariously, edging their mounts ever closer, the horses' powerful hindquarters bunching and flexing, steam rising from their hot, sweaty hides.

'What else ya got for us?' asked the first man, and it occurred to me, from the way the others deferred to him, that he must be their leader.

'How 'bout a lead bullet?' said Rhoda Magruder, her voice carrying clearly across the yard.

For one intense moment, the bushwhackers all froze, their horses tossing their heads as the men reined in sharply. Then their gazes turned toward the back gallery.

She stood at the top of the steps, her big revolver held in a steady, two-handed grip, the muzzle trained squarely on the chest of the black-bearded man in the gold-trimmed frock coat and black felt hat. She had filled out in the weeks she'd been with us, so that she now looked more her age, her glorious red hair wild around her head.

'I got one bullet fer each of you varmints,' she said, thumbing

back the hammer. 'Way I figure it, y'all are a waste of good ammunition, seeing as how I reckon you're too scrawny and tough to
make good eatin'. But I'm willin' to make the sacrifice, if'n you
insist on pressin' the point.'

Black Beard threw back his head and laughed, and after a moment,
his companions joined in. 'Little lady, I reckon you couldn't hit the
broad side of a barge with that thing.' He leaned forward to rest
one forearm across the pommel of his saddle. 'But it was right kind
of you to sashay out here and spare us the trouble of comin' in
there after you. You ain't a bad lookin' woman, if a man likes red
h—'

I jumped as the report of a pistol shot echoed across the yard.
The black-bearded bushwhacker pitched backward off his horse, his
chest blooming crimson, the smoke from the burnt powder drifting
on the cold wind as Rhoda Magruder thumbed back the hammer
again.

'I got me five more bullets. My daddy taught me t'shoot by
picking off the squirrels running along the top of a fence rail, so if
yer countin' on me missin' yer ugly hides, yer all plumb stupid.'

I knew for a fact that she only had three more bullets. But the
men didn't know that. They looked at each other, their horses sidling
nervously beneath them.

'Y'all can just turn around and ride right out of here. And don't
even think of comin' back. I see yer ugly faces again, I swear to
God, I'll cut off all yer preckers and feed 'em to the hogs. Now
git.'

Without even bothering to pick up their fallen leader, the bushwhackers snagged the reins of his riderless bay and dug their spurs
into their own horses' sides, the churning hooves flinging up tufts
of brown grass as they galloped toward the road.

'Think they'll be back?' I asked.

Rhoda shook her head. 'Nah. Them kind's cowards. They'll just
move on to whoever they reckon'll be an easier target.'

'Too bad you didn't shoot more of them,' I said, and to my
surprise, Rhoda laughed.

'What we gonna do wit him?' asked Mahalia, nodding toward
the dead bushwhacker who lay sprawled on the frozen earth, one
leg crumpled awkwardly beneath him, his unseeing gaze fixed on
the white winter sky above.

'Reckon there's enough hungry critters to take care of him quick

enough, if we drag him down into that coulee back there,' said
Rhoda. 'But he can jist bleed all over the yard fer now, as far as
I'm concerned. Ain't no sense lettin' Christmas dinner git cold.'

That night, the wind blew away the clouds, leaving the sky a clear
blue-black panorama of infinity glittering with a universe of stars.

I stood at my dormer window, wrapped in a ragged quilt against
the cold radiating off the glass, my gaze on the black shapes of the
live oaks and pecans shifting in the darkness. Somewhere out there,
hungry wild animals were doubtless already tearing at what was
left of the dead bushwhacker. I tried not to picture it, but I couldn't
help it.

Before we dumped him in the coulee, Rhoda Magruder had calmly
stripped the body of anything useful – which meant everything
except his ragged, stained drawers. Mahalia and I both expected
Mama to insist that he ought to be buried, and I spent most of
Christmas dinner dreading another midnight visit to the swamps.
But she didn't. I wasn't sure if it was because he wasn't a Federal,
or because she didn't feel so personally responsible for his death,
or if the events of the past six months had simply altered her attitude
towards the proper disposal of inconvenient corpses.

Clutching my quilt tighter, I stared up at the cold night sky.
Despite the little pine tree on the ruined piano and the turkey dinner,
it still didn't feel like Christmas. I wondered if I'd ever be able to
celebrate Christmas again without remembering those howling,
jeering, unwashed men, or the pulpy red mess Rhoda Magruder's
bullet made of Black Beard's chest.

I decided, probably not.

'"Peace on earth, and good will toward men",' I quoted softly,
one hand coming up to touch the icy, frosted windowpane. I thought
about what my mother had said, that most bushwhackers and
jayhawkers probably belonged in a lunatic asylum. It seemed to me
that if this war kept going long enough, the same could probably
be said about most of us.

I was about to turn back to bed when I thought I saw something
move in the yard. I paused, my breath rasping in my tight throat,
my eyes straining to see in the darkness. But the night was full of
shadows, the moon a faint silvery sliver tossed by a fitful wind. I
told myself it was just the product of an overactive imagination that
saw a boy's familiar way of moving when nothing was even there.

But it was still long before I slept. And in the morning, I crept down the stairs early to open the front door.

A sack of real, honest-to-God flour and a bag of coffee leaned against the jamb. And in case I wasn't sure who'd left them, there was also a fistful of arrows fletched with turkey feathers and crafted by a boy-man who could move as silently as a moonbeam over frosted ground.

Forty-Nine

We could have hoarded the flour and coffee, and feasted on it in secret for months. I knew there were some who did such things. But not many. These days, when folks got their hands on a supply of flour, they threw what we called a biscuit party. It was sort of like a recipe party, only a whole lot more satisfying.

The appointed day dawned overcast but blessedly warm, and the ladies of St Francisville came wearing their best salvaged or carefully preserved dresses, with darned gloves and homemade palmetto hats decorated with sprigs of holly and mistletoe. Even habitual sourpusses like old Mrs Mumford and Jane Gastrell were there, smiling something fierce and near giddy with anticipation. I don't think there was anything we'd come to pine after more than honest-to-God wheat flour. There were lots of substitutes, but after a while they all just sorta stuck in your caw and left you dreaming of the real thing.

While Mahalia and Rhoda Magruder whipped up batch after batch of flaky, golden-brown biscuits, the ladies crowded into our ruined parlor and dining room, and even spilled out onto the galleries. Each was careful to only take one biscuit at a time.

'Mmm,' sighed Maisie Sparrow, her eyes closing as she bit into her first biscuit. 'I done died and met the Lord, and he's handed me this here biscuit at the pearly gates.'

Beside her, Jemma Huber held her own biscuit in her hands, a look of wonder suffusing her face. 'Me, I'm just gonna stand here and look at this biscuit and smell it. I'm afraid if I try to eat it, it's gonna disappear.'

'Jemma,' said Rowena Walford, 'the way you save everything,

that biscuit's going to be a rock before you get around to eating it.'

Everyone laughed, including Miss Jemma, who opened her eyes and took a tentative nibble.

There was no denying the biscuits would've tasted better with butter melting into their soft white goodness. But some of the ladies had brought with them clay crocks of honey and preserves, and shared them generously. Nobody asked where the flour came from. We all knew the only flour that ever appeared in our parts came from the Yankees, sometimes through speculators, but most often from raids on the Federal supply lines. And the less said openly about that sort of thing, the better.

I walked amongst the ladies with trays of hot biscuits and listened, faintly smiling, as they all talked at once.

'. . . he was shoving all my dresses and the children's clothes, too, into pillowcases, and I said to him, "What use does a man like you have for such things?" And he looks up at me like I'm daft and says, "Ain't I got a wife and four children up North?".'

'. . . don't know what it is about Yankees and crockery,' said Margaret Mason. 'It's like they've got an aversion to it or something. They see a plate or a bowl, and they've just got to smash it. By the time they were done, there wasn't an unbroken piece in the house. I'm eating off a part of what used to be a platter, while Mercy uses the side of one of my big old crocks—'

'. . . a bunch of 'em grabbed Ada Wolfe's pretty young gal, Heidi, when she was comin' back from her grandma's last week. Took Ada two days to find her, barely alive and all covered in her own blood down by the creek. Tried to keep it quiet, of course, but how can you, with the poor thing doing nothing but alternately laughing and crying and saying, "Please don't; oh, please stop,"? Mind's gone—'

'. . . they said he died real quick and easy, but that's what they always say, isn't it? Whether it's true or not—'

'. . . I've just about got Danny's uniform ready; all I need is to find a couple more buttons. He's only turned fifteen, but with his brothers all dead, he feels somebody from the family ought to be fightin' for our independence. Me, I was hoping this damned war'd be over before he was old enough to go. But I can't stand in his way. All I can do is pray—'

My tray was empty again, but for a moment I simply stood in the doorway to the parlor and let my gaze drift over the familiar

faces of the women. I could see the Widow Carlyle and Delia
Stocking, Sophie Gantry and Trudi Easton – even Amelia Ferguson
was there. After little Theodore died, I thought for sure she'd die
of grief or lose her senses completely. But she was starting to get
out more and more.

These women had been a part of my life for as long as I could
remember. And yet I'd always felt somehow apart from them, alien-
ated and alone and isolated. I wasn't sure when exactly that all
changed. We'd been through so much together, years of increasing
suffering and brutal want. Somehow it had forged a sense of unity,
a bond of commonality and deep affection as precious as it was
unexpected. We had starved together, frozen together, feared and
grieved together. We'd shared our food, our joys, and our sorrows;
we read each others' precious letters, knew the intimate details of
each others' lives that in times of peace were kept hidden and
private. With life stripped down to its most basic elements, it was
hard to remember the differences that had once divided us. We now
understood that our fears and hopes were all the same. And I knew
a rush of affection for these women that both humbled me and
buoyed me up and strengthened me.

I suppose it was a version of the comradeship known to fighting
men – that uniquely masculine bond forged by war that historians
and poets and novelists were always lauding. But the likes of Homer
and Sir Walter Scott never talked about what *we* experienced, about
the bonds formed amongst the women and children left alone in
times of war to face hardship and deprivation and danger, to confront
marauding armies and battle every day to find food and stay warm
and simply survive.

'Amrie,' said my mother, gently recalling me to the task at hand.
'More biscuits.'

Fifty

Nobody celebrated New Year's Eve anymore. As glad as we were
to see the back of 1863, the thought of what 1864 might bring was
too frightening to contemplate for long.

A couple of weeks later, on a cold January afternoon, the Federal

gunboat *Lafayette* subjected St Francisville to the worst bombardment we'd yet endured. We heard later that the commander, Foster,
claimed he'd given the women and children of the city twenty-four
hours to evacuate before he started firing. It was a lie. For what
seemed like forever, frantic mothers sheltered their shrieking children as best they could in cellars and behind brick stoops as hundreds
of exploding shells and whistling rockets rained down on us.

We were told the bombardment was in punishment for the recent
arrest in the area of a Confederate deserter. The problem was, no
one could figure out how the Yankees even knew the deserter had
been nabbed, let alone why they should care what happened to him.

It had been a long time since I'd given much consideration to
the Federal messenger who'd drowned down on Thompson's Creek
or to the 'Dear Madam' who lived amongst us. But I now found it
hard to think about much else. I refused to believe that one of the
laughing, warm-hearted women who'd filled our house and shared
our biscuits could somehow be a traitor. And so my suspicions
turned, inevitably, to the one woman who would never throw a
biscuit party: Hilda Meyers.

It was no secret that Hilda Meyers had all the flour she could
eat and never shared it with anybody. She had taken the dreaded
Oath of Allegiance without a second thought, and was in constant
communication with a son who lived in New Orleans and was said
to be in thick with the occupation authorities. I'd only recently
learned that she even had a son. It'd come as something of a shock,
for there was nothing the least bit gentle or maternal about Hilda
Meyers.

I was careful not to voice any of these suspicions to my mother.
But a few days later, Castile hurt his leg while helping Reverend
Lewis stabilize the church after the Federal bombardment, and the
subject came up when I went to see how he was doing.

I found him in his tack room, fixing a shelf that had been jarred
loose in the same bombardment. I said, 'I thought Mama told you
to rest that leg?'

He settled on a stool beside the stove and gave me a grin. 'I'm
restin', I'm restin'.'

I made him a cup of real coffee with the beans I'd brought him,
then sat and listened while he told me about how the reverend
reckoned it was a miracle that his Pilcher organ had come through
another shelling without hardly a scratch on it.

I said, 'Seems to me that if the good Lord was working miracles, them Yankee shells wouldn't have hit the church at all.'

Castile 'tssked' and shook his head. 'Child, child; you gotta have faith.'

'Why?'

'Cause that's the only way a body's ever gonna make it through this world of woe.'

'*Huh.*'

He smiled with his eyes and took another sip of his coffee. 'I hear yor grandma's doin' poorly.'

'She ain't said nothin' to me.'

'Well, she wouldn't, would she? That ain't your grandma's way. But Mahalia says yor momma thinks her heart is givin' out on her.'

I found the idea that something could be wrong with Adelaide too fantastical to consider. The woman was an indomitable rock, as constant and indestructible as all get out, and too mean and ornery to ever be ill.

I said as much to Castile, but he just got that pained expression on his face – the same one provoked by my mockery of Reverend Lewis's determined belief in miracles. 'One of these days, Amrie, you gotta see your way to get over this.' He pointed to his ruined face. 'If'n yor grandma dies and you ain't forgiven her, you're gonna feel bad the rest of yor life. Guaranteed.'

'Nope.'

He shook his head, but to my relief let the subject slide, saying, 'You hear what happened to Old Aunt Sylvia?'

Sylvia Chew was a *gens de couleur libre* who'd been putting flowers on her children's graves when the *LaFayette*'s shells started falling. She'd taken refuge in the church, but when part of the roof came crashing down on her, she'd run outside screaming to duck inside the Polk family's big mausoleum. A minute later, a whistling billy tore through the side of the tomb, burying her in bits of coffins, bones, and torn shrouds.

'She says to me, "What's the world comin' to, when even the dead ain't allowed to rest in peace?"' Castile laughed and drained the last of the coffee.

I said, 'Who you reckon told them Federals about that deserter?'

He lifted his shoulders in a shrug. 'I dunno. Word gets around.'

'I think it was Hilda Meyers.'

Castile grunted. 'Few years back, you and Finn was convinced she was a witch.'

I squirmed with all the discomfort typical of anyone reminded of the foolishness of their younger self. 'She ain't never supported this war, and you know it.'

'Yor momma and daddy ain't never supported this war, neither.'

'But they would never betray our friends and neighbors!'

'And you think Hilda Meyers would?'

'Don't you?'

He stared down at his empty mug for a moment, the scars showing grey against the darkness of his cheeks. 'I reckon Hilda Meyers got more reason than most to hate war and the sufferin' it brings on folks.'

I shook my head. 'I don't understand.'

'She already been through one war before comin' here. At a place called Cry-Mia.'

'The Crimea? You mean, in Russia? I always thought she was German.'

'Well, she is, but I hear tell her people settled in Russia long ago. I don't know too much about that. All I know is they had them a big war a few years back. Lots of folks fought in it – the Russian Bazaar and the King of England, and even a bunch of them Mohammedans.'

I nodded. I was vaguely familiar with the Crimean War, mainly because I'd grown up hearing my mother talk about Florence Nightingale.

Castile said, 'Part of the deal them Germans made when they settled in Cry-Mia was that they weren't supposed to be forced to fight. But war has a way of making governments forget whatever promises they done made to people.'

'Why? What happened?'

'Hilda had five sons once. The reason she's only got the one left is because the three oldest died fighting in that Cry-Mia War. Then they come after the fourth, only he refused to go. So they strung him up and hanged him dead, right there in front of her.'

I swallowed hard. 'What about the fifth?'

'He was still too young for them to take. But he wasn't gonna be for long. So after his brother was hanged, Hilda sold what she could and caught a ship with him for New Orleans.' Castile reached over to throw more wood into the stove. 'She lost most everybody she loved and everything she had to war before this war ever started. Ain't no wonder she feels about it the way she does. But that don't mean she's passing information to the Yankees.'

'Well, somebody is.'

Castile looked troubled.

'What?' I prodded.

But he only shook his head and refused to be drawn on the subject any further.

A few days later, I was bringing him a crock of Mahalia's soup when I was surprised to find Josephine's little girl, Calliope, playing with a half-grown orange and white kitten on the stoop.

'Hey, Calliope,' I said. 'Your mama here?'

The little girl looked up and shook her head. 'She done gone.'

'Gone where?'

The little girl shrugged her thin shoulders. 'I dunno. She says I'm to stay with Paw-Paw till she come back.'

I stared at her. Paw-Paw was an Acadian word for 'grandpa', although lots of other folks in south Louisiana used it.

I looked up to find Castile standing in his open doorway. 'I didn't know she was—'

'Here,' said Castile, reaching for the crock; 'let me take that soup from you.'

'Josephine says Calliope is Leo's,' Castile told me some time later as we watched the little girl spoon chunks of Mahalia's soup into her mouth. 'I think I can see my boy's mother in her – around the eyes, and in the way she holds her head when she's studying on something. But maybe that's just because I want to believe she's his. I like thinkin' something of my boy is livin' still.'

'Josephine's run off from Bon Silence?'

Castile nodded. 'Last night. But so many of the little ones've been dying in them contraband camps that she didn't want to take Calliope with her. Says it's one thing to risk her own life, but she ain't got no right to risk Calliope's.'

'Miss Rowena could just take Calliope away from you.'

'She could. But I don't reckon she will. Child that young ain't no use to her. She's just one more mouth to feed.'

I lowered my voice. 'You think Josephine will really come back for her?'

'Maybe, when this danged war is over. Truth is, I'm kinda hoping she don't.'

I was silent for a moment, my gaze still on the child, who'd finished her soup and was playing with the kitten again. 'I always heard Josephine was old Gilbert Vance's daughter. Miss Rowena's half-sister.'

'So they say.' He scrubbed a splayed hand down over his face. 'There's somethin' you gotta know, Amrie. Somethin' Josephine said before she left last night . . .'

And so I listened, while a warm breeze chased away the lingering rain clouds, and Castile told me the tale Calliope's mother had relayed to him.

She'd come to him when the wind was thrashing the sweetgum and buckthorn trees in the coulee behind his house, and lightning forked across the black night sky. She'd brought away with her the child and the kitten, and nothing else.

'Why now?' he'd asked her, his voice practically drowned out by the endlessly rumbling thunder. 'Why you runnin' off on a night like this, girl? Ain't no sense in it.'

'I got my reasons,' she said, cold rainwater dripping from her hair, her face showing stark and wet in the sizzling blue-white flashes of lightning.

'What you done?'

'Never you mind what I done. You better worry 'bout what your friends done. Mizz Rowena, she *knows*.'

'Knows what?'

Josephine gave a brittle laugh. 'You sayin' they ain't told you?'

'Told me what?'

'You remember BobbyTi? Tall, skinny man run off from Mizz Rowena last June?'

'Yes.'

'Most folks think BobbyTi run because he wanted to be free. But BobbyTi's a coward. He run because he scared. He found out somethin' about Mizz Rowena, somethin' she don't want nobody to know. He was afraid she was gonna have that crazy mulatto she got as an overseer kill him.'

Castile just shook his head and smiled.

'You laugh. That's 'cause you don't know Mizz Rowena. Folks think she's as soft and sweet as vanilla pudding, but that's just what

she want them to think. Truth is, that lady'll do anything for Bon
Silence – and I do mean anything.'

'What you sayin', girl?'

'I'm saying that when BobbyTi run off, he picked a night just
like this. Figured the dogs'd have a hard time tracking him. He had
an old skiff he'd found washed up on the levee after the spring
flood, and he'd hid it down by Cat Island. He was sliding down the
side of the bluff when he seen two women and a boy burying a
couple dead men in a hollow where a big old oak got blown down
in a storm. Now, BobbyTi, he figured it was an omen, a sign of
what was gonna happen to him if he stuck around. He didn't stop
running till he reached the contraband camp down by New Orleans.'

'What's any of this got to do with me?'

'I'm gettin' to that. See, after a while, BobbyTi heard about how
the Federals was all afire to find some missing captain and his
sergeant, and he knew then what he'd seen.'

'How'd he know that?'

'Because the men those women was burying had on blue uniforms,
that's how. Ain't no other Yankees disappeared around here I heard
about. Have you?'

'No.'

'Now, it took BobbyTi a while to sort out how he was gonna use
what he knowed, but it finally come to him. You see, BobbyTi, he
was missing his wife and children somethin' fierce. So he comes
back up here and he offers Mizz Rowena a deal: says if she'll let
his family go free, he'll tell her something that'll make the Yankees
right grateful to her.'

'I don't understand. What's Mizz Rowena got to do with the
Yankees?'

Josephine shoved the wet hair off her forehead in an exasperated
gesture. 'You just don't get it, do you? *That's* what BobbyTi found
out abut Mizz Rowena last June – the reason he run off in the first
place. I told you, that woman'll do anything for Bon Silence. As
soon as the Yankees moved into New Orleans and started confis-
cating plantations, she got it into her head they was gonna take Bon
Silence. So she been sending them messages full of whatever they
want to know. Don't matter to her who she betrays or who gets
killed, long as Bon Silence is safe.'

'And did she let BobbyTi's family go when he told her about
them two dead Federals?'

'She did. But here's the thing: BobbyTi, he told Mizz Rowena it was too dark that night for him to see the faces of the women burying them Yankees. But that weren't exactly the truth. He seen them clear enough when the lightning lit up the night. And that boy? He weren't really a boy, but a girl dressed up in boys clothes.'

Castile shook his head. 'I still don't understand what any of this has to do with me.'

And so she told him.

After Castile finished talking, I just stared out at the yard and watched the wind lift the moss hanging from the limbs of the live oaks and stir up little whirlwinds of dust.

He said, 'Why didn't you tell me, Amrie? Why didn't you let me help y'all?'

'We didn't tell anybody. We didn't want anyone else to suffer for what we'd done.' From here I could see a weed-choked cane field and the burned-out ruins of the old Sprague place. I said, 'You think BobbyTi will tell anybody else on us?'

Castile shook his head. 'Your daddy saved BobbyTi's life once, when he was real sick. He ain't gonna tell on y'all.'

'The Federals might make him tell.'

'Josephine said he ain't goin' back to New Orleans. Said now he's got his family, he's headed up to Ohio. Ain't no way them Yankees are gonna know it was you, Amrie. But y'all gotta be prepared for what's gonna happen when they dig them two up, because you know they gonna do it.'

My lungs felt oddly tight, and I sucked in a deep breath trying to ease them. 'What you think they'll do then?'

He didn't say anything, just crimped his lips into a tight line.

But we both knew that whatever it was, it was gonna be bad.

Fifty-One

That night, after the others had all gone to bed, Mahalia, Mama, and I sat down to figure out how to deal with Josephine's disclosures.

Mahalia was all for digging up the dead men and dumping their bones in the river. But Mama decided that was too dangerous.

'For all we know,' she said, 'the Federals could have already set a watch on the bayou. If we go anywhere near that tree, we'll simply betray ourselves.'

'So what are we gonna do?' I asked.

'There's nothing we can do except wait and see what happens. If Josephine is telling the truth, BobbyTi didn't betray us. And now he's gone.'

'But Josephine knows. She could tell someone.'

'Yes.'

A silence fell, filled only by the keening of the wind and the low, mournful howl of an abandoned dog somewhere in the distance.

Mahalia shook her head. 'I still can't believe that Rowena Walford's been secretly dealing with the Federals all this time. And her husband a colonel in the army.'

'I doubt she's been telling any of his secrets,' said Mama. 'We're the ones she's been betraying.'

'Dear Madam,' I said softly. It pricked my conscience that I'd been so sure the unknown correspondent was Hilda Meyers. I'd hated her bitterly for something she wasn't doing. God help me, at one point I'd even started to doubt my own mother.

Mahalia got up to throw another hunk of wood on the fire, then stood looking down at the crackling flames, the golden light dancing over her face. 'What you reckon the Federals are gonna do, once they find them bodies?'

'I suppose they'll start looking for two women and a boy.'

'Good thing I wore Simon's clothes that night,' I said. But then I started running through the families in the neighborhood, figuring up how many contained two women and a boy, and wondering if by our silence we'd be putting someone else at risk.

I don't think any of us slept that night.

That Sunday dawned crisp and mostly clear, with scatterings of thin, rippled clouds that looked like the frozen waves of a celestial sea breaking on a shallow shore.

Mama, Mahalia, Althea, and I were the only ones who walked into town that day for church. Rhoda Magruder was a holy-rolling Baptist and didn't cotton much to the Reverend Dr Daniel Lewis's sedate, cerebral style of preaching, while Adelaide announced she'd decided to just sit home and read her Bible. I saw the shadow of concern that passed over Mama's face when she said it; Adelaide never missed Sunday services.

Grace Church was uncommonly crowded that morning, despite the Federals having done their best to demolish it. The gallery was too unsafe to use, so the *gens de couleur libres* and what few slaves were left just sat in the back. Mahalia took Althea with her, the little girl's white-blond hair gleaming in the sunlight that streamed in through the breaks in the roof.

By now, folks were used to seeing the child with Mahalia and didn't take no real notice. Truth was, I'd seen quadroons as fair as Althea. And it occurred to me watching the little girl contentedly take her place amongst her caramel, café au lait, and ebony-skinned neighbors, that race was a fluid thing whose arbitrary lines could be as divisive and deadly as the man-made borders drawn by politicians and generals on a map.

Althea still didn't speak, and Mama was beginning to worry that she never would. Mama had a theory, that seeing and experiencing awful things left an impression on people's brains that could be permanent. It was a theory I didn't like.

I looked around that shattered church, at the women, children, and aging or crippled men huddled there, and I felt a swelling of despair within me. Our lives were never going to be the same again, no matter who won the war or when it finally ended. *We* were never going to be the same again.

'Let us pray,' said Reverend Lewis, recalling my wandering thoughts. I tried to focus on what he was saying, but I found I couldn't believe any of it any more. I remembered how he'd told me once that what people really ought to pray for was simply inner peace and strength. I was trying to focus on that when the thunder of horses' hooves and the rough voices of shouting men drowned out the reverend's words.

I saw him hesitate, felt the raw, skin-prickling fear that swept over the congregation as two blue-coated soldiers strode into the church, spurs and sabers jangling in the sudden, frightened silence. They clomped up the altar steps and swung around to face the congregation, their rifles cradled at the ready.

'Gentlemen,' protested Reverend Lewis. 'This is a house of worship. I must ask you to respect—'

'Shut up,' snapped one of the men, a whipcord thin sergeant with blond whiskers, pale eyes, and a fiercely sunburned nose. 'This church service is over. Everybody outside. The colonel's ordered the whole town to assemble in front of the courthouse. *Now.*'

There were a few whispers and murmurs, but nobody thought of disobeying. You don't argue with loaded rifles in the hands of men accustomed to killing without hesitation or compunction.

As we filed out the church into the cold sunshine, I reached out to tightly clasp my mother's hand. Federal soldiers were everywhere, rounding up people at bayonet point and herding them toward the ruins of the courthouse that stood across the street from the churchyard. It had been completed only a few years before the war, a once grand affair of red brick with two soaring pedimented white porches and an elegant bronze-covered cupola. Now it was in even worse shape than Grace Church, its roof collapsed, its brick walls showing big holes.

As we drew nearer we could see a wagon pulled up out front, two ominous forms lying beneath an oilcloth in its bed. At the top of the courthouse steps stood a Federal colonel, a portly man creeping into middle age, with thinning fair hair and a jowly, mustachioed face. His uniform was magnificent, a well-tailored, double-breasted, navy frock coat topped by a caped overcoat of sky blue wool that he wore open to display his sash and ceremonial sword.

'I am Colonel Ogden O'Keefe, of the Fourth Wisconsin Volunteers,' he said, his voice ringing out over the crowd.

I glanced at my mother. We'd all heard of Colonel O'Keefe. A judge and local politician before the war, he'd been appointed colonel of the 4th Wisconsin Volunteers by the governor himself. He was known as much for his habit of appropriating other people's fine paintings and expensive furniture as for his marked incompetence on the battlefield and a willingness to allow the troops under his command to plunder and pillage without check.

'Seven months ago,' he said, 'two men under my command disappeared while in your area: Captain Gabriel Dupont and Sergeant Jules Boyle. They have now been found.' He flung out one gauntleted hand toward the wagon, where a private stood waiting at the bed. The colonel's face had darkened now to a deep, righteous crimson, his voice rising to a thundering roar as he intoned dramatically, 'Behold your handiwork!'

At his nod, the private flung back the oilcloth. The heavy, sour stench of decay wafted on the wind, a reek that mingled bayou mud with the unmistakable pinch of old death.

I'd seen Gabriel Dupont in my dreams many times since that fateful June day. Sometimes he came to me looking much as he had the morning I'd killed him, his cheeks flushed with heat, the wool of his uniform sticky and dark with his blood, his dead eyes glittering with an undying rage and a hellish thirst for revenge. At other times, the hands he raised to me were ghastly things, their swamp-stained bones held together more by skeins of algae and wisps of Spanish moss than by skin and sinew. But in my dreams his hair was always shining and gold, his face whole and firm and unmarred by mud or time or the creatures of the earth.

I had never imagined him like this, a muddy wet brown lump of decaying flesh and rotting wool. Someone had obviously poured buckets of water over the corpses' heads, trying to wash away the worst of the muck, because I could see clumps of Gabriel Dupont's golden hair adhering to what few patches of scalp still clung to one of the brown-stained skulls.

A chorus of horrified gasps arose from the assembled towns-people. Someone screamed, and several children began to cry, their mothers hurriedly pressing their little ones' faces against their skirts.

'You see before you the sad remains of two brave, loyal men,' intoned Colonel O'Keefe as the crowd shifted restlessly, some surging forward to get a better look at the dead men, others trying to put distance between themselves and the grisly sight. The move-ment wrenched me away from my mother's side. I looked frantically around and spotted Mahalia standing with some of the other *gens de couleur libres* near the street and clutching Althea to her. Her stark, frightened gaze met mine.

'Brave, loyal men,' the colonel was saying in stentorian tones, 'laid low in the prime of life by the foul hand of murder. Two women did this. Two women and a boy. They were seen while vainly endeavoring to conceal the evidence of their foul deed in the swamps below your city. Seen, but unfortunately not identified.' He let his gaze drift over his now silent audience. 'Yet these men must and will be avenged.'

He drew an ornately engraved gold watch from his pocket and held it up. 'You have fifteen minutes to surrender these men's murderers to me. If not, my men will destroy your town. By the time we are finished, there will be not a house unburned, not a tree standing, not a dog or blade of grass alive.' He paused to let his words sink in. 'Fifteen minutes.'

No one doubted him. The Federals had wrecked this kind of vengeance on hapless civilian populations over and over again across the South. Someone began to cry, a quiet, helpless sobbing that sounded unnaturally loud in the awful silence. I felt my stomach seize up with a vicious ferocity that left me panting. I was trembling, the brilliant intensity of the sunlight hurting my eyes. I knew I had to say something, to own up to what I had done and stop what was about to happen. But I felt frozen, unable to speak, unable to move.

Say something, I told myself. *You have to say something!*

Colonel O'Keefe made a show of lifting his watch again to flick open the case.

Then my mother's voice rang out loud and clear. 'I did it.'

She pushed her way forward, the crowd falling aside to let her through. She didn't even look at me as she passed. At the base of the steps she paused, her features stark and strained with emotion, her head held high, her chest visibly jerking with the agitation of her breathing. 'I did it. I killed them, and my sister Emma and her child helped bury them. But you'll need to wreck your vengeance on me alone, because they're both dead now.'

A loud murmur rose up from the crowd, a hum of disbelief and protest. But there was something else there too, something I recognized as relief tinged with guilt and embarrassment, that my mother had had the courage to sacrifice herself for them while they stood silent. I suspect no one actually believed she'd had anything to do with the death of those two men.

And the truth was, she hadn't killed them. Mahalia and I had, and I couldn't let my mother take the blame for something I had done.

'No!' I cried, struggling to work my way forward through the crowd. 'She's only saying that to protect me. I killed them. She had nothing to do with it. Arrest me.'

The colonel nodded to the officer beside him, and for the first time I realized that I knew him: it was Luke Beckham, the lieutenant who had sparred with my mother with a strange familiarity that both baffled and disturbed me.

As Beckham hesitated, I heard Amelia Ferguson shout from somewhere near the street, 'Don't listen to them. It was me. I did it. My Micajah and I killed them when he was home on leave last year. There wasn't anybody else but us.'

A faint titter of disbelief swept through the ring of watching blue-coated soldiers.

'Now, now,' said Margaret Mason, stepping forward. 'That's very kind of y'all to be trying to protect me, but I can't let you take responsibility for what I did. My old father-in-law and I killed them, not long before he died.'

I felt the prick of tears sting my eyes and burn the bridge of my nose. I wanted to scream, *No; don't do this! You don't understand; we're not being noble. We're just taking responsibility for what we actually did. Don't put yourselves in danger to save us!*

'Nah,' said Cyrus Pringle, moving to stand beside Miss Margaret. 'Don't believe any of them. It was me. Don't know who told y'all it were a woman. Ain't nobody ever mistook me for a woman before.'

'Shut yer trap, Cyrus,' shouted Maisie Sawyer. 'I did it, and you know it.'

My mother's gaze met mine, her eyes glistening as, one by one, the women with whom we had starved and mourned, laughed and cried through all the dark years of this wretched war now stepped forward to take our guilt as their own.

'I did it.'

'No; I did it.'

'It was me.'

'*Me!*'

I watched the colonel's flush of satisfaction fade to chagrin and bafflement before shifting slowly to rage. And I thought, *He's going to burn the whole town anyway. With everyone taking responsibility, what other choice does he have?*

Then Hilda Meyers pushed her way forward, her iron-gray head towering over almost everyone else, her homely, uncompromising features set in scornful lines. 'They all lie, of course,' she said, her accent unusually thick and guttural.

Everyone fell silent, the only sound the wail of a babe quickly hushed.

'You *dummkopf*,' she said, 'what alternative have you left them? They can either lie, or vatch their town burn.' She nodded to the rotting corpses in the wagon. 'You describe these *schmucks* as brave and loyal. But they weren't. The men whose deaths you seek to avenge were *wystlings* who brutalized the women of this parish for months. I almost said, while you turned a blind eye, but the

truth is, you knew vhat they were doing all along. You knew, and
you approved of it. For you, vomen are as much the traditional
spoils of var as mules and pianos. "Bounty and Beauty" is your
battle cry, yes? And yet because our vomen's shame has traditionally kept us silent, you think your own mothers, vives, and daughters
vill never come to know vhat you have done here. Vell, I promise
you that if you burn this town, I vill not keep silent. I am too old
to vorry about false notions of honor or to believe all the foolish
myths ve use to convince ourselves that var is something grand
rather than a simple act of collective madness. You burn this town,
and I vill tell the vorld of your licentiousness. The Fourth Visconsin
vill be as infamous as the Tribe of Benjamin after the outrage of
Gibeah.'

'Madam,' blustered the colonel, 'I will not stand here and listen
to your lies and threats.'

I saw Lieutenant Beckham lean forward to say to him quietly,
'Excuse me, sir, but it seems to me that we do not know for certain
that the information we received was entirely accurate. I mean, it's
more than a bit unlikely, wouldn't you say, that a couple of women
could murder two armed men and drag their bodies into a swamp?
Perhaps the contraband who claims to have seen it all is actually
the man we're after.'

'But he's long gone,' muttered the colonel in a furious aside to
his aide. 'What do you suggest I tell the governor?'

'Coulda been bushwhackers,' shouted Castile from the back of
the crowd. 'They been plaguing us something fierce for a while
now.'

We all exchanged glances, but nobody said a word. The bushwhackers hadn't really operated in our area until after the fall of
Vicksburg and Port Hudson. But hopefully this pompous, puffed-up
colonel didn't know that.

Colonel O'Keefe smoothed one splayed thumb and forefinger
down over his carefully waxed blond mustache. 'Bushwhackers,
you say?'

'Sounds reasonable, sir,' said the lieutenant.

The colonel nodded thoughtfully, obviously already plotting how
he could present the corpses of some random bushwhackers as the
murderers of his governor's nephew.

For one telling moment, I saw Lieutenant Beckham's gaze shift
to meet my mother's. And I thought, *He knows. He knows or at*

least suspects the truth about us. Then he looked away, and I told myself it was an illusion, a creation of my own guilty conscience.

The colonel cleared his throat and raised his voice again. 'Your cooperation in helping to solve this reprehensible affair has won your town a reprieve. But let this be a lesson to you: the vengeance of the United States is as swift and awful as that of the Lord. Suffer not the handmaidens of the devil to dwell amongst you, nor the temptations of sin to entice you into wickedness.'

If that was from the Bible, I didn't recognize it. Maybe it was just meant to sound biblical. All I knew was that I was sick of men quoting the Bible and using God to justify whatever loathsome actions their greed and hatred motivated.

Someone shouted, 'Mount up, men!'

We watched in silence while the colonel and his men turned their horses and filed up Ferdinand Street. A breeze gusted up, bringing us the smell of the river and swelling the branches of the live oaks in the churchyard against the sky.

The wagon was the last to pass, its big, iron-rimmed wheels bouncing and clattering over the ruts to rattle the swamp-stained bones of the men who lay within.

Fifty-Two

The incident was never discussed – at least not openly – by those of us who lived through it. The emotions it provoked were too raw and intense: fear and gratitude, heroism and cowardice, all wrapped up in a sense of unity and community so rare and beautiful that it sometimes takes my breath, still, to think of it. We simply tucked it away into our collective memory and went on with our lives.

A couple of days later, I talked myself into walking down Ferdinand Street to Hilda Meyers' emporium. She did most of her trade from under the counter these days, selling goods that came through speculators and were bought by those few amongst us who still had money to spend and who didn't know – or pretended not to know – their origins.

She was busy straightening some boxes on a shelf over her head when I walked in. But at the sound of my tread, she turned. 'Vhat are you doing here?' she demanded gruffly.

My throat felt like I had a fishbone stuck in it, so that I had to work to push my words out. 'I came to say I'm sorry.'

A shadow of surprise mixed with something else wafted across her lumpy, unattractive features. 'Sorry? Vhat for?'

'For all those years of tormenting you. For thinking you were a witch and . . . and worse.'

The flesh beside her small dark eyes crinkled with what might have been amusement. 'I am a vitch. I have a broomstick, and I have been known to chase naughty children on Krampusnacht and whip them.'

I huffed a soft laugh and turned to go.

She stopped me, saying, 'Vhat do you hear of the thatch-gallows?'

I swung to face her again. 'You mean, Finn? They say he's with Scott now.'

She nodded. 'I always like that boy. He has *Tapferkeit*.'

I contemplated her words all the way home. It was just one more revelation to me of the extent to which the realities of our world and the people in it can differ from our own imperfect perceptions of them.

I turned fourteen that summer, while the Federals burned and pillaged their way up and down the state of Louisiana.

By that point, most folks knew the end was near; it was just a matter of when. Things had reached such a pass that the government in Richmond decided to free the South's slaves and arm them to fight the Federals.

But it was all too late.

That fall, Trudi Easton announced she was going to teach school and she didn't care if her husband approved of it or not. I volunteered to help her with the little ones and also taught French to some of the older girls. There weren't any older boys. By that time, every able-bodied male between fifteen and fifty was off fighting. And dying.

'You ought to consider becoming a teacher,' Miss Trudi said to me one afternoon after we'd let the children go for the day. 'You've a gift for it.'

I looked up from straightening the crude benches – the Federals had burned our desks on one of their raids – and shook my head. 'I want to be a doctor. A *licensed* doctor.'

I thought she might be scandalized at the suggestion that women ought to be licensed to practice medicine, just like men. Instead, a wistfulness pulled at her features that made me wonder what dreams she'd once cherished that the prejudices and assumptions of our age had killed. Then she smiled and said, 'If any woman can do it, Amrie, you can.'

In November, the Federals overran and burned Camp Moore. They also pulled up the more than eight hundred wooden grave markers in the cemetery there and burned them, too. I thought it was just about the lowest thing I'd ever heard of an army doing.

Then General Sherman started his march to the sea.

Finn O'Reilly never came back to St Francisville. I saw him only once more, in the fall of 1864, when a strong force of Federal cavalry landed at Bayou Sara and skirmished with Colonel Scott's First Louisiana Cavalry all the way up to Woodville and back.

I was sitting beside Simon's grave when the Confederates came galloping through town. I ran to the churchyard gate, reaching the street just in time to see a familiar figure mounted on a big, rangy roan charging down Ferdinand Street.

'Finn!'

He reined in hard, his horse jibing at the bit as he wheeled. For one intense moment, his gaze met mine. In the year or more since I'd seen him, he'd grown tall and lean, not a boy any longer but a man, with a piercing green gaze and the shadow of a beard darkening his hard jaw.

He raised his hand to his hat in a jaunty salute, his lips curling in a bittersweet smile. Then someone shouted at him, and he touched his spurs to his horse's flanks and was gone.

The end came with a curiously mingled sense of disbelief and inevitability. Impossible not to feel relief that the moment we'd known was coming for so long had finally arrived. But it had been more than six months since we'd heard any news of Papa, and it was hard to exalt at the thought of his homecoming when we weren't even sure if he was still alive.

Rhoda Magruder and her children left us in mid-April and headed back up to Mississippi in anticipation of finding her husband there. Uncle Tate wrote that he'd be coming just as soon as he was well enough to travel. But as April turned to May, and more and more shattered, ruined men stumbled home, our fears about Papa became a dread that we refused to acknowledge even to ourselves, let alone to each other.

That's when I took to bargaining with God again. At night, I'd stand at my dormer window staring out over the empty, moonlit drive, and pray. *Please, God; I promise I won't question your wisdom or goodness ever again. I'll try to simply find peace and strength in your divine existence. Only, let Papa come home.*

Please?

He came to us in the gloaming of the day, when the jasmine splashed a riot of snowy blossoms across the crumbling brick foundation of the cistern, and the mockingbirds sang gloriously from the spreading limbs of the live oaks lining the drive.

Mama and I were trying to put up a new rail fence around the vegetable garden when the sound of tired hoof beats brought our heads up. I saw her straighten slowly, one hand coming up to push the loose hair off her forehead as she turned toward the lane. The setting sun spilled its last golden light across the fields, and a breeze was blowing up warm and sweet from the river.

Horses and mules had become more common in the area now that the armies were disbanding and men were making their way homeward, some to be welcomed with joy, others to find only blackened, weed-chocked walls and sunken graves. I told myself it could be anyone. But I couldn't stop the leap of hope that thrummed through me.

And then I saw him, a dusty, too-thin figure urging a familiar chestnut into a lope as he swung in through our gate.

'Anton?' whispered Mama, as if afraid to believe what she was seeing, afraid of the bitterness of disappointment if she were wrong.

And then she was running, hands fisting up her rough homespun skirts, knees pumping high. 'Anton!'

He reined in sharply, his head turning toward the sound. I saw the wonder that spilled across his face, the joy that was almost palpable. He threw himself off his horse to catch my mother in his arms and lift her up, her momentum spinning them around and around. His laughter intermingled with hers, and she wrapped her arms around his neck and hugged him with a fierceness that caused my own step to falter. Theirs was an intensely intimate moment, and I was an intruder witnessing it.

Then he looked over and saw me.

'Good God,' he said in wonder. 'Amrie? Is that you?'

I'd been ten when he left, a child in pinafores and pigtails. I was nearly fifteen now, my childhood left far behind me.

'Papa.' I felt shy, embarrassed, unsure of anything. He was different from the father I remembered. Not simply older, but harder, rougher, with a brittle edge that hadn't been there before. I found myself wondering what he saw when he looked at us. Had he expected us to be the same?

And I knew, then, that he would never grasp the true horror, desperation, or fear of the war we had lived, just as we would never fully understand the things he had seen or the things he had done. The last four years had changed us all, each according to our own nature, in some ways for the better and, inevitably, in other ways for the worse.

But he was alive, and whole, and home. When I closed my eyes and listened to his soft, familiar laugh, I felt my heart begin to lighten.

And I smiled.

Author's Note

This story had its origins in a desire to explore the ways in which the women of a patriarchal society such as that of the antebellum South coped when virtually every able-bodied male in their community marched off to war, leaving them alone to face deprivation and a brutal occupation. How did white women who had supposedly been placed on a pedestal adjust to single-handedly running farms and businesses in an increasingly harsh and dangerous environment? How did enslaved women and *gens de couleur libres* react to their shifting circumstances? The answer, of course, is that they coped extraordinarily well. In many ways the tradition of the South's 'steel magnolias' was forged in the holocaust of that war.

But as I read the hundreds of journals, memoirs, and letters those women left behind, I began to notice an undercurrent of something that surprised me. It is one of the commonly accepted truisms of Civil War historiography that rape was extraordinarily rare in the Civil War. More honest historians acknowledge that Union soldiers looted and burned their way across the South, often torturing and murdering civilians as they went; but, we are assured, they stopped short of rape. Why? The answer is, they didn't.

Open, contemporary accounts such as Celine Garcia's description of the brutal rapes at Clinton, Louisiana, or William Simms's report of the scores of women gang raped in Columbia, South Carolina, are relatively rare, although actually more common than we are led to believe. But subtle references abound. Consider the frequent use of the phrase 'plunder and pillage'. We all know what 'plunder' means: theft. But the word 'pillage' has traditionally been used to refer to wanton destruction accompanied by rape. There is no reason to assume it meant anything different to those who used it during the Civil War.

Other frequently used euphemisms included the expression 'the greatest indignity possible committed upon the women' or 'the worst insult imaginable', or simply 'horrors'. These and similar phrases can be found again and again in the diaries, memoirs, reports and, especially, the private letters of the period, yet their meaning seems to sail over the heads of modern historians. Likewise, when Southern women write of 'lascivious' solders 'rampaging through town', one must wonder exactly what historians think those men were doing to earn such an adjective.

Because of the importance placed by patriarchal societies on female chastity and fidelity, women have long sought to hide their rape. This is especially true in times of war, when it is unlikely the perpetrators of such crimes will ever be brought to justice. The reasons for such concealment are numerous and multifaceted, and include women's perceived need to safeguard their reputations and protect themselves from shame, scorn and societal rejection. But equally important is the recognition that rape is a tool of war, a deliberate attempt by invading armies to punish and humiliate their enemies. By concealing their rapes, the women of the South were refusing to be complicit in the 'shaming' of their fathers, husbands, brothers, and sons; they were safeguarding not only their own honor but also the honor of their community and their men. The people of the time knew what was going on. But in the Victorian era, one spoke of such things obliquely, if at all.

Interestingly, the rape of enslaved women and free people of color was more often acknowledged and has given rise to the fallacy that Union soldiers raped black women but not their white counterparts. However, this conclusion shows a pronounced lack of understanding of the times, when the reasons for the concealment of the rape of white women were not generally seen as applying to black women. Simms, for example, mentions only the rape and murder of black women in the sacking of Columbia; to admit that white women were also brutalized would have impugned the reputation of every white woman who survived Sherman's infamous march to the sea.

To put the events of the Civil War in perspective, consider that close to a third of all modern female United States veterans admit having been raped or sexually assaulted *by their own fellow servicemen*. There is no reason to assume that the nineteenth-century United States Army – the same army that perpetuated such atrocities as Sandy Creek and Bear River – behaved better in their rampage through the homeland of what had become a hated enemy. The historian Crystal Feimster has recently been attempting to reassess the prevalence of rape in the Civil War; E. Susan Barber and Charles Ritter have also addressed the issue.

New efforts are likewise underway to reassess the accepted casualty figures for the Civil War. General consensus is that the long established figure of 625,000 dead is a drastic undercounting; the true number is probably closer to a million or more. Few have seriously attempted to assess civilian casualties; the figures sometimes given for the South as a whole are often lower than civilian casualties in the state of Missouri alone. Even the most casual reading of the period's diaries and letters will show that the excess mortality amongst Southern civilians was staggering.

While this is a work of fiction, I have sought to set it against an accurate framework of the events that actually occurred in the St Francisville area. The winters of 1862-63 and 1863-64 were indeed abnormally cold. I have at times combined several similar incidents in order to avoid repetition, but the battles for New Orleans and Baton Rouge, Vicksburg and Port Hudson were essentially as portrayed here, as were the various gunboat assaults on St Francisville and Bayou Sara, the theft of the wharfboat, the landing of General Banks's army, the Yankee Doodle parade of the *Brooklyn*'s landing party, the battle at Centenary College in Jackson, Louisiana, and the lynching of black troops that followed it. The Union major in command at Jackson was indeed James Moore Hanham, from Woodville, Mississippi; the Hanham Variation in chess is named after him. The Masonic burial of Commander Hart likewise actually occurred and is still commemorated in St Francisville by an annual reenactment known as the Day the War Stopped. The initial visit of the *Katahdin*, while modeled on other such incidents, is my own invention, as is the killing of Gabriel Dupont and Jules Boyle, and the events that flow from it.

In the course of writing this book, I read innumerable memoirs, dairies, and letters. The most useful were those written by Louisiana women, such as Celine Fremaux Garcia, Kate Stone, Sarah Morgan Dawson, Eliza McHatton-Ripley, Clara Solomon, and Sarah Lois Wadley. The experiences of the women and children caught in the siege of Vicksburg are vividly detailed by Lida Lord Reed, Mary Webster Loughborough, Emma Balfour, and Dora Richards Miller. Lara Locoul Gore's memoir of her family provided the inspiration for Castile's brand. Martha Turnball's *Garden Diary*, edited and annotated by Suzanne Turner, was an invaluable source for nineteenth-century gardening and the passage of the seasons in St Francisville.

The remembrances recorded by men who served on both sides of the war in Louisiana were also useful, especially David Hughson's *Among the Cotton Thieves* and Thomas Wallace Knox's *Campfire and Cottonfield;* also the diaries of Lawrence Van Alstyne, George Hamill, Felix Pierre Poche, and Howell Carter.

I drew additional inspiration for various incidents from accounts written by women who experienced the war in other parts of the South, including Lucy Breckinridge, Phoebe Yates Pember, Eliza Frances Andrews, Constance Cary Harrison, Susan Chancellor, Mary Ann Harris Gay, Dolly Lunt Burge, Emma LeConte, Julia Morgan, Cornelia Peake McDonald, and Catherine Hopley. Accounts left by women who served as nurses in the hospitals of both the North and the South include those of Louisa May Alcott, Adelaide Smith, Cornelia Hancock, and, especially, Kate Cummings. I also relied on *Doctors in Gray* by H.H. Cunningham, as well as *The Medicinal Book of Augustus Ball; Thomas Ellis's Leaves from the Diary of an Army Surgeon*; and Marlin Gardner and Benjamin Aylworth's *The Domestic Physician and Family Assistant.*

The classic work on shortages and substitutes in the Civil War remains Mary Elizabeth Massey's *Ersatz in the Confederacy.* Also valuable was *The Confederate Housewife*, edited by John Hammond Moore

The Reverend Garette Hale's sermon using Christianity to justify slavery is based on the works by John Henry Hopkins, George Fitzhugh, and their many contemporaries. The comparisons of abolitionism to communism and socialism were indeed made at the time.

The standard reference for the Civil War in Louisiana remains that of John D. Winters, along with the works of J.D. Bragg and, for the era of 'Spoons' Butler, Chester Hearn. I also relied on more local works such as those by Dennis Dufrene; Lawrence Estaville, Jr; Samual Hyde, Jr; Chistopher G. Peña; Donald Frazier; and Powell A. Casey. Terry Jones's *Lee's Tigers* was useful for keeping track of Amrie's father. Samuel C. Hyde's work on the Florida Parishes provided thought-provoking insight into the effects of the violence and anarchy of the Civil War on the subsequent culture of the area. I have also been influenced by Liddell Hart's famous essay on the dangerous legacies of guerrilla warfare, and by Chris Hedges's writings on war.

David Goldfield's *America Aflame* was invaluable for helping to put many of the events and attitudes of the Civil War into context.

James Marten's *The Children of the Civil War* provided the true tale
of children frightened into being good by threats that God would
withdraw His protection from their soldier father. Also useful were
Kenneth Greenberg's *Honor and Slavery*, and Stephen Ash, *When
the Yankees Came*. Walter Brian Cisco's *War Crimes Against Southern
Civilians* is considerably more partisan but is valuable for his cita-
tions of documents contained in the government's voluminous *War
of the Rebellion: a Compilation of Official Records of the Union and
Confederate Armies*.

For understanding slavery in the antebellum South, few sources
match the WPA's *Slave Narratives*. Also useful for insight into
Louisiana's slave laws and the world of the *gens de couleur libres*
were Taylor's 'Slavery in Louisiana During the Civil War;' *The
Forgotten People: Cane River's Creoles of Color*, by Mills; Hall's
Africans in Colonial Louisiana; and Solomon Northrup, *Twelve Years
a Slave*.

A number of historical studies on women in the Civil War should
also be mentioned, such as Waugh and Greenberg's *The Women's
War in the South;* Ott's *Confederate Daughters*; Faust's *Mothers of
Invention*; Sullivan's *The War the Women Lived;* and *Occupied
Women*, Whites and Long, eds..

When discrepancies exist between official military reports and
civilian eyewitness accounts, I have tended to go with the civilian
accounts. For instance, reports from the Federal fleet claim the initial
bombardment of Baton Rouge was provoked when 'forty guerrillas'
opened fire on an officer rowing his laundry ashore; but civilian
accounts say only four youngsters were involved. Since it is likely
that forty men shooting at a rowboat would have inflicted considerably more damage than the few wounded that resulted, I have gone
with the local accounts. Local reports of civilian casualties likewise
tend to be more accurate. Porter's claim that the occupants of St
Francisville were given twenty-four hours to evacuate before the
devastating January 1864 bombardment is contradicted by the
accounts of those who lived through it. Doctoring of official accounts
was common; extant correspondence between General Banks and
several of his commanders in the field provides examples of
commanders attempting to resist the general's insistence that all
references to rapes and other atrocities against civilians be removed
from reports. I also received valuable information and assistance from
Daniel at Centenary College in Jackson, Louisiana, as well as from the

staff of various area battle sites, including Camp Moore, Port Hudson, and Vicksburg.

Bayou Sara was rebuilt on a much smaller scale, but eventually succumbed to successive floods and fires and has disappeared. Although no longer as prosperous as they once were, the towns of St Francisville, Jackson, and Clinton still exist and preserve hundreds of antebellum homes and other structures that were repaired in the decades after the war.

CPSIA information can be obtained
at www.ICGtesting.com
Printed in the USA
BVOW03*1002280617
488044BV00005B/60/P